Prais... **GLEN ERIK HAMILTON**

"If you like Lee Child's Jack Reacher,
you will absolutely love Van Shaw."
–Deborah Crombie, *New York Times* bestselling author

"If you're not reading Glen Erik Hamilton, you oughta be."
–Chris Holm, Anthony Award-winning author

"Glen Erik Hamilton's character,
Van Shaw, is a street savvy, modern-day
Robin Hood with the bare knuckle fighting skills
of Rocky Balboa . . . [a] creative series."
–*Iron Mountain Daily News*

A DANGEROUS BREED

"Exceptional."
–*Publishers Weekly* (Starred Review)

"A thriller tour de force.
The past collides violently with the present,
and the result is a Pandora's box of secrets spilled open.
It's taut, compelling, and it's so well written.
But here's the kicker. At its core, it's really all about family.
This is a bulldog of a story that, once it sets its teeth in you,
refuses to let go."
–William Kent Krueger, *New York Times* bestselling author

HARD COLD WINTER

PAST CRIMES

By Glen Erik Hamilton

PAST CRIMES
HARD COLD WINTER
EVERY DAY ABOVE GROUND
MERCY RIVER
A DANGEROUS BREED

GLEN ERIK HAMILTON

A DANGEROUS BREED

A NOVEL

wm

WILLIAM MORROW
An Imprint of HarperCollins*Publishers*

Essential Business Copyright © 2021 by Glen Erik Hamilton.

A DANGEROUS BREED. Copyright © 2020 by Glen Erik Hamilton. All rights reserved. Printed in the United States of America. No part of this book may be used or reproduced in any manner whatsoever without written permission except in the case of brief quotations embodied in critical articles and reviews. For information, address HarperCollins Publishers, 195 Broadway, New York, NY 10007.

First William Morrow mass market printing: April 2021
First William Morrow hardcover printing: July 2020

Print Edition ISBN: 978-0-06-297852-3
Digital Edition ISBN: 978-0-06-297853-0

Cover design by Richard L. Aquan
Cover photographs © nexus 7/Shutterstock; © Mark Owen/Trevillion Images (man)

William Morrow and HarperCollins are registered trademarks of HarperCollins Publishers in the United States of America and other countries.

21 22 23 24 25   CPI   10 9 8 7 6 5 4 3 2 1

For Bruce and Marjorie,
who raised a large and wonderful family,
and made room for one more.

A DANGEROUS BREED

PROLOGUE

We WERE IN THE air, falling backward. The black water of Puget Sound coursed ten feet below, glints of moonlight defining gentle waves. For an instant there was no sound at all.

Then the police car hit hard and speared below the surface, bobbing swiftly back up to slap the waves flat. The impact threw me face-first into the clear plastic barrier separating the rear of the car from the empty driver's seat. Blood erupted from my lip.

I yanked myself upright, hampered by handcuffs that bound my wrists behind my back and the heavy bulk of the man lying half across me. The car window pressed his head into an awkward angle, deforming his cheek. A puff of breath condensed on the glass.

He was alive. For now.

We began to dip forward, borne down by the mass of the cruiser's V-8. Seawater bubbled and splashed into the front compartment. In seconds it had swamped the pedals. A briny reek overwhelmed the tang of blood in my mouth. I twisted in my seat, trying to feel for the tiny piece of bent metal I'd dropped in our fall.

The car leaned toward the icy deep as if eager for its

embrace. Half a minute, maybe less, before the roiling water would fill the interior.

I pushed at the unconscious man with my shoulder, trying to gain a few more inches of space, but there was nowhere for his body to move. The cold lent a razor sting to every gasp of air. My grasping fingers brushed the hard plastic seat, only to slide away again.

Heavy diesels churned nearby. The barge from which we had fallen began moving away from the sinking car and toward the shore. Four miles off, the city sparkled in the clear night. I had one final glimpse of those glittering lights before the waves shrouded the windshield outside and darkness consumed both of us.

Me, and the man I'd met for the first time barely one week before. A week of violence and death—and the hard proof about the identity of the man about to drown alongside me.

My father.

CHAPTER ONE
Thirteen days ago

BULLY BETTY'S GRAND REOPENING was a triumph threatening to collapse into tragedy. By midnight the main room of the bar was almost bulging at the seams, a crush of two dozen warm bodies past any sensible capacity.

Word about the new location had spread, and then some. Betty's first weekend on Capitol Hill attracted her kind of crowd. Queer techies. Theater vamps wearing tailored tartan suits. Horn-rimmed creatives with enough side hustles to fill a résumé. A combined target demo that might be narrow anywhere but Seattle. All the revelers temporarily free from their holiday obligations and end-of-year deadlines. Ready to shake themselves slack.

"Van." A-Plus, shouting from ten feet away. I read her perfectly glossed lips more than I heard the words over the din of a hundred other voices: "Two sour ales, three tequila shots with lime, two house bourbon." She flashed French-manicured fingers to make sure I caught the count.

A-Plus and the other bartenders handled the showy job of making cocktails. I pulled all the pints and poured bottles with both hands to keep the river of well drinks flowing. Factory work. The arrangement suited both sides. They kept the tips, and I didn't have to make small talk.

Betty had allowed a few concessions to her loyalists in the new place. At the corner of the bar nearest me, a muted television streamed a rerun of the U-Dub women's basketball game against Oregon State. The Huskies had an ace power forward this year who was expected to turn pro a year early. I knew all this because the knot of women glued to the action had been singing the player's praises since tip-off.

"All that technical crap, like executing the game plan," one fan in a sleeveless T-shirt proclaimed. "The team can learn that shit from the coach. But *that*." She jabbed a finger at the screen. "That's fuckin' *mean*. You can't learn mean." Her nugget of wisdom prompted affirming whoops from the others.

Betty had noticed my self-imposed exile, of course. She'd thrown me the side-eye, but that was all she had time for. Too busy keeping order, nostrils flared for anyone vaping, making sure Maurice on the door was confirming that every pretty face matched with an ID photo.

"I'll have a gin fizz," a woman said to my back, over the babble of the crowd.

I knew the voice and angled my gaze downward before I turned around.

The bar counter was tall. Addy Proctor was not. Only her head and shoulders could be seen above the edge.

Her cherubic crinkled face poked out from the hood of a cherry-red quilted parka lined with fake fur. A scowling circle.

"Do I look like I know how to make a gin fizz?" I said.

"No more than I look like I belong here." Her neck trapped in the parka, Addy turned her whole body to examine the throng that moved like wheat stalks in wind every time the door opened to admit just a couple more. Drops of rain suspended from her fur collar broke loose. "I'm a gnome among mermaids. Look at these children. It's marvelous."

"I'm working," I said.

"You can spare a minute for an old woman up past her bedtime. If you can't make a decent drink, pour me a vodka. Something that pairs nicely with a fixed income."

I ignored Addy's restriction and pulled the Woody Creek Reserve from the top shelf to fill a shot glass for my former neighbor. A-Plus brought another stack of orders. I waved her toward the taps to fend for herself, ignoring the gorgeous pout she fired my way.

"You haven't returned my phone calls," Addy said, sniffing at the vodka.

"It's been busy." I nodded to the bar. "Betty lost her lease. We wanted to relocate before the end of the season."

She frowned. "That's not the cause. You've been a damn ghost since you got back from Oregon, and that was over two months ago."

I didn't want to talk about Oregon. I had been practicing hard to not even think about what had happened there, and I had finally reached the point where I managed the trick most hours of the day.

"I've come by your house," I said. "At Thanksgiving, with Cyndra." Cyn was Addy's foster kid.

"You came, you brought a pie, big whoop. You spoke about ten words, Van. It hurt her feelings. I know Luce getting married must have been tough for you—"

"What do you want, Addy?"

"Fine. Cyndra went to L.A. to have Christmas with her father. Which means she spent the holiday in a convalescent home with Mickey, who is nowhere near a suitable host for her, dad or not. She'll be on the morning flight back. You're going to help me welcome Cyndra home and make sure she has some fun. Starting with taking her to her team practice tomorrow afternoon." To underline her point, Addy downed half of the shot glass.

Betty had spotted our conversation and angled her path toward us through the crowd. I was reminded of an icebreaker, its armored prow shoving aside tons of frozen floes.

"If I say yes, are we done?" I said to Addy.

"For now," she muttered, understandably distracted by a seven-foot sylph in green sparkle makeup using the bar mirror to freshen their mascara.

"Bring your next luncheon group here," I teased.

"Please," Addy said. "I lived through Haight-Ashbury."

Betty reached us. She had no problem making room for herself at the counter. Besides wielding shoulders as wide as mine, twin ebony boulders covered in purple tattoos advertising the combined Aztec and Ghanaian heritage she claimed, Betty possessed a force of personality that encouraged the world to make way, or else.

"You got to be Addy. Hello," Betty said, giving our parka-encased guest the once-over.

"I must be. I'm surprised Van has mentioned me. Congratulations on your new place."

"I'll exhale when it's still standing in the morning. I'd forgotten how wild the Hill can get." Betty turned to me. "Maurice is taking over the taps."

I shook my head. "He made me a deal. He's on the door. I close up."

"Big Mo doesn't frighten off drunks. Dickless wonders keep cruising past and hollering shit at the clientele."

"That's harassment. Can't the police help?" said Addy.

Betty and I both looked at her.

"Or is that a foolish question?" Addy finished, eyeing me.

She knew enough of my personal history to predict my opinion. Being raised by my grandfather, a professional thief and onetime armed robber, had lent me a different true north on my personal compass. Betty had suffered her own challenges with the cops, like pretty much anyone black and queer and raised in poverty. Maybe that shared suspicion toward the rest of the world was why she and I got along.

"I'll take care of it," I told Betty.

"Don't forget about Cyndra," Addy said. "Tomorrow morning. And we're not done talking about this."

Betty offered me a penlight to use when checking licenses. "No one paying you for conversation here. Go scare somebody."

I retrieved my jacket and gloves from the back room.

Addy wanted to know what had been bothering me since my return. She'd assumed it was my ex-girlfriend, Luce, tying the knot earlier that month. Wrong guess, Addy. Thanks for playing.

I had made some choices in Oregon that I couldn't ignore, or walk back, if I had cared to try. I hadn't. Living day by day had been tough enough these past weeks without worrying about something as ephemeral as atonement.

On my way out into the cold, I reflected that the basketball fan had been dead wrong, too.

Someone *could* learn to be mean. Start as young as I had, and there was no limit.

CHAPTER TWO

ONE NIGHT JUST BEFORE the start of the school year, Cyndra had found a movie on cable about young women competing in roller derby. She used her own money to buy a digital copy that same night and pasted her nose to the screen, watching the film six more times before Monday rolled around.

Within a week her skateboard had given way to quad-wheel boots. Cyndra would have worn the skates to bed if Addy had allowed it. They found a junior league team called the Screaming Mimis. When I arrived at Addy's on Sunday morning to pick up Cyn for practice, she was already outside in the cold, gear bag over her shoulder for added weight as she did calf raises on the porch step. She heard my car pulling up and sprinted to meet it.

The Mimis' derby league was flat-track, meaning the skaters competed on smooth concrete. Parents had arranged a fund drive to have a new floor poured in an old cinder-block warehouse near Northgate. I'd handed Addy a short stack of cash to donate. She knew better than to ask where the money had come from.

At fourteen and undernourished much of her child-hood, Cyndra weighed about as much as a loaded sack of groceries. But what she lacked in size she made up for with speed. She was a favorite jammer among the newer players, the fresh meat. Jammers scored points by making it past the opposing team's blockers, who did their level best to knock the jammers on their asses. Sportingly.

I sat against the sage green blocks of the warehouse wall, watching Cyn lean into the curve, picking up velocity, angling for the inside, and then suddenly juking right to find daylight between two blockers who hadn't linked arms. She whooped elatedly. A fraction too early, as her skate caught another player's and she fell, skidding two yards, her plastic kneepads and wrist guards rasping harshly on the concrete. I winced. But Cyndra popped back up as if the impact had been a cool breeze.

Speed, and guts.

The instructor, a slim woman with a dark braid and a band of tattoos spiraling up her right arm, blew her whistle to bring the girls in for a lesson. They gathered with a clomping of wheels like pony hooves on hard dirt.

I turned my attention to the stack of mail Addy had given me. My old house, the home I'd shared with my grandfather Dono as a boy, had been up the block from Addy's. Mail still trickled in at that address. The family that had bought the property and built their own house on the land left anything sent to the Shaws under Addy's welcome mat.

Grocery fliers and tool catalogs made up most of the stack. One expiration notice of union membership for nonpayment of dues, forwarded by a mailing service to

Dono—or, more accurately, one of Dono's aliases. My grandfather had always maintained a couple of identities. Handy for emergencies, and for purchasing items unavailable to people with felony rap sheets.

I nearly missed the last envelope, which had been tucked into a bulk-mail magazine of coupons. I glanced at the handwritten address. And then stared at the name.

Moira Shaw, it read.

My mother.

My mother had died when I was six years old. A distracted driver tapped the wrong pedal at the wrong moment and jumped the curb in downtown Seattle. I wasn't there. My daycare worker brought me to the hospital. No one had really told me what was going on. Not until Dono arrived. He took me to his home that same night, and there I stayed.

Moira Shaw. I barely remembered her. Dono hadn't kept pictures. Hardly ever spoke of his only child. Seeing her name again, for the first time in I couldn't remember, felt like I'd swallowed a small but very sharp icicle.

I headed outside, ducking under the rolling door the Mimis kept partway open to allow some ventilation in the airless warehouse. Drizzling rain, a near-constant in December Seattle, coated my face and hair. I opened my car to sit in the driver's seat.

The return address at the top corner of the envelope was a stick-on label with a Christmas theme, green holly and candy canes. From a John and Josephine Mixon in Redmond. Our house address had been handwritten on the envelope in purple ballpoint.

I opened the envelope and removed the single sheet

of paper. Only the salutation and a phone number at the
bottom had been written with the same purple pen. The
rest of the text was a typed copy.

> *Dear Moira,*
>   *I hope this note finds you! We are just
> starting to plan the Emmett Watson High
> 30th Reunion (WOW!) for sometime next
> summer, and would love to include you.
> Please call me at the number below to let
> us know!*
>   *Go Paladins!*
>
>   *Sincerely,*
>   *Jo Mixon (Gerrold!)*

Just a form letter, sent by someone so far out of the
alumni loop that she hadn't even heard Moira Shaw had
died almost a quarter of a century before.

I had only a few sparse facts about Moira's life. Her
own mother, Dono's wife, Finnoula, had also died while
Moira was still young. The Shaw women traveled tough,
short roads. Moira had gotten pregnant and left Dono's
house a few years after that.

So far as I knew, she'd never spoken a word about
who had knocked her up. Out of shame, or maybe to
keep Dono from murdering the guy. Probably the latter.
That secrecy had driven a wedge between father and
daughter.

Cyndra's practice was about to end. I tossed the letter
from Jo Mixon on the passenger's seat and stepped out
into the cold mist.

GRANDDAD KNELT TO WRESTLE the heavy bench grinder free from the other tools crowded under his worktable. He muttered curse words with every tug. My homeroom teacher, Ms. Heffler, had put the word involuntary on last week's spelling assignment, and Granddad's swearing was the first example that came to my mind. I didn't write that down for my practice sentence, though. I wasn't that dumb.

While Granddad set up the grinder, I opened the cardboard box of papers he'd told me to sort. We were making space. We called the little room carved into the hill below our house the garage, but only about half of Granddad's truck would have fit inside. Mostly the garage was his workshop and a storage place for whatever he didn't want in the house. The box of papers he'd given me was so full, it bulged at the sides. The cardboard was soft to the touch and smelled like rags left out in the rain.

Make three piles, he'd said. One for records from his contracting business, one for home stuff, and one for instruction manuals or anything else that didn't fit the other two piles. I pulled out a handful of papers and started looking through them.

"Finish that fast," Granddad said as he tightened bolts through the worktable to hold the grinder in place, "and I'll teach you to use this. About time you worked with something other than hand tools."

"What are you making?" I said. He had brought a sack of metal rods from the hardware store.

"Some disposable punches. For knocking out hinges and locks and the like."

"What locks?"

"Never mind that. Get to it."

I turned back to the papers. It wasn't tough to sort them. Usually the first page of each bunch told me what pile the papers belonged to.

Then I found one lone page, stuck in the middle of a manual for a power wrench. A lined sheet of notebook paper, with a girl's handwriting.

Moira Shaw
Ms. Cullen, Room 17
Native American Tribes of the Northwest

Mom?
I stared at the loops and slants of the letters. This had been hers. She had written it, touched the paper with her own hand.

Paragraphs in the same writing covered both sides. She'd gotten an A on the paper. If there had been more pages to it, they were missing. The top corner of the paper was torn, probably where a staple used to be.

I knew Ms. Cullen. She taught fifth grade at Bertha Landes Elementary. My school.

"Did Mom go to Landes?" I said.

"Eh?" Granddad looked up. "What's that?"

"It's Mom's. Was Mom's." I showed him. He took the page from me. "Did she go to my school?"

"She did." Granddad's eye moved over the paper.

"You never said."

He didn't answer. Just held the page by his fingertips, like it would rip if he pressed any harder. Granddad had big hands, even for somebody as tall as he was, and I was suddenly worried he would decide to crumple the fragile page to dust.

"Was she at Hovick Middle School too?" I said quickly. "That's where I'll be going."

"Next year. I'm aware." Granddad set the homework sheet on the upper shelf with his router set.

"Because maybe some of the teachers remember her—"

"You've work to do."

I knew better than to keep talking. I went back to the box, rummaging through the stack even faster than before, hoping to discover more of Mom's stuff. Our house didn't have anything of hers inside, not even a photo of Mom as a kid.

But I reached the bottom of the box without finding anything else of hers. The realization made a lump in my chest. I looked around the garage. Maybe there was another pile of old papers. Or books or toys or anything that might have been hers. All I saw was more of Granddad's tools and a lot of paint and varnish cans.

"How come we don't have any pictures?" I said. "Of Mom, or Grandma Fi? Or anybody?"

"Because I don't want them around."

"Why not?"

"Pictures are false. Better my haziest memory than the clearest photograph." He hadn't turned away from his task of putting a new wheel on the grinder.

Weird. But then a lot of things Granddad did were strange. Or scary. My friends from school didn't like to come to our house. Only Davey Tolan was brave enough, and that's because his home wasn't much better.

Later, when Granddad went up the stone steps to the house to grab us coffee and a Coke, I stood on a stepladder to reach the upper shelf and Mom's school paper. I folded the page into a square and slipped it into my back pocket.

When kids at school talked about their parents, I avoided the subject. If they didn't get the hint or a teacher asked me a direct question, I just told them my mom and dad were dead and that usually shut them up fast. At least half of that answer was true, anyway. Maybe all of it.

Granddad wasn't going to say any more. But Ms. Cullen or some of the other teachers might. They'd met her. Mom. I wanted to learn whatever they could tell me.

Anything would be more than I knew now.

IN THE WAREHOUSE, THE whole derby squad was on the track, doing laps. Their trainer with the thick dark braid of hair stood in the center, shouting out the elapsed time from a stopwatch. Two minutes. Two-thirty. The skaters pushed harder, racing to achieve some goal unknown to me. The older teens skated in a line, with long fluid strides that ate up the track, weaving like a Chinese parade dragon around kids like Cyndra, who doggedly ground out their own laps in disorganized and gasping clumps.

Impossible to say who tripped first. One girl went down on the far side of the track, and then three and four, most of them just tapping the concrete with their kneepads before bouncing right back up.

Cyndra stayed down, cradling her arm. In an instant I was running the length of the hangar.

The trainer reached her first. Two members of the squad around Cyndra's age hovered anxiously as the woman helped Cyndra stand and roll to the outside of the track.

"I'm sorry," one of the girls kept saying.

"Not your fault, Jaycie," the trainer said. "Take my stopwatch and call out when they hit five minutes." The girls reluctantly skated back to the track. The woman held out her hand to Cyndra. "Let me see."

Cyndra uncurled her arm. Her fingers were bright pink, the same color as her face, and scraped raw. "I'm fine," she said. The reflexive answer of any kid embarrassed by sudden attention.

"Uh huh. Make a fist." Cyndra did, carefully. "Good. Wiggle your fingers."

"What happened?" I said.

"Somebody ran over it," Cyn said. "It's okay." She used her other hand to quickly wipe her eyes.

"It is," the trainer agreed, "though you need some antibiotic. C'mere." She led us over to the bench, the two of them floating on wheels, me thudding behind. When the woman knelt to fish an equipment bag from under the bench, her black-coffee braid fell to one side, revealing her derby name stenciled in block white letters on the back of her ebony tank top: PAIN AUSTEN.

"What do we always say, Mortal Cyn?" she asked.

"Fall small," Cyndra answered, giggling despite herself.

"Got that. Best way to protect your extremities." The

trainer sprayed Neosporin on Cyndra's knuckles. "I haven't seen you here before," she said to me.

Cyn remembered the manners Addy had been working so hard to instill. "This is Van. He's . . ." She hesitated. What was I, exactly?

"Family," I said.

Cyndra nodded vigorously. "Yeah. An' this is Pain."

It was the trainer's turn to grin. It was a good grin. A little crooked, a little self-mocking. She was long of leg and strong-looking in the way naturally slender athletes develop over time, as much sinew as muscle fiber. Kneeling with one leg up and balanced on her skate's toe-stop seemed to be no effort for her at all.

This close, the spiral of tattoos on her arm and shoulder was identifiable as a loose line of small birds in flight. Each bird varied slightly in size and radically in style, from photorealistic black and gray to eye-poppingly bright cartoon. The flock winged its way from her wrist all the way up and under the strap of her tight tank top. Her skin beneath the ink was tan, whether by genes or the sun. Not every part of her figure was slim.

She caught me looking. "My name's Wren," she said, nodding at the bird tattoos before turning back to Cyndra. "Teddy bears or pop art?"

"Art," Cyndra said. Wren took two bandages with Warhol soup cans and Elvises printed on them and applied them to Cyn's ointment-covered knuckles. "There. Better than new."

"Can I finish?" Cyndra said, looking at the track. The other skaters had collected by the aluminum bleachers to stretch and rehydrate.

"You better. You owe me laps."

Cyn dashed away, injury forgotten.

"She's fast," Wren said as we watched her bank hard into the curve, "for being so new to it."

"Making up time," I said.

"You're her stepbrother or something?" said Wren, eyeing me. I knew what she meant: that Cyndra and I looked nothing alike. Cyn was small and blue-eyed and fair, at least when her hair wasn't dyed. I was none of those things. I'd inherited Dono's Black Irish looks through Moira.

"It's an unusual situation," I said. "You've met Addy? Cyndra's guardian?"

"Talk about unusual. She's amazing. She told me she had a tryout with the Bay Bombers back in like nineteen-sixty-something."

I hadn't known that but didn't doubt it. Addy seemed to have lived enough lives for a dozen octogenarians.

"None of us have other relatives," I said, "except for Cyndra's dad, who's down in California. Addy was a neighbor of my grandfather's. We all sort of adopted each other."

"Chosen families can be the best. If you want to help out Mortal Cyn, she could use some resistance training. You look like you've seen the inside of a gym."

"Once or twice."

"Show her how to use the weights. Nothing too heavy. Just build up the endurance in her back and legs."

"Core strength. To get up every time she falls."

"You got it." Wren's eyes were a lighter shade of brown than her hair, a splash of cream mixed in the coffee. With tiny flecks of gold near the center. "Come to practice again. Let me know how it goes."

"I'll do that."

She glided away to join the girls, who had collected by the aluminum bleachers to shed their gear and goof around, not in that order. One of the older teens handed out popsicles from a cooler. Wren waited until Cyndra had finished her laps, then she had the skaters shout out the team name three times to close practice. Kids or not, they could yell like drill sergeants.

RAIN PELTED DOWN, BOUNCING like hail off every hard surface. Cyndra and I ran for the car with me carrying her gear bag. She shook water out of her hair while I turned the defroster on full blast.

"You want food?" I said.

"Uh huh."

"Dumb question."

"What's this?" Cyn said, taking the letter to Moira off the seat.

"Junk mail." The AC had cleared the fog of condensation from the bottom few inches of windshield. Good enough to see the road. We pulled out of the lot, the Barracuda's wheels splashing through a newborn river of water in the gutter.

"Are you gonna call this person?" Cyndra pointed at Jo Mixon's number.

"I'm not going to the reunion."

"Yeah, but . . . your mom, right? This woman knew her."

"If she really knew my mom she'd know Moira was dead."

Cyn frowned. Whatever point she was making, I was

obviously too dense to grasp it. "Well, what about your dad? You said you never met him. She could know."

"Not likely."

"But there's a chance. Like, you have to call her."

I should have expected this. Ever since I'd made the mistake of telling Cyndra about my unknown parentage, she'd romanticized it into thinking I might be the love child of an exiled duke.

"Cyndra," I said. "Give it a rest."

"Promise me."

"Yeah. I'll call her. But no more about it."

"And you have to tell me everything she says."

"You want to walk home?"

She sat back, satisfied.

A gust of wind rocked the car. At the next stoplight I pulled up the NOAA weather streaming app, letting the monotone male voice of the running forecast play while we drove. After a few minutes the looped recording cycled around to report on the coastal stations nearest Puget Sound. Winds up to forty knots with a small craft advisory in effect for everything south of Port Townsend.

"I have to go to the marina," I said. "Do you want me to drop you off first?"

She looked alarmed. "But food."

"On it."

The rain hadn't discouraged many diners from the eternal line outside Dick's on Broadway. I left Cyn in the warm car playing on her phone while I snagged us two burger-and-shake combos. Double patties for both of us. Cyn could eat nearly as much as me.

We parked in front of Addy's quaint yellow house

and ate in the car, dumping our fries into a collective pile in the cardboard tray. Cyndra held her Deluxe with one hand and deftly texted with the other.

"Your trainer Wren says I should teach you how to lift weights," I said. "Cross-training, you know?"

"When?"

"Whenever we want. I can take you to my gym. Once we know what size weights you need, we'll figure out something to use at home."

"D'you like Wren?" she said around her next mouthful.

"I just met Wren five minutes ago."

"But she's pretty, right?"

"You want to tell me about Elias?" Elias was a name I'd heard Addy mention at Thanksgiving. Mention only once, because the topic had made Cyndra flush bright pink from her hairline to her throat, as she started to now. "Okay, then."

Détente assured, I told Cyn to give Addy's dog, Stanley, the last bite of my burger and to tell him it was from me. She hauled her bag out of the back and kicked open the fence gate to run to the front door. Addy, ever prepared, opened it before Cyndra reached the porch. I waved to them and pulled away.

The letter to Moira slipped off the dashboard on the first turn and fell onto the steering column. Refusing to be ignored.

Addy and Cyndra weren't my relatives, but neither were my brothers in the Rangers. Both were a kind of chosen family. The difference was that Addy and Cyndra and I had chosen each other, and the Army had chosen the guys in the 75th Regiment, after we'd survived the levels of hell that made up the selection process.

Blood, though. Dono had been the only blood relation in my life that I had known, beyond scattered and unreliable impressions of my mother.

Moira had become pregnant at barely sixteen. She hadn't told Dono about her boyfriend, but it was possible that she'd trusted a friend. And anyone who was that close a friend had probably gone to Watson High with her.

This might be my best shot at ever learning who my father was. If I wanted to know. I'd gone a long time and done just fine without that knowledge.

Air blowing from the car's vent caught the letter and sent it flying. I snatched it out of the air without thinking. Like I'd been terrified to lose it.

CHAPTER THREE

I RACED THE RAPIDLY SETTING sun toward the west. About as far west as it was possible to go in Seattle, to the big marina at Shilshole Bay. The gale warning on the NOAA broadcast meant enough wind after nightfall to bang boats against docks and maybe shake them free from their moorings. My speedboat was one of the last possessions of my grandfather's that I still owned, and I didn't want it sunk by a storm.

The wind wasn't waiting for darkness, already pushing the rain half sideways and the Barracuda insistently to the left, as the muscle car's wide tires sluiced through the streams flowing across Leary Way. The copper-colored Barracuda was a recent acquisition. It still felt disconcertingly low to the ground compared to Dono's old Dodge pickup, which time and wear had finally forced me to set out to pasture, if an exorbitantly priced space in a long-term garage could be called pasture.

I parked in the marina lot and dialed the number written in purple pen on the letter.

"Hello?" A woman's voice, sounding rushed, like

she'd snatched the phone up while dashing between rooms.

I explained who I was and about how the reunion letter had found its way to me. The voice belonged to Jo Mixon. She made appropriate sounds of dismay when I informed her that Moira had died long ago.

"Why I'm calling," I said, when her torrent of words slowed, "I was wondering if you could put me in touch with anyone who knew Moira then. A school friend, or even a teacher."

"Oh. Let me think."

The noise of rain on the car roof and kids arguing in the background on her side provided a strange kind of hold music.

"Here we are," she said finally. "I had the yearbook out as part of all the work for the reunion. This is who I was trying to remember. Stasia Llewellyn. She and Moira were joined at the hip, you know?"

"A yearbook? Is there a photograph of Moira?"

"With the seniors?" I heard her flipping pages. "No, I don't see that. She *was* in school."

But maybe she had been pregnant with me when class-picture time came around. Not keen to capture the moment.

"I don't have any contact information for Stasia," Jo Mixon said. "I'm sorry."

I told her that was fine and asked her to spell Stasia Llewellyn's name. As we said goodbye, I was already pulling up a browser to search for Moira's friend.

Luck was with me: a Stasia Llewellyn-Wiler on Face-book, from Seattle and now living in Philadelphia. Her family pictures focused almost exclusively on a flock of children who ranged from grade school to college. A job profile on two networking sites listed her as a senior comptroller, whatever that was.

I sent Stasia a message, repeating the basic information I'd given to Jo Mixon and asking her to call me whenever it was convenient.

At dusk on a wet Sunday the marina was nearly deserted. The floating docks bobbed well below the parking level. I had to watch my step on the wet ramp. Cabin lights of a few liveaboards gleamed through the masts and radio antennae like lanterns in a forest.

One bright cabin belonged to Hollis Brant on the *Francesca*, two docks over. I'd just reached the speedboat when he stepped out from the aft door and waved one broad hand in greeting. He may have shouted something as well; it was hard to tell from a hundred yards away over the drumroll of rain pelting on my jacket hood. I waved back, aware that I'd been avoiding Hollis as much as I had Addy and Cyndra lately. He'd broken things off with his latest girlfriend, Gloria, too. Small wonder he might be craving any company, even as lousy as mine was these days.

The narrow spearhead bow of my twenty-foot speedboat rode high at rest. A consequence of the big Mercury outboard weighing down its stern. Dono had installed the engine and its muffled exhaust not long before his death. The boat had no name, only the registration numbers on the sides. It was painted shark-gray and originally intended for very fast and quiet runs across the Sound and up into the San Juan Islands, usually in the dead of night.

In the weeks since Oregon, it had become my refuge. When the apartment grew small and people became loud, I busied myself with scut work aboard or day trips out on the Sound, even sleeping some nights in the shallow triangular sarcophagus of its tiny cabin. The rhythm of the waves eased my restlessness.

I tied two more fenders as an extra defense between the boat and the dock and had begun checking that each snap of the canvas covering the cockpit was secure when Hollis came rumbling down the ramp. His sole acknowledgment of the foul weather was a canary-yellow slicker thrown over his T-shirt and shorts. Water dripped from it onto his short ruddy legs and sandals. Hollis gave the impression of being ninety percent upper body, all chest and shoulders with a hard round belly and ape-like arms. Even his hair under the slicker's hood was a shade an elder orangutan would admire.

"Hullo," he said as he hurriedly closed the last steps. "It's something when the Sound gets angry, isn't it?"

"Easy to enjoy a storm when you're in the harbor."

"Now that's a bit of truth. But this is the exception that proves the rule. I'm damned glad you're here."

"What's wrong?"

"Best I explain where it's dry. If your hatches are sufficiently battened, let's get the hell inside, shall we?"

We walked through the mounting rain to his dock, Hollis taking every third step double-time, as if to urge me to move even faster. Something was chipping away at his normally carefree façade. By the time we boarded the *Francesca*, he was practically jogging.

Hollis's home was a fifty-foot Carver, outfitted for comfort and modified to hide many things that were better left unseen by harbormasters and customs officials. Hollis was a smuggler, an expert one. He'd been a frequent accomplice of my grandfather's as well as his closest friend.

I hung my dripping coat in the enclosed aft section as Hollis opened the door and almost rushed into the main cabin, leaving a trail of rainwater across the faux teak parquet.

"Hollis—" I began, and then I saw what held his concern.

A tall heavyset white man with bristly brown hair lay on the main settee. He was shirtless, his left rib cage covered with a flat rectangle of folded cloth. Blood had seeped through at least two spots at the lower edge of the thick pad. He didn't stir at our approach.

Hollis grabbed a waterproof first aid kit from the table and unlatched it to take out a roll of clean gauze, winding it rapidly around his hand to make another pad.

"The damn wound's still bleeding," he said. "I've tried taping it shut, but no."

"I'll look. You start talking sense. Did you do this?"

"Hell no. The man's a friend of mine."

I knelt down beside the wounded man. His airway and breathing both checked out normal, and his pulse was steady. Pupil reaction when I lifted his eyelids looked fine, too. I didn't see any sign of an injury to his head.

"How long's he been out?" I said.

"Almost since I found him. He was more asleep than awake. I managed to get him up and walk with him onto the boat, but then he went out completely. That's when

I took off his coat and saw how much he was bleeding. Scared the hell out of me."

I set the man's arm carefully to one side. The cloth pad turned out to be two of Hollis's undershirts, folded and held to the man's abdomen by strips of athletic tape, which I peeled away. Underneath, more tape and wads of gauze made a red clotted lump. A sharp smell and yellow streaks on the skin underneath were evidence that Hollis had done what he could with iodine as antiseptic. As I looked, a drop of blood escaped the sodden bandage and fell onto the settee's blue upholstery.

"His name's Jaak," Hollis said, "a sailor on the Finnish freighter *Stellar Jewel*. I sailed out on the Sound earlier this afternoon to meet him. Just a bit of information and a sample product to show me, nothing major. He was supposed to borrow a boat and meet me in Smith Cove. Instead I found one of the freighter's launches drifting near shore, with Jaak lying inside. Out cold. It took all I had to drag him aboard."

Pulling back the bandage with a finger, I saw a long seeping cut across Jaak's side, with a wider puncture at one end. A blade had stuttered along the hard ribs until it found the softer flesh below.

"Stab wound," I said.

"That much I know."

"So why aren't we talking to paramedics right now?"

"Because the man's got no sailor's card on him, no visa to be onshore. If I take him to a hospital he'll be reported as illegally entering the country. At the very least he loses his job, and maybe the poor fool spends some time in jail here *and* in Helsinki to boot. But if we can get him back to the *Stellar Jewel* in one piece, his mates can cover for him. I'm sure of it."

"Well, I'm sure that he needs surgery. Soon. Look here." Hollis stepped forward, and I showed him a purplish blotch where blood was pooling below the puncture, blurring the skin down almost to Jaak's kidneys.

"He's hemorrhaging inside," I said, grabbing latex gloves from Hollis's kit. "We have to staunch the bleeding as much as we can. I need clean sponges. And duct tape."

"Tape's with the tools here," Hollis said, removing a small tackle box from shelves in the galley. "I think I've some new sponges in the cleaning supplies."

"Tear them up into pieces. About the size of a marble. Wash your hands well first."

He hurried to comply.

"I can patch him, but field medicine doesn't cover sewing up whatever's sliced inside." Keeping light pressure on the wound, I used my other hand and my teeth to tear off strips of duct tape, setting each one aside. I couldn't figure why Jaak was unconscious. He wasn't especially pale, and his pulse was solid. Not so much blood loss that a man his size should pass out. "He needs a doctor."

"I have an alternative to visiting an E.R." Hollis nodded. "I was about to give up on the idea, but then you arrived. Evidence of a grand design." He brought me a cereal bowl filled with small ragged chunks of orange sponge.

"Hold the towel there," I said to Hollis, indicating below the wound. "This will be messy."

When I took pressure off, the stab wound opened again. Blood flowed down Jaak's stomach, even as I swiftly began packing the puncture with pieces of sponge. The orange bits immediately swelled and grew saturated with blood. I pressed each of them gently into Jaak's body, counting on the swollen weight of the massed sponges to slow his internal bleeding. Six pieces, seven, and then the wound would take no more.

I pinched the two halves of the puncture together and used the last chunks of sponge to mop most of the blood from his skin. The last of the gauze went on next. It would keep the wound clean of duct tape residue. I layered the strips of tape in Xs, counting on them to keep the skin over Jaak's ribs from pulling apart. If the injured sailor was going to have surgery within the next couple of hours, I didn't want to attempt suturing the wound and risk tearing his lacerated skin further. My makeshift bandage would stem the flow. If it held.

Hollis climbed to the helm on the flybridge above the cabin and started the *Francesca*'s engines. A moment later his VHF radio began blaring the same weather broadcast I'd heard only an hour before. I looked out the cabin window. Between the rain clouds and the dusk, the sky was already a step beyond black. Wind buffeted the masts outside, making their halyards clang like muffled gongs.

"Hollis," I called.

"I know, I know. But we only need to sail as far as Vashon Island."

"In a gale."

"If you don't want to get involved—"

"Come on." Hollis and I had known each other long enough that the question was insulting. "What's on Vashon?"

"A physician called Claybeck, in a lovely beachfront home with its own dock."

"Tell the doctor to get ready," I said, peeling off the gloves. Jaak's blood had changed the latex from sky blue to deep violet.

"Thanks," Hollis said. "I'll cast off."

"*I'll* cast off. You get us moving. The faster we get across the Sound, the less chance we'll all finish this day by drowning."

CHAPTER FOUR

IT TOOK AN HOUR to cross the furious Sound to Vashon Island. A full sixty minutes, as each ten-foot swell coming from the north lifted the *Francesca* like a bubble to speed beneath us, leaving the boat heeling precariously to starboard as it fell into the trough behind. Hollis did what he could to follow a course that kept the stern at an angle to the current. Allowing the looming walls of water to slam straight into the transom might have swamped us.

"How's he doing?" Hollis shouted from the flybridge above. I caught the gist more than his actual words, smothered as they were by the laboring of the diesels and the latest wave's reverberating boom against the hull.

I felt Jaak's throat for his pulse while keeping a tight grip on the rope I'd used to lash the unconscious man to the settee. One hand for yourself, one hand for the ship, always. Especially when the weather was trying its hardest to toss you on your head.

"The same," I yelled back. I checked Jaak's pupils one more time. No dilation. His leg had twitched against the rolling of the boat a moment before, so I was halfway sure the sailor wasn't about to slip into a coma. But there was no way to know how much blood he might be losing inside. Small blessing that he was out cold. The boat's rocking was almost painful even without a knife wound in your gut.

"Five minutes," Hollis said. "Then we should be 'round the point and out of the worst of this."

"What about the doctor?" I said, leaving Jaak and climbing the step to join Hollis at the wheel. He held his balance against the ship's motion as if the seas were as smooth as glass. "Can he meet us at the boat?"

"She," Hollis corrected. "Claybeck's a woman. I've been trying to reach her. No cell signal way out here but I've tried her on the satellite phone, and still nothing."

"But she knows we're coming."

"She knows I might turn up with a patient."

"Christ, Hollis."

"Options were limited, lad. I called Dr. Claybeck straightaway once I found Jaak. She told me she'd be at her house after nightfall. But with the storm and Jaak passed out, I had nearly resigned myself to calling an ambulance and giving them some half-assed story about finding him unconscious at the marina."

And then I showed up and Hollis decided to gamble on Claybeck being home. God help the sailor if we crossed the Sound in a storm only to find an empty house.

"What's your business with a freighter from Helsinki?" I said.

"You'll laugh. Video game controllers. A new model, with built-in memory and some sort of kinetic whatsit for the player's movements. People will spend thousands on the latest generation to get the edge on their competition. What do they call it?"

"E-sports."

"Right. South Korea's crazy for those. An acquaintance of mine in Vantaa found a couple of dozen extra controllers lying about their R&D department and got them to Jaak, who was going to show me a sample today. If all looked proper, I'd buy the rest tomorrow. But then—" He shrugged and glanced toward the cabin where the unconscious sailor was secured to his blood-dappled settee. "Fate had other plans."

I looked at the indistinct shape of Vashon Island, off our starboard. The scattering of lights onshore helped differentiate the black of the landmass from the dark sea below and clouded sky above. We hadn't rounded the point yet, but already the waves rolling the *Francesca* were decreasing in size.

"Doc Claybeck's home is just four miles along," Hollis said, reaching for the satellite phone he'd tucked into the chart holder. He let the phone ring as he nudged the throttle forward. The *Francesca* responded as if she'd been waiting for the moment, her bow lifting to keep pace with the rapid current. No one answered the call. I went below to ready Jaak to move.

I guessed the sailor's weight at about two hundred and fifty pounds. I could conceivably get him off the boat and into Claybeck's place, but only by lifting his substantial bulk in a fireman's carry over my shoulders. That would put a lot of pressure on his gut, which sounded like a bad idea. Hollis and I would have to try hauling Jaak using a blanket. I went below to the *Fran-*

cesca's staterooms and found a duvet that looked thick enough to handle the load without tearing.

By the time I'd readied the makeshift stretcher, Hollis was easing back on the *Francesca*'s speed and turning us sharply toward shore. Through the windshield I could see a stubby dock outlined by footlights every few feet along its length. Beyond the dock, a broad house stood at the top of a rise. A lamp glowed from behind one long picture window. The rest of the house was dark.

"Not promising," I said, loudly enough for Hollis to hear me.

"But the dock lights are on." I could imagine Hollis gesticulating encouragingly. "Tie us off and I'll try calling the doctor one more time."

I stepped out the aft door into the driving rain—the island did nothing to block that—and made my way carefully along the narrow side deck to kick the fenders to hang over the rail before picking up the coiled and sopping bowline. As Hollis brought the *Francesca* alongside the dock, I jumped down and wrapped the line around the nearest cleat. A surge shoved the ten-ton boat into the floating dock, crushing the fenders between nearly flat. The planks groaned with the pressure. I hurried to tie off the stern. My head was already soaked, hood or no.

"Anything?" I called to Hollis. He began to shout a reply from up on the bridge, but my attention was distracted by movement from the rise leading to the house.

Dogs. Large dogs, running at top speed. Running at me. Their claws made hasty scrabbling clicks on the first wooden planks of the short dock as they lunged, fangs bared.

CHAPTER FIVE

I MOVED AS QUICKLY AS I ever had in my life, jumping high to catch hold of the *Francesca*'s deck rail and vaulting in a single motion onto the boat. Without pausing I reached up to grab the chrome handrail on the side of the flybridge above me and practically ran vertically up the cabin windows, hooking a foot on the handrail and hauling myself upward.

Below me, the dogs jumped to snap menacingly at the air and ran in circles on the dock. The side deck of the *Francesca* was only a foot wide—too narrow for the beasts to leap aboard easily, but their jaws could reach just fine. Every jump brought them close enough for me to count their teeth. They looked like some sort of shepherd or Malinois mix, big-chested with pointed ears and tawny fur and black faces. Big enough to tear off a man's limb if they wanted to. They wanted to. They didn't bark but instead whined with spine-chilling eagerness.

I was perched in a crouch with my feet on the slick metal handrail and my arms holding on to the side of the boat for dear life. Like a treed cat. Me on the outside of the flybridge, Hollis gaping at me from the other side of the polyurethane window.

"Van?" he said.

"You might have mentioned the damn dogs," I shouted.

"I didn't know," Hollis said. "They weren't around the only other time I've been here."

I risked standing up on the slippery handrail to climb to the aft of the boat for a better grip. I was stuck between the dogs and the pouring rain, but at least I wasn't in danger of falling to the dock. My escape seemed to urge the hounds into trying to leap aboard, their claws scraping the fiberglass hull with every attempt.

"I've got an air horn," said Hollis. "And a gun, if we need it. But—"

"We're not shooting the dogs. Any other ideas?"

My phone rang. I wasn't in a position to reach for it.

"Look there." Hollis pointed.

Another light had appeared up at Dr. Claybeck's house. The right size and shape for an open door, down at ground level.

The dogs stopped jumping. In another instant, they were running as fast as they had come, up the dock and the short hill and presumably into the house. The rectangular light went out. I hadn't heard a whistle or any other signal.

After a moment I climbed down to the side deck. Hollis met me outside. We both kept a wary eye on where the dogs had gone.

"The doctor must have called them off," he said, turning to put the satellite phone to his ear. "Maybe I can reach her."

"No need." I nodded toward the house. In the dim, a

distant figure of a tall person in pale clothes stood out like a phantom. The figure raised one arm and held it aloft.

"That her?" I said.

"Let's say yes," said Hollis. "Jaak can't wait forever."

We lifted the unconscious sailor onto the duvet and wrapped him like a tamale. Only his face showed from the folds. With Hollis taking his legs and me at his head, we carried Jaak aft—both of us grunting with effort—and down onto the swim platform, from where we could step to the dock and begin making our slow way toward the house. The pale figure stayed where it was. No sign of the dogs. My forearms ached with the effort of gripping the duvet.

Flagstones in the lawn helped us climb the hill to the house. Hollis's breath was coming short and fast.

"We can rest if you want," he said. Then another two gasps later: "Better than dropping him."

I nodded and we set Jaak down gently on the soaked grass. We were close enough now for me to be sure the figure in the cream-colored rain jacket was a woman. Hollis waved exhaustedly to her. In her middle years and over six feet tall, she had curls that might be ash-blond under the jacket's ivory hood. She hovered outside the closed door, barely shielded from the weather by a stunted overhang.

"Doctor," Hollis managed.

"You shouldn't have come," the woman said. "Take him to a hospital."

"We're here now," Hollis said. Rain dappled Jaak's slack face. "At least have a look—"

"He's not my concern. Leave." Claybeck held herself stiff upright, as if guarding against the cold and the occasional gust that splashed water over her boots.

"Why tell us now?" I said. "Hollis has been trying to call you for hours."

"I'll let the dogs loose again."

"He could die before we reach the mainland. If we go back to the boat, it'll be to call nine-one-one. You're in this now. Help him."

Before she could answer, the door swung open behind her. A slim man with a thigh-length tan leather coat and a hard expression on his darker face appeared from one side of the doorway. He pointed the blunt barrel of a machine pistol at me. Hollis stepped back reflexively.

For an instant, nobody moved. I watched the gun, anticipating the minute flex of the man's trigger finger that would send half a dozen rounds tearing through my center mass.

A young woman stepped past the gunman, blocking his field of fire. Her platinum hair had been highlighted with blue tips that brushed the shoulders of her trench coat. She took in the sodden sight of us for a moment before nodding assent to some private decision.

"I have a better idea," she said. "Come in out of the rain."

CHAPTER SIX

THEY MADE US LEAVE Jaak on the wet lawn while the glowering man patted Hollis and me down. His leather coat had a band collar and only buttoned partway down his chest, as much poncho as jacket. I guessed him to be Indian or Pakistani, or some nation close to those borders. He removed my wallet and multitool and even the change from my pockets. Then he knelt to check Jaak himself.

When they were satisfied, the white woman with the bicolor dye job ordered us to carry Jaak into the house. Dr. Claybeck remained at a distance, observing our progress without comment.

We hefted Jaak's limp form through a mudroom lined with cedar planks and into a finished basement, though unlike any basement I'd ever seen before.

The square room had been outfitted like a very small but completely modern emergency care clinic. Two hospital beds and one steel-topped surface that might serve as an operating table took center stage. A rack on one wall held equipment like defibrillators and vital-signs monitors that I recognized, and a lot more that I didn't. Cabinets and refrigerators completely covered the far side of the room. Each shelf was fully stocked with a pharmacy's worth of pill bottles, surgical tools, and other supplies.

One of the beds was occupied. A man, fully clothed in an expensive-looking metallic gray suit and fawn shirt, and a ventilator mask covering most of his face. Elastic bands around his forehead and neck held the clear plastic wedge in place. Tubes connecting the mask's valve to the ventilator flexed and shuddered minutely with every breath. A sweep of brown hair started high on his scalp and reached down to his shoulders. His eyes were closed.

"Set him on the table," Dr. Claybeck said to us. It was her first utterance since the blonde and the gunman had appeared. Hollis and I made one last heave to set Jaak carefully on the steel surface.

"Leave him." The blonde strode across to grab Claybeck's arm. "See to Bilal."

"Bilal is stable—" the doctor protested, as the blonde shoved her toward the man in the ventilator mask.

"Then keep him that way."

Claybeck looked on the verge of spitting right back. She didn't give the impression of a woman who would be pushed around, literally or otherwise. But she made work for herself by checking the ventilator machine.

"What the hell's going on, Paula?" Hollis said. "Setting your animals on us and now this?"

"I'm sorry." Claybeck spared a glance for him. "Saleem and Aura let my dogs loose to try and force you to leave." She indicated the man with the machine gun and the blonde. "I convinced them that unless I turned you away directly, you'd keep trying. I underestimated your stubbornness."

"Sorry we didn't take the hint," Hollis growled at the blonde, Aura. "This is madness. Why not tend to both of them?"

Because there was no point, I had realized. Whoever the man called Bilal was, his presence here was meant to be kept secret. Now that we had seen him, Saleem and Aura might have no intention of letting us leave.

The man called Bilal opened his eyes. Wide eyes, very dark and completely alert. The mask and tubes gave the impression of a large translucent snake against his face. It was unclear who was eating whom.

He motioned to the mask, and Aura began to remove it.

"He needs that," Claybeck said. They ignored her.

Saleem motioned toward the opposite side of the room with his gun. "There. Sit down there," he said in a heavy South Asian accent.

Hollis and I sat on stools against the wall. The stools weren't metal, like the table, but they were solid enough chunks of wood. Aura seemed distracted with Bilal. If Saleem came close, I would have a fair chance of putting his lights out with the stool and taking his gun before Aura could effectively retaliate.

Except Saleem was a watchful fucker. He kept his distance from Hollis and me. His Steyr machine pistol was more than capable of cutting us both in two from across the room.

Aura helped Bilal prop himself up on one elbow. His bronze face was long and square and creased with temporary furrows left by the mask and permanent ones that spoke of heavy concerns. He took a long breath, maybe testing his lungs. I guessed Bilal's age at late forties. His brown mane showed no gray. Maybe he went to the same salon as his girlfriend, who must be twenty years younger.

"Your names, please?" Bilal said to Hollis and me. His voice was deep and casual, with the same accent as Saleem's, though not nearly as pronounced.

Saleem answered for us. "The old man is Hollis Brant, who the doctor told us about. The big one with the marks is Donovan Shaw." He stepped forward to offer Bilal my driver's license. The picture on the license didn't show my marks—the scars that divided my left cheek into three distinct sections, and the smaller ones that bisected my eyebrow and creased my jaw on that same side—as starkly as real life.

Bilal tapped the license with a blunt finger.

"Donovan Shaw," he said. He met my gaze. "Perhaps you shorten that? To Van?"

An answer wasn't required. Bilal knew me, or at least recognized my name. Which was unsettling, since I'd never seen the man before.

Bilal nodded to the unconscious Jaak. "Who is the man on the table?"

"Only a merchant sailor," Hollis said, doing enough nervous fidgeting for both of us.

"And if he dies? What is that to you?" Bilal sat up, swinging his feet to touch each woven leather shoe gingerly to the tile floor. Aura stood prepared to catch him if he tottered.

Hollis grunted. "He's a friend."

Bilal stood up with almost exaggerated slowness and buttoned his suit jacket. "You go to considerable risk for your friend. Sailing through storms. Friendship is important to you. Correct?"

"Yes," said Hollis. He glanced at me, maybe feeling the same apprehension I had about the direction of Bilal's questioning.

"Good. Friends are very useful. I would like to be your friend. Yours and Mr. Shaw's."

"Let the doctor look after our guy," I said, "and I'll buy the first fucking round."

Saleem spat a threat. No translation required.

"Everyone may leave the doctor's home healthy tonight," said Bilal, as if neither of us had spoken.

"In exchange for what?" I said.

"Two necessities. One is that you will not mention our meeting here. To anyone, in any capacity. You have never heard of my name."

"I'd be happy to forget the whole damned night," Hollis said, "you especially."

Bilal looked at me. I nodded agreement. He murmured something to Aura, who walked out of the room. Her steps retreated swiftly up a flight of stairs.

"My second condition is a transaction," Bilal continued. "The doctor is in my employ tonight. Exclusively. I've paid well for this. If she saves your sailor friend, then it stands to reason I should be recompensed for her time and effort."

"How much do you want?" Hollis said.

"Not money," I answered for Bilal, who was looking at me with the same focused expression as when he'd clicked on my name.

"Not money," he agreed. "I have a task for you, Mr. Van Shaw. For this service, all three of you will have your lives. A good exchange, I think. Until then—"

Aura's quick steps tapped back down the stairs and into the room. She carried a computer sleeve under one arm. Saleem crossed to hand her my cell phone. Aura removed a tablet from the sleeve and plugged my phone into it with connecting cables. Her face showed absolute concentration, as if we'd all gone for a walk in the storm and left her alone to work. It was a face I might have found cute in different circumstances, heart-shaped and with a snub of a nose between blue eyes that matched Bilal's for size. But the circumstances did a lot to ugly her up.

After a minute she handed the tablet to Bilal and pointed to the screen. "They're the primaries."

Bilal nodded as he read. "Addy Proctor. Cyndra O'Hasson. And"—he looked up at Hollis—"Mr. Brant."

My scalp felt like worms were crawling over it. Saleem noticed and smirked.

"These are the people with whom you are most in contact," Bilal continued. "People you care about. I could list more."

"You've made your point. Here's mine: If you touch them, you're dead." I glanced at Saleem. "I'll go through this one and anyone else like fucking butter to get to you."

"You misunderstand. I do not need to touch them. This"—he tapped the tablet—"is a toy. Useful, but not the extent of my capabilities."

Aura had glowered slightly when Bilal dismissed the tablet. Had it been her work?

He continued to scroll down the screen. "You have biometric sign-in for your bank account. Foolish. Though perhaps not so big a fool. You have a surprising amount of money for someone employed at a tavern, Mr. Shaw."

Bilal said it like a shared joke, like we both already knew the punchline. Damn.

"I can harm your friends without resorting to violence," Bilal continued. "Without even being in the country. Without even being *alive*, Mr. Shaw. My team could carry on ably, should anything happen to me. Debit accounts. Retirement savings. Legal status. Even medical records. Imagine Mrs. Proctor going to her doctor and being prescribed the wrong medicine. Or incriminating texts from Miss Cyndra appearing on the phone of someone arrested for selling drugs. These are simple things. It can get much worse."

I stayed silent. I didn't trust myself not to snarl like one of Claybeck's attack dogs.

"Good," said Bilal. "You understand."

He extended a hand and Saleem passed him a cell phone. Bilal held it out to me.

"You will keep this close. It must be answered when I call."

"What's the job?" I said.

"I will tell you the particulars when time allows. Soon."

I still didn't move to take the phone. To the left of us, Saleem stiffened. Aura shifted into view on Bilal's other side, the pistol back in her hand.

"Van," Hollis urged.

"If I don't like the job, I won't do it," I said to Bilal.

"Then we will renegotiate," he said, as if he'd expected that very answer. He looked pointedly at Hollis. "I'm certain we can agree on terms."

"Mr. Nath," Dr. Claybeck said, one hand on the wheeled cart of instruments. "The patient."

"Of course. See to him."

The doctor checked Jaak's breathing and pulse, then took scissors from her cart to begin cutting his bandage away. Bilal and the others moved to the door. He motioned for Aura to go ahead of him and then paused in the doorway. Saleem tossed the items he'd taken from us on the spare patient bed.

"You cannot clap with one hand. Do you know this expression?" Bilal said. "It means out of assistance comes great things. We are associates now. We cooperate."

Or else, I thought.

The gunman, Saleem, took the rear, his eyes on us until his boss reached the top of the stairs. Then he, too, was gone.

CHAPTER SEVEN

HOLLIS AND I GATHERED our possessions and joined Claybeck at the steel table.

"Who the hell was that bastard?" Hollis said to her.

"Priorities." Claybeck had donned gloves and a surgical apron. She peeled away the tape and gauze that had held Jaak's wound closed over the massed wad of sponge pieces. "What happened?"

"His name's Jaak," said Hollis. "He passed out shortly after I found him, stabbed. Almost four hours now."

"My work," I said, indicating the bandage. "I'd guess Jaak had lost at least a pint of blood by then. Maybe more inside him."

She frowned as she began to pick out the crimson-soaked bits of sponge with tweezers, dropping each one to the floor. "Military, I suppose."

"How's his blood pressure?"

"Still there. Now leave, please. Wait upstairs." The doctor's voice cracked slightly, but her hands moved without pause.

We followed the same path that Bilal and his soldiers had taken. The stairs led to a living area so long it was practically a meeting hall. The picture windows we'd seen from the dock offered a view of the Sound and the distant lights of Dash Point on the mainland, all blurred by rain washing over the glass with every gust of wind. Crepe paper streamers adorned the room in preparation for what might be an early New Year's party, if that year was 1963. Every low-slung chair and walnut credenza screamed Camelot. Only the computer monitor sitting on an elegantly curved desk in the corner fit this century.

"A time capsule," Hollis said, delighted by the display in spite of what we'd just been through.

A whine and fervent scratching from the opposite side of a nearby door revealed where Claybeck's dogs had gone. We beat a fast retreat to the farthest end of the living room. Hollis headed for the loaded bar cart and clanged through the bottles to see what was on hand. The cart was identical to the one downstairs with the surgical tools. I looked out the window at the evergreens. Their top reaches lashed to and fro like bullwhips. The cell phone Bilal had given me made a heavy lump in my pocket.

"Your choice of health care sucks, Hollis," I said.

"Don't you think if I'd known—" Hollis started. "Never mind. I'm sorry. Let's have a drink and start the fucking healing process."

He poured two generous quantities of a brown liquor and brought them over to sit on the seafoam-blue couch. After a moment I took the matching chair and accepted the glass from him. We drank. Rye, smooth enough to soothe a consumptive's cough.

"This isn't her fault," Hollis said after a few moments. "Doc Claybeck. She's trapped."

"Trapped by what?"

"By who. The doctor had—still has, my mistake—a daughter. That poor girl was born with a devil's truckload of what we used to call birth defects. I don't know what the kinder term is now, but whatever you choose to say, the child is afflicted, even though she's long since grown. Vision and hearing troubles, mental and sometimes emotional troubles, too, since her brain stopped developing after a point. She needed a lot of care. More than the doctor and her eventual ex-husband could pay for."

"So Claybeck borrowed."

"After a fashion. Paula Claybeck had an acquaintance from Seattle's social elite. This person offered to hire the doctor at an exorbitant salary to be on call as a private physician. For whomever the acquaintance chose."

"For people like Bilal. Get there quicker, Hollis; I don't need a damn yarn right now. What are you not telling me?"

"Fine, fine. Doc Claybeck's benefactor"—Hollis layered some uncharacteristic venom into the word—"is Ondine Long."

I stared at him.

"Exactly." Hollis nodded. "Once in, Paula was in all the way."

Ondine Long was a broker. A facilitator. She might not deal directly in drugs or gambling or flesh or set up scores herself, but she knew who could and would make the introductions for a percentage. Her connections reached from corner boys to the legislature. She donated generously to symphonies and charities and the right politicians. A spider, if the spider never had to leave the center of her lavish web to feast on a morsel from every insect that happened along.

Ondine and I had crossed paths before. After the dust had settled, we had both tacitly agreed to give one another a wide berth.

"How are you in the know on Claybeck's story?" I asked.

"All that medical equipment you saw downstairs? I was the one Ondine tasked with obtaining it for Paula. Best if the AMA didn't start asking why a surgeon would be outfitting her home like a trauma center."

I had to chuckle. "And you held on to Claybeck's number."

"Who knows when a man might need a physician? Besides." Hollis looked a little sheepish. "She's a handsome woman. Though I never did call her, until tonight."

"Hell of a first date, Hollis."

He sighed. "At least Bilal is gone. Do you think he can do what he claims? Empty everyone's bank account and all that cyber witchery?"

I wasn't certain. Bilal's trick of phone hacking had been impressive. He might have made an educated guess at my net worth from text notifications of past deposits still in my history. The rest of his assertions sounded a few ticks above knocking down the privacy barriers on a cell phone. But his knowing everyone in my contact list was enough to me to take Bilal at face value.

The doctor had spoken his last name: Nath. A place to start. I'd have to learn everything I could about the man and find something that would allow my own brand of renegotiation.

We turned at the sound of Dr. Claybeck coming up

the stairs. She had taken off the apron and was wiping her hands on a paper towel.

"Jaak was very fortunate," she said before she reached the top step. "No penetration of the organs that I can determine. But it's a serious puncture. Something thicker than the average pocketknife. Do you know what it was?"

"No," said Hollis. "Some of the sailors carry fixed blades for their jobs. Those can be sturdy."

"I've sewn up his subcutaneous tissue and the surface laceration separately, with some staples, given how jagged the injury was. I've also typed him and given him a unit of blood. Plus antibiotics." She shook her head in judgment of my field care. "If anything kills him it will be the imminent infection. His vitals are good but we'll have to watch him through the night to make certain."

"We?" Hollis said. "I'm no medic."

"You can manage to work a blood pressure cuff," the doctor said, dry as parchment, "and check his pupils. I'm not confident that he doesn't have a concussion. It's disturbing that he's been unconscious most of the night. That's not normal, even for someone in shock from being stabbed."

"What's wrong with Bilal Nath?" I said.

Claybeck looked uncertain. "I can't—"

"I promised the fucker I would forget he was ever here. That includes forgetting you said anything about him. Why would he pay Ondine Long to see you?"

She glanced reprovingly at Hollis. He'd been indiscreet. "Nath has ALS."

"Lou Gehrig's disease."

Claybeck nodded. "He had an attack last night and

couldn't breathe properly. And for whatever reason, he refused hospital care."

"Perhaps he doesn't want anyone knowing he's sick," Hollis mused.

"That's possible. Or he won't admit it to himself. He's on riluzole and other medications, but he's going to go downhill quickly without full treatment."

"How quickly?" I said.

The doctor raised an eyebrow at my tone. "Hoping your problem will solve itself?"

I grunted. "I won't be that lucky. Bilal has something specific in mind for me. He won't waste a second if he's going to die soon."

"The progression of ALS can vary hugely. Stephen Hawking lived for over fifty years after his diagnosis. But"—Claybeck shrugged—"most patients succumb within five. I believe Bilal was diagnosed at least three years ago, and his limbs are showing signs of recent atrophy. My best guess is that he has a year at most."

"So we all take a long vacation," Hollis said, trying to break the mood. "Maybe Jaak can arrange a sea voyage. Speaking of our friend . . ."

"I'll take first watch," I said.

"No," said Claybeck. "I won't be sleeping anytime soon. And I want to stay close to the patient for another couple of hours in case he needs another unit of blood."

I wasn't so sure sleep was in the cards for me, either. But after the doctor led us past the door with her ravenous dogs and down the hall to the house's spare rooms, I lay down on one of the beds and closed my eyes. An old habit from the Rangers: Rest whenever you can, because the next opportunity might be a long time coming.

CHAPTER EIGHT

D R. CLAYBECK SHOOK ME awake. Her face so slack with fatigue I thought she might collapse onto the bed next to me.

"Jaak is stable," she said. "You shouldn't have to do more than check his pressure every hour. You know how?"

I did. The doctor left immediately for her own room, her dogs padding after her. I washed my face in the guest bathroom sink and headed downstairs.

Jaak looked about the same as when I'd last seen him, save for a much cleaner bandage strapped to his side. He was snoring lightly. I took that for a good thing.

My watch read five minutes past three in the morning. I checked my phone and remembered that it had rung earlier in the night, during all the chaos. Stasia Llewellyn-Wiler, from Philadelphia. Moira's school friend had left a brief voice mail saying she was happy I'd gotten in touch and that she'd try me again tomorrow. Which was today. I texted to let her know I was awake on the West Coast.

The other cell phone, the one Bilal had given me, felt hot in my chest pocket. Right over my heart.

Goddamn it. A day ago I had my life in order. A tenuous state, but at least I was putting the recent past behind me. Now I was keeping watch on one of Hollis's smuggling cronies and owed a favor to some gangster connected to Ondine Long, of all people. What the fuck was I doing wrong?

Maybe it was karma. My ex, Luce, for all her pragmatism, had liked the idea of karmic balance. Do some good, and trust in the ripple effect to benefit you and yours somehow. I didn't believe justice worked so efficiently.

I didn't believe in ghosts, either. But somehow the men I'd killed in Oregon managed to haunt me, at least a little.

My pocket buzzed. For an instant I thought it was Bilal, wasting no time in putting me to work. But the vibration came from the other pocket, and my own phone. Stasia, calling back right away.

"It's Van," I said. "Moira's son." Those last two words sounded very strange coming out of my mouth.

"Van, it's Stasia Wiler. This is amazing. Truly. It might sound very odd to you, but I've thought of you so many times over the past twenty years or so. Almost every time I remembered Moira. How are you? Or maybe *who are you* would be a better question, after so long."

"I'm good," I broke in. "I wanted to ask you some questions about Moira."

"Naturally. I could talk for an hour about she and I and barely scratch the surface. Wait—" Stasia interrupted herself. "All I can think about is how much you might look like her. Could we switch to video?"

Her call was already sending a request to activate my camera. Best that Stasia didn't see Dr. Claybeck's clinic and the sleeping trauma patient. "Give me a second," I said.

I'd spotted a set of baby monitors on the rack of medical equipment earlier in the night—an odd fit with the rest of the gear—and now I had an inkling of how Claybeck used them. I set the monitor next to the sleeping Jaak and brought the parent unit with me as I jogged back up to the cavernous living room to turn on the lights. If his snoring changed, I'd come running.

I accepted the video request. Stasia's face came into the frame. Lean and equine, with subtle makeup in place despite the early hour and auburn locks barely tamed with a large tortoiseshell clip. Her eyebrows popped into view over the lenses of her glasses.

"Oh, my God!" Stasia said. "You are very definitely Moira's boy. Your hair. And something in the mouth, too. Those are so her. Not your eyes. Hers were brown, too, but not nearly so dark . . ."

"The eyes skipped a generation."

"Her father, yes, yes. Donny? Is he still alive?"

"Dono. Donovan, I'm named for him. He died a couple of years ago."

Stasia rubbed her forehead with a fingertip. Behind her, I could make out a bookshelf loaded with thick three-ring binders and framed degrees on the wall next to family photos. A home office, maybe. "I'm very sorry." She sighed. "Man. Moira's dad. He was . . . an intimidating guy. Of all the ways Moira impressed me, the biggest might have been standing up to her father."

"When she became pregnant? I was also hoping you

knew something about her boyfriend back then. Dono—and I—never found out who he was."

She laughed, a little shakily. "Well, nothing like starting a conversation with the easy topics. I don't know how much you know about Moira—"

"Just north of zip. Don't worry about offending me."

"Then I'll begin at the beginning. Moira and I met in middle school. She was very smart. We both liked to get good grades and had our hands raised in class constantly, even if the teachers called on the boys nine times out of ten." Stasia paused to reflect.

The storm outside had finally passed. A low cloud cover cast an ashen pall over the night sky.

"We were closest then," Stasia said. "High school sort of tugged us apart. Even though she'd already skipped a grade in elementary, Moira was enrolled in AP courses. And there were boys."

"She dated a lot?"

"Not her, me. I had the hormone crazies and didn't make as much time for Moira. We still saw each other, but . . ." Stasia made a face. "Between my having fun and her being such a private person, it wasn't the same. She sort of withdrew."

That was the Shaw way. Keep to yourself and guard your flank. My own circle of friends in school could have been counted on the tines of a pitchfork.

"Not your fault," I said. "Kids drift around."

"That's why it was so surprising when Moira asked if she could come stay with me and my family, just before our senior year. I was stunned. But happy she'd asked, even if I didn't really know why. All she would tell me was that she couldn't live at home anymore. That she and Dono were arguing all the time. She implied without actually lying to me that their fights were about whether Moira would go to college right away or take some time off."

"And you took her in." My glass of rye whiskey was still sitting on the coffee table, half full. I picked it up, less to drink than to feel its solidity.

"My parents were fine with Moira living with us for a while. She was still pulling all As and they considered her a good influence, you know? And they might have been nervous to talk to Dono about what was going on."

"I could see that."

"So we started school and came home each day and that was pretty much all for two weeks. Then I found Moira crying in the closet, not for the first time, and I told her I was going to go to the police unless she told me what was happening. That did it. She fessed up that she was four months pregnant. Of course I insisted that she tell me who the boy was, but no way. She hadn't even told Dono who he was. Hence her extended visit."

"Dono kicked her out." My fingers were tight around the whiskey glass. I made myself set it down.

"No. At least I don't think so. My guess is that their fights were about him pressuring Moira to give up the boy's name. She seemed scared of what Dono might do."

I could understand that, too. My grandfather was scary enough when he was calm.

"And she never hinted at who he was?" I said.

"No. Not for lack of my asking. But Moira wrote letters. I found her scribbling feverishly at my desk once, and she swept the letter into her backpack and made me promise that I'd never go hunting through her stuff. And I never did. She was so furious. I'd already seen the words at the top of the page but pretended I hadn't: *'Dear Sean. I'm sorry but I can't. If Dad ever asks you—'* That was all I caught."

Sean. My father's name was—might be—Sean.

Then the *other* critical point hit me.

"'If Dad ever asks you'?" I said. "So Dono knew this kid?"

"I suppose he must have. But that doesn't mean Dono ever realized Sean was dating Moira. I remember thinking about that and mentally going through every boy I had ever met, trying to recall one named Sean. I'd promised Moira I wouldn't look through her things, but not that I wouldn't try my best to figure out who her secret boyfriend was. It was pointless. Eventually I accepted that if I wanted to stay friends with Moira I had to let it drop."

Dono would have done the same, I realized. Considered every boy in Moira's life, trying to figure out who was to blame. Moira must have been damn good at keeping her life private.

"Moira stayed with us first semester," Stasia said. "She kept up with school, too, even though—people were cruel. Students and even some of the teachers. I don't know how she stood it. But the longer it went on, the tougher Moira seemed to get. She was so brave. I remember she was going to church every week. I suppose that helped her."

"Church?" I said. "Like, Catholic?"

"Yes. We were Presbyterian, so I don't know if we're

talking about attending full Mass, or if Moira was just going to a cathedral to sit and contemplate. It was new for her. Discovering or rediscovering her faith. Did she take you to church as a boy?"

"I don't think so. At least I don't remember that." Dono had rejected religion early on, a collision of tough corporal schooling and his tougher defiance. I suppose Grandma Fi might have been closer to the church. And that Moira would have been christened or baptized or whatever it was when she was a baby.

Damn, maybe I had been, too.

"Wait, you said Moira stayed with you first semester?" I said. "Where was she after that?"

"Her own place. Before Christmas, when she was just a few weeks away from popping, Moira told my parents and me that she'd be getting an apartment starting in January. We thought that was crazy. She was still sixteen. How could she live alone? How could she pay for it? But there it was."

"It must have been Dono's doing. A compromise, if Moira wouldn't return to their house on Roy Street."

"You're probably right. I couldn't change her mind about moving out. Moira's apartment was only a few blocks away from school. I visited her at least once every week through the rest of the year. Partly to see the baby—you—but also to study. It wasn't completely selfless: I brought her homework when she had to skip, and Moira got me through Physics." Stasia shook her head. "She was so proud of you. Babies don't do much during their first months, but man, she talked to you like you could understand every word. You'd babble back and she'd pretend you were interrogating her like on a cop show. I would fall over laughing. She could be very funny, Moira. Very wry."

More droll than Stasia knew. Dono had played a game like that with me, too, one where he was the cop and I had to avoid being trapped by questions. It had been good practice. Had he taught Moira the same lessons?

"What about other friends?" I hoped my mother had another confidante, anyone she might have talked to about Sean.

"If there was anyone, I never met them. I'm sorry."

"And Sean never came around."

"No. I don't think he did. Perhaps Moira thought she was better off without him."

Perhaps. Dono knew Sean: my thoughts kept circling back to that. Most of the people Dono had known were not straight citizens.

Stasia asked me what I'd been doing with myself since I'd learned to walk. I gave her a sanitized version of my life, as quickly as politeness allowed, and turned the conversation back to my mother.

"After graduation things trailed off," Stasia explained. "I headed to college at Penn. I know Moira was aiming for college herself when you were a little older, but I don't recall her ever taking any classes." Her voice trailed off.

"Before she died," I finished for her.

"When I heard, I was so upset. I called around and someone told me Dono had taken you in, so I assumed that Moira and Dono had healed their relationship."

No way to ask either of them now.

"Oh, wait," Stasia said quickly. "You'll want to see this." She left the frame for a moment. "Here. From our junior year, before all the trouble started."

She held up an open book to the camera lens. A yearbook, the headshots of the students in black and white. It took some trial and error for Stasia to position the heavy book so that I had a clear view of the second row, last picture.

Moira Shaw.

Dono hadn't kept family photos. I was seeing my mother's face for the first time all over again. She was fifteen years old, and a stranger to me.

Except. The black hair and the cheekbones and just the way she was smiling at the camera, with a hint of *can-you-believe-we're-doing-this* in her tilted eyebrow, rang as true as a sledgehammer on a gong. Embarrassed and awkward and beautiful in spite of and because of all those things.

"I'll take a picture and send it to you," Stasia was saying, "and if I find any others—"

"Thanks," I said, my voice thick. And then again: "Thanks."

"You never got to know her." Stasia caught a tear as it rolled from under her glasses. "You should have."

I coughed to clear my throat. Stasia Llewellyn-Wiler and I both took a moment.

Stasia wished me a happy new year. I returned the sentiment. We ended the call. I picked up the glass of whiskey and downed its contents without tasting a drop.

My mother. Barely half the age I was now, with an infant son, living on her own and finishing high school.

Whatever trials I'd conquered in my own personal life, they were vying for second place behind Moira's survival.

"MIZ CULLEN?" I SAID.

She looked up from the stack of math assignments on her desk. "Hello, Van. Davey wasn't here today." Ms. Cullen was my best friend Davey's homeroom teacher. I had Mr. Rigby this year.

"No. I mean, I know. I wanted to—" I glanced outside at the hallway, making sure again that it was empty. "Um. You knew my mom? When she was here? Moira Shaw?"

Ms. Cullen blinked. "Moira?" She looked past me at the open door to the hallway herself. "Well, yes. Of course."

"And, did she—was she, like, good in school?"

Ms. Cullen looked at me for a moment, then motioned to the door. "Why don't you close that, Van? We can talk better."

I didn't really want to shut the door, though I wasn't sure why. Maybe because if it stayed open I could turn around and leave faster. But I closed it anyway and sat down in the first row where Ms. Cullen pointed.

"Your mom was a very good student," Ms. Cullen started. "She liked to read a lot. You read, too, don't you?"

I nodded. Granddad made me, keeping the TV off, but I probably would have read, anyway. We had a lot of books in the house.

"Well, Moira was especially good at book reports.

She would tell the class about scenes she had read and get other children excited to read the same book. That was a real gift." Ms. Cullen took her glasses off, which made her squint a little. She opened her drawer to get a cloth and began cleaning the lenses. "Moira's father: Do you live with him now? I think I heard that."

"Uh huh."

"I see." She finished wiping the glasses and set the cloth down. She cleared her throat. "Do you and he ever talk about your mother? Or your grandmother?"

I shook my head.

"Can't pretend I'm surprised. I met your grandmother a few times, at parent-teacher conferences. She was—very smart. Very direct. She wanted to make sure Moira had everything she needed in school. She dressed very well. A lovely green linen dress one day. And she wore her hair up, with chopsticks for hairpins. It's very funny, what people remember after so long. Oh, Van." She got up and took a Kleenex from the box on her desk and handed it to me. "Blow your nose, sweetie."

I did, and I wiped my eyes on my wrist.

"It's okay, dear. Of course you want to know about Moira, and your grandma. Do you want to keep talking now?"

"No."

"That's all right. I'll see if I can remember more. It was—well, there have been a lot of students but I'm sure there's more in the back of my head. You come back when you're ready."

I nodded, already hurrying to get out.

"And Van? I won't mention this to your grandfather. Okay?"

I hadn't even thought about Granddad. Man, if he learned what I was doing, I was toast.

"Thanks," I managed. I opened the door and closed it tight behind me before I ran down the hall.

I STRODE DOWN THE hall to Dr. Claybeck's second spare bedroom. Like the living area, it was of another age. Hollis made an unkempt lump under retro Mondrian sheets.

"Hollis," I said, clicking on the bedside lamp. The bulb glowed beneath a fabric lampshade patterned with starbursts. "Wake up."

"Whazzit? My turn?"

"No. Did Dono know anybody named Sean? Back when Moira was a teenager. A young guy, I'm guessing."

"Who's—wait. What are we talking about now?"

I forced myself to rewind and told Hollis about Moira's reunion letter, and my conversation with Stasia. The room smelled of Lemon Pledge and faintly of Hollis himself. I must have needed a shower just as much.

When I finished, he was sitting upright, his eyes wide.

"Jesus God. You think this lad could be—"

"Sean," I pressed. "Did Dono know someone named that?"

"Your man didn't socialize much. You know as well as I do. Much less with young people. Most of the men he met were in our line of work, one way or another."

"So what jobs was Dono pulling that spring? Was he into house scores? Smuggling anything with you?"

"Easy now, I'm thinking." He leaned back against the robin's-egg headboard and scratched his tousled head. "That was during one of the big tech booms. I remember Dono stole a truckload of stuff from Microsoft right off the loading dock. Housing prices going up, lots of expensive development materials. And new players in town . . . Oh."

"Hollis."

"Give me a moment. Fats. No. Gut."

"Gut?"

"Gut Burke. He was a fat man, hence the nickname, though I don't know if anyone dared call him that to his face. Fergus Burke, or Gus or Gut. A very bad sort. He had been some kind of muscle for one of the families. I think he was new in Seattle, from back east."

"And Dono worked with him?"

My grandfather had kept himself at a long distance from organized crime, as a rule. It was the main reason he and Grandma Fi had left Boston for Seattle in the first place. The East Coast was too mobbed up for an independent operator like Dono.

"Or Gut Burke was buying something. Don't recall exactly what that might have been. The point is, Burke had brought his son with him. A teenager. I can't swear to it, but the boy might have been named Sean."

"You're not sure."

"It was thirty years ago, Van. And your grandfather told me all of this secondhand. But Moira was around. Burke and his lad came to the house unexpectedly, which pissed your grandfather off to no end, let me tell you. He never liked conducting business with family nearby. If he hadn't been so royally furious and ranted to high heaven about it, I might not have remembered the incident at all."

"So they met: Moira and Sean. If it was Sean."

"They must have. Dono and I talked about the strangeness of Gut Burke taking his son along on the errand. Learning on the job."

Just like I had with Dono. I wondered what sort of skills Sean had perfected as Gut Burke's apprentice.

"You've got a contact in the FBI field office downtown, right?"

"Yes." Hollis's voice was cautious.

"I want to meet him. After he's pulled everything he can find on Gut Burke and his son. And," I amended, "on Bilal Nath and his soldiers, too. Might as well get all of my shopping done at once."

"Van, that's not—I've been a long time earning my man's trust. He's a jumpy fellow. He can't just type in names and have NCIC spit information out without people noticing. They track these things. You're asking a lot."

"Less than a sharp poke." I nodded toward the stairs leading down to the clinic.

Hollis flushed. "I suppose I do owe you for tonight. It's Monday. I might be able to reach him this morning."

"Call him now. I'll make it worth his while if he comes through. A bonus if it's fast." I had come into a lot of money early in the year, through circumstances that required me to spend the cash quietly. I still had some of that slush fund left for emergencies. And this had been one rainy goddamn day.

Hollis got up to put his pants and sweater on over his

sleeping attire of boxers and undershirt. I idled impatiently in the hall.

"Did you sleep?" he said.

"Some."

"I imagine . . . since you came back, that hasn't come easy."

My pacing stopped. "What do you mean?"

He hitched up his trousers, a kind of embarrassed shrug. "You've told me your combat experiences gave you nightmares for a long while." Hollis glanced down the hall and lowered his voice another notch. "After what happened with those maniacs in Oregon, it stands to reason you'd have some trouble putting that aside. In your dreams, I mean."

I looked at him, understanding. That *would* be the normal response.

It just hadn't been mine.

"My dreams aren't troubling me, Hollis," I said. "The thing that troubles me is that I haven't been dreaming at all. Not since I came back. I killed those men and I've been sleeping like a baby ever since."

I couldn't put an exact name to Hollis's reaction, but the closest expression might have been wariness. Like realizing the docile neighborhood mongrel was showing flecks of foam around its jaws today.

CHAPTER NINE

JAAK REGAINED CONSCIOUSNESS SHORTLY after dawn. I roused Hollis and Dr. Claybeck. The sailor's English was limited but serviceable, which was a grace as none of us knew any Finnish and Hollis only a few phrases of Swedish, most of them dealing with the possibility of being arrested and protesting innocence. But we all collaborated to piece together the story of what had happened to Jaak the evening before.

He had been preparing to sneak off the *Stellar Jewel* to meet Hollis when a ship's petty officer named Kauko had caught him. Instead of turning Jaak in, Kauko had offered a deal. Kauko had been planning to take one of the freighter's launches to pick up other sailors north of where the *Jewel* was docked on Harbor Island. He offered to hide Jaak in the launch and ferry him to meet Hollis. In return, Jaak would share the profit from the deal. Trapped, Jaak couldn't refuse.

Things had taken a turn. During the ride on the launch, Kauko had pressed Jaak to share drinks from a flask. Jaak began to feel groggy. By the time he realized he'd been drugged, it was too late. He had a rough memory of staggering toward Kauko and the petty officer looking at him in terror. Then nothing. Dr. Claybeck theorized that Kauko had doped Jaak with Rohypnol or some similar benzo compound.

Kauko's motives were less clear to all of us. Jaak told us that Kauko had stolen his entry visa. Perhaps that had been his intent all along, to filch the document to make his way onshore and maybe use Jaak's name to start a life in America. But when the roofie hadn't knocked the large Jaak out quickly, Kauko had panicked and stabbed him in self-defense. Thinking his shipmate dead and himself a murderer, the petty officer had bolted.

Claybeck okayed Jaak to be moved, and Hollis agreed to take the sailor back to his freighter. If Kauko had returned to the *Stellar Jewel*, Jaak would confront him and take whatever punishment came for leaving the ship.

"What do we owe you?" Hollis asked Claybeck.

"Peace and quiet," she said. After her short sleep the doctor looked slightly refreshed, if just as aloof. Only Jaak received any hint of warmth. "Make sure your ship's doctor takes you to a hospital," she reminded him.

We left. I risked Claybeck's ire to leave my number and asked her to get in touch if she heard from Bilal again. She didn't refuse outright, which was as much as I could hope.

A rippling chop greeted us on the Sound, but compared to the previous night, the *Francesca* barely felt the waves. Hollis dropped me off at a marina in West Seattle. After dozing through a Lyft ride, I was back in my own car and headed for home. I needed rest and food before I met with Hollis's FBI contact later in the day.

And, I decided, I needed to talk to someone who

could tell me if I was insane for even considering digging up family secrets. For wanting to know who my father was, if the son of a bitch had abandoned Moira and me thirty years ago.

"YOUR *FATHER*?" ADDY SAID. The pan she was removing from under the oven clanged against its drawer. "That's tremendous!"

"Keep it down," I said. A glance into the living room confirmed that Cyndra was still engrossed in a *Fortnite* mission with other gamers around the world, her over-ear headphones in place. Addy's excitement was enough; I didn't need Cyn getting overstimulated, too. She'd think the whole situation was romantic. The long-lost family, reunited. "I don't know if Sean Burke is my father. Just that he might have known my mother."

"How could you not have mentioned this before? That you were tracing your roots?"

"I've barely started. And if Burke isn't the guy, I might be finished just as fast." I wasn't even positive yet that Gut Burke's son and Moira's Sean were one and the same.

"Don't downplay this. You might actually find a blood relative. Someone other than your grandfather, for the first time since you were small. It's huge."

I went back to dicing potatoes. When I'd first met Addy, her antique set of Henckels kitchen knives had been so dull they were more useful as bookmarks than cutting tools. Addy was a good cook but terrible at maintaining things around the house. I had borrowed a manual sharpener from Luce's bar to hone the blunted edges of the knives and bought Addy a sharpening steel to use regularly. She never touched it, but the steel was there when I visited.

"What are you going to say to him?" Addy said as she plopped a roast into the pan. The three of us were having a pre–New Year's Eve dinner together, since she and Cyn would be joining one of Addy's coterie for the holiday itself.

"That's the big question," I said. " *'Hey, did you knock up Moira Shaw when she was statutory?'* "

"They were children. Teens make mistakes."

"A mistake Sean Burke had years to make up for."

"How do you know he didn't try? The only way to find out is to talk to the man. I'm sure you've already searched online."

I had. There was no shortage of Sean Burkes in the world, and a handful on the West Coast who might be the right age. But the field would narrow once I learned more about Fergus Burke. Gut's only online presence was a two-line notice of a conviction in Everett for DUI and solicitation, almost twenty years ago. A great anecdote to tell about my possible paternal grandfather.

"It's only a big deal if I let it be," I said.

A deal I would be smart to postpone. My shadowy bloodline wasn't important right now. Not with Bilal Nath holding me at his beck and call. That had to be my priority.

"Addy," I said, "how long are you and Cyndra staying with Dorothy?"

She paused in her grinding of peppercorns and rosemary. "Just sleeping over at her home after the ball drops, and then breakfast on New Year's Day."

"Could you extend it?"

"What's going on?"

"It would be better if you and Cyn were out of this house for a while." I took a breath. "Somebody with hostile intentions hacked my phone. There's no direct threat. But I'd feel better if you were harder to locate for a few days."

Addy set the mortar and pestle down. A small action, but Addy pausing her bustling flow sent as much signal as a shout. "Any threat feels direct enough, Van. If you don't see that, I don't know what I can do for you."

"I just want to take precautions."

"This is a caution. A *pre*-caution would be avoiding situations like this in the first place. And you seem incapable of doing that. No, don't say anything." She held up a hand. "I accept the part of you that's prone to trouble. You know that. You also know it's not me or you I'm concerned for."

"I do."

She looked toward the living room, and Cyndra. "I will ask Dorothy if we might stay a couple of days. It'll give us a chance to go through some donation ideas she's been on me about."

"Thanks."

"You'll recall I once did some volunteer work with addiction therapy. Friends and family support groups."

Surprised by what seemed like a swerve in topic, I blinked. "Yeah."

"Something we always taught: the first and primary reason that a family member should cut ties with a loved one is when safety is jeopardized," Addy said.

From the backyard, a crow cawed its harsh laughter.

"It's foolish of me to expect you to change," Addy continued. "But if your choices mean Cyndra is forced to live with any kind of fear, or risk to herself? That's an easy decision to travel a hard path, as my Magnus used to say. That girl has experienced enough trauma."

I nodded. What else was there to say? I would take that path, too, if I were in Addy's place.

CHAPTER TEN

RUNNING WITH ADDY'S DOG, Stanley, was like being tethered to an enthusiastic horse. Not only did the huge mixed breed resemble an especially pale and muscular pony, but I was also very conscious that if Stanley suddenly chose to switch directions, there wasn't a hell of a lot I could do about it.

Fortunately, Stanley limited himself to occasional arm-yanking tugs at the leash as we jogged. He probably wondered why our pace was so leisurely. He knew I could run faster, even if it would never be as fast as he would prefer. But I didn't want to be early. So we had taken the long way from Addy's house, coasting down the steep slope of 24th Ave and winding around Interlaken, descending even farther to arrive at the edge of the arboretum, our breaths making steam-engine puffs in the late afternoon air. Traffic was light but rushed. I kept a watchful eye for cars slaloming through the boulevard as fast as the curves allowed.

In another five minutes we reached the Japanese garden. I bought a ticket and let Stanley investigate the lawn before we entered. Normally he'd mark his territory, but he'd depleted himself during the first mile of our run.

Inside, the garden was nearly empty. Just me and Stanley and a few families with young children. Hollis's friend from the FBI hadn't arrived yet.

Within a few months the garden would be a riot of colors and scents. I wasn't much on horticulture, but I remembered the vibrant pinks of the azalea bushes and an almost bittersweet lush smell of the cherry trees in full bloom from walks I'd taken as a kid, whenever the big house I shared with Dono became uncomfortably cramped. Now the garden looked subdued, patiently waiting for the celebration of spring to start.

A small boy, encased in a puffy coat and pompom hat, screwed up his courage to take two steps away from his parents and toward Stanley, who wagged his tail in greeting. I made him sit, and the boy reached out. Stanley landed a lick on his hand before the boy began scratching the dog's tea-saucer-sized ear. A blue Prius, so new it shone like a sapphire, pulled into the parking lot.

I led Stanley down the long path that looped around the narrow park. On the far side was an open-air shelter, overlooking the largest of the garden's ponds. I sat on one of its benches and waited. The owner of the Prius made his cautious way through the gate and eventually toward us.

Stanley huffed as the man drew nearer. I patted the dog's side and fished in the pockets of his harness for a bully stick. The harness held everything from waste bags to hand wipes. Stanley could have easily carried a cooler full of beer, too, but Addy drew the line at that. I gave the stick to Stanley. He seemed assuaged as he lay down and began to gnaw at the rawhide.

I removed a small receiver from the other side of his harness, switched it on, and put it in the pocket of my running jacket.

"What kind of dog is that?" the man said, stopping ten yards away. The comforting mass of a rhododendron still between us.

"Part mastiff, part Komodo dragon," I said.

The man nodded, not really listening, his head moving to and fro as he scanned the park. He was skinny enough to seem taller than he actually was, with old-fashioned glasses that reminded me of Scrooge counting pence.

"We're alone," I said. "Unless there's a police diver hiding in the koi pond."

He actually glanced at the surface of the water. His name was Panni. For the purposes of our meeting, I was told to call him Mark if I had to say his name out loud. Hollis had said Panni would be more comfortable if we used aliases, and I was trying to make friends here. Panni was probably only a year or two out of grad school, finding his criminology degree of limited use in a low-level position in the Records department of the FBI's Seattle branch office.

After another moment of reconnoitering the lily pads, Panni sat down on the bench beside me. While his jaw was so hairless that it might never have seen a razor, his embroidered skullcap bulged with long locks tucked beneath it.

"How do I know you're not wearing a wire?" he said.

"You can check if you want."

He thought about it. Maybe it had already occurred to him that if OPR, the Bureau's version of Internal Affairs, were on to him, they would have busted him the moment he tried to leave the field office with confidential files.

"Never mind," he said.

"And I'll trust you, too." The little receiver in my pocket hadn't emitted the buzz alerting me to any cellular or two-way signals within a dozen feet. Panni wasn't wired.

"I don't know why we couldn't go through our mutual friend," he said, sitting next to me on the bench.

"Because our friend isn't always available," I said, "and if I need information quickly in the future, it's better that you and I know each other." I patted Panni on the back.

"I can't do this a lot," he said. I wasn't sure if he meant logistically or emotionally.

"Let's just take care of today."

"So how do we . . ."

"You leave what you brought on the bench. Then you go to your car and find yourself a party."

He frowned. "What about the rest?"

"It's already in your pocket, Mark."

He pressed his elbow against his North Face ski jacket and was rewarded with the crackle of paper from the folded envelope I'd placed there. His eyes widened.

"Happy New Year," I said.

Panni fumbled in his jeans pocket and set a black thumb drive on the bench. He managed to take long strides on his way back out of the garden, despite being clenched enough to hold a broomstick lodged where I couldn't see it.

I scratched Stanley's flank as I reached into his harness again for an adapter cable. I plugged the thumb drive into my phone and began to read the files Panni had brought.

The first document was Bilal Nath's travel visa to the United States, including an image of his passport. He was a citizen of Pakistan, with a listed residence in London. He'd entered the country on a flight from Heathrow to Miami in mid-November. The next two pages of search results confirmed Bilal had no arrest record in the United States and a check with Interpol had drawn a similar blank.

But the next file was a surprise. A State of Florida marriage license. Bilal Nath and Aura Kincaid had been married in Miami only a week after Bilal had arrived in America. The gangster and his girl were newlyweds.

Aura's record wasn't quite as clean as her husband's. Arrests for identity theft in her home state of Washington, and again in Florida, which also included a count of wire fraud. Cybercrimes. Unsurprising, given that code she'd created to strip-mine my phone for all its data. She hadn't been indicted on the first rap and had gotten off with probation for the second.

The sentencing statement noted that the judge had been lenient given Ms. Kincaid's ongoing health concerns. It didn't elaborate on what those problems had been, but if they'd been serious enough to make a Dade County judge pause, I guessed Aura had been afflicted with more than a hangnail.

She'd been married once before Bilal, too, I noticed. To a Timothy Gorlick, while she was still living in Washington. Their divorce had been finalized right before her move to Miami.

That was the sum total of information on my new and unwanted acquaintance. I had gleaned a few biographical facts, but nothing that might give me any leverage to shake Bilal loose. Stanley caught my angry curse and raised his head.

Bilal had hired Dr. Claybeck through Ondine Long. It was a sure bet Ondine was also the person who had first dropped my name to Bilal, although I had no idea why. Nothing good, that was equally certain. Whatever motive that witch might have had for mentioning me, my best interest wouldn't be a factor.

I closed the files on Bilal to open the second folder. The information Panni had been able to find on Fergus Burke.

Gut Burke's federal rap sheet was the largest file. It had been linked to records in various counties and states. I didn't know if that efficiency was Panni's good work or courtesy of Homeland Security tying information across sources.

Fergus William Burke, aka Big Gus, aka Gut Burke, aka George Bergin. White male, six-foot-one, 260 pounds. Born New York City, died twelve years ago in Longview, Washington, only days shy of age sixty.

So he was dead. If Gut Burke had been my paternal grandfather, he was just another relation lost to time, never to be known.

But that was making the very big assumption that Burke had any connection to me at all. I scrolled ahead, looking for his family and known associates.

There. Three relatives. Wife Iva Burke, divorced with no year listed. Daughter Kathleen, deceased. She had her own criminal sheet as a separate file on Panni's drive. Katie Burke had been arrested in Berkeley twice for possession of heroin and died of an overdose at age twenty.

And son Sean. Sean Burke.

Hollis's memory had been spot-on. My mother, Moira, had known him.

The news was big enough that I let the file labeled SEAN_WILLIAM_BURKE _09790467A sit unopened and full of its own portent, while I read more about his father, Gus.

Gut Burke had racked up enough arrests to force me to scroll down twice to see the whole list. He'd been in handcuffs before he'd had his first zit. Assault, burglary, armed robbery, possession with intent, suspicion of extortion, suspicion of kidnapping, suspicion of murder more than once. Leaving aside a host of short jail terms, two of those arrests had earned Burke prison time. Four years in Sing Sing for manslaughter, six in San Quentin for selling cocaine. East Coast, West Coast.

Mug shots of Burke at various ages showed a man who was almost fully grown and next door to good-looking at sixteen, with a strong nose and chin and dark wavy hair, who had slid downhill fast. Like a time-lapse of Dorian Gray's portrait. It wasn't just the weight gain that ballooned his already thick neck. The skin on his cheeks blossomed into rosacea and his countenance became darker in a different way.

Burke looked exactly like what he was: a thug, a crook, a killer.

The attached Bureau dossier gave me some color commentary to back up all the stats. Gut Burke had been an enforcer for the Westies, the Irish-American mob in Hell's Kitchen, who started as competitors of the Italians and ended as little more than attack dogs working for the Gambino family. Seeing the writing on the wall, Burke had pulled up stakes and fled to California in the early 1980s. The Feds had tried to make him turn state's evidence when they nabbed him for trafficking drugs, but Gut hadn't taken the deal.

Burke had moved again, to Washington State, just after his parole from SQ ended. The dossier showed registered addresses in Olympia, Longview, Tacoma. Never anywhere longer than five or six years. And no arrests after his relocation to the Northwest. Had he suddenly quit? Or changed his methods?

Which renewed my curiosity about what business Burke might have had with Dono thirty years ago. Despite a few similar notes in the melody of their criminal records, the two men didn't have much in common. Burke was a few years older than my grandfather had been, and from NYC, while Dono had come to the States through Boston. Dono was a thief, with no interest in dealing narcotics and especially not in murder for hire, which looked to be Gut Burke's specialties. And Dono had assiduously avoided working with gangs. If crime could have hermits, that would have been my grandfather.

My fingers hesitated over Sean's file. The more I learned about the Burkes, even reading between the emotionless lines of the official record, the less I liked.

My grandfather had raised me to be just like him. A

thief. Dono Shaw wasn't without his own scruples, and he'd loved me. I'd bought into the idea—the delusion—that he and I were justified in what we did. That I was a good person despite my crimes.

I'd grown out of that way of thinking.

Gut Burke couldn't by any stretch of the imagination be considered good, not ever. Was his son the same?

I opened his file.

Sean Burke's driver's license and two passport copies were on the first pages. He was forty-seven. He traveled internationally with enough frequency that he'd filled the first of the passports within a few years. Trips to Canada and Russia, mostly, and a handful of former Eastern Bloc nations as well.

I studied Burke's face. The photos were straight-on and impassive, as with most DMV and passport pictures. It was a squarer face than his father's but with the same strong features and the same pugnacious set to the jaw.

He didn't look a ton like me, except for the shape of his skull and perhaps the ears. Dark hair and eyes, sure, but not so dark as the Shaw bloodline with their black hair, and eyes close enough to that shade that a drunk girl in a bar near Fort Benning had once poked me in the chest and proclaimed them obsidian. I'd known my whole life that my looks resembled Dono's. Everyone who'd seen us together had remarked on it.

Burke and I were similarly sized, though. Over six feet, and big in the shoulders and chest from what I could gauge from his headshots and his license. That hadn't been the case for Dono. My grandfather had been even taller, but rangy. More a wiry strength than the muscle mass that came naturally to me. I noted Sean had kept his weight down as he'd aged. No one was likely to call him Gut after his dad.

He was also married. To Natalia Burke née Morozova, no children. Real estate records showed they owned a house right here in Seattle, a two-bedroom suburban in Bitter Lake bought ten years ago for four hundred and ten thousand and probably worth twice that now, thanks to Seattle's insane real estate boom.

Married, and settled. That surprised me, and the fact that I was surprised made me wonder whether I was trying too hard to fit Sean Burke into a preconceived notion. I exhaled a breath I hadn't realized I'd been holding. Maybe Sean had escaped the pull of his father's gravity, as I'd more or less escaped Dono's.

I continued to page through his records and stopped abruptly, thinking at first that the copies of Burke's U.S. travel documents had been duplicated.

But no. I was looking at a copy of a second passport for Burke. With the red-and-gold cover of the Russian Federation.

That must have taken some doing, even with a Russian wife. Did Burke somehow arrange for dual citizenship? Was that even recognized by both countries? It hadn't seemed to set off any red flags during travel. He'd logged at least two trips to Asia per year, with entry points at Pushkin International in Moscow and also to Kiev in the Ukraine. Family visits? Or working?

Sean held a Washington State business license under the name SWB Consultants. I clicked away from the file to make a fast search. If the business was still operating, it was unusual. I couldn't find any online presence for SWB or Sean Burke. No social media, no company website, not even a Yelp review.

He did have a criminal record. A single arrest by the SPD, for suspicion of assault when he was barely eighteen. I checked the date against Gut Burke's file. Sure enough, father and son had been busted together. Neither man had been indicted.

The last part of his rap sheet was especially curious, an appended section of only two sentences. Sean Burke had been questioned by the ATF two years ago. Any inquiries were directed to the federal agency's Seattle field office. No further details on the investigation were provided. I suspected that the official record had been classified, which would make sense if the case was still considered open.

Burke might be a suspect. Or a witness, or even just a technical expert the Feds had consulted for information. No way of knowing. But those two lines had become a cloud obscuring any clear picture of Sean Burke.

The final three pages were almost identical, each one a federal firearm transaction form. Burke had purchased two SIG Sauer M17 pistols, and one bolt-action SSG 3000 rifle by the same maker, all within the past four years. I knew the M17, had even tried it out on the range in the Army when the model was in contention to replace our standard issue Beretta. SIG Sauer had eventually won that bid. The M17 was rolling out by the tens of thousands to Army and Air Force personnel.

Burke wasn't a veteran. Why pay top retail to own pistols that would become as common as weeds within a couple of years?

The SIG rifle struck me as even stranger. A sniper rifle used by law enforcement, and an odd choice for the casual gun enthusiast.

I recalled something else about the rifle. Something that turned the nagging tap at my mind to frantic scratching. The SSG 3000 had a rare feature, a barrel that could be replaced in just a few minutes. Useful, if you wanted to try out different calibers.

Or maybe swap out the rifle's original barrel to muddy the results of a ballistics test.

I could think of at least one private sector occupation that would find that feature useful. A job that might reward tactical proficiency with a model of handgun you could acquire with comparative ease almost anywhere in the world.

Combine those facts with frequent travel. A vague registered business. And a family history shadowy enough to make mine look like a bunch of Peace Corps volunteers.

A shooter. Not a grunt like Gut Burke, weighted down with a rap sheet that would attract attention in any town he settled in. But a professional killer, careful and prepared.

Had Sean Burke gone straight? Or, like Dono after his young wild years, had he refined his approach over time to become much better at the work he'd done all his life?

Hell. I was probably building an elaborate house of cards. Maybe Sean Burke had buddies in the Army whom he liked to go shooting with, or he had found some price break on weapons from his favorite manufacturer.

And he lived in Seattle. My possible next of kin, my father, might have been living less than ten miles away from me all these years.

Ten miles, a drive of no more than twenty minutes. I could be at Sean Burke's house just that fast.

I unplugged the drive and filled Stanley's harness with the various pieces of electronics once more. The bully stick long since devoured, he hopped up, keen to be on the move.

So was I, I realized. I had enough raw energy suddenly firing my blood to sprint like a wolf chasing prey.

I just wasn't sure which direction I should go.

CHAPTER ELEVEN

CYNDRA WAS THE FIRST to hear Bilal's phone ringing. I got up from the little circular table Addy used
for sit-down meals, which had become more frequent
occurrences now that Cyn lived with her, and retrieved
the phone from my jacket pocket.

"Yeah," I said.

"This is Shaw?" Bilal's gunman, Saleem, I guessed,
based on the accent.

"You give these phones out to a lot of people?"

He paused, maybe uncertain whether he was being
mocked. "We are at Eastlake and Roanoke. Come here."

"Later. I'm busy."

Another delay as the line went completely quiet.
Maybe Saleem covered the phone with his hand while
he conferred with Bilal or Bilal's new wife, Aura.

"We can come and find you," Saleem said finally, "at
the Proctor house."

My jaw tightened. I had to give them intimidation
points for efficiency. Bilal could track the phone's location, and he'd already matched it to Addy's home. Sure
as shit I didn't want these assholes anywhere near Roy
Street.

"Half an hour," I said, and hung up. I could be terse, too.

"Who was that?" Addy said from over her sliver of mince pie. Addy liked food, would try a bit of everything, but she claimed she'd reached the age where she couldn't eat as heartily as she once enjoyed.

"Someone I have to see." I returned to the table and tucked in to the last of the roast. "Start the movie without me. I'll come back to catch the end if I can."

"But it's Mad Max," Cyndra said. "And Furiosa."

"I've seen it before. We all have."

"Too much for me," said Addy. "So much violence." Her tone implying something other than the film.

"It's not that bad," I said, answering her question. "Save me some dessert. Cherry, not that weird spiced stuff you call pie."

Addy didn't rise to the joke, lame as it was. Cyn didn't look entertained, either.

"You're still off school." I nodded to Cyndra's gear bag lying in the corner of the living room. "How about you and me go to the gym in the morning? Like Wren said?"

"Okay," she answered, only half looking up from her plate.

"I'll be back as soon as I can."

Neither of them said anything to that. I swallowed the final bite and took my dishes to the kitchen before leaving. Setting a fine example.

I KNEW THE INTERSECTION of Eastlake and Roanoke. About a block away was a good Italian restaurant called Pomodoro that stayed open until midnight. I'd taken Luce Boylan there once. And another woman much more recently, on a date that had ended in a one-night stand. The meal was worth seconds, the sex not so much. We'd both agreed to feast elsewhere.

As I drew near, Bilal's phone rang again. Probably tracking my progress. My electronic leash had a fucking choke collar on it.

"I see you in your car." Saleem again. "Leave it and come down to the corner." I spotted him in his leather coat on the stone steps leading to the tennis courts at Rogers Playground. I'd played some baseball on the diamond there as a kid. Never enough time on any league team for me to become much of a batter; life with Dono had interfered with the schedule demands of organized sports. But I could run fast enough and throw hard enough to get by at center field, the same position my idol, Ken Griffey Jr., played. The notion of beaning Saleem with a fastball gave me an ounce of pleasure.

I left the Barracuda two blocks from the park and walked down. Saleem stayed on the steps, maybe to keep us eye to eye. His jacket was open, and his right hand hovered near the buckle of his braided belt.

"Nervous?" I said.

Saleem's only reaction was in his eyes, which blazed. His chiseled face might have approached handsome if it ever relaxed. But there was an intensity, maybe life-long, that had drawn the fine ligaments under his skin taut, like the rage within was consuming him.

He angled his head at Eastlake. "There."

I looked. A Mercedes G-class utility vehicle in glossy lunar blue idled at a fire hydrant. The rear door opened and Bilal Nath stepped out. Aura, a white winter cap covering her azure-tipped hair, joined him. Another man I couldn't see clearly through the tinted windows sat in the driver's seat.

"We can walk from here," Bilal said, as if he was looking forward to the exercise.

"Walk where?" I said. No one bothered to answer.

Aura took Bilal's arm and they crossed the street, headed down the slope toward Lake Union. Saleem didn't move until I did. I followed Bilal and Aura, Saleem followed me, and after a moment the rumbling Mercedes made a caboose to our little train.

"You were born here. In this city," Bilal said. "Is it still home, after all of the travels serving your nation?"

An unsubtle flex. Bilal had done some homework on me, maybe by asking Ondine Long. Between tracking my location and this, it was clear that my new acquaintance liked to show off.

"Where's home to you?" I said. My own background check on Bilal Nath could remain my secret.

"Karachi, originally. I, too, am a city person. But so much larger a place. Seattle seems a small town to me."

Aura squeezed his arm. "It's your way. You want everything available, every hour of the day or night."

"Yes, I do. Here."

We reached the end of the block. There had once been a small marina here, one of a handful on this side of the lake, along with the community of houseboats just a hundred yards south. In place of the former docks, a swath of water had been filled with tons of rock and sand to extend the land and construct a building. A new enough project that the sign of the architectural firm was still planted proudly outside, above shrubs that retained their unnatural geometric squareness straight from the nursery. The building's exterior cladding carried the look of brushed steel. With most of its lights on inside, the whole structure gleamed like a pale opal in a dim room.

CERES BIOTECHNOLOGIES, the angled silver letters above the fourth story read, over a symbol that was a combination DNA helix and sheaf of wheat.

Aura and Bilal looked at the building. Their expressions took me a moment to place. Hostile, certainly, and tinged with something close to loathing. The temperature on the street dipped another ten degrees each time a breeze whipped off the water. Neither of them took any notice.

Bilal pointed to the building's upper stories.

"Ceres holds something which I require. You will take it from them, and then I will consider your debt paid," he said.

"What is it?"

"That is not your concern right now. Your task is to gain access to the building. And to disable any protective countermeasures."

Countermeasures? Like booby traps? What could a biotech firm have that a gangster might find valuable?

"Not a chance," I said.

"This is your answer? I can send Saleem and Juwad to discuss better terms with your friend Addy, perhaps."

"I'm not bargaining. I'm telling you that this whole idea is dead on the starting line. Look." I nodded at the building. "There's a guard at the front desk at this hour, and another man just walked past that window on the third floor. So we can assume twenty-four-seven security. There are cameras and keycard entry. That's what we can see from here. There are bound to be other barriers inside, especially in restricted areas. Fingerprint access. Voice recognition."

I was laying it on thick. Angling for whatever advantage that might give.

Aura looked at me with the same antipathy she'd given the shining offices of Ceres. "You're supposed to be good."

"Good enough to know a bad thing. If Ceres handles government contracts, they could have a direct patch to the FBI. Any vaccines and viruses, they'll have extra precautions."

"We do not want viruses," Bilal said. "I am not a terrorist."

"It's not a disease we're after. Or a weapon," said Aura.

I glanced at the Ceres building and back at them, my doubt readily apparent.

Not a disease, but perhaps a cure. Bilal was sick and going downhill fast. Was Ceres working on a vaccine for ALS?

"How valuable is this thing?" I said. "Why is Ceres so worried about theft?"

"The safeguards are to prevent accidents, not theft," Aura said.

"Wife," Bilal said to her.

"He'll know eventually, Bilal," she replied. "Better to tell him now, so he can be ready."

She turned to me. "What we need is on the fourth floor. In cryobank storage. Extreme cold. Ceres does keep some materials on-site that might be infectious. So each individual storage tank has a safeguard. A controlled burn that will destroy the contents in the event that the tank is ruptured, before its contents can thaw."

"If you know all this, why do you need me?"

"Knowing is different than being able to do something," she said. "I promise you: what we want will not hurt anyone."

"Then there shouldn't be any problem telling me what it is."

"No." Bilal put his hands in his pockets. He looked drawn. Either the nighttime walk or our argument was pushing the limits of his energy.

I wanted to tell them to fuck off. That if they were foolish enough to come after Addy or Hollis or anyone near me, I'd dump their carcasses into the trunk of their hundred-K Mercedes along with Saleem or whoever else got in my way and bury them all in concrete.

But that would be the wrong play. Something in Bilal's and Aura's shared attitude resonated that they didn't just *want* whatever was locked away in Ceres, they *needed* it. An edge of desperation. They might not flinch if I forced their hand.

And that urgency was a crack in their armor. A place to start prying, if I could find enough time.

"It'll take research," I said. "I'll need the building blueprints, and make my own version of the external alarm, for practice. See if I can reverse-engineer it to figure out what might be waiting inside. I'll have to watch the building to learn the guards' patterns."

"Wednesday night," Bilal said.

Forty-eight hours. New Year's Eve. "Impossible."

"I do not care," he said. "This is as much time as you have. If you require a team, I will provide them. Take it by force if you must. But do not fail. Do not try to evade this. I will avenge any disobedience on you and every person in your life. Do you understand?"

Saleem was behind me. I didn't have to look to know he had a hand hovering near his Steyr machine pistol. The driver of the idling Mercedes might be aiming a second gun at my head right this second.

And despite the odds, I was still angry enough to be half a tick from making a move.

"We're clear," I said through my teeth.

Bilal nodded. "There is a number programmed into the phone I gave you. Call that when you are ready."

"Don't wait," Aura said. "Find out what you can tonight, while you're here."

The driver, Juwad, rolled down the driver's window. He had a phone to his ear. "Sir. The restaurant valet has called."

"Our table." Bilal shrugged. "I suppose everyone is short on patience tonight. Tell them two minutes."

He stepped to the Mercedes and held the rear door open for Aura—a damn gentleman—and went around the other side to board himself. Saleem stayed where he was.

"I do not trust you," he said to me when the doors of the big car had closed.

"Likewise," I said.

"Bilal and his *wife*"—Saleem bit off the word like a piece of rot from an apple—"believe they require you, as if you have magic. They are wrong. I can take what he wants from this building without you. And I will be ready to kill you. I will enjoy it."

He might have meant he *would* enjoy it, if I stepped out of line and Bilal gave the order.

Then again, maybe the gunman's vision of the future was clearer than mine.

CHAPTER TWELVE

THE BIG MERCEDES PULLED away. I waited until it was out of sight around the curve of the road before taking out my phone.

Aura had one thing right: I should learn whatever I could, right away.

Faregame was a rideshare company I'd used before. Local and a little more flexible than the bigger providers. I requested a car. Within ten minutes, a baby-food-green Chevy Volt covered the last block on Eastlake doing forty and stopped within an inch of the curb.

"Hey," I said, leaning into the back. The driver was a young dude, with a wall of curled hair and a mustache bushy enough to outstretch the tip of his nose in profile. "I got a problem. My friend left her phone and I have to stay here." I held out Bilal's phone with a fifty-dollar bill and a scrap paper receipt from Analog Coffee I'd found in my pocket wrapped around it. "Take this to the destination I wrote down and keep the fifty."

"I don't know, man."

"Same as dropping me off. Only instead of a person, it's the phone. Read the note."

He looked at the piece of scrap paper. I'd written: *Addy: Call me on your phone to let me know this arrived safe. Thanks. V.*

I pointed at the driver. "Once she calls I'll tip another fifty. Right?"

"Shit. Okay, I guess."

"Thanks. You're saving my life."

The Volt sped off, and the phone with it. Bilal could track my movements all he damn well wanted tonight.

I backtracked to the Barracuda to retrieve some tools. My car was known to Bilal and way too noticeable. I needed another ride.

Within a month after the Barracuda had come into my possession, I had constructed flat hidden compartments between the trunk space and the backseat. One compartment held my kit of various electronics, including a cigarette-pack-sized transponder that could get me arrested just for owning it in the United States.

It wasn't by chance that I'd modified the car, or that I owned the illegal gadget. Over the past few weeks I'd been investing a lot of time and money in building the kind of tool collection that Dono might have once used, with me working right alongside him. Call it preparedness. Since I'd returned to Seattle from the Army, I'd been in situations where the right gear might have made a difference. If I wasn't going to change my life, I could at least update my methods.

Halfway up the block, a dusty white Camry was reversing, the driver having spotted an open space at the curb. He began to parallel park.

I preset the transponder for the low frequency common to that generation of Camry sedans as I walked toward him. The device started by mimicking the car. It sent a signal, and the smart key in the driver's pocket dutifully replied with its unique ID, which the transponder captured. Reverse the process, and the transponder would act as the key itself. All before the driver had set the parking brake.

Once he'd hustled away, burdened with his briefcase and what looked like groceries for dinner, I pressed the transmit button. The car unlocked and its engine started.

I had to admit using the transponder wasn't as much fun as boosting older cars by hotwiring their ignitions, but you couldn't beat it for expediency.

While waiting for the Faregame driver, I'd searched online for restaurants. Specifically eateries with valet parking, within only a couple of minutes' drive of Ceres Biotech. I was counting on Bilal's penchant for precision and his demonstrated taste for the finer things.

There weren't many top-end dining options this far from downtown. Two at the south tip of the lake were closest. I drove the Camry one mile down Fairview and pulled into the parking lot shared by the restaurants.

Luck was on my side tonight. The big Mercedes GLE was easy to spot in the reserved parking section of a steakhouse. I waved no thanks to the approaching valet and U-turned to find a spot in the self-park lot that allowed a view of the restaurant entrance.

My phone rang. Addy.

"You have a strange version of sending flowers," she said.

"I would have if there had been time. Thanks."

"The young man delivering your phone seemed very perplexed. I take it you're not coming home soon."

"No," I confessed. "At least one more errand to run. If that phone I sent rings, don't answer it."

"I wouldn't dream," Addy said.

I sat in the white Camry, its engine running, watching the restaurant. Now I knew why Bilal had been talking to Ondine Long, and how my name had come up: he'd needed a thief.

A fractional part of me, a shadier part, felt some pride that the criminal broker with all her connections had placed me in the top echelon. But, then, I didn't know the criteria. Maybe I was only in the top tier of guys with professional burglary skills whom she also considered disposable. She sure as hell wouldn't shed any tears if Bilal had me aced.

Bilal and Aura kept dinner short. Within an hour, the valet pulled the Mercedes out of its parking spot. I kept the Camry's headlights off as I slowly drifted toward the exit to the street.

Saleem and Juwad were the first out the door of the steakhouse. Juwad was an inch taller and much heavier than his slender partner, with the blocky build of a powerlifter and hair gelled so liberally I could see its shine from forty yards away. Saleem tipped the valet and let the man open the door for Bilal and Aura when they joined the party. He and Juwad kept watch on the surroundings. I was glad the Camry was partly concealed behind the Chandler's Cove sign and its ornamental bushes, and that the engine's purr was soft. Only when their master and mistress were safely within the car did the two bodyguards climb in.

A careful team. I would have to be equally cautious. I waited until the Mercedes was half a block away before following.

Bilal was only in Seattle for a while, he'd said. That implied a hotel. I hoped it would be one of the larger chains downtown, where I might have a better chance of following his team on foot without being spotted, at least far enough to determine which floor their room was on.

But instead the Mercedes jogged left onto Boren Ave, cruising through the easy late evening traffic. I stayed three blocks back, confident in the Toyota's smaller size and my knowledge of the city to allow me to catch up if I became trapped at a stoplight or they made an unexpected turn. Boren took us both over the interstate and diagonally up the west side of my home turf of Capitol Hill.

I nearly lost them, anyway. Juwad turned right on Madison. When I followed fifteen seconds later there was no sight of the big car, even though I had a clear view down three full blocks of the wide street. I craned my neck from side to side, slowing to a crawl even as cars angrily revved to drive around me.

There. In the tight turnaround in front of the Hotel Neapolitan, their Mercedes partly hidden behind hedges that shielded the hotel entrance from the busy intersection.

I kept rolling down Madison and left the Toyota in an alley just behind the hotel, then ran back toward the entrance. Bilal and Aura and the rest were already inside.

It had been a long time since I'd seen the small lobby of the Neapolitan. At least one full remodel ago. If I strolled in unprepared I might run smack into any one of Bilal's crew.

This would have to do for now. I knew their car and their hotel and at least two of their soldiers. More intel would follow soon.

Very soon. I'd just burned two of my allotted forty-eight hours. I could almost hear the tick of that clock over the stolen Camry's purr.

Bilal had suggested hiring a team to knock over Ceres Biotech. I liked that idea. I could make good use of the right people. Even if their goal wasn't quite what the venomous Mr. Bilal Nath had in mind.

CHAPTER THIRTEEN

I WAS TOO AMPED UP after my confrontation with Bilal to consider rest. Bitter Lake, and the home owned by Sean Burke, was only a few short miles up the freeway. And the night was overcast and dark. Ideal for reconnaissance.

The Camry had served its purpose. I drove it back to Roanoke and marveled at the small miracle of the same spot at the curb being available as I parallel-parked and turned the wheels to touch the curb on the incline, just as they'd been when I first saw them. If the owner was especially observant, he might puzzle over how the odometer had gone up and the gas gauge had gone down overnight. But the placement of his car would offer no clues.

After driving the boosted Camry so gingerly, it was a pleasure to make the Barracuda growl as it merged onto the freeway. I supposed I would get habituated to the muscle car before long, but for now it had that new toy feel. Its former owner, for all his sins, had kept the engine in fighting trim.

Burke's address was walking distance from the lake itself, midway along a short street called Amsbury that ended in a cul-de-sac of homes. Each eighth of an acre allowed for a swath of front lawn beside a two-car driveway and an unassuming strip of backyard behind each house. Almost aggressive in its normalcy.

The residential street meant I could cruise at a slow pace without drawing attention. I drifted by the Burke home—what Dono would have called a ranch house, one story, low-slung, and shaped like a shallow L—and followed the curve of the cul-de-sac at the end of Amsbury to return for another pass.

No cars in the driveway. One light on behind curtains at the far tip of the L, probably a bedroom. No security company sign. Standard deadbolt on the door, maybe a Schlage. The lawn was so well groomed I suspected weekly landscaping rather than an owner's touch.

I drove away from the street, in case anyone had been tracking the Barracuda's progress from their living-room window, and parked to examine my toolkits in the trunk for the second time that night.

The houses on Amsbury Street had no mailboxes. USPS had consolidated delivery for its own convenience into a stand of metal postboxes emblazoned with the familiar blue-and-white eagle logo at the end of the road. A Douglas fir, its drooping branches still holding zealously to its needles in winter, sheltered the mail stand from view of the houses. From the truck I removed a lockpick gun and traded the transponder I'd used on the Camry for a larger wireless scanner. I pocketed the scanner. The pick gun I could make use of immediately.

The mail stand offered three sizes of postboxes, ranging from envelope width for standard mail to large enough to suit residents who didn't want packages left on their doorsteps. A label on one of the bigger mailboxes matched Burke's house number. Maybe he collected stamps and received an entire bushel of correspondence from around the world every day. Or maybe he bought his ammunition online.

USPS didn't invest heavily in the latest lock engineering. I had the pins clicking into place in less time than it had taken me to walk from the car to the mail stand. The little metal door swung open.

I'd expected to see an empty box, or at most a couple of letters. Sufficient to fulfill a burglar's standard precaution and verify whether the Burkes had been home recently.

Instead I had to extend a quick hand to stop a short tower of paper from tumbling out onto the wet ground. Loads of mail. Junk circulars, political fliers, coupon books, enough volume to fill half the available square footage.

The postmarks at the bottom of the pile were from more than a week ago. I had hit the jackpot. The Burkes must be on vacation for the holidays.

Then I just as quickly revised my guess. Vacation would mean a hold on their mail, not renting a bigger postbox. This must be a common thing for Burke and his wife, being away from home for long periods.

He had his Russian passport. Maybe they were abroad. Conducting whatever business paid for ranch houses and large postboxes in a sleepy neighborhood.

My quick memorization of the environs from online maps told me Burke's house bumped up against one of the trails leading down to the lake. I walked up the street to find a gap in the treeline. One leap over a sodden ditch to the trail, and a fast stroll through the dark, and I was looking at Burke's slash of backyard, its fence shrouded by blackberry brambles and creeping ivy.

The same single light still shone from the house, increasing the depth of the shadows in the yard. I saw no cameras or motion sensors or other signs of security beyond the simple lock on the sliding-glass door. The Burkes kept their curtains drawn. They had planted rows of short cypress trees on either side of the property, as a privacy screen from their immediate neighbors. All the better for me. No water dishes or chew toys or fecal land mines on the grass that signaled a dog, either. This was about as clear a coast as I could hope for.

I was nervous, and I realized why. Burke could be my father. A narrow chance, but a chance nonetheless. A better person than me might consider breaking into his immediate relation's home to be crossing a moral line.

Burke might also be someone who put bullets into people for money. That was a more pressing reason to be jumpy.

Trail maintenance near the lake didn't include limbing up the lower branches of the fir trees. It was much easier to climb one of the tall evergreens and drop ten feet down into the backyard than to fight through the brambles. I landed on the strip of bark that bordered the lawn, just a soft rustle above silent.

For a moment, I didn't move. The house remained equally still.

My first stop was the window with the light shining behind it. A deep blue curtain obscured the interior of the room. I watched, and listened, until I was ninety percent confident that despite that lamp's claim, the room was empty. And likely the entire house with it.

At the sliding door, I removed the scanner from my pocket. A slender silver box the same size and shape as a surge protector, the scanner was similar to the receiver I'd used when meeting Panni from the FBI at the Japanese garden. It made a sweep of low-band wireless frequencies, nothing more than 900 MHz, looking for a spike in activity. Low frequencies are best at penetrating walls and furniture, ideal for silent alarms. The scanner's digital readout remained blank as I swept it across the edges of the doorframe.

I made a visual check as well. No telltale contact pads around the sliding door or the nearby window. No motion sensors under the eaves. Peering through the glass I could see straight through to the front door on the other side of the slim house, partly illuminated by the streetlamps on Amsbury shining through a vertical strip of pebbled glass at the doorframe. I didn't see an alarm keypad on the nearest wall. Could it be this easy?

There was still a tiny possibility that someone was in the house, asleep. I rapped softly on the glass. A minute went by before I used the pick gun to unlock the door. It slid open with the slightest of shudders.

The scanner in my hand stayed dormant. I slipped my wet running shoes off and stepped inside.

Spotless. Both my entry, and the home as well. The Burkes must have a housecleaner as well as a landscaper.

It wasn't a flashy house, like Dr. Claybeck's midcentury marvel. Most of the furnishings looked like they had been acquired through catalogs, and not so long ago. The watercolors on the walls, too. As clean and uncontroversial as a home prepared by a Realtor to show prospective buyers. All the dishes put away. No clutter on the countertops. One lone raincoat hanging on the line of pegs by the front door, but no messy shoes below. Even the roll of paper towels on the kitchen wall looked fresh from the plastic, the first sheet still stuck to the ones below. Only the black-painted ceiling beams offered a hint of individuality.

I left the back door open—in the event I had to suddenly bolt—and stepped softly down the hall.

The bathroom and two identical bedrooms followed the same pattern. Very clean, very colorless. Men's toiletries in the bathroom, but not so much as a whisker stub in the bone-dry sink or soap scum in the tub. The dresser drawers and closets held men's clothes. Not enough of them to fill many washing machines at the laundromat. Sweaters, mostly XL, a couple of sport coats in 46R, and two pairs of lace-up dress shoes, one brown and one black, sized eleven-and-a-half. Same size as the sneakers I'd just removed.

Most of the clothes looked lightly used, but not enough that any of the garments were truly broken in. Even the socks neatly folded in the dresser had their creases from the original packaging.

From Panni's records I knew Burke had bought the house ten years ago. He might have moved in yesterday, for all it showed. And he'd apparently left his wife, Natalia, back in Smolensk or wherever she was from.

I spent a few more minutes searching through hall closets and under kitchen counters. There were only a handful of things beyond the expected linens and appliances. Some camping gear and old stereo equipment was about as intriguing as it got. The spare bedroom lived up to the name. Spare. No filing cabinet or computer or other personal records. In a kitchen drawer I found bills from the past quarter for the house's water and power, its trash pickup, its landscaping. I used my phone to snag a picture of each.

Locking the back door behind me, I put on my shoes and left the Burke home—no longer an accurate word for the place, I was sure—via the side of the house to Amsbury Street. A quick walk put me back at the Barracuda.

I took a moment to sit and muse about the strangeness of it all.

The house was spitting distance from deserted. For what reason? Had Burke moved, separated from his wife, and now the house on Amsbury was just an investment waiting for the market to bubble again? Was it a safe house in case he needed to crash somewhere in an emergency? That didn't match. It didn't make sense to use his address of record as a refuge.

But the idea redirected my thoughts back to the stack of mail I'd seen in Burke's postbox. No magazine subscriptions. No bank statements. No cards or personal letters. Only junk that might as well have been addressed to Occupant.

I recalled my impression of Burke's home being ready for an open house showing. Realtors had a word for that: staged. That was what Sean Burke's house was. Just a bare façade of a dwelling, there to provide an impression but nothing more. Soulless.

As I drove down Amsbury Street one last time, my skin prickled. It took me a few seconds to catch up to why.

Burke's house had contained no photographs at all.

That simple fact shouldn't have surprised me, not with how impersonal the rest of the interior had been. But the similarity to the home I had once shared with my grandfather was positively spooky.

CHAPTER FOURTEEN

I'D DISCOVERED MY GYM through a Facebook group that provided community info and general bullshit sessions for the 2nd Ranger Battalion at Fort Lewis. Most of the group's posts concentrated on activities near the base, but there was usually a mention when a brother got something going in Seattle. One of those Rangers was a former second lieutenant from 1st Bat named Twelvetrees, and one of those somethings was his venture into training MMA fighters.

The LT's business had suffered a rough start. His first location had been burglarized of all its brand-new equipment. When Twelvetrees had posted on the battalion group, it was to ask if any brothers had old punching bags or dumbbells or gloves they could spare, or at least lend, while his stable of fighters got ready for their upcoming bouts.

My curiosity had been piqued. I exchanged messages with Twelvetrees online. He'd said he hoped the cops were able to trace the gear; that he'd etched *12T* on every piece. I wasn't as optimistic, given the smaller scale of the theft and the manpower constraints of the

SPD, but I kept that to myself. I told the lieutenant I'd do some hunting.

Almost everything that had been stolen was heavy. The punching bags—the largest of them two hundred pounds—would have required more than one person to take down and carry. It didn't take intuitive genius to guess a truck or van had pulled right up to the door, with two or three men inside. At least one of them had been familiar enough with the gym to know it was worth knocking over.

The free weights would be worth far more if sold as a set. I tried eBay and Craigslist and other sources for new listings. I checked pawnshops I knew might not give a crap about the provenance of their inventories. I came up blank.

Then it dawned on me: Who would want a metric ton of fighting gear?

I asked Twelvetrees if he'd had any prospective clients who'd come from other gyms but never signed on. He remembered a guy from Lacey who claimed to have a few pro fights and was looking to become a trainer. The guy had told Twelvetrees that he would come back to work out and talk more, but that was the last the LT had seen him. With a little mental digging, Twelvetrees recalled the dude's name—Hepp—and that he'd had a shaved head and a tattoo of flames on the side of his neck. It gave me somewhere to start.

A gym called World Class Warriors had opened two weeks prior in Lacey. It had a basic webpage with address and hours and photos. One of the photos showed an instructor working with kids, his flame tattoo stretched as he extended his neck to call out instructions.

I took a drive. World Class Warriors was open. Hepp's bullet head was visible toward the back, leading a group in abdominal exercises. I paid ten bucks for a pass and waited until the evening class let out.

Hepp caught me scratching at the red paint on the dumbbells, exposing the etching underneath. *12T.* He protested, vehemently. I knocked him down, twice, along with one of his more foolhardy middleweight fighters, before holding a seventy-pound dumbbell suspended over Hepp's throat while I explained to him how he was going to spend his night. The alternative would be a squad of highly motivated Rangers making an impromptu sortie to Lacey.

It took Hepp three hard hours to load my truck with the stolen gear, working alone. By the end, all of the fight was out of him. I let him keep the ten bucks' gym fee but warned him that if Twelvetrees so much as saw a cockroach in his newest place, it would be Hepp's fault.

Two days easy work, and I'd earned myself a lifetime membership, along with a key to unlock Twelvetrees Fitness at any hour.

Which was how Cyndra and I found ourselves in the former auto-body shop at nine in the morning, working on the basics of the deadlift. In the opposite corner of the gym, two fighters named Oscar and Cannonball shadowboxed in the ring. I showed Cyn what the movement looked like before rolling a ten-kilogram barbell with no plates on it in front of her toes.

"Keep your spine straight," I said, "and pull a little on the bar. Feel the muscles in your back engage?"

"Uh huh. I just pick it up?"

"Push with your legs. Let them do the work of getting the bar off the ground."

She did. We refined the motion a few times before I put a five-pound plate on either side of the bar. Twelvetrees had positioned the plate racks to conceal bolts still jutting from the concrete floor, remnants of the auto shop's hydraulic lifts. The gym still smelled faintly of oil from its past life.

"I can lift more than *that*," Cyn said.

"Sure. But try this ten times first. Take it slow."

She did. By the last rep her face was crimson and she had to concentrate every second to keep her back from arching.

"What's it for?" she said after a couple of breaths.

"Darn near everything. But especially your back and legs. Perfect for derby. Get some water; we'll try bench press next."

"I can do more."

"You'll feel it tomorrow as is. Tell me about Los Angeles."

"Huh? It was fine."

"'Fine' like fun, or 'fine' like you got through it?"

"Mostly got through it. Dad's happy. And I got to see some of the kids I used to live with."

In their foster homes. "Are they solid?" Meaning were they leading what most people would consider law-abiding lives. Cyndra was the daughter of a former crook and, just like me, had grown up with a skewed perspective. Hell, mine was still skewed. I was just aware of it. And trying to keep Cyndra from falling into her old habits.

"Yes," she said. "Farrah got a job at the Northridge mall. She sells big pretzels."

I grinned. "How many'd you eat while you were there?"

"Like six."

My phone rang. I practically leapt across the rubberized mats to grab it off the apron of the ring.

Willard. Finally. I had reached out to my grandfather's onetime criminal cohort last night, letting him know it was urgent. With every hour that had ticked by since, I'd grown more convinced that Willard was occupied with his own work and wouldn't respond.

I told Cyndra to practice her flexed-arm hang on the pull-up bar while I took the call.

"Got your messages," he said in his meat-grinder voice. "All three of 'em. You ever sleep?"

"When there's time." The two fighters in the ring had begun working with the mitts. I walked toward the entrance so I could hear Willard over the pop of Cannonball's fists on leather.

"Time you don't have. That came through loud and clear, during your second voice mail, I think."

"It kept cutting me off. I figured the faster you had the details, the faster you could get to work."

Willard rumbled his discontent. "*If.* If I get to work. This is a long list you gave me. Genesee Architectural Cooperative. H&L Construction. Blueprints, electrical plans . . ."

"They built Ceres Biotech within the last year. And I need whatever specs you can find on their security company. By this time tomorrow."

"It's the holidays, Van."

I wondered if my grandfather had had an equally difficult time getting Willard to commit to a job. Not that the huge man was unwilling. Just deliberate to a fault.

"No rest for the wicked," I said. "I can give you eight grand for the intel, and another twelve if you'll back me up during the score."

"A fool and his money, huh?"

My cash reserves from my unexpected windfall had dwindled rapidly. Getting my neck out of the noose seemed a good reason to blow the last of it.

"Give me a couple of hours," Willard said. "By then I'll know if any of this is even possible."

"As long as I'm pushing my credit, there's other help I need." I took a breath. "From Elana."

"Fuck you," Willard said, loud enough I glanced up to see if Cyndra had overheard. She'd grown bored of hanging from the chin-up bar and had gone back to more deadlifts, with more weight. "You keep my niece out of this."

"It's just some snoop work. Hollis or I would be recognized."

"Let me do it."

"You stand out like a bowling ball in a fish tank," I said. "Elana can be there and gone fast enough."

"Are you asking or telling me?"

"Call it a courtesy notice."

"Some courtesy. Every time you call me I get the same feeling. As though I'm reaching into a garbage disposal to fish something out, and your finger is poised over the switch."

He hung up.

When I turned around, Cyndra took a flash picture of me. "There."

"I should have put your phone at the top of the climbing wall. Least you'd have to work for it."

She held out the phone to show me. Video of her lifting the barbell, already on TikTok. She swiped the screen and I saw myself, looking startled, for an instant before Cyndra pulled it away to continue tapping messages in the app.

"Wren says hi," Cyndra said. With enough innocence for a platoon of angels.

"Say hi back."

"You should. Here. Text her."

"I'll text her you're slacking off to DM your whole school. You'll be doing laps for a week."

Cyn scowled. "That's not fair."

"Fair is what you make out of what you get. Let's go to work."

JUNIOR YEAR, PART ONE

I was late for registration at the start of the second semester, having overslept because Dono and I had been out late the night before to case a gated community in Magnolia. All of the shop electives I had wanted were full. Technical theater with Ms. Nasgate was the best of what was left.

I figured I'd just make the most of it, work the spotlight, and maybe practice my rewiring skills on the electricals in Watson High's auditorium. If I wanted Dono to teach me more about greasing home security systems, I had to master the basics, and I was forbidden from messing with our house since I'd accidentally shorted everything out over winter break.

But on the third week, when we were breaking out into different teams for the spring show, Ms. Nasgate had a different plan.

"Costumes?" I said.

Yvette Friel next to me laughed. Enjoying my pain.

"You'll be good at it, Van," Ms. Nasgate said. "I

saw how quickly you sewed on that button during our orientation week. Very deft. Imagine what you can do with a machine."

Jesus, had that been some kind of audition? I kicked myself for doing the job so fast. "Yeah, but . . ."

"No nonsense about costumes being just for girls," she replied, though I wasn't going to say that. *Think* it, maybe.

Ms. Nasgate turned to our group of ten. She'd had the students move our desks into rough circles for each team. Theater in the round, which we'd just learned about, as she gave instructions.

"We'll start with fixing some of the basic pieces that need some TLC. In theater, we always try to repair and modify, not to replace. It's cheaper and it requires more ingenuity." She showed us plastic storage bins labeled VESTS and PETTICOATS and other costume bits. "Then we'll move into using those pieces to design costumes for the show."

Damn it. A whole month of frills and frocks.

Yvette was whispering something to her friend Kayla, both of them glancing my way. They noticed that I had noticed.

"You should really wash your hands first," Yvette whispered to me, like she was sharing an important secret. And of course I was dumb enough to look at them, which prompted more laughter. They weren't wrong; I had dirt under my nails. Not the point.

I guess my disappointment showed, because halfway through stitching a rip in a pants seam,

Ms. Nasgate called me to her desk. She brushed the ends of her scarf behind her shoulder. She always wore a silk scarf around her neck, and the scarves always had gold in them, I guess to go with her short straw-colored hair.

"I know you're not happy with this assignment, Van," she said. "Do a good job, and I'll let you take your pick of teams for the senior variety show."

"Okay."

"You really might be good at costuming. Your mother was."

That brought me up so short I almost fell over. "What?"

"That's right. She had my class and she volunteered for one of her graduating class's projects. A quilt that used to hang in the library, with squares from every student who worked on it. You've seen that."

I was struggling to keep up. Teachers just didn't mention my mom out of the blue like this. Sure she'd been in a lot of the same classes as I took now. But she was dead, which always made people nervous. Plus I knew she'd been pregnant with me while in school. That *really* closed teachers' mouths, at least around me. Pregnant during her last year, because she'd skipped a grade and graduated just after she turned seventeen.

Which meant . . .

"When she was on the senior project, was she, um . . ." I put my grimy hands out like a pregnant belly, praying that Yvette and Kayla weren't watching.

"She was. Never let that slow her down much. Now finish fixing those trousers, and I'll ask Marli to walk you through setting up a sewing machine before end of class."

"Wait. You said the quilt used to hang in the library?"

"Oh. I'm afraid it went missing last year. I'm very sorry." Her face fell. Maybe realizing no one had thought to mention to me that something my mom had made was just hanging there all this time.

"Missing like stolen?" I said.

Ms. Nasgate hesitated. "We're not sure." Which meant yes.

I went back to my seat. My fingers worked on the stitching while my brain tried to picture what the quilt had looked like. I *kinda* remembered it, hanging above low shelves near the dictionary stand, but who looks at junk on the walls in the library? I hadn't even clocked that it was gone. It wasn't like I spent a ton of time there, anyway.

Kayla and Yvette were already slacking off, talking through plans for the party Yvette was going to throw this weekend after the school's midwinter carnival. I knew about her parties, though no way I'd ever been to one. If you weren't rich or in Yvette's drama clique or able to help her popularity in some fashion, forget getting on that list.

Mom had made a quilt. Or at least part of one. I wished I'd known that before. And why the hell would somebody steal a quilt? Some of those antique ones from like Amish people went for a lot of money—Dono had considered taking a quilt during a house score last year before rejecting it as too traceable—but this was a fucking high school project. Who cared? I mean, *shit*.

My fingers tightened on the needle and it slipped and jabbed me through my jeans. It hurt. I didn't mind. Pain could be better than feeling.

CHAPTER FIFTEEN

AFTER DROPPING CYNDRA OFF with Addy I invested two hours casing Ceres Biotech. My eyes tracked the patterns of movement around the building while my brain gnawed bitterly on the problem of finding a way into the cryobank on its fourth floor without getting myself or any of the Ceres employees killed. I didn't doubt that Bilal Nath meant what he'd said. If I couldn't crack Ceres by stealth, he'd resort to force. The security guards were armed. They might be dumb enough to resist. It wasn't tough to imagine the ever-angry Saleem going to town with his Steyr, cutting through any opposition like a scythe.

When I got the message from Elana Coll, the distraction was a relief.

Meet Neapolitan lobby at 4. Dress right.

Dress right? I guessed Elana meant I should look like someone who belonged at a four-star hotel. I didn't own business clothes. The best I could manage would be chinos without noticeable stains and a better shirt than the flannel I had on now.

I was due to meet Willard at noon. He'd chosen to combine business with his midday meal. That meant

Zane+Wylie's steakhouse downtown, and me picking up the tab.

The hostess at the Z+W reception was too classy to look askance at my barn jacket and workboots ensemble.

"Reservations?" she asked.

"Loads," I said, scanning the tables on either side of the elongated bar running down the center of the restaurant. The guy I was looking for was easy enough to find. I just looked for a wall wearing a suit and tie.

Willard was the kind of size that people remembered, long enough to tell their grandchildren about. He was tall, sure, and broad and thick in an ancient world sort of way, when muscles came from hard labor and harder warfare. But beyond those stats there was a solidity to Willard, a colossal weight of presence that made him more awe-inspiring than any individual statistic.

He had chosen a seat at the back, taking up a full half of a four-top table. On the wall behind him a giant black-and-white photograph formed a mural. The photographer had captured a trio of cowboys riding away from the viewer in three-quarter profile. Willard's suits were custom-made, by necessity. This one was houndstooth in brown, giving his shoulders the look of a fence that the horses had just leapt.

"How's the prime rib?" I said, sliding into one of the chairs opposite.

"Lean," Willard rumbled, "like my prospects."

"What happened to that roadshow casino you were running?"

He grunted. "Some muttonchopped little jagoff in

Portland lost forty grand in one night and went crying to daddy. A city councilman. So low on the political ladder that a quick donation kept my name out of the official record. But it wiped half my capital. No more traveling circus for the foreseeable."

"Menu, sir?" the waiter asked, looking as selectively impartial as the hostess.

"A shot of rye straight up, please," I said. Dr. Claybeck's liquor selection was about my only good memory of that night. Willard nodded assent. The waiter left, pants cuffs flapping in haste.

"The card games will come around," I said. "People need their vices."

"Your vice seems to be the same as your granddad's." Willard cut into his ribeye. "Crazy schemes."

"Don't tell me you never made a profit with Dono."

"I made out fine. But I also flirted with a fucking ulcer." He swallowed his bite of steak. "Ceres Biotech. We might have some headway there. Ceres built their new headquarters on artificial landfill and on the water. That raised the hackles of some local activist groups. They pushed the city's environmental review board, which forced the members to put the building plans under a microscope. And then they had to share those plans with the EPA and Public Relations, given the stink. So there's no shortage of copies floating around City Hall."

"Blueprints?" I said.

"Blueprints, electrical, hazmat evaluations. A lot of it is public documentation. A citizen could put in a request and get most of it in two or three months."

I saw where he was heading. "How much to get it today?"

"Three large to the right guy. He'll spread it around a little. I'll pick the papers up from him late tonight."

Crime really didn't pay. "All right." I put an envelope on the table, which Willard made disappear with superb dexterity for a guy with hands the approximate size of shovel blades. "That's your eight. Take the palm oil from that and I'll make it up on the back end."

Willard took another small bite, his lantern jaw barely moving to chew. "And what are you gonna do, while I'm attempting all this legwork?"

"I'll be talking to a couple of people. Ondine Long was the one who gave my name to Bilal Nath. I want to know why."

He lowered his fork. Willard didn't give away much—he was probably a hell of a poker player, along with running illegal gambling joints—but his misgivings were plain enough.

"Bad on top of worse," he said.

"You know, that might be the first time I've seen you nervous."

"Ondine'll kill you before Bilal Nath can if she thinks you're any kind of risk."

"So I'll have to count on my charm."

"Stupid." Willard frowned. "Ondine's not why you're hiring Elana." It sounded like an order.

"No. I wouldn't put your niece near Ondine."

"Elana." He made a rumbling sound in his throat, half sigh and half growl. "I got her a straight job last summer. This guy owed me a favor. His firm was a headhunter for pharmaceutical reps. You know those women who talk doctors into buying products? Elana's smart, attractive, knows how to read people. I figured she'd be good at it."

"She turned it down?"

"No, she signed on. Took it serious. She memorized the shit out of the product catalog in just a couple of weeks, and the clients fucking loved her. Then she quit after two months. She said of all the things she'd ever done, pushing drugs was the lowest." Willard drank the last of his wine. "Maybe she took the job just to prove she could do it. To me or to herself. I dunno."

"I'll find Ondine on my own."

"She moved somewheres out by Broadmoor, I think. But tonight she'll be at SAM."

"Sam's a boyfriend?"

"SAM. The art museum, genius." He pointed in its direction, just a handful of blocks away. "The trustees are throwing some big gala for benefactors or some shit tonight. Ondine goes every year. Hell, you can find her name on the wall of diamond-level donors, or whatever they call it."

If Ondine was attending an event surrounded by the wealthy and powerful, it wasn't for the pleasure of their company. Patronizing the museum at her level must mean elite privileges, special access. And special influence.

"I'll talk to her there," I said.

Willard actually laughed. It sounded like a stump grinder in action. "They wouldn't let you onto the front steps. It's black-tie, Van. Do you have a tuxedo?"

I'd never even *worn* a tuxedo. My expression confessed as much.

"What I thought," Willard said. "Plus it's invitation only. God knows how much you have to donate to get on that list. Forget it."

"Who does your suits?" I said.

"Go to hell."

"Just a tux off the rack will do."

"You say the words *off the rack* to my guy, he'll kill you. Or himself, or both. This'll cost you." When I didn't flinch, Willard grumbled again and took out his phone.

"I need a business suit, too," I said, remembering Elana's text.

"Jesus. You really have to find the limit, don't you? Hang on."

He began texting someone. The waiter brought the bill in a calfskin folder. I had just enough in my wallet to cover it.

CHAPTER SIXTEEN

I MADE A QUICK STOP at the Barracuda to retrieve more cash from another of my hiding places, this one inside the driver's seat. The address Willard had given me for his tailor was off Blanchard, close enough that a fast walk would get me there sooner than driving. Lines of pedestrians snaked to and from their holiday plans, everyone's urgency matching my pace. I skirted the light at 4th Ave to the next block.

Forty yards behind me, a weighty guy in a zip-front running jacket and matching black pants jogged across Stewart to beat the traffic. Active wear or not, he didn't look like jogging came natural to him. His jowls bounced a bit as he hustled along.

I turned onto 3rd. He did, too, matching my pace exactly. A block later I paused at Virginia as if deciding which way to go. Jowls stopped, instantly preoccupied with his phone.

He wasn't alone. Another man, this one with a shock of sandy hair looking like a lit matchstick atop his puffy blue hiking coat, had halted abruptly on the other side of the avenue. He gazed with furious interest at the window display for an eyeglass store.

When I moved, they moved. I rounded the corner onto Virginia and immediately sprinted to stretch the distance between us.

Bilal's people? These were white guys, and excepting his wife, Aura, all of Bilal's soldiers I'd seen so far were South Asian. I considered leading the two men on a roundabout chase, maybe corner one and get some answers, but I was in a hurry.

At the next block a thick column of people had formed outside the Moore Theatre, waiting for entry. The marquee read: DEC 30 / 2 SHOWS: CRATER + SKATING POLLY. I wasn't clued in to the bands, but they had drawn a big enough audience that the line for the matinee filled the sidewalk from wall to curb, all the way down the block and onto the next. I dove into the first rows.

"Hey," a woman said.

"Sorry, dropped my keys somewhere," I said, shuffling past and removing my barn jacket while keeping an eye on the corner. My pursuers appeared on the opposite sidewalk. I kept my head down as they scanned the streets, the crowd of theatergoers, and then the streets again with increasing desperation. I kept up my sham of searching the pavement as I edged farther back into the throng.

After another thirty seconds Jowls pointed, and his lean partner speedwalked down Virginia toward the water, in the direction they'd last seen me going. My friend in the tracksuit took a more deliberate route, walking along the avenue for a closer look at the crowd. But the mass of people had started to move, and I let myself shuffle along with it, no one giving a damn if I was cutting in line so long as they got inside themselves.

Jowls gave up and hurried after his partner. A little extra exercise for him tonight. I waited until he was out of sight, then bolted up the avenue.

Who were these guys? They could be cops—Jowls had that plainclothes vibe, not quite matching the vibe of the civilians around him—and they knew at least the basics of tailing someone, even if they needed more men or more practice. But there was no reason for cops to be following me.

At least no reason that I knew.

Which flipped me back to the other side of the coin. Bilal might have wanted me followed, to make sure I was complying with the plan to break into Ceres Biotech. Maybe he'd hired help, knowing his men would be recognized. I might not be the only one building a team.

The more worrisome question was how they had tracked me here. Had they been watching the car? Or Willard? I kept to the shadows, metaphorically speaking, on my way to the bespoke tailor.

His shop was called Giuseppe's, and it was shaped like a wide hallway between two much grander Belltown stores. The wizened Italian guy who unlocked the shop for me either spoke little English or was so angry at being rousted from his home to fit me for a tuxedo he refused to speak. He just pointed.

I put on the black tux with the notched lapels he had indicated. He pinned the hem and the sleeves within a flat minute, and disappeared with the jacket and pants into the back of the shop.

By the time I'd used my phone to read what I could learn about the Seattle Art Museum gala online, Giuseppe had returned, placing two zippered clear garment bags on the counter along with a pair of black patent-leather shoes. He hadn't asked my shoe size. He hadn't measured me for a shirt, either, and I could see the top edge of a white collar on a second hanger under the tux.

I glanced at the second garment bag. A two-button suit in light wool, in slate blue with a subtle gray check paired with another white shirt and a tie the color of rust on iron.

"Should I try them on?" I said. Giuseppe's glance was withering. It softened marginally when I put fifty hundred-dollar bills beside the register.

As he locked the door again, I surreptitiously opened the zipper and glanced at one of the suit sleeves, to make sure I wasn't being conned. There had been no sound of a sewing machine from the back room. The cuffs had been hand-stitched, each loop precisely the same distance from the last. The old tailor would be hell at lockpicking if he chose to change professions.

I took a circuitous route back to the Barracuda, buying a pair of shoes to match the blue suit and slipping out the back of the store. Spent ten minutes checking the surroundings before approaching my car. And another twenty examining both interior and exterior with a penlight for tracking devices. I wasn't certain that Jowls and his matchstick buddy had started tailing me at the car, but if they knew my ride and were trying to find me again, the Barracuda would be an easy choice. I even checked my own hidden compartments, in case they'd used those against me.

When I drove away, I circled the blocks around Belltown until I was sure I was alone. The feeling that I wasn't safe proved impossible to shake.

CHAPTER SEVENTEEN

ELANA COLL LOOKED AS comfortable in the lobby of the Neapolitan as if she were a guest in their Marchesa Suite every night. It wasn't hard to imagine the owners making some arrangement with her whereby Elana would adorn the lobby during peak hours just to add some millennial appeal to the classical surroundings. She had the right look: very tall, very green-eyed, and swathed in an LBD that flirted with being too L.

If the owners knew how often those green eyes focused on the jewelry of other guests, they would rethink their options. Elana was Luce's best friend, which said something about her magnetism all by itself. Luce was about as ethical as a human could get. Elana was never happier than when she was breaking a law.

"Hey." She looked me up and down as I approached, my new shoes squeaking. "You took me serious."

"As a heart attack. Why are we standing where every person and camera can see us?"

"Because guests of the hotel have no reason to hide." She held up a wine-colored keycard between her first two fingers. "Room 502."

"You checked in?" I sat down in the gold velveteen chair opposite hers.

"Technically Solange did. Personal assistant to Mr. Gilles Foster."

I tamped down my impatience. Elana would have her fun.

"Mr. Foster has a number of personal assistants in various cities," she said, with the tiniest of smiles. "One of them is my friend Winnifred, whose professional name is Solange."

"Okay. And Foster stays here when in Seattle?"

"He usually stays at the Fairmont, but Solange made a special request. She finds the Neapolitan much sexier."

"Where are the lovebirds now?"

"Gilles's plane arrives from Montreal in two hours. Solange checked in early to make herself presentable. Two keys. Your friend Bilal and his wife are in suite 501, and his two angry-looking associates are in the adjoining room 503."

"What else?" Elana looked too smug.

She waggled the key. "502 is the room on the other side of 501. Solange told Gilles she likes the eastern view. The Neapolitan has it so that entire families—or celebrity entourages—can occupy a floor without ever stepping into the hall."

The lock of a connecting-room door would be a whole lot simpler to open than the door off the hall. And much more private. "Nice."

"Say it."

"You're very good. Do you also know if Bilal and his team are at home?"

"I was with Winnifred half an hour ago when they left. We went down to the lobby after them. They took their car."

I winced inside. "How much have you told Winnifred?"

"Just that Bilal is a bad guy and I promised we wouldn't steal anything. Strictly fact-finding. And we need a lookout."

"You're the lookout."

"Hell I am. I'm going in." Elana stood up before I could protest further. "Besides, you need me to make introductions."

The Neapolitan's elevators had retained their old brass accordion gates as accent pieces after their modernization. Elana paused as I opened the gate for her.

"You're going to be cool, right? About Winnifred?" she said.

"Yeah."

"Some dudes get all flustered around sex workers. Just don't embarrass me."

"I'll try not to faint."

Suite 501 was at the end of the short hall, flanked by 502 and 503 on opposite sides of the corridor. Elana tapped softly on the door to 502. Winnifred-slash-Solange answered her knock immediately. She was nearly as tall as Elana, every inch the corporate businesswoman. Her blouse and skirt would have passed the dress code of any bank. As she glanced my way, a slight magnification of her blue eyes revealed her glasses weren't just for costume.

"Van, Winnifred," Elana said, striding into the room.

"Hello," I said. "Elana said she talked you into keeping watch."

"I offered," Winnifred replied. "Just tell me what you need."

A murmur at the back of my brain wondered if that would have sounded provocative even if I hadn't known her profession. "Set up in the lobby where you have a view of the entrance. You've seen their Mercedes. Text Elana if it pulls up."

"That's all? I expected something more . . . covert."

"The simplest plans are the best." I was already examining the deadbolt on the adjoining door. A thumb turn allowed me to unlock our side. There would be a similar knob in Bilal's suite. As a backup for the hotel, there was also a keyhole that would spring both mechanisms. I set to work with my lockpicks and drew the bolt back.

"Whoa!" Winnifred said at the sound of the click. She was still putting on her shoes.

"We won't be long," Elana said. Winnifred nodded and hurried to the hall. We waited three minutes before Elana's phone buzzed to signal that Secret Agent Solange was in position.

Aura and Bilal had evidently told housekeeping to let the room alone. A twisted rope of bedsheets lay at the foot of the California king, and the soft pillows still showed deep depressions from their most recent nap. The towels on the floor of the bathroom were damp and the air in the small tiled space humid. They had showered before heading out for the day.

"Don't touch anything," I said. "They can't know we were here."

"What are you looking for?" Elana said.

Anything that might give me some chance of slipping the leash Bilal had fastened around my neck. Something that could help me stall him for a while or get him arrested and booted out of the country. A box of plutonium would be nice. Call the FBI with an anonymous tip and let them take over.

It didn't take long to check every drawer and every piece of luggage in their room. Nothing unusual, not even a gun. The room safe under the dresser was open and empty. On the nightstands were books—two in what might be Urdu, with translated promotional quotes on the back from prominent European politicians. The books on Aura's side were slightly flashier—a paperback suspense novel and a thick well-thumbed tome on health and pregnancy. Looked like the newlyweds weren't wasting any of Bilal's limited time.

In the bathroom, I found half a dozen prescription bottles from a Miami pharmacy for Bilal, treatment for his ALS. An evil part of me whispered that I could return and doctor the pills just a little. But Bilal had warned me that even death wouldn't stop his vengeance if I crossed him. Even if I could set aside my scruples—*no different than Oregon*, the insidious voice whispered—it wouldn't set me free.

Aura was taking a prescription as well. The largest of the bottles held fifty or more cream-colored time release capsules. A drug called olaparib. I was familiar with a wide variety of pharmaceuticals thanks to time spent in Army hospitals and in therapy, but olaparib was new to me.

The judge that had granted Aura probation on her

identity theft charge had referred to health concerns. I'd considered whether Bilal might be sending me to steal a vaccine for his incurable disease. But maybe Aura's own troubles were their real motive.

The only items of interest were two new-looking HP laptops on the desk. Bilal might be conducting business while on the road. If he'd been at all careless, the computers could be hard evidence. But I had no way of hacking past their log-in screens here, on the fly. I'd have to leave them. The idea of abandoning something so potentially useful made me grind my teeth.

Elana was admiring a set of black pearl earrings Aura had left on the room's lone table. "What did you say this guy does? Hacking?"

"Something related to that. I don't have a handle on him yet," I said, running my fingertips over the back of the dresser to see if anything had been taped there. A last-ditch effort. "He's more skilled than the average black hat."

She tilted her head to see the pearls from another angle. "Must be. These could pay my rent for a year."

A high-end hacker must have high-end enemies. Small wonder Saleem and Juwad went everywhere Bilal and Aura did. Saleem struck me as someone with advanced training—maybe maroon berets or some other Special Service branch of the Pakistani armed forces. And devoted to his boss's continued good health, at least against anything that could be cured by a well-aimed bullet.

The connecting door to 503 was unlocked. Saleem and his buddy kept their room considerably neater, though again without a hotel maid's help. The blankets on both twin beds had been pulled back into place, and the surfaces of the dresser and table were bare. I set about searching, faster now. We'd already spent more time in the rooms than I'd intended.

The safe in Saleem's room was closed. I punched the LOCK button twice to enter administrative mode, then tried 9999 as the factory default. It didn't work. I tried all zeroes and then all ones, with the same result.

"Shit," Elana said, thinking we were stymied. I pulled the safe out slightly to see the top. A small metal plate stamped with the safe company's name decorated the center of the front edge, fastened in place with two hex screws. I used my multitool to remove one screw and swung the little plate aside to reveal a tiny cross-shaped keyhole.

I grinned. A manufacturer's lock, to open the safe if guests forgot their codes. Elana leaned over my shoulder as I began to work the lock with the slimmest of Dono's old picks.

Her phone buzzed, making us both jump.

"They're at the valet," she said.

Dammit. The lock clicked and the door came open with a whine of the bolts drawing back.

"Get ready to run," I said, as I scanned the safe's contents.

Boxes of 9 mm ammo. Two empty magazines for Saleem's Steyr. All squeezed to one side. Filling most of the safe's cubic foot was a white cylinder with a narrower top, like a large metal water bottle. A logo on its side read CXS-3001. I took the bottle from the safe.

"In the lobby now," Elana said, waiting by the adjoining door.

The top of the bottle unscrewed. Removing it drew out a green plastic plug. The rest of the interior was filled with some kind of soft insulating foam.

"Van," said Elana.

No time to take pictures. I replaced its screw top and set the bottle back in the safe, held the thick door shut, and began tweaking the lock with one hand. Elana cracked the door to 503 to peer down the hallway. The lock gave way and the servomotors buzzed as the bolts glided back into place.

A ping came from down the hall. The elevator, reaching our floor.

"Go," I said, screwing the metal plate down with my fingertips. Elana closed the hallway door and raced to Aura and Bilal's room. I shoved the safe back into position and almost leapt after her, closing the adjoining door and crossing in a rush to meet her in 502.

Relocking the connecting door gave me more trouble than it should have. From the hallway we heard the scuff of feet on carpet and light thumps as the door to the suite opened. Saleem's voice, asking a question. I made myself relax. The mechanism gave a faint click as the deadbolt sprung back into the frame.

Neither Elana nor I moved. Just listened, as Bilal's door thumped closed, followed seconds later by the sound of Saleem and Juwad opening their own room.

We slipped out to the hall and padded silently to the stairs. It was three flights before Elana spoke.

"That was perfect."

"You have a strange dictionary."

"I meant the timing. This might be the best holiday treat I've ever had. What's next?"

We reached the lobby. I gave Elana a moment to talk to Winnifred privately. I was busy with thoughts of the insulated bottle in Saleem's hotel safe.

It had clearly been designed to transport something under extreme cold, which made sense for biological material. Whatever Bilal wanted me to steal from Ceres, I was going to carry it away in that.

Reason it out: Bilal Nath is a hacker, dealing in information. Maybe Ceres made a breakthrough and Bilal found out about it. He's stealing a sample to sell, or to ransom.

Elana interrupted my conjectures. Her emerald eyes sparkled with enthusiasm.

"When I asked what's next, I meant it," she said. "Willard let on that you have a score tomorrow night. I'm there."

"No. It's a one-person job. And dangerous."

"Willard also said that limpdick will kill you if you don't do it and might kill you if you do. So you obviously need friends."

What I needed was a minor miracle. For Bilal to have a heart attack, or suddenly get religion, or become homesick for Karachi. But none of that was going to happen. Whatever was protected in Ceres's cryobank had brought him to Seattle, and it would remain Bilal's singular focus until he'd acquired it. I'd seen his and his wife's expressions when they looked at the biotech company.

None of my options were sunny. Run, and Bilal would come after my people, either by sending his killer Saleem or through more devious online attacks. Hand over the goods and I would be beyond expendable. Ensuring my silence would become the new priority, at least for the few moments until Saleem squeezed the trigger.

The sun had gone down while Elana and I had been inside the Neapolitan. It wouldn't be long before the museum gala opened its doors. I still had to figure a way to storm the gates and find one particular benefactor.

Ondine. She knew Bilal; she'd set him up with Dr. Claybeck. Odds were good that she also knew something about his plans on her home turf.

Crashing the gala would be a challenge. Convincing Ondine Long to help me might be impossible.

CHAPTER EIGHTEEN

I CHOSE A PARKING GARAGE a block away from the museum and drove up the ramps until I reached the top level. A modicum of privacy for me to change clothes for the second time that day.

The tailor's efficiency hadn't stopped at the shirt. Hanging along with the tuxedo pants under the jacket I found a black silk cummerbund and bow tie. The cummerbund I could figure out. The bow tie was beyond my ken. It took a quarter of an hour and a couple of YouTube instructional videos for me to finally get it tied to where it didn't look like a bat had squashed itself against my throat.

The tux made me the most overdressed guy at the Starbucks on 1st Ave. Watching the SAM entrance from across the street, I saw museum staff—employees drafted into putting on their finest and working the holiday—just inside the arched portico, using scanners to read QR codes off paper invitations and cell phones submitted by the guests. Security in blue blazers stood discreetly to one side.

There were cops, too. During my passes along the sidewalk, I'd seen a team of uniforms on the long low flight of granite steps inside the museum, pausing to chat by the Chinese statues of seated rams with the nonchalance of patrolmen on easy duty. I wouldn't be sneaking in.

A knot of revelers waited at the crosswalk. Doyennes and dignitaries who had noticeably started their evening at dinner, with wine. Their dress was formal, their laughter considerably less starched. The ivory edge of an invitation showed from one pooh-bah's tuxedo pocket.

Tempting, but risky. If the code on the invitation was unique to the guest, or their name was printed on the card, I might be finished before I started. These people looked like longtime supporters who might be known to museum staff.

Someone closer to my age, maybe. Like the half-dozen suited-up college kids under the legs of the Hammering Man statue, having a last vape before going inside. Maybe their families were donors, or maybe they were tech prodigies with a yen for modern art. Just so long as they had their invitations.

I tossed the dregs of my Sumatra and crossed the avenue, pretending to be as engrossed in my phone as most of them were. In the half light of the winter street, it was an easy task to review their screens as I paced. A blast of wind off the harbor steps made the nearest girl shiver.

"Let's go," she said, her teeth chattering either by natural reaction or to deliberately emphasize her point.

Her date nodded without looking up. She nudged him impatiently before his screen changed to display the black mottled square of the QR.

"Could you grab my picture?" I said, abruptly holding out my phone. "I promised my folks they'd see me in the tux."

They looked startled but the boy complied, and he even angled himself where he'd capture the moving statue in the background.

"Thanks a lot," I said as he handed the phone back. "Have fun tonight."

I looked at my phone and swiped away from the picture of me grinning sheepishly to see another app. The black square of the invitation code appeared, every pixel as crisp as the original.

It was a simple program on the surface. Simple, but highly illegal. Similar to the old applications that traded contact information or photos when two enabled phones bumped each other, this function stole a screenshot from the nearest unlocked phone on command. In this case, an image of the kid's invitation code. I'd bought the app off an anonymous hacker from Hong Kong, thinking it would be useful for snagging texts or emails should I ever have need. But I could be flexible.

I quick-marched to the entrance, wanting to make sure my copy was the first one seen. A pass of the scanner gun over the phone resulted in a satisfying ping. All good.

The docent secured a black plastic bracelet with the SAM logo around my wrist.

"That's your pass," she explained, showing me the strip of flexible metal on the underside. "You can come and go now if you like. Don't forget the director's presentation at eight o'clock in the forum."

I examined the bracelet. Classier than an ink stamp

at a club. I wondered if its metal band also signaled if a guest was permitted in the VIP sections. There was bound to be a private room somewhere. Rich people loved exclusivity. The more select their daily lives were, the more they coveted reaching that next level. Ondine lived on the next level.

A loose line of volunteers—flanked by SPD officers in crisp navy—ushered all of the entrants to the nearest escalator and up to the museum's main forum, the launching pad of the party. I went with the flow.

It was early yet. Most guests hadn't advanced beyond the forum, enmeshed in politely chatting clusters. A coat-check service in the corner was doing brisk business. I wove around the knots of people.

Elana would have coveted the jewelry adorning the necks and earlobes of many of the matrons. She could pass for a member of this class, probably creating a whole backstory about being the heiress to a lumber empire. My sharp tuxedo aside, I would have more trouble blending.

The forum took up half the length of the long block on 1st Ave, a room as tall as a terminal in a regional airport. There were a few nods to the season in the holly branches placed on the front desks and at the corners of video screens behind the receptionists. Restrained, unlike the art installation that had many of the two hundred guests craning their necks upward.

A representation of an old-growth tree, suspended horizontally. One hundred feet or more from its fan-shaped roots to the wiry upper branches at the far end of the hall. Its trunk had been segmented every fifteen feet or so, and the pieces rocked fractionally on their guy-wires in response to some movement in the air above us. It made the longest branches appear to be stretching toward the high windows of the lobby. As if straining to rejoin nature.

A plaque on the wall told me the piece was crafted from over a million pieces of reclaimed cedar, off a plaster cast of a living tree. But the dappled surface looked less like wood to me than the skin of some great snake, cast off and wrapped around crooked tubes. Elegant and eerie.

The thought of serpents brought me back to my purpose here. I went hunting for Ondine.

On the third floor, the galleries had been opened to allow guests to wander freely about the twisting metal sculptures and abstract images in oil and aluminum filling the walls.

Hard to envision Ondine gazing at modern art, unless it was brought directly before her after being liberated from a private collection by someone like my grandfather.

Up to the fourth level. More galleries, with bristly costumes and ceremonial masks from Africa. More guards, too, wandering with slack expressions between rooms.

One of the more imposing sentinels held his post by a red velour curtain that had been set up to block a wide entryway off the rear hall. A glowing screen past his shoulder read WYCKOFF PORCELAIN ROOM. As I watched, a crisp white-haired member of the gentry approached. The guard moved the curtain aside to admit him before the man had to break his stride, without so much as a nod exchanged.

That would be the place. But from the look of the guard, I wasn't going to bluff my way inside.

I still carried the burner backup phone I'd been using since Bilal had hacked mine. I stepped into one of the side galleries to mess with the burner's settings and downloaded a Migos song that Cyndra had been playing in her room before dinner the other night, until Addy had protested about the lyrics searing the paint from the walls.

Down the hall from the Porcelain Room, past a collection of Catholic triptychs, I found a gallery dedicated to textiles from the Restoration Era, or replicas thereof. Gowns ten times as elaborate as any on the museum guests. I waited until the nearby guards circled away to check the adjoining exhibits before slipping the burner into the folds of an especially lavish bodice.

Nothing I could do about the cameras, which would have caught my tuxedoed image near the gown and my profile leaving the gallery. But then I didn't plan to stay and admire the culture all evening.

One minute later the timer I'd set went off, and Cardi B's voice-over began to echo through the galleries at the highest volume the little phone could manage. It was a shame I hadn't had time to patch into the museum's sound system. Cardi's words were hard to make out from the adjoining hallway, but I imagine most guests got the tone if not the precise words describing her riding her man like a BMX bike.

Guards hurried toward the textile gallery as if hot coals were frying their feet. Curious patrons joined the rush. The sentinel at the Porcelain Room resisted the pull for a slow count of three, then strode across and into the gallery, looking ready to crush the offending device in his meaty fist. I was through the red curtain in seconds.

True to its name, the room was like being inside the world's largest and most expensive china cabinet. Each dish and cup and tureen individually mounted within slim cocoa-brown display cases. Whatever viewing benches the room usually housed had been replaced by chairs and couches with velvet upholstery, arranged into seating areas around hexagonal glass coffee tables.

On a loveseat at the far side was Ondine Long.

She'd spotted me before the curtain had stopped swaying. Her soft smile for her companion—the stiff gentleman I'd seen enter the room earlier—didn't change, but her eyes held mine for an extra second before turning back.

If I gave her a few minutes, she might gracefully extricate herself from the conversation. Minutes I didn't have. I wove through the standing knots of guests, absorbed in their close discussions over drinks they had acquired from some unseen server.

"Ondine," I said.

The starched man looked up, thrown by the intrusion. Was I some impertinent waiter?

Ondine hardly moved. She wore a green dress made of some kind of silk, high-necked and so restrained in its cut that it had to cost as much as a decent used car. Her hair was coiled in an equally minimal arrangement. Only her makeup was a touch too visible. I wasn't precisely sure of Ondine's age—her blend of Asian and Western heritages and the very best surgery complicated any attempt at analysis—but suspected that she'd had a professional apply her mask, and the artist's hand showed in the work.

"Good evening," said Ondine, as if she'd been expecting my visit for the past week. "Van, this is State Senator Werring. Senator, Donovan Shaw."

"Hello," the senator said, without another glance at me. "Ondine, I think if you'll consider the party's point of view, you'll understand why your support—"

"I promise you I'll consider every perspective, Lyle. And I'll have an answer for you by Monday. If you'll excuse me."

"Of course. I'm overdue to check in with my campaign staff." Werring stood up, adroitly turning the dismissal into the next move of a man of action. "Mr. Shaw."

I nodded, choosing the seat on Ondine's right rather than the chair directly opposite. The angle let me keep half an eye on the entryway.

"I'll be astounded if you've begun patronizing the arts, Van," Ondine said. Her words and expression and tone all projecting calm politesse. I wasn't fooled.

"You've branched out, too. Playing kingmaker." I nodded to the chair the senator had recently occupied.

"The recall election. Many candidates and very few days before February."

"Time is short all around. Tell me about Bilal Nath."

The corners of Ondine's mouth twitched, which passed for disapproval.

"I didn't realize you two had met," she said.

Apparently neither Bilal nor Dr. Claybeck had shared the details of that stormy night with Ondine. No point in pulling Claybeck further into quicksand.

"He tracked me down," I said, "with the offer of a lifetime."

"I'm willing to discuss this matter tomorrow."

"Tomorrow I'll be busy dealing with the grenade you've dropped in my lap. We'll talk right here."

Her direct gaze might have unnerved a more anxious guy. Or a less angry one. Having me tossed out of the museum would attract the kind of attention not in keeping with her stature. And she couldn't be sure I wouldn't tell the cops about the connection between her and Nath. Even if they didn't believe me, it would be on record, and Ondine would find that unacceptable.

"Start at the start," I said. "Why did Nath hear my name?"

"He inquired about people with your skill set. I gave him my top recommendation. But he wasn't satisfied. He needed someone immediately and wanted options. I provided him with a short list of names—including yours—but cautioned that for various reasons they may not be to his liking. You, specifically. I told him that you weren't manageable."

"So why mention me at all?"

"What is it that Bilal wants to acquire?" she said, instead of answering.

"He didn't tell you?"

"No. He was very closed about his intentions, even though it might have helped me find the best contractor for the job."

Contractor. Like I would be remodeling Nath's kitchen.

"He won't tell me what he's after, either," I said. "What's he into? His regular business?"

"That's not relevant."

"I'll decide what's useful. If Nath is my problem, then I'm yours."

"You are not as formidable as you imagine."

"Try me."

Ondine waited, still as one of the porcelain figurines in the nearby display case, until a tangle of guests had moved out of earshot.

"Bilal Nath started as an early online entrepreneur. Mining personal search histories to encourage small payments from individuals, in the days before the Internet had many ramparts in place."

Even with Ondine's oblique language, I grasped the extortion. *Send $500 or we will email everyone in your contact list these sick webpages you've visited. Everyone will know you're a pervert.* A scam with a very low success rate, but minimal cost and no risk at all if carried out from beyond the reach of U.S. authorities. Run the job on a few million addresses, and even if only a tiny portion of one percent paid up, you'd still be rich.

"I already knew Bilal was a hacker," I said.

"On a higher level than most, if not all. He transitioned into more targeted ventures before long," Ondine said, "aimed at celebrities and public figures. I'm told he has a team in Lahore, which he hires out to acquire private information for political movements in South Asia and perhaps elsewhere. Nath is very adept at circumventing defenses."

She didn't make it sound like a compliment. An inkling that where Bilal Nath was concerned, Ondine's customary detachment might be shaded with something else.

"Yeah, I had a demonstration of his skills," I said. "So what does an international blackmailer need that he can't buy or coerce?"

Ondine turned over one palm, as if considering the question moot. "You may have also noticed that Bilal is ill. Perhaps he desires something of emotional value."

I thought of the cryo bottle I'd seen in their hotel room. Something personal?

The door to the Porcelain Room opened and the thick-necked sentinel strode in, along with an equally brawny guy in a black suit and tie. He looked at Ondine. And me.

"Yours?" I said, looking at the grunt in the funeral wear.

"My driver."

"Surprised he wasn't lurking near the soup tureens to protect you."

"I have Jessica for that." I looked where she indicated. A fortyish Latina woman wearing a claret-colored dress and more sensible shoes than a formal party demanded stood off my left shoulder. Her hand rested, relaxed, at the open top to her Kate Spade handbag.

"Diversity in bodyguards," I said. "Good for you."

"Our time is up," Ondine said.

The museum guard was holding the burner phone I'd left in the antique French gown. A glance at his ruddy glowering face told me he'd seen the security video and identified me.

"So it is," I said.

I stood up. Jessica moved to a position beside Ondine's loveseat.

"How's the employee health plan?" I asked her. "Just in case I hire on."

"Profit sharing is the real draw," she said. "Nice tux."

"Let's go." The guard, at my elbow.

"Can't take me anywhere," I said. Jessica smiled minutely. Ondine looked undisturbed by anything around her, like she might already be weighing the merits of contributing to Senator Werring's campaign.

I walked out the open door, past Ondine's driver. The guard followed close enough behind to pick lint off my collar. Two more guards joined our procession as we paraded down the escalators to the portico where I'd first come in.

"Your wristband, asshole," the guard said.

He wanted to take a swing at me so badly it was making his fingers twitch. I held enough pent-up rage myself that I was tempted to ask him if he wanted to take it outside, where he could make a move free from any cameras or easily horrified party guests.

But I'd started the trouble tonight. And this poor furious goon wasn't my enemy. I tore off the wristband and handed it to him and left.

Outside, the hammer of the giant statue rose and fell, rose and fell. I finally turned toward University Street and began walking. Just a well-dressed mutt, looking a whole lot better than he felt.

I was tired. Which was no excuse for not having spotted Ondine's bodyguard Jessica, despite the signifiers of her practical shoes and the handbag large enough to hold her piece and as many extra magazines as she could want. Sloppy.

I unraveled my bow tie and unbuttoned the top buttons of the tuxedo shirt, grateful that I didn't hold a job where a necktie was a daily requirement. I barely held a job at all. My gig at Bully Betty's was just marking time. Betty had recognized it before I had. I didn't need the income—though I would soon, the way I was burning through my savings—and as much as I liked the people at the bar, pulling drinks and keeping the peace weren't any challenge.

Bilal was a threat. And threats were a kind of challenge. The kind that kept me sharp, focused on something important, feeling the way I wanted to feel. I wasn't suicidal, but I would have to be dense not to recognize the pattern of my own behavior. I liked the action.

My grandfather had, too. Dono was never happier than when he was planning a score. Afterward, when the excitement and urgency had abated, he'd sink into what he called his black dog days. Growing morose and surly for no accountable reason.

Screw it. Solve the problem right in front of you, Shaw. Get Bilal Nath off your back. Then you can sweat the small stuff, like the rest of your life.

On a normal night, the garage where I'd left the Barracuda would have been nearly empty. But with half the hotels and restaurants at the heart of the city hosting end-of-year events, every parking space from the stadiums to Belltown was filled. I wound my way through the packed rows on the sloping roof level. I was five yards from my car when a tapping sound came from the dark at my nine, pebble on pavement.

I dodged to one side, ducking down behind a blue

minivan. Was it Bilal, or Saleem? How had they tracked me here?

"Hold it." A man's voice, on my opposite side. Very close. He'd suckered me. "Get your hands up. Now."

I showed my palms. The man stepped out from the shadows of the elevator stand.

Sean Burke. In the flesh. With an arctic expression on his face and one of his recently acquired SIG Sauer pistols in his hand. A suppressor extended the barrel like an accusing finger, pointing dead square at my head.

CHAPTER NINETEEN

BURKE WAVED ME TOWARD the other side of the elevator stand. Where someone returning to their car would be less likely to spot him holding me at gunpoint. Or emptying his clip into my heart.

He walked steadily sideways as I approached, keeping at least a dozen feet between us. When I reached a spot in the center of the nearest handicapped space, with an SUV blocking us from the rest of the lot, he motioned for me to stop.

"If you want my wallet, man, you can have it," I said.

With his left hand he removed something from his pocket and flicked it so that it landed at my feet. A thick square of folded paper.

"Pick it up," he said.

I did, and unfolded it.

It was a picture of me in black and white, taken from a foot or two above the level of my head. The distance was tricky to gauge due to the fish-eye lens. But there was no mistaking my face, with my concentrated expression and every scar sharply detailed as I came toward the lens. Taking my first shoeless step through the sliding-glass door of Burke's cul-de-sac home in Bitter Lake.

There were more papers, more pictures. Me in Burke's hallway, rifling through the closet. Me in the bedroom, opening a dresser drawer. Each image taken from roughly the same elevation. Each a prosecutor's dream.

Not that I thought Burke had any intention of involving the cops.

"In the ceiling beams," I said.

Burke nodded. "Triggered by pressure plates in the floor." If he had much emotion about our situation, he was keeping it to himself.

The black paint on the beams had struck me as odd at the time. Now I knew why. It would have been almost impossible for me to spot a tiny camera lens in rough wood painted black. Especially at night. The part of me that wasn't screaming at myself for fucking up admired the simplicity.

"You're not a shooter," Burke said. "You didn't bring a gun to the house. Who are you, Shaw?" he said.

He knew my name. Son of a bitch.

"Hey, I was just looking for cash, man. It won't happen again, I swear."

"Burglars don't leave flat-screens and stereos behind. And your car is registered to some dead shitheel in Oregon." Burke lowered his pistol until it pointed at my left knee. "Last chance. Who do you work for?"

The elevator motor started. Neither of us moved.

Burke wasn't bluffing. I tensed, waiting for the hot round to fracture my kneecap and shred the ligaments around it into wet mush.

A car alarm beeped and parking lights flashed from the lower slope. In the instant Burke's eyes flicked in that direction, I dove and rolled under the SUV. I came up on the other side and kept moving, bolting for deeper cover. Expecting gunfire to follow at any second. I heard laughter instead, and happy curses, as a small group of teenagers made their loping way off the elevator. On the row below us, the car whose alarm had beeped roared to life.

I risked a look over the nearest hood. Burke was gone.

Maybe he had stepped into the open elevator. Or maybe he was waiting until the new arrivals had left to emerge and finish me off. I ran to the Barracuda, diving into the driver's seat, leaving thick black stripes on the asphalt in my haste to be away.

Driving out of the garage gave no relief. I expected Burke to appear from behind every car, around each corner. Only when I was on the street and roaring south did I unclench.

How had he found me? How the hell did he know who I *was*, even with the pictures from his camera trap at the house? It had been less than twenty-four hours since I'd darkened his doorstep. *Goddamn.*

Once I'd passed the stadiums and was sure no one was following, I pulled over and stepped out of the car. The way I was going I'd smash into a lamppost, or get busted for reckless endangerment.

My new tuxedo was beyond repair, torn and stained by my roll across the oily pavement. I could feel my knee seeping blood. I tore off the jacket and shirt and replaced them with the old flannel I'd started the night with.

Idiot. The only reason I wasn't ending the night in a hospital or a morgue was dumb luck, emphasis on the *dumb.* I had been a step too slow in every single dance tonight.

I called Hollis. Maybe misery could do with company.

"You alone?" I said.

"For the moment. Matty and Fran from J dock are on their way over. We've a trip planned south to Cannon Beach after the new year."

"I just met Sean Burke."

"The man who might be—"

"The man who might be. We didn't get into that."

"So what's he like?"

"Calmer than me. But he was the one holding the gun." I told Hollis what had happened.

"Sly devil," Hollis said, "with his hidden cameras."

"In a home that might as well be a worm on a hook. An entire house, set up just to see who comes knocking."

"Who does that?"

Somebody with serious enemies. If I had walked into Burke's house with a gun in my hand, he'd have assumed I had broken in to kill him. In which case he might have ended me straight off, no need for interrogation.

"I can't get distracted by Sean Burke right now," I said, more to myself than Hollis. "Bilal Nath is still dead set on forcing me to crack Ceres Biotech tomorrow night. It's more than just business for him, I'm sure. And I don't think I can shake him loose in time."

"And you need help."

"I need a third option."

I told Hollis what I had in mind.

"That's possible," he said, "but are you sure you

won't want a little—what do you soldiers call it—fire support?"

"Willard will be there if things get hot. My last resort."

"Matty just stepped aboard," Hollis said. "I can come by your apartment in the morning."

"I'll come to you."

"You all right?"

"I'm rattled. Between Bilal knowing where all my friends live and Sean Burke tracking me down hell knows how, I'm not sure where safe ground is. Better to keep on the move."

"Get some rest, lad," Hollis said. "We'll sort it out."

He hung up. I knew he was right. I'd been on the move and on edge all day, and tomorrow would be worse.

The last day of the year. Time for resolutions. And fireworks.

JUNIOR YEAR, PART TWO

Seeing my friend Davey Tolan in the library was like spotting a coyote at the off-leash dog park. Out of place, and very likely up to no good. He was alone at one of the study tables, reading or pretending to read our English assignment of *Brave New World*. Really he was drawing robots and shit in his notebook like always.

"Davey," I said, sliding into the chair opposite him. "The fuck?"

He smiled like he already knew the punchline to a joke I was telling and flicked his eyes toward a group of girls at another table I'd passed on the way in. "Kate Barra."

"Huh?" I knew who Kate was. Honor Society, in every AP course ever invented and probably creating more they hadn't. High-Quality Life. "You're not horny for her."

Davey leaned in so far he practically lay across the table. His dark hair flopped over his face. "I am since I saw her running in gym class. Katie

Girl's exercise necessitates an industrial-strength sports bra."

I snorted. Davey's dick was like a compass with a magnet nearby. Unpredictable. "She'll never go for it."

"You have no faith at all. One, Kate has agreed to help me with algebra. Two, she broke up with Pel Rosario last weekend. Time is ripe and so is she."

How did Davey track all this stuff? Every time I thought he and I were roughly equivalent in our social status—somewhere north of the burnouts and south of everyone else—he proved he was tapped in. And despite my scoffing, I knew damn well Kate Barra might be in his range. Davey had those kinds of looks. Girls had been into him since before we knew what girls were.

"So that's why *I'm* in the library . . ." Davey said, nudging.

"You remember a quilt? Used to hang on the wall right there." I pointed to where a bunch of watercolors from Ms. Pico's art class now covered the wall.

"That is maybe the weirdest question you've ever asked me."

"Do you?"

"Whoa." He mimed raising his hands to ward off a blow. "Yeah, sure I do. It got ripped off last year. So?"

"My mom made part of it."

"Oh. And it's gone now. Man, that sucks." He thought about it as I stared angrily at the watercolors. The library smelled a little like old wool, even though the school had dehumidifiers running all year long to keep mold away.

"You talk to Colten?"

"Who? Colten Gulas?"

"He got fucking reamed by Mr. Lindhoff when the quilt disappeared. 'Cause I guess Colten was watching the library, part of his detention or some shit. So either Colten left when he wasn't supposed to, or he knew who took the quilt and wouldn't squeal."

Mr. Lindhoff was the guidance counselor. I didn't like him, and I probably wasn't one of his favorite people, either. "Why's Lindhoff care so much?"

"Dude!" Davey laughed. "He cares 'cause Ms. Nasgate cares. They're *boning*, man. How do you not know this?"

Because I rarely gave a thought to school, except to finish it and get away. I was starting to see the downside.

"I'll find Colten," I said.

"I figured. You got that look, like you're biting on aluminum foil. But you'll have to wait. The dork's been out of class past three days."

"He sick?"

"Dunno."

"You know where he lives?"

"Man, you are caffeinated today. I don't. He sometimes skips last period to hang with Singer Boeman's Club for Shitheads, so maybe he's skipping the whole week."

I remembered Singer. The school's dealer of tiny bags of pot or coke or whatever pills he'd been able to steal from somebody's parents' bathroom. Boeman and most of his bunch had graduated or finished their credits during summer makeup sessions last year.

"Kate's friends are leaving," Davey said, shrugging into his black leather jacket. My cue to make space. "I'm gonna see if she wants to go to Yvette Friel's party this weekend."

"Bet you don't even get a hand in her sweater," I said, standing up.

"You *should* have my back, dude," he said. "Kate says Eden Adler likes you. I might be in a position to make that miracle happen."

"Bullshit."

"I mean it," he said. "Swear to God. She's no Kate"—he subtly mimed huge globes on his chest—"but if that's your type, go for it."

Eden Adler did not require a double-whatever-letter bra. Eden Adler didn't require anything but being Eden Adler. And Davey really was just trying to help.

"Thanks, man," I said.

"If we all go out, you're payin'."

It was a Wednesday, which meant Mr. Lindhoff was in his office. Early in the school year he had come around to all the homerooms to introduce himself and had mentioned that most guidance counselors served two or three high schools depending on size. He meant the size of the schools, but I guessed it could also mean the size of the district budget.

Probably because he wasn't there more often, his office was for crap. More a long closet with a high window, like a jail cell, and so narrow he would have to turn sideways to go between the wall and his desk, which was not exactly huge itself. Below the window, a hanging magazine rack was packed solid with brochures on universities and voc-tech schools, instructional packets for writing college essays, GED forms for students dropping out, and reams of other stuff I'd likely never give two shits about.

Lindhoff's eyebrows popped over his bifocals as I entered. The idea of him and Ms. Nasgate as a couple was weird. She wasn't young or anything, she'd been at the school for like twenty-five years. But Lindhoff seemed old. Like dentures old.

"Mr. Shaw?" he said. "Rethinking our talk about colleges?"

Right. Lindhoff had said something to me about my grades holding up for two-year colleges and maybe state school if I applied myself. I had forgotten what I'd said to get away from him at the time.

"Sure, but . . . I wanted to ask about the quilt from the library. The one that got stolen."

"Ask what, precisely?"

"Did Colten Gulas ever say who took it?"

He removed the glasses entirely now. I'd gotten his attention, which may not be the best thing.

"Why," he said, "do you want to know?"

Oh shit. I saw the leap he'd made. Now Lindhoff thought I was worried Colten had ratted me out.

Sometimes the truth really does set you free.

"My mom. She's dead." I let that hang in the air for a moment. Lindhoff nodded impatiently, but his expression eased back a little. "She made one of the squares, Miz Nasgate told me." *A one-two punch for sympathy, throwing out my mom and your girlfriend, dude.*

"I see. And you're hoping to recover it." He cleared his throat. "I'm afraid that's a dead end, Mr. Shaw. Colten said he never saw who took it."

Which was different than not knowing. I caught that, and Lindhoff saw me catch it.

"At this point it would be best to consider it lost," he said. "That's my belief as well as the school's. Do you grasp my meaning?"

"Yeah." Don't go beating up Colten for answers, or the guidance counselor will guide me right into a suspension.

"Good. And I'm sorry. I remember your mother. Moira, wasn't it?"

"Yes."

"Unusual name here in the States. She and I talked about college options for her, even after her surprise." He nodded toward me. "A very good student. I think she was looking at community schools, something that might allow her flexible hours. Do you know if she ever went?"

"No."

"'No, you don't know,' or 'No, she never attended college'?"

Lindhoff could be such a dickwad. "I don't know."

"Hmm. Priorities, perhaps. Still, a bright young woman."

He turned back to his paperwork. I left him.

At least Lindhoff hadn't given me the old speech about doing a good job because Mom would have wanted that. People had been telling me that shit my entire life, like they'd known her at all.

And he hadn't been convinced by Colt's story. While I didn't like Lindhoff much, I had to admit he wasn't a dummy. If he thought Colten Gulas knew something about the quilt, then I'd bet he was right. Suspension or no suspension, I was going to find out what that something was.

CHAPTER TWENTY

RETURNING TO MY APARTMENT was too big a risk. Even though I'd kept my name off the lease, Bilal Nath had access to enough information that he might conceivably track me to my overpriced studio off Broadway. And there was no telling where Sean Burke and his silenced SIG might pop up again. Or the pair of men who had tailed me earlier in the day.

Less than a week ago, my biggest concern was how to mend fences with Addy. Now I was dodging at least three different menaces while setting up a score that might get me killed. I needed a new life plan.

The speedboat should be safe ground. Officially I'd sold the boat after Dono's death and it was registered to a marine supply company in Everett. Which in turn was owned by a real corporation in Hong Kong, although those papers were false. I was subletting its moorage with cash. That made enough of a smoke screen that I could close both eyes to sleep.

In the morning, I rose to find the cloud cover had lightened to the point where I could at least guess at the position of the sun. The docks smelled of Canada geese and algae and clean ocean air every time the breeze picked up.

The *Francesca* wasn't in its slip. Hollis might be off-shore, out of the reach of Bilal. I texted him the number 16 and tuned the VHF radio to that hailing channel. I'd finished changing clothes when his voice came through the tinny speaker.

"Benning Boy, this is *Francesca*." Fort Benning in Georgia was the home of the Ranger Regiment.

"*Francesca*, this is Benning Boy. Reply seven-one."

"Seven-one," he confirmed. We switched frequencies.

"Smart thinking calling on the radio," Hollis said once we'd exchanged call signs again. "I've been nervous about using my cell phone since that—" He stopped himself from cursing over the airwaves. "Since our spot of trouble."

"Where are you?"

"A few miles north. Have you heard from our large friend?"

I'd received a text from Willard overnight.

"I'm meeting him at ten," I said. "You remember the place where Albie used to watch the ponies?"

There was a moment's pause. "I do. It's still around?"

"Sort of."

"I can tie up at a guest slip in Edmonds and probably get there by then."

"See you there. And thanks."

"Don't thank me. My head might just as well be on that same chopping block, you know."

At a diner on Seaview Avenue, I drank too much coffee and picked at an egg breakfast, as I concentrated on reading details online about the CXS-3001 container I'd seen in Saleem's hotel safe.

I'd been right about it being designed to transport biological material. The CXS-3001 was touted by the manufacturer as a new generation intended for small-scale transport, and top of the line. The heavy base of the aluminum bottle could receive a pressurized cartridge of liquid nitrogen that would charge the foam inside within minutes instead of the hours necessary for larger, older models, the advertising claimed. So charged, the bottle's insulation and vacuum plug would maintain the temperature south of one-hundred-fifty degrees below zero, Celsius, keeping its contents viable for at least ten days.

Time enough for Bilal to escape. Far out of the reach of any law. He'd claimed he wasn't after anything that would cause harm, but I trusted that about as far as I could fastball the runny egg yolk on my plate. Even if I were stealing some prototype vaccine that might help him avoid a slow death from ALS, who knew how that theft might set back research at Ceres, or how many lives a lost cure would impact?

I had to go through with the job or suffer the consequences. That, or call the FBI now and have them ready to bust all of us the moment I stepped over Ceres's gleaming threshold. I'd keep Hollis and Paula Claybeck out of the story if I could. But if that was impossible, so be it. Better to have them in a cell than dead, or enabling the deaths of who knew how many others.

Would calling the cops even solve the problem? We'd all be stuck in holding tanks until Bilal's lawyers arranged to cut him loose. Probably much sooner than I would be arraigned and make bail. He could be out and making his next move within hours, and I'd be trapped, unable to protect anyone.

Yet I couldn't let Bilal Nath get hold of whatever he was after. Regardless of the risk to me or Hollis or even Addy and Cyndra.

The whole puzzle was giving me a headache. I swallowed two aspirin from my pocket, which reminded me of Bilal and Aura's lineup of prescription bottles in their hotel bathroom. What had Aura's been?

Olaparib. I looked it up. A cancer cell inhibitor. Commonly taken as a long-term maintenance drug to help prevent recurrence. The description I read mentioned particular use for patients with advanced ovarian cancer after prior lines of chemotherapy, once the tumor had diminished or disappeared.

I knew just enough to understand heavy chemotherapy could impact or even end a woman's fertility. A book on pregnancy had been on Aura's nightstand. Was she healthy now, or waiting until her body could handle carrying a baby to term? Were they racing against time with Bilal's worsening health? Any way it shook out, I didn't see how knowing she was afflicted could help my problem.

First things first. I'd meet Willard and Hollis, and we'd see how tough a nut Ceres would be. Then, unless I had some brilliant idea before nightfall, I'd drop by the FBI field office downtown and hand whatever agent had pulled holiday duty a shiny gift for the new year.

LUCE'S LATE UNCLE ALBIE Boylan had loved to gamble. He never had enough money or credit to get himself deeply into hock, but he seemed to get as much joy out of betting five dollars as five hundred. The bar he'd fronted for my grandfather—who had called the shots behind the scenes—didn't carry the cable channel showing the action at the old Longacres track. So to watch whatever horse race he'd bet that week's spare change against, Albie would toddle down to Alaskan Way and a billiard hall nestled under the viaduct.

Over the years the pool hall had been sold and partitioned, with half the space becoming a coffeehouse, which was eventually halved again into a sort of lunch bodega for commuters and tourists coming off the ferries and looking to grab a fast bite. But the television stayed in roughly the same place on the wall, upgraded to a flat screen now and showing a singing competition on Telemundo. I bought a Coke to claim space at the window counter.

Willard crossed the street at Marion, walking without hurry. He carried a long cardboard mailing tube, which looked a little like a drinking straw in his fingers. I joined him at a bench outside, for privacy. Willard's ass wouldn't have fit on one of the bodega counter stools, anyway.

He opened the mailing tube and slid a thick roll of papers out. The blueprints were the largest, but some of the other plans were nearly poster-sized as well.

"You've already looked," I said.

"Sure. And the headline is: Don't Do It. Check this." He unrolled the stack and leafed through to pick one batch of pages. Eleven-by-seventeen sheets, and thick. Electrical schematics.

He flipped to an interior page and held it out to me.

"Fourth floor. Everything's pretty much normal until you see that they've wired the cameras separately. I think that's because this section"—he pointed to one quarter of the building—"has got its own power supply that switches on in case of an outage."

"That'll be the cryogenic storage bank," I said. "Can't have things melting during a blackout."

"Well, that room's cameras and alarm are completely enclosed. Even if you manage to patch into the building system somehow from outside, or make the lights go out, that piece of real estate keeps right on humming. The guards downstairs can still see everything that happens in that section. And I gotta assume the system can still make a cellular call to nine-one-one, too."

"Aura Nath said that Ceres has controlled burn safeguards to destroy their biological matter in case of a breach."

Willard actually smacked his heavy brow. "Controlled burn. That explains it. I was trying to figure why they had this." He flipped to another page. "It's a tiny room off the cryogenic unit. Hypoxic air generator, the label says."

"Fire suppression," I realized. "The oxygen level in the cryo unit is kept low. In case a controlled burn is set off. The flames destroy the virus or whatever it is, then sputter out from lack of oh-two before anything else catches on fire. I saw hypoxic chambers in the Army. They have them for high-altitude training. And computer data centers, so they don't have to use water sprinklers."

"So you can't breathe inside the cryo room?"

"There's enough oxygen in the air for humans. Might give you a headache after a while."

"Christ. Now I get why Nath wanted a pro."

I sat with the thought. Being a professional meant being a realist. And realistically, Ceres was a bitch.

Gulls cried overhead. Just a few weeks ago their caws might have been drowned out by a constant sonorous drone of traffic right over our heads. But the old viaduct was closed. If I listened hard, I could hear the scrape and crunch of the claw machines south of us as they tore down the two-story highway. Route 99 now went far under our feet. It had taken billions of dollars and nearly that many delays, along with the biggest drill in the world, to bore two miles of tunnel through the heart of the city. The whole waterfront would soon be repaved and redesigned, once the highway was gone. I guessed it wouldn't be long before market forces pushed the bodega out, too. Maybe the perpetual TV would carry on as a marker.

I thumbed through the schematics Willard had brought. The challenge with complex defenses, overlapping means of security, is that they add extra wrinkles that can go wrong. Your backups wind up needing backups. Somewhere in Ceres's design there was a flaw. Maybe systematic, maybe human. But what could I exploit with just a few hours to prep?

Nothing. Time to face facts. I had to bring in the law. Maybe I could convince them that I wasn't a terrorist myself.

I heard Hollis coming before I saw him. He was

breathing hard and sweating lightly, even with the morning chill.

"I misremembered which block," he said, before coughing violently into his hand. "Thought you might have left already."

"Ceres is a wash, anyway," said Willard.

"Van?" Hollis asked.

I shrugged. "With time, it's beatable. But Bilal Nath is expecting me to show up in nine hours."

Hollis settled onto the bench with a sigh. "I hesitate to suggest it, but there is the nuclear option."

"Killing Nath," Willard said.

I'd thought about that, more than once. It was an option. Even if it made my mouth taste bile.

"I know he claims to have an axe ready to fall on your head if he suddenly dies," said Hollis, "but do you believe him?"

"Ondine gave me Nath's bona fides. Even she respects him. And Bilal has a whole team to avenge him, not counting Aura."

"So he means what he says," Willard noted. "There's a contract on you, unless he cancels it personally."

"And I can't force him to do that. He's already dying. I don't know what he fears."

"He loves his wife, you told me."

"Yeah," I said. "But going after Aura is a fool move, even if I could stomach it. Threaten Aura, and Bilal will just spirit her off to Karachi or Indonesia or anywhere else out of our reach. Kidnap her and Nath comes after Cyndra or Addy in return. There are too many ways for him to retaliate."

"Which leads us back to Ceres Biotech," Hollis said, glancing at the blueprints. "What about a takedown? Masks and shouting and make one of the guards hand over the goods?"

"That stinks," Willard said. "What if there's employees working late, or another guard wandering the building?"

"I know it's a lousy idea," said Hollis. "I'm not a damned beginner. But we're down to the dregs here."

"Here's an employee roster," Willard said, finding a stapled bunch of sheets in the pile. "All the security is contracted through Markham Protective. I've got some history with that company. They're good, but they follow the same procedures with every client. We could pull the old gag of telling the guard we've got thugs watching his family."

I glanced at the top sheet, less because I was honestly weighing Willard's idea than to grasp at straws. The roster started at the Ceres executive board and went down by department and rank from there.

One name, just below those of the CEO and the president, caught my eye: Timothy Gorlick, MD, PhD. Chief medical officer, co-founder.

Gorlick. I'd seen that name before. On Aura Kincaid's civil records from my new buddy Panni at the FBI.

Aura had been married to Timothy Gorlick shortly before Bilal Nath. And she'd fought ovarian cancer. Had she been struck with it before she and Gorlick were divorced?

"You all right?" Willard said to me.

"We'll figure a way out of this, lad," said Hollis.

I barely heard them. I was getting an inkling of what Bilal Nath wanted. Why he and Aura were so ruthless in their determination.

And, more important, how I could turn that against them.

"Willard," I said, "walk me through everything you have on Markham Protective. Start with their camera circuits."

CHAPTER TWENTY-ONE

TWO HOURS LATER, I left Hollis and Willard to the tasks we'd agreed upon. For me, that started with retrieving gear I kept hidden in storage.

My apartment was a studio. Hiding burglary tools there was out of the question. During the past weeks I'd set up a workshop inside a multistory storage unit on the Hill. Not in my own name, of course. There were plenty of DIYers using their units for home repair jobs and side businesses, so nobody looked twice at the occasional whine of a drill or the shriek of metal being cut coming from my own space. I'd slipped the manager extra to clear out a unit way at the back, with plenty of privacy.

I wasn't blind to the ways my life had begun to echo my grandfather's. Hidden places, extra identities. I hadn't chosen Dono's life of crime for profit. I'd carved my own path, winding as it might be. But the methods I used were the ones he'd taught me. Plus my own innovations, some courtesy of my Ranger training.

Duffel bags and backpacks of various sizes lined shelves I'd built from two-by-fours and plywood. I opened four of the bags to retrieve items from within.

A keycard programmer. A set of fiber-optic cables and splicing tools. A laptop computer, and a wireless transmitter similar to those used in home theaters. A device that looked very much like a paintball gun. And a short prybar, in case brute force was called for.

Burke. I hadn't given much thought to the man during the past few hours, which was a freakishly odd thing to say about a guy who'd aimed a gun at my face the night before. There was no question in my mind that he would have shot me, save for my extremely good fortune that he'd been interrupted.

He hadn't gotten the answers he'd demanded. He'd try again. Although Burke knew my name, it was my motive for seeking him out that really concerned him.

Burke was a killer. So was I, if I were being honest with myself. Besides the rough similarity of our dark hair and size, he and I had violence in common.

Like me and Dono, Burke had apparently started on the same path as his brutal elder. Gut Burke had been a murderer and enforcer. Whoever Sean worked for now, himself or some racket, he was operating on a higher level than roughing up shopkeepers who had fallen behind on their protection payments. Which made him that much more dangerous.

If Burke learned he might be my father, would he be less likely to murder me, or more?

The keycard programmer looked like an oversized calculator. In the side pocket of one of the duffels I kept a bag of blank RFID keycards. I distracted myself from further thoughts of Sean Burke by getting to work with the programmer and the specs Willard had acquired on Markham Protective Services. I'd have to hope

Markham had stuck to their cut-and-paste approach to installation. If Ceres had sprung for an extra level of security, those bells and whistles might bring every guard running the moment we stepped inside.

When that task was complete, I spent another half hour double-checking my plans. Ceres's system was good. I could be better.

Finally, I packed the tools I'd chosen into a rucksack, wrapping each piece in a towel as padding. It would be heavy but manageable once strapped to my back. And silent, which was at least as important.

The rucksack rested on the passenger seat as I drove the old blue Dodge down Interstate 5. Rattles and pings all the way. The truck saying it was grumpy at having its rest disturbed, or peeved at being left alone so long. Maybe both. Maybe it was confused.

I switched on my blinker to move out of the fast lane, taking advantage of a gap in traffic to glide over three lanes in one go. A hundred yards behind me, a low silver Acura moved, too, abruptly jogging one lane to his right and then holding, as if the car had reacted reflexively. He dropped back as I accelerated.

Another half mile along, I moved into an exit-only lane for the next ramp. After a slow five-count, the Acura steadily crept over the last two lanes, until he was on my tail.

I drifted out of the exit lane, and of course the Acura followed.

Damn it. Who was this guy? My gut said police. He followed like police, like he had the basics of mobile surveillance down. Patient enough to keep his distance in the easy sightlines of the freeway, but maybe more accustomed to being one of two or more cars in a rotating pattern, plus air support. Hell, he might have exactly that kind of backup, and there was a police radar plane tracking me right now.

And me with a rucksack full of suspicious tools on the seat next to me, some of them worth a Class 3 felony. If my new admirer realized that I'd clocked him, his next move might be to pull me over. All my plans for Bilal Nath and Ceres Biotech would be smoked.

So my new first priority was to ditch this sucker before he got smart.

The next exit led to Highway 518 and SeaTac. I drifted onto the ramp without changing speed in the slightest, letting the Acura have plenty of notice. He followed me as I merged onto 518 and off again almost immediately, following the exit for International Boulevard.

This close to the airport, long-term parking lots dominated the landscape. I chose one called Renny's FastPass Parking—*The Business Traveler's Best Friend!*—and pressed the button at the gate to receive a ticket. The gate lifted, and I sped inside.

I would have to count on my pursuer hesitating. Should he follow me inside or wait and see if I left? What if I boarded a shuttle for the airport? I swung the Dodge around and up the ramps to the third level and into an open space in a row of parked cars. In an instant I had my door open and was grabbing the rucksack with my other hand. I dropped to the ground and began to low-crawl under the cars in the row, as fast as I could, dragging the ruck with me.

At the fifth car, I turned faceup and shimmied so

that I could reach the exhaust pipes leading to the mufflers. I unclipped the rucksack straps and fastened them around the pipes, pulling them tight so the ruck was suspended off the ground. It would have to do. I crawled back to the Dodge, whose engine still idled expectantly.

As I walked to the stairs, I glanced at the fifth car from the truck. A Nissan Altima, not that I'd been able to tell that from just its undercarriage. The rucksack below was essentially invisible, unless someone leaned way over and looked for it.

I made it down one flight of stairs. Two plainclothes cops—as recognizable by their flat affects as from their aggressively business-casual shirts and trousers and sport coats on a holiday—met me at the second landing.

"Mr. Shaw," said the one in the lead. "Come with us."

CHAPTER TWENTY-TWO

THEY DIDN'T HAVE TO show identification for me to know they were legit, but I asked them to do it, anyway. The bigger one, the cop who'd first spoken, tugged his ID off his belt to flash it for a full two seconds. Walter Podraski. A detective sergeant with the state. A big guy, almost as large as Bilal's goon Juwad, but with the added spread of middle age.

And jowled. Podraski had been the man tailing me on foot after my lunch with Willard. His partner's sandy hair was less windswept now that they were off the downtown streets.

"What's this about?" I said.

"Nothing serious," the partner said. In addition to being much leaner, he was slightly better dressed than Podraski. Nordstrom Rack instead of JCPenney. His hair and stature were boyish, but up close I realized both men were the same age, well north of forty. He hadn't offered his ID and he wasn't showing much deference to Podraski in answering my question. My antenna buzzed Fed.

"Driver's license," Podraski said. I took it out of my

wallet and showed it to him. "This is your current address?"

"I sold the property. I'm staying with a neighbor
down the block."

"Where are you headed?" the federal cop said.

"To that Thai place up the road." Name and address
and where I was going officially exhausted, what they
could demand of me, or bust me for if they caught me
in a lie.

"So why not park there?" the Fed asked.

"Am I under arrest?"

"This won't have to go that way," said Podraski. "We
just want to clear some things up."

On another day, I would have smiled. They'd already
decided to haul me in. Playing nice was just to dangle a
carrot and get me talking. One way or another, I wasn't
walking free. Which meant bad things for my appointment with Bilal Nath in just a few hours.

If I made a show of cooperating, maybe I could figure
out what this was about. A state detective and a Fed was
an odd combination to be tailing anybody.

"All right," I said. "Where we goin'?"

Just up the boulevard, as it turned out. They stuck me
in the backseat of the Acura—undoubtedly the Fed's
personal car, as he was driving and there were stale
Cheerios wedged into the rear seatbelt buckle—and
drove a quarter mile to a WSP station right off 518.

While Podraski stayed behind to clear things with
the admitting officer, the Fed ushered me through a
long room of cubicles that might have been any office
in America, save for the PSA posters and the holstered

weapons on the uniformed desk workers. Our destination was an interview room with three chairs and one camera, high on the wall.

"I didn't catch your name," I said to him once we were seated. The room was cramped. They are always cramped, and hot, and boring, increasing pressure on the interviewee every way possible. There was no table between us. The better to get personal, establish a rapport.

"It's Rick. What do you do for a living, Mr. Shaw?"

"I just sold that property, Rick."

"So you're between things?"

"You don't need to wait for your partner?" I nodded toward the closed door.

He shook his head. "What have you been doing the past couple of days?"

"Enjoying the holiday."

"A day off from all that free time, being between jobs and all." Rick the Fed grinned, like I was clearly making the right choices in life.

Podraski opened the door, closed it behind him, and took the last chair. No notebooks, no visible badges or guns or other signs of authority. Just us dudes, hanging out.

"You don't look like someone who sits at home playing PS4 all night," Rick continued.

"I'm more of an Xbox guy."

"First-person shooters? Since you don't have the real thing anymore?" Podraski said, taking over the lead. "I know another vet when I see one."

Making friends already. "You?"

He smiled. "A long time ago."

"Let me guess," I said. "MPs."

"Nope, just plain old Eleven Bravo." Infantry. "You do any contract work after serving? A lot of guys sign up for that now, I hear. Private security. Bodyguarding."

"Not yet."

"If I was as tough as you, I'd be cashing in."

"Could you tell us where you were two nights ago?" Rick said.

And there it was. Two nights ago I'd been breaking into Sean Burke's house.

"Sure," I said.

"So where was that?"

"I probably should have a lawyer, right? If we're talking about a crime?"

"We're not accusing you of anything, Van," Rick said. "Maybe you saw something we should know."

The lure, sparkling in the water. Detectives love for perps to try and fool them. *I was there, yeah, but it was this other guy . . .*

"What would I have seen?" I said.

"We just need some facts and then you can go. Where were you again?"

"'Cause this sounds like I'm a suspect. What happened?"

"It's probably a mistake," Podraski broke in. "People ID the wrong guy all the time."

I was supposed to ask who saw me, where they saw me, jump up and down protesting my innocence. Innocent people protest. Guilty ones get quiet.

"We just want to help," said Rick.

Podraski nodded assurance. "You're a combat vet. I know what it's like coming home after being down-range. It ain't easy. You have to find your place again."

"Gotta have a purpose," I said.

"So we're on your side here. Whatever you're into, we can put in the right word for you. If you need protection, you've got it. If you help us in return."

Protect me. From whom? From Burke?

"I'll call my lawyer," I said, "and he'll come here and then we'll talk."

"You don't need to do that," Podraski said.

Rick held up a hand. "Your lawyer might not be on your side. Who pays for his services?"

Now that was an odd question.

I took out my phone. "I'm calling."

"Bad choice," said Podraski. He stood and plucked the phone out of my hand. "Now we have to stick you in a cell until you get smarter. Stand up."

I complied and we went through the business of frisking. The cold strategic part of my brain noted that Podraski was overconfident. He had his main piece clipped over his right kidney. I could have relieved him of his weapon and shot both men before they had Chance One. But I wasn't a lunatic. I stood quietly while the state detective emptied my pockets and handcuffed me. They left the interview room.

My immediate future was clear: They would toss me into a holding tank, drag their feet through the booking process, and then allow me to call for a lawyer once everyone had left for New Year's Eve and I would be guaranteed a long uncomfortable stay. My lawyer was Ephraim Ganz, who had been Dono's attorney for a long time. Ganz was damn good at his job, but the last time I'd left him, he'd been delighted to see me go. I wasn't positive he'd even take my call.

I was going to be a no-show at Ceres Biotech tonight. That was a given. I could only pray Bilal Nath didn't immediately leap to hunting down my friends in retribution.

An hour later they returned. Ready to try a new tack. Podraski read me my rights, signifying that their questioning was about to become official. I confirmed I understood. Podraski took the chair this time, Rick at the door.

"You were in Bitter Lake three nights ago," Podraski said.

"I want to call my lawyer," I repeated.

"We've got witnesses."

This was curious. And a little unsettling. Once I'd asked for an attorney, the cops should have shut down their fishing trip. Unless they'd decided to ignore the rules.

I glanced at the camera on the wall.

"Just us talking," Rick confirmed.

"Now maybe you were only casing the place," Podraski said. "That's barely trespassing. You could get off with a warning. Were you there?"

I counted the checks on the chest pocket of the detective's blue jacket.

"A guy with your service record for his country, any judge will probably go easy. Just talk to us."

Thirty-two stitches. I counted them twice more as the silence stretched out. Silence makes most people uncomfortable. They rush to fill it. I was happy to meditate on Podraski's fabric halfway to forever, just to see how long it took them to give up.

"With the holiday it could be three days before you make bail. We haven't booked you yet. There's still a way out of here."

The more they are desperate for you to talk, the more lenient they'll pretend to be. One of Dono's lessons.

"Somebody hired you," Rick said. "He's the one we want."

"Forget it," Podraski said. "This guy's an idiot. His granddaddy was a moron, too."

I'd have lost a bet with myself on how long it took them to bring up Dono. I'd have guessed the next round of questioning.

"Grandpa had multiple falls," the detective continued. "One of which sent our poor baby here to foster care. Boo hoo. Surprising they didn't keep you in the system for good, instead of throwing you back into the lion's den."

That had been the path I'd been on. A life shuffling between overtaxed foster families. But social workers could be bribed as readily as any underpaid government employee. Dono had found a way to get me home.

Podraski pointed at my chest. "Bet your granddaddy taught you some stuff about B&E, didn't he? In between fondling you at night, I mean. That why you went into the Army? To get away from that sick freak?"

Get them scared, get them angry, get them talking. I pretended I was holding an ace-high straight and willing Podraski to throw in his chips.

"Maybe you liked it," he said. "Maybe you want to go to jail, get another taste of that."

A sharp knock at the door made Rick jump. He stuck his head out and the desk officer murmured in his ear. The Fed's expression fell in surprise. He left the room without another word.

"Just between you and me," Podraski said, once the door was closed. "You kill a lot of guys?"

He sat a little crooked in his chair, the result of the piece pressing into his back. If he'd been at his desk or in his car, he would have removed it for comfort.

"Were you good at it?" he continued. "Maybe I've got you wrong. Maybe you're a stone-ass motherfucker. That what you are?"

I denied him the tough-guy stare he was so clearly expecting.

"Okay. Silent Sam. Stay quiet and take the fall. Nobody's gonna pay you for it."

The door opened and Rick came back in. Followed by a familiar face.

Familiar, if not entirely friendly. John Guerin, SPD.

"Shaw," he said, nodding at me. He still had the mustache, which was a shade darker than his prematurely white hair. In his glasses and crisp dress shirt he looked less conspicuously like a cop than either of the other two men. More like a very intense bonds trader. I guessed a lot of crooks were fooled by that, until it was too late.

"Detective," I said.

"Lieutenant," he corrected.

"Congratulations."

"What the fuck is this?" Podraski said.

"I've had the same question, Sergeant Podraski," said Guerin, "ever since I got your call yesterday asking for background on Mr. Shaw here. You didn't give me much context. Then I catch wind that two of our patrolmen ran into you in Bitter Lake a few nights ago, where you were conducting what they were told was a routine interview."

"You're out of line. This is a state matter."

"So you said over the phone. I called Captain Fisher in District Two just to make sure we were coordinating our efforts effectively. He told me he wasn't familiar with this particular joint operation, but that he was sure you'd be in contact with our North Precinct soon, so they could understand why you were conducting investigations in SPD's yard."

Podraski looked like he was about to retort before Rick the Fed cut him off.

"This isn't worth your time, Lieutenant." He waved a hand. "Or the trouble it will bring."

"See, now that could be interpreted as a threat," Guerin said. "I wouldn't want to get the wrong impression. Why don't we leave Mr. Shaw here and make sure we're all on the same page."

He held the door open. After a moment they acquiesced and left the room.

"Don't suppose you can get them to take these off?" I nodded to the handcuffs behind my back.

"I'm not sure you don't belong in them," Guerin said, and he closed the door.

I might see the sky again today after all. I didn't know what kind of jurisdictional dance Guerin was doing, but it was clear enough that Podraski and Rick had overreached somehow.

But right this minute, I had nothing but time. I thought

back to the schematic I'd seen of the Markham security system, how the alarms on the cryobank worked, and the controlled burn safeguards for the bank's contents. I rehearsed each step in my mind and considered contingencies. A lot was riding on Hollis and Willard. And Elana. I'd found a role for her to play after all.

Two hours, I decided. That was how much time I would need before going anywhere near Ceres's cryo chamber. An hour to access the utility shed on the roof, then another hour of work there before I dared to go inside the building itself.

It would be getting dark outside now. My spare minutes were burning fast.

The door opened. Podraski came in, tossed a gallon Ziploc with my personal effects in it on the table, and removed my handcuffs. Then he left again, leaving the door open.

I pocketed my things. Bilal hadn't tried to call me while my phones were in police hands, which was a minor blessing. A state trooper waited for me just outside the room. "That way," he said, pointing toward the exit at the far end of the cubicle farm. I obliged.

My two hosts, Rick and Podraski, had vanished somewhere, along with Guerin. Passing by a conference room, I heard voices, fragments of overlapping sentences dueling in anger—*that's not what I—hang on a damned minute—might wind up like Santora with—*

It would be poking the bear to intrude. But I was too curious about the whole episode, not least why they had suddenly let me go without booking me. I opened the door and stuck my head in.

Podraski and the Fed stood in close and what looked like intense conversation with another man in a blue suit and conservative tie. A much better suit than Rick's, just as Rick's had been better than Podraski's. His suit and the professional styling of his silvered brown hair added up to brass. Rick the Fed's boss, maybe, or someone even higher up the chain.

All three men turned. The combined force of their surprised glares almost made me grin. Instead, I said, "Sorry, wrong door," and vamoosed.

Guerin was waiting in the lobby. I was feeling like a relay baton, passed from one cop to the next.

"How'd you know I was here?" I said as we left the building and followed the entrance roundabout to the station lot. A brilliant stripe of magenta filled the western sky, backlighting the hills between the station and the airport just beyond. Far-off jet engines combined into a constant whispery moan.

"Friends. After Podraski called me yesterday, digging into your sordid history, I was curious. Then more so once I learned he was running some job on Seattle turf. I asked a contact of mine in WSP dispatch to watch for your name. Podraski may play loose with jurisdictions but he's not an idiot. Before they pulled you over, he called it in."

I grasped what Guerin meant. I had a family background and military record that would make any cop extra vigilant. If I'd turned out to be some trigger-happy head case, maybe even left Podraski and Rick the Fed dead at the scene, at least their compatriots would know who was responsible.

"Guess I owe you some thanks," I said.

"Save your gratitude. Tell me what you were doing in Bitter Lake."

"Question is, What do *they* think I was doing in Bitter Lake? They seemed convinced somebody hired me to be there."

"They don't know you like I do. You work for yourself." His eyes narrowed behind the rimless glasses. "Like your grandfather."

"And they didn't book me," I said, looking back at the patrol station. "They could have held me for at least a day and done their best to put me through the ringer if they'd gone through with putting me on the record. That strike you as weird?"

"Whatever you're chasing, drop it," said Guerin. "It will not end well."

"Who's the Fed?" I said. "FBI?"

"That's exactly the kind of thing I mean. I won't be around next time to stir up shit."

"They warned you off, too," I said, realizing. "How does that happen?"

He exhaled, a soft whisper of breath out of his nose. On Guerin, that might have been a shout.

"Okay," I said, raising a hand to signal a truce. "Let's trust each other. I'll tell you why I might have had reason to be in Bitter Lake, and you tell me what kind of minefield I've apparently wandered into."

"Your problem, Shaw, is that you imagine you're my equal. Podraski and me, we're cops. You're a repeat offender, with no fixed income or residence. And even that assessment is generous."

"What if my answer changes your mind? About trusting me?"

"Only one way to find out. Talk."

"Thirteen Coins. Tomorrow. I'll call you with the time."

"Bullshit."

"Best I can do. I have a hot date tonight."

Guerin frowned. He knew I wasn't lying when I offered to share information. He also knew I wouldn't be pushed into doing so sooner than I wanted to.

"Tomorrow," he said. "Don't make me hunt you down."

Enough people were doing that already. "Deal."

"I feel sorry for the girl." He walked away.

Renny's FastPass was close enough for me to jog back. The run blew off some excess energy from being trapped in the stifling interview room. And it gave me room to reset my mind toward Ceres Biotech. Two more hours before I was due to meet up with Hollis and Willard. I could just make it.

Back on the top parking level, I made sure I was alone and ducked under the Nissan to retrieve my rucksack. At least the owners hadn't returned and driven it home with them. That would have been the last nail in my coffin.

I paid my ticket at the machine and pulled out of the FastPass lot, only to realize how close that comparison had been. The lot lay directly across from a cemetery.

My Dodge pickup was old, without any hands-free phone functions or Bluetooth or even a CD player. I waited until the next light to call Hollis.

"You're late," he said.

I didn't want to tell Hollis I'd been arrested. He got edgy enough before a job.

"I need a license-plate check," I said. "Silver Acura TL, probably owned by a guy in federal law enforcement. First name Rick, unless he was bullshitting me." I read Hollis the number of Rick the Fed's car.

"FBI? Is this some other horrible problem for us to handle before tonight?"

"Nothing to do with Bilal. I think this team might be on to Sean Burke."

"Ah. Well." Hollis hesitated. What does one say when talking to a friend about a possible-father-and-probable-hired-killer? "Personal information will be restricted from DMV if he's federal law. Our friend Panni might have the right access. But he might not be around until after the holiday."

I said that was fine. We had more pressing concerns. Like surviving Bilal Nath long enough to see the new year.

But back on the highway, my brain wouldn't stop chewing on what had just happened. A weird kind of catch-and-release, with Rick and Podraski hauling me in only to change their minds at the last minute. Was that solely Guerin's doing? Or had something else prompted them to cut me loose?

The superior who'd been reaming the two cops had looked familiar. A little overly groomed, too. Like he spent time with the media. A slick suit. Athletic, but in the way that a youngish CEO might be fit, thanks to diligent personal trainers and nutritionists rather than pursuing any sport.

Then it hit me where I'd seen him before. On television. The slick guy was one of the candidates for governor in the recall election. I couldn't remember his name, but knew he was some kind of federal attorney. Holy shit.

It made for easy arithmetic. Federal prosecutors plus special agents plus state detectives added up to major trouble for Sean Burke. And anyone dumb enough to be close to him.

JUNIOR YEAR, PART THREE

I waited until Mr. Grennon, coach for the Watson Paladins' not so lauded baseball team, was deep in conversation with the batter on deck about reading the slider or some shit like that before I leaned out from under the bleachers to tap Davey in the back of the head with a thrown pebble.

He whipped around. When he spotted me skulking, he had a hard time not cracking up as he meandered to take a seat in front of me. It was a preseason workout, nominally voluntary. None of the players carried themselves with the intensity of real practice. Recent rain had turned the baseball diamond into clay. It smelled like I imagined a newly turned farmer's field would, all loam and earthworms.

"I got your message," I said. "What's up?"

Instead of answering, Davey just grinned wider and looked off to right field. Past the fence, Singer Boeman and his pack were hanging by their twin Pontiacs. First time I'd seen that bunch in over a year. They were spread out. Watching cars leave the lot, and the students drift out of the main entrance.

"Those morons," Davey said, scraping dirt out of his cleats. "What the hell are they doing here? They graduated. Or almost."

Leaving school had lost them their pissant revenue stream. Singer himself had tagged me as a kid who could probably keep his mouth shut during my freshman year. He'd sidled up, all chill, asking if I wanted to buy a little somethin' for me or maybe to share with my friends. I hadn't.

Later that first semester, Singer had made me a different offer. To deliver a bag for him and keep ten bucks as my fee. I'd almost laughed, his approach was so lame. He was at least bright enough not to make a big thing of it when I turned him down a second time. No point in making an enemy when your whole business model relied on being approachable.

Colten Gulas had started hanging with Singer's group the next year. And then Singer and most of his buds graduated. Maybe Colten had become their go-between for Watson High.

"Think they're waiting for Colt?" Davey said, echoing my thoughts.

"Or hunting for him."

"Hey, where you goin'?"

Across the field. If these dipshits were looking for Colten, we had at least one thing in common.

The outfield had been mown just before the last

rain. By the time I jumped the fence, my sneakers were covered in wet green clumps of grass.

Singer Boeman sat on the hood of his car, which was discernible from the other white GTO because of the large rust-speckled dent in the driver's door.

"Hey," I said. "You seen Colten?"

"What the fuck you want?"

Which I'd just told him. "Colten. Where is he?"

"You seen him?"

Jesus. I was starting to think Singer hadn't graduated at all, just frustrated the school to the point where they handed him a paper with writing on it and told him it was a diploma.

"I owe him money," I said.

"Shit, he owes us." Singer's guys had noticed our conversation and begun to walk from each end of the short block toward us. Whatever we were doing had to be more interesting than watching the crowd. Burn Burkley was one of their gang. The only one of the four still enrolled at Watson. He saw Yvette Friel off and on, and it was a toss-up which of the two of them was less appealing. Good faces and rotten insides.

"Dudes," Singer said to the bunch. "He's looking for Coltie, too. Paying his debts like a man." He pounded the car hood in mock glee. Singer had been a running back for Watson's football team, and he still had the compact muscularity that seemed to extend all the way to his close-cropped brown curls.

"Give us the money," Burn said. "Cut out the middleman."

"What about Candace? You seen her?" one of the others asked.

"No," I said. Candace was a friend of Colten's; they hung out behind the portables smoking. Which was probably also where Davey got most of his news. It made sense that Singer's boys would look for one to find the other.

That might work for me, too. I knew another crowd Candace hung out with.

"Forget it," I said, walking away.

"Hey," Burn said, moving to intercept. "The money."

Singer stayed on his car, but the two others instinctively edged closer with Burn. Pack mentality. Younger or not, I was sure I could take any one of them. Singer was strong but smaller than me, and Burn tall but not much else. And I knew I was meaner. But four on one, forget it. They'd pound me like bread dough. I coiled, ready to hurt the first idiot who got close and then run like hell.

A whistle sounded from nearby on the baseball field. The guys surrounding me flinched back at the signal of authority. Grennon had gathered the team in the outfield for wind sprints. Davey was watching our little drama, a look of concern on his face.

I ambled away before Burn got his courage back. Davey looped near the fence after his first sprint. Not breathing hard yet; he could run like a rabbit.

"Anything?" he said.

"Maybe. We saw Candace on Broadway last week, right? Hanging with the street kids by the Rite Aid?"

"Yeah. Oh, Candy and Colten. They've been hooking up. You think she knows where he is?"

"Where he's hiding. Singer and the others are looking to get paid. Money or blood. Normally I wouldn't care, but I want my shot first."

"I'll come with you—shit, I can't. Ma and Michael have this thing at the church tonight, I gotta go, too. And dinner after."

"Don't sweat it. Candace and Colten might not even be around."

And besides, this was something I wanted to do alone. Family business.

CHAPTER TWENTY-THREE

CERES BIOTECH'S CHUNK OF man-made land extended out from the natural shore about thirty yards. The lake side of the building blazed with another of their slanting silver logos at the very top, big and bright enough to be seen from the opposite shore of Lake Union. Environmentally friendly LED lamps on the corners of the roof cast wide cones of light over the face of Ceres. And created equally broad contrasting shadows. At the building's north side, the dilapidated marina looked like a rotting stump in a polished smile.

Hollis guided the speedboat past the remnants of docks and pilings as I tightened the chest straps on my rucksack. We'd placed black electrical tape over the running lights. Sailing low and dark and quieter than a car engine, thanks to Dono's muffled outboard. Water traffic was heavy tonight farther out on the lake. Boaters readying to watch the fireworks display at midnight at the south end.

Ceres Biotech had constructed a patio area made of all-weather planks spanning the rear of the building, for employees to lunch outside and indulge in the view when weather permitted. The patio extended out over the water. Hollis nodded to me and slowed the boat to a drift.

I jumped from the bow to the composite slats of the deck and sprinted toward the side of the building opposite the abandoned marina. The south side, the one facing the houseboat community next door, was out of the question. It wouldn't do to have some host or his holiday guests step out on the balcony for a toke and see a guy scaling the building next door.

Four corporate stories and related sublevels made at least ninety feet from ground to roof ledge. It looked even taller from where I was standing, looking straight up.

Given a rope and a little training, climbing a sheer surface isn't that hard. The Army had given me all the practice I could want and more on hard terrain, including but not limited to inching up and rappelling down icy mountains in Georgia during Ranger School.

A black 9.9 mm rope made a thick bundle at the top of my ruck. I couldn't use pitons and a hammer on the building wall. But the thick lampposts extending a yard from the roof offered another method.

I had packed a cable string launcher under the rope. Cable installers used launchers to shoot pull lines through tight spaces in ceilings and under floors, or across wide gaps. The launcher looked almost identical to a paintball gun, up to and including the laser sight and the thick cylinder under its barrel. But instead of paint capsules, the cylinder held a spool of coiled filament. The end of the filament was fixed to a plastic dart like a crossbow quarrel. The launcher could shoot the dart half the length of a football field. Shoot the filament, tie its line to the heavy cable, and pull the cable through from the other side.

The launcher would work equally well for my needs. I hoped.

No doors on this side of the Ceres building meant no need for cameras. I turned on the cable launcher's laser sight, aimed it at a spot just above the horizontal lamppost four tall stories above me, and pulled the trigger. The launcher made a sound like a partly deflated balloon popping, and the red filament flashed into the air with a descending whistle.

It took me a moment to spot the dart in the shadows, now dangling twenty feet below the lamppost. I fed it more filament, and the dart gradually lowered to meet me on the grass.

It was a quick task to attach my climbing rope and pull the rope up and over the thick pipe of the lamppost and down to the ground again. I held the two ends and yanked hard, then leaned with all my weight. The lamppost didn't waver.

I checked my watch. Eight-forty. Twenty minutes wasn't enough time to scale the roof and complete my preparations up top. I'd have to meet Bilal first.

Without my rucksack. I didn't want Nath or his devoted retinue getting the idea to examine its contents. I tied the loop of climbing rope to the ruck and hauled it skyward. Its bulk created a dark lump under the lamppost, like a shy gargoyle.

Somewhere just out of reach of the lights from shore, Hollis waited in the speedboat, idling while he watched my progress through binoculars. If there was any sign of police presence, he would signal me. Willard was watching the other side of the building from a hiding place along the lakefront paths. That was as much backup as I would have. If trouble erupted inside, I would be on my own.

The phone in my chest pocket buzzed. Bilal. He was early. Maybe edgy.

"I'm here," I said.

"Two blocks south." Saleem's voice, sounding as usual like speaking to me was beneath him. "Opposite a place called Zoo. Now."

I knew the Zoo Tavern. I'd boosted a Harley Shovelhead on consignment for one of their regulars when I was a teenager, working side gigs without Dono's knowledge. That job had gone smoothly. Maybe this was a good omen.

I walked the two blocks on Fairview, just another Seattle dude in a fitted black jacket, gray jeans, and black jungle boots. Half the people in the city dressed like they were about to go for an extended hike. Tactical wear for burglary fit right in.

Bilal's Mercedes SUV waited at the lot's accordion fence. Juwad hoisted his heavy frame from the driver's seat and gestured for me to raise my arms. He removed items from my pockets as Aura and Bilal stepped from the rear of the car.

Saleem was already out. He'd been watching me from the opposite side of the road for the past hundred yards.

"You are ready, I trust?" Bilal said. Juwad handed him the short lengths of climbing cord and the large steel carabiners he'd taken from my jacket. "What are these?"

"That's how I'm getting inside. I still don't know what I'm supposed to do once I'm in there," I said, taking the cords back. "Time to level with me. What is it you're after?"

"We're changing the plan," said Aura. She motioned to Saleem, who approached. "Saleem will go with you. He knows what we need."

I stopped. "That's not possible. This is a one-person job."

"Make it possible," Bilal said.

Saleem had a small rucksack of his own. Its rounded contours told me he was carrying the CXS-3001 cold-storage bottle I'd seen in their hotel room. The bulge under his coat was evidence that his machine pistol would be along for the ride, too.

"Look," I said, "if you want this job to go right, I can't be dragging your man through the whole building like some fucking toddler."

"You think I'm a child?" Saleem said. "Say that again and I will see you dead."

"Stop," said Bilal. "There is no question: Saleem will accompany you. Once you have given him entrance to the fourth floor, he will take over."

"We can't trust you," Aura said. "But you will have to trust us. Get Saleem inside, and once you're done, you and your friends will be safe. I swear."

She was either a damned good actress or telling me what she thought was the truth. Maybe her husband had convinced her I'd be allowed to skip merrily away once the job was done.

Shit. My plan had been to grab Bilal's prize from the cryo chamber and make a very hasty exit out the other side of the building, to Hollis and the speedboat. Leaving Aura and Bilal and his thugs literally staring up a rope, waiting in vain for me to climb back down. I had bet the farm that what Bilal and his wife wanted was so valuable to them, so irreplaceable, they would be desperate to make a deal once I had it in my hands.

Adapt, Shaw. You know more than they do. Use that.

I looked at Saleem. "I hope to hell you can climb." His lip curled in contempt.

"We will be nearby," Bilal said. "Do not disappoint me."

Disappointment was the least of my intentions. I repocketed the cords and carabiners.

"Come on," I said to Saleem. We retraced my path up Fairview. I paused before approaching the building.

"Do not stall," Saleem warned.

"Shut up." I watched the lobby of Ceres Biotech, and the floors above. New Year's Eve meant no regular employees were around, and the cleaning crews had completed their jobs earlier that night. Only the pair of guards held the fort. I checked the time. Twelve minutes past nine o'clock.

"Why are we waiting?" said Saleem, shifting his weight from side to side.

"That," I said. One of the guards passed in front of the windows on the third floor.

Hollis's surveillance yesterday and today had confirmed the guards made their rounds once every hour on the hour, taking the north stairwell all the way up to the fourth floor, making a loop, and going down the south stairwell to the next floor and continuing that pattern to the ground level. The other guard would be stationed at the front desk, so that someone was on the monitors at all times.

The fourth floor should be clear for most of the next hour.

"Let's go," I said.

He followed me around by the old marina and onto Ceres property, to the shadows of the back corner. I had the momentary urge to bounce his skull off the building wall and carry on by my lonesome, but only Saleem knew exactly what Bilal wanted. And what Bilal wanted, I needed.

I tied two of the cords from my pocket into Prusik knots around the climbing rope, one cord with a loop for my foot.

"This is not—" Saleem began. He was staring with wide eyes at the sheer face of the building.

"I told you to shut up. Pay attention." I made him stand with legs apart as I used the last and longest length of rope to tie a rappel seat around Saleem's waist and thighs. It was undignified as hell for him, made worse by the thought of what he was about to attempt. I clicked the carabiners at his waist, then grabbed the lower cord on the climbing rope to show Saleem.

"Like this," I whispered, putting my boot in the loop and pushing down until it was tight. Holding the climbing rope and top cord with my hands, I used the loop like a step to climb off the ground. I showed Saleem how to alternate between the two cords, shifting weight from hands to feet to move each cord a foot or two at a time and climb the rope.

It was steady progress if you knew what to do and stayed calm. Otherwise it was exhausting as well as treacherous. Saleem would at least have the rappel seat to keep him from plummeting to the ground. I jumped down and slid the two knots down to knee level and held them out to him.

"There must be another way," he said.

"You wanted to join the party," I said, threading the rope through the carabiners at his waist. "We go in through the roof."

"But if I have this"—Saleem shook the rappel seat—"how will you climb?"

Nice of the shithead to worry. He might have considered the question before now.

"The hard way," I said. I tied another Prusik above the two already around the rope. Better to have the stronger climber up top, to lend help if needed. Assuming I made it to the top.

I put on my climbing gloves, half-fingered gauntlets with thickly padded palms and edges that would save my skin if not my neck. With the nitrile gloves to prevent fingerprints making a second layer underneath, at least there was no risk of my hands getting cold.

The ninety feet above me looked like nine hundred in the dark. Damn it. I could do this. One vertical step at a time.

I put my boot in the new loop, pulled it tight, and lifted myself two feet off the ground. Winding the loose rope below around my other leg let me take some weight off the loop and shift it higher. Not much higher. Maybe six inches. This would be a tough go.

When I was ten feet off the ground, I motioned to Saleem to get moving. With a moment's fumbling he got his foot into the loop and began to make upward progress. I left him to it and concentrated on my own climb.

Ten more feet. Twenty. The guards would both be back in the lobby now, passing the time, so there was little chance they might look out an upper window and see two figures spidering up the side of the building. But we were slow. Slow enough that it would be a race to see if Saleem and I would make it to the roof before the guard began his next round.

From blocks away, zippering pops from a string of firecrackers rent the air. Harbingers of the bigger show to come. As long as no one was looking our way, I'd take it.

I heard a whispered exclamation from Saleem below me and smiled. I had tied the rappel seat loose enough that it would creep up and squeeze his balls like a vise. A dick move, but I was feeling ungenerous.

At the third story I spared a glance at my watch. Nine-forty-six. Shit. I moved faster, risking holding more weight with my arms to get an extra few inches with every move of the loop. A gust off the lake, honed by cold to a knife edge, made the rope sway. My breath was fast and rasping in my throat. After another few minutes of back-straining effort I pushed the hanging rucksack aside to touch the thick bar of the horizontal lamppost.

Now for the really dangerous part. I shook the corded loop loose from my foot and hauled myself up, hooking a knee over the post. The roof ledge with its silvery alloy weatherproofing was within reach. I grabbed it with one hand and with a grunt heaved my upper body onto the ledge.

Mostly. I began to slide backward, scrabbling at the ledge for a solid grip, finally finding it and rolling my body onto the roof's gritty surface.

No time to celebrate. I stood and looked over the edge. Saleem was still back at the start of the third floor.

Too slow. I clutched the climbing rope with my gloved hands and pushed at the roof ledge with my foot, hauling Saleem upward three feet in one yank. I heard his faint gasp of alarm. I pulled again, moving fast before my arms had a chance to give up in angry protest. In another minute Saleem's head appeared at the edge, his hands reaching frantically for the ledge. I grabbed his shoulders and almost threw him onto the roof.

We were still for a moment, me standing, Saleem on his ass, both of us breathing too hard to speak.

"You are—" Saleem attempted, then let his malevolent stare finish the thought. I leaned over the ledge to untie the rucksack.

At the center of the roof, a steel shed with its large satellite dish looked like a square head wearing an especially wide-brimmed hat at a rakish angle. The shed housed telecom and transmission equipment for the dish and its nearby cellular tower. I carried the ruck to the shed.

Saleem watched as I picked the lock. "The way in is over there."

"With cameras on the other side. Be my guest."

I opened the door. A series of hinged metal housings like large fuse boxes lined the walls of the shed. I searched for one specific box and opened it to reveal a forest of cables inside, each with a tag denoting its purpose. At least the Ceres engineers knew their jobs. I began unloading my gear from the rucksack.

"What are you doing?" Saleem pressed.

I cursed silently. Answering would at least keep him from talking more.

"The security cameras and alarm around the cryo chamber are completely enclosed inside the room, including their own power source," I said as I stripped the rubberized covers off three of the coaxial cables within the box. "But keeping the two systems physically separate means that the chamber's cameras are forced to transmit their images wirelessly. That's hard to do through an entire building. Impossible with medical equipment around, and there's a few tons of that downstairs. That's why hospitals restrict cell phone use in some wards."

I tapped a wireless transceiver below the cable. "So what Markham Protective does is send that wireless signal from the cameras here instead. The cryo chamber is right below us. This transceiver grabs the signal and feeds it into the main system. The guards see the image on the monitors. What we're doing"—I connected my own fiber-optic band to the stripped cable—"is tapping into that same signal, copying the still image, and feeding that to the monitors instead."

I wasn't sure Saleem understood. But he stayed quiet as I opened a laptop and plugged it into the transmitter I'd taken from my storage unit. Markham liked a cookie-cutter approach to their systems. I'd soon know for sure if they used the same frequency for all their wireless cameras. A screen came to life on the laptop, allowing me to fine-tune the transmitter's frequency using the keyboard.

And there it was. A full-color view of a plexiglass door, with a clear plastic bar handle and words stenciled in white on the surface. Only in reverse. We were looking at the image from the camera inside the room, pointed outward. The mirror-image words read: CRYOGENIC FACILITY—AUTHORIZED ADMITTANCE ONLY—NO PHONE, COMPUTER, OR OTHER ELECTRONIC DEVICE USE PERMITTED.

Two other cameras on the same frequency broadcast images of different corners of the chamber. It was the work of a minute to capture the images and feed them to the cable I'd spliced into the system. The monitor downstairs would cycle through the three incoming feeds, showing each in turn. Now the guards would see a chamber as placidly unoccupied as it had been all night. So long as we could make it into the cryobank without being caught on the building's hallway cameras, we'd be invisible. And I had a plan for that.

Saleem had regained his energy and squandered it by shifting from side to side. "We must go."

"We begin after I've disabled the alarms," I said. "If you're bored, check the perimeter. Make sure the guards haven't found our rope."

The Ceres guards didn't patrol outside, but Saleem didn't know that. Watching me type was only increasing his stress. After a moment, he strode to the edge of the roof.

That's it, you jackoff. Take your time.

I pulled up the output from a different network cable. Despite what I'd told Saleem, it wasn't the cryo chamber alarms. Thanks to Willard's homework, I already had a way past those. What I was working on now was something new to me.

Ceres Biotech boasted cutting-edge environmental controls, monitoring and fine-tuning every inch of their building's climate via a central source. Green and clean, including the cryo chamber. And its fire-suppression system.

It took me twenty minutes before I was sure I had the functions tweaked to work the way I intended.

Reasonably sure. I'd never tried a stunt like this before, and there would be no rehearsal. Saleem was back at the shed.

My ruck was mostly empty now, save for some basic tools. The laptop would stay behind, happily fulfilling the tasks I'd set in motion. Eleven-twenty now. The guard should be done with his latest round of the fourth floor.

I texted Hollis. Confirm clear? A moment later the magic word Clear appeared on my phone.

The lock on the roof door offered less resistance than the one on the telecom shed, and it wasn't alarmed. I reached out a hand to stop Saleem. "Not yet."

My next text was to Willard: Ready for delivery.

The wait was longer this time. I ran the mental movie of what would be happening four flights below us.

Elana, dressed in a FedEx polo and probably one of her many wigs, walking up to the main door. The guard, seeing a delivery person dropping off a package at a late hour on a holiday—not unheard of in the age of twenty-four-seven service—and leaving his post to take receipt.

Saleem's very short patience ended. He grabbed my shoulder, his grip surprisingly strong for a slender guy.

"Do not play games," he said. "I know you are planning to betray us. I will leave you dead right here."

"Your bosses promised I'd live."

Delivery now, Willard's text confirmed. Saleem eyed it suspiciously.

"Bilal will not weep for you. And I do not care what the woman says. Go."

I opened the door and hurried down the stairs. Saleem followed. The cold-storage container in his backpack thumped lightly with every step.

His other hand rested inside his unzipped coat. Quick access to his machine pistol. Positively salivating to rip me to pieces, once my duty to his master was complete.

CHAPTER TWENTY-FOUR

AT THE FOURTH-FLOOR LANDING, I stuck my head out to check the surroundings. Branching hallways curved gently in three directions, each with its own array of conference rooms. Every second ceiling light was out, conserving energy after hours. I could make out the entrance to an atrium halfway down the center hall. That should be the fastest path to the cryo chamber. I ran toward it, Saleem on my heels.

Elana would detain the guard as long as she could manage, which was considerable given her looks and charm. She'd take her time ascertaining that Timothy Gorlick, MD, PhD, chief medical officer, did in fact work at Ceres Biotech. She would bid the guard to sign here, initial here and also here, and did his family have any plans for New Year's Day?

I didn't pause at the atrium, trusting my memory of the blueprint. Right, and then left, and the chamber should be at the far end. Yes, there was the clear glass door. We raced to it. The second guard would be returning to the lobby before much longer. One glance at the monitors and he was sure to notice Saleem and me, dashing around the halls like mice in a maze.

The black square of a standard RFID keycard reader waited beside the clear door, its light blinking red. I could beat the reader with only a few minutes' work, but thanks to Willard's intel on Markham Protective, I didn't have to take the time. The keycard I'd programmed at my storage unit had Markham's proprietary master code. One swipe to make the light flash green as the magnetic locks on the door opened with a satisfying clunk.

I stopped to take in the sight of the cryogenic chamber. Oblong tanks, each about thirty inches high and painted a dull olive green, squatted in loose rows. Tubes connected each tank to the power station and a central cooling unit, maintaining their interiors at far below freezing. The machinery gave off a rumble that got down to the bones, like the lowest note on a double bassoon, playing forever.

Stickers in four languages warned of extreme temperatures and danger to exposed skin. More signs on the walls prompted employees to follow safety procedures—masks, glasses, aprons. An eye-wash station occupied one corner.

On the western wall, air vents made a row of black meshed columns. That would be the hypoxic air generator. The chamber's air smelled of something akin to menthol, maybe a byproduct of the constant adjustment to the oxygen levels.

I checked my watch. Eleven-thirty-eight.

Deep breath, Shaw. This would be close.

"You're on," I said. "Show me which tank." Saleem reached into his pocket to remove what looked like a stun gun. My instinctive tension eased when he used the device to scan the bar code label under the lip of the closest tank. He moved on to the second, then a third.

"This one," Saleem said. He stepped back to give me access to the tank. The lid read WARNING—PYROGUARD SEAL B-16—REMOVE ONLY WITH AUTHORIZATION. A list of instructions followed.

"I can remove it," I said, "but there might be a fail-safe inside. Don't make any quick moves. One mistake and this thing will torch every microbe in the tank."

He nodded irritably.

The truth was the lid was designed to activate in the event of breakage, not wired with an alarm like a combination safe. Removing it was just a matter of releasing the pressure seal in the proper order as indicated. But I didn't let Saleem in on that. I took another deep inhalation, as if I were nervous that the entire room would explode any second, and began removing screws.

In another minute I had pried the lid loose. A swirl of white vapor escaped from under the lip, cold that made my fingertips tingle even through the gloves.

Under the red lid, around the lip of the cryo tank, were six numbered indentations, most of them holding a hook at the end of a slim metal rod that extended down into the vat of supercooled nitrogen.

"Okay," I said. "Here's the tricky part. Show me which card is the queen."

Saleem got the gist if not the reference. "Move over there," he said.

"I have to check the inside of the tank—"

"I am not a fool. There is no other alarm. Stand by the wall." He drew the Steyr to make his point.

I went, cursing to myself with every step. Would he

finish me right here? Once Saleem found the right vial, once he was sure of what he had, my odds of leaving this room were as low as the core temperature in the tanks.

How much time would it take? It was already eleven-forty-four. I made myself relax. Tensing up was the last thing I wanted now.

Saleem holstered the pistol and opened his backpack to remove the CXS-3001 container. When he lifted the cap a translucent wisp rose along with the vacuum plug. He set the container aside to draw a rod out of the cryo tank. At the other end of the rod was a rack of metal trays, dripping with liquid nitrogen. Tendrils of vapor swirled around the exposed tray as if trying to draw it back down into the tank.

Using a pair of rubberized tongs, Saleem selected one slim vial—like a crystal straw—from the tray and slid it with infinite care into the container.

I felt a sharp pain like someone pressing the tip of a blunt pencil between my eyes. That was the first hint. The rest of the symptoms came fast on its heels. An unconscious quickening of my breath. A slight blurring of my vision around the edges.

I concentrated on Saleem. He managed to set the cryo container down before heeling to one side. I shoved off the wall to launch myself toward him. He heard me coming and turned. His hand drew the machine pistol.

Too slow. I caught his wrist in my left hand and gripped tight, pressing the pistol against his stomach. He had realized what was happening, and his eyes were insane with fury.

We stood locked for a moment as he strained to aim

the gun and I fought equally hard to keep that from happening. I let go of his shoulder with my right hand and punched him in the solar plexus. It wasn't a great punch. I was already weakening. But it was enough. Saleem grunted and his lungs expelled the last of his air.

My legs began to buckle. Saleem's gave out first. He slumped to the floor, his brain shutting down from hypoxia. I clumsily grasped his gun and staggered with it toward the entrance to the room. Fell to one knee. Black rushed in from the sides of my eyes.

Come on. Move. It's right there.

I crawled the final two yards and dropped Saleem's gun to press both hands on the door and push it to one side. The plexiglass slid open a crack.

I fell with my face at the gap and drew in huge lungfuls of air. It was warm and stale, and nothing could have tasted better in that instant.

My plan had cut things too close. Almost fatally. But I'd had no chance to practice, just guessing at the direction the wheels I'd set spinning would roll. I'd used Ceres's environment controls to override the hypoxic generator. At eleven-forty, my laptop had ordered the generator to make the chamber's oxygen level plummet from its usual sixteen percent down to zero. Within five minutes, the chamber was lethal. Within ten, we'd have both been dead.

I couldn't rest. Saleem might regain consciousness any second. I picked up his gun and stood, carefully, to walk with increasing confidence back to the open vat of liquid nitro. As good a place as any for the machine pistol. I dropped the gun into the foggy mix and watched as it sank to the bottom.

The cryo bottle waited on the counter. I glanced inside it, at the delicate vial that had led to all this trouble, before screwing the cap back on.

Saleem coughed and sat up. I hit him again, much harder this time, with an elbow to the side of his head. He crumpled back to the tiled floor.

I was tempted to leave him where he lay. But that would be shortsighted. He was a foreigner caught in a secure biotechnology facility. Homeland Security would grill him like a cheap steak, and maybe the NSA would have their turn, too. It wouldn't take long before he gave up my name.

Instead I wadded up a pink protective glove from the counter to stuff into Saleem's mouth, and I bound his wrists and ankles with electrical cord cut from peripheral equipment around the cryobank. When I was sure he couldn't worm his way loose, I dialed a number on my burner phone and let it ring while I pocketed the phone again.

It would take about ten seconds. I hoisted Saleem over my shoulder. I waited an extra count of ten more, to be sure, before opening the door.

Downstairs, the package Elana had dropped off with the front desk would be hissing and smoking. The guards, if they had any sense, would get far, far away from it. And the monitors.

I ran for the north stairwell, Saleem over one shoulder and the cryo bottle tucked under my arm like a football.

It was a balancing act, moving as fast as I could down three flights without dropping either burden or falling ass over teakettle. At the very bottom of the stairs was a fire exit. I was past caring if I set off any alarms. I slammed the pushbar with my hip and ran for the water.

Hollis saw me coming. Before I had reached Ceres Biotech's rear patio deck, I heard the muffled rumble of the speedboat's engine and the splashes of water thrown up by her propeller as the boat surged forward.

Saleem had revived. He began to struggle madly against his bonds, and I let him drop. He landed on the slats of the deck with a pained grunt. He couldn't talk with the wad of pink glove in his mouth. But the frenzied rage in his eyes spoke volumes.

The deck ended at the water. I stopped, gasping for the air that my body still seemed desperate for after the trauma of the chamber.

"Shaw!"

The shout came on the wind. I turned to see Bilal at the corner of the building, fifty yards away. Aura joined him, coming into view almost at a run herself.

She took in the sight of me, of the boat drawing near the dock, of the precious cryo bottle in my hand. She dropped her bag and sprinted toward the dock. Hollis drew alongside and I stepped aboard. Her scream of *No!* was as much lupine howl as human voice.

"Go," I said. I could make out Bilal continuing to shout, maybe to his wife, maybe to me. Then the waves slapping the hull drowned them both out as we sped away.

To our port side, a salvo of brilliant, strobing explosions filled the shoreline. White first, then yellow and blue curlicues snaking upward. The delighted whoops and screams of spectators on their boats carried over the muffled bangs of the pyrotechnics. Midnight. The new year.

"Where to?" Hollis said over the growing cacophony. "Back to the *Francesca*?"

"No," I said. "Call Doc Claybeck. Tell her we're on our way."

"What happened? Christ, are you shot?"

"I'm fine." I hefted the thick bottle. Sudden starbursts of red and orange filling the sky gave its enameled sheen the look of a flaming torch. "I need a professional opinion. To confirm that what I just stole is as unique as I think it is."

CHAPTER TWENTY-FIVE

HOLLIS PILOTED THE SPEEDBOAT through the floating audience and billows of white smoke that drifted over the lake, taking us toward the locks. This night's crossing to Paula Claybeck's house was much faster than our previous trip and heralded by the explosive show. The highest rockets of the finale were visible as we exited the ship canal and entered the Sound.

Claybeck seemed no happier to see Hollis and me this time. We stood on the dock while her dogs sniffed us, until they were satisfied that we weren't an immediate threat. Claybeck warned us that the hounds were jumpy given the late hour and the unfamiliar noise of the fireworks. They growled faintly as if in agreement. Hollis looked like he was about to lose his latest meal.

Twenty minutes later, we were all in Claybeck's basement clinic—Hollis and me seated on the same bench where Saleem had held us at gunpoint, the two dogs sharing a padded bed, gnawing on chew bones that looked uncomfortably like human femurs. Claybeck's tall frame arched over a microscope as she examined the frozen contents of the cryo tube.

"I can't be certain without thawing them," she said, "which I can't do safely here."

"Best guess," I said.

Claybeck tapped the microscope. "Three mature human eggs. Unfertilized, and viable."

"Eggs?" Hollis said. "Like, for pregnancy and such?"

I nodded. "Aura's."

"Then why in hell—" Hollis snorted his exasperation. "Van, why would her eggs be in a biotech company? And why would she have to steal them?"

"I think because these are her last," I said. "Aura has a prescription for cancer cell inhibitors. The drug is most commonly used for cases of ovarian cancer."

"That's possible," Dr. Claybeck said, frowning. "Malignancy requires removal of the ovaries in nearly all cases. She might have harvested her eggs beforehand, knowing the risk."

"It's a theory that matches what we know, with some guesswork," I said. "Aura was married before Bilal. To a Timothy Gorlick, who happens to be the chief medical officer of Ceres Biotech. Maybe the divorce was an angry one. Maybe there's a custody battle over her eggs. For some reason they wound up at Ceres's secure facility rather than some easy-to-crack cryo facility somewhere."

Claybeck shook her head. "A custody dispute between exes might make sense if these were embryos. If they were created by both—Gorlick, you said?—by him and by Aura together. Then he might have a case. But unfertilized eggs should be her property alone."

"Should be. But Gorlick had them hidden. And Aura had to go to extreme measures to get them back." I rose and walked over to the sink at the wall to turn on the left tap. The flow might have run straight off an iceberg. I splashed the icy drops over my face and the back of my neck. The drips off my skin tasted like sweat and something more sour.

"Bilal deals in information," I said. "High-level hacking. If Gorlick somehow arranged to keep his ex-wife's eggs, out of spite or whatever reason, Bilal could figure out where they had been moved. And he would know how to hire somebody like me to steal them."

"Maybe that was the attraction," Hollis said dryly. "Aura's a lot younger and prettier than Bilal."

"He's dying. She can't have kids, except with the eggs. No wonder they're in a hurry."

"So what will you do with them?" Claybeck said, replacing the delicate vial into the thermoslike tube.

"Her eggs are irreplaceable," I said. "Bilal and Aura want them far more than they want me dead. We can cut a deal. Fast, before Bilal tries to grab anyone I know off the street to trade."

Hollis folded his arms. "Who's to say Bilal won't have you killed the second you hand the eggs over?"

I looked at Dr. Claybeck's dogs, gnawing on their bones.

"We'll enlist some help of our own," I said. "A bigger animal."

BILAL HAD TRIED TO reach me, of course. Yanking desperately on the electronic leash. The log on the phone he'd given me showed unanswered calls starting two hours ago. He'd dialed the number every sixty seconds, then every five minutes, until about half an hour ago when he'd given up. I called him back on a burner phone from the speedboat.

"Where are you?" he said.

"Somewhere you can't trace the call."

"Return immediately. Or I will—"

"Aura's eggs look healthy," I interrupted. "So far as I can tell. I could let them sit on the counter for a while, see if they twitch a little after they thaw out."

He was silent.

"Right," I said. "Now you listen. No more threats. You want Aura's eggs, I want you gone. We're going to make a different agreement, with insurance to make sure you hold up your end."

"Please." Aura's voice. Not on speaker. She'd taken the phone from Bilal. "They won't last forever in the container—"

"I'm aware," I said. "Just like I know these are the only eggs like them on earth."

"We can pay you. Whatever you want."

"The things you love will stay safe, so long as everything I love stays safe. You get me?"

"Yes," she said. "I understand."

"I'll call and tell you where to meet."

I turned the phone off. Pocketed it. Walked back to Claybeck's house while I tried to quell the churning in my gut.

I was the aggrieved party here. No question. Bilal and Aura had fired the first shots. And they would be merciless if it got them what they wanted.

That didn't make me feel much better about holding a cancer survivor's only hope for children over her head.

Back in the basement clinic, I took the cryo tube from Claybeck. "Thanks," I said.

"Normally I would bill you, but I'd rather be free of this entire situation immediately." She turned off the microscope and went to sit on the floor with her dogs, who shifted themselves to lean against her before slipping back into their postsnack dozes. "With a guarantee of no more midnight visits."

"I'll lose your number," I said.

"Would you mind if I didn't, Paula?" Hollis said. "So long as I promise to call at a more civilized hour?"

Dr. Claybeck looked at him. "And for a more civilized reason."

"Of course."

She nodded fractionally. Hollis's smile could have woken the dogs, it was so bright.

CHAPTER TWENTY-SIX

I SLEPT ON THE SETTEE in the cabin of the *Francesca*, waking at midmorning. Much later than I'd intended. My eyes felt nearly as gritty as my mouth. The action of the previous two days had wrung me dry.

Hollis's snores from the main stateroom below almost made the plates in the cupboards rattle. He'd left a note on the galley counter in his large loopy scrawl. *License plate Richard Martens, ATF.*

Rick the Fed was ATF. Not the FBI after all.

I knew enough about the ATF to know that the modern bureau focused primarily on the last two components of its complete name: firearms and explosives. I also knew the ATF was tiny compared to other branches of federal law, with only about fifty active agents for every state, on average. A victim of the U.S.'s tortuous gun laws—no politician who wanted to keep their job could argue for more funding for a bureau that half the country considered a sworn enemy to their civil rights.

So what was Sean Burke into that could be worth Special Agent Rick Martens's time, given the severe manpower constraints of the Seattle field office?

I showered and brewed a pot of coffee, downing two large mugs and an equal amount of water before I approached feeling human. Raiding Hollis's dresser, I found a T-shirt advertising Baja California Sur that was relatively stain-free.

I texted Guerin that I was headed for 13 Coins. He would know without asking that I meant the one near Union Station.

Growing up, I'd taken full advantage of the twenty-four-hour restaurant in its old location on Boren, where it had been since before my grandfather had come to town as a young man. At fifteen years old I was as likely to get kicked out of the place for making a nuisance as be allowed to order a Monte Cristo at three in the morning.

The new location retained a few familiar touches, just like Bully Betty's had when the bar was moved. Swivel chairs at the counter, and the absurdly tall booths with quilted leather backs. But it lacked the amiable seediness of the old place. Too wholesome.

On the holiday, between the breakfast and lunch hours, I had my pick of seats. I chose the swivel chair at the farthest end, where the counter curved and I could watch for Guerin to come in.

I checked the news while I waited. The break-in at Ceres Biotech had earned a few lines from most of the local outlets, most of them quoting the SPD spokesperson that police were confident suspects would be apprehended before long. Ceres had officially stated that nothing in the facility had been taken or damaged during the attempt.

Which was a lie. But did the people at Ceres know it

was a lie? Had Timothy Gorlick, MD, etc., hidden his ex-wife's eggs in Ceres's cryo chamber without anyone at the company being aware?

The top story on most webpages was the tightening race in the recall election for governor. It was the Democratic candidate whom I'd seen at the state patrol station, giving hell to ATF agent Martens and Detective Podraski. U.S. Attorney Palmer Stratton.

I looked up Stratton's specifics. Seattle native, son of a long-term congressman and grandson of a female state senator. A graduate of Whitaker Academy, one of Seattle's toniest prep schools, followed by Cornell for undergrad and law. Photos from a quarter century ago showed Stratton at college wrestling tournaments and standing proud in an NROTC uniform. Stratton served five years with Naval JAG, which seemed to be a family tradition after his father and grandpappy. Then back to Washington State to fight for good and right.

The Strattons went back a long way. From the looks of it they'd been rich and connected every step. Boards of directors, charity funds, hosting events for the Seattle archdiocese. I found numerous photos showing Margaret Stratton, the candidate's mother and wife of the late congressman, as the regular guest of honor at an annual sailing regatta named for the family.

The scion Palmer had gone the public service route in becoming a federal prosecutor, but that was plainly just a stepping-stone to the family business of politics. In another few weeks he might be governor. Onward and upward.

Guerin walked in at half past ten, surveying the room with the almost arrogant confidence I associated with cops. Some of them lost that swagger when they stopped wearing the badge. I suspected Guerin had it before he'd even entered the academy.

"Lieutenant," I said, as he took the chair next to me.

"Let's keep this tight," he said. "I spent enough time yesterday fielding phone calls about you."

"Phone calls from whom?"

He flagged down the server and ordered coffee and a plate of egg whites and wheat toast. I ordered the Italian scramble, just to balance out the level of cholesterol in our party.

"You first," he said. "Bitter Lake: Why were you there?"

"Sean Burke," I said.

He very nearly blinked. Enough of a reaction that I knew the direct approach had surprised him. But I wasn't done yet.

I showed Guerin the letter from Jo Mixon about the reunion. "This got me following a trail. About Moira—my mother—and maybe my father, too."

Guerin stared. It took a lot to throw the veteran cop, but I might have managed it.

"Burke is your father?" he said.

I waited until the waitress had placed our mugs of coffee in front of us. Neither of us moved to pick them up.

"I don't know," I said. "Dono had dealings with Sean Burke's father, Fergus, around that time. I know through a school friend of Moira's that she knew Sean. They seem to have had a relationship of some kind, enough that Moira wrote him letters. Beyond that . . ." I shrugged.

"Good Lord Almighty," Guerin said. We both sat for a moment.

"Dealings," he said at last, "with Gut Burke. You happen to know what kind?"

"Whatever they were, the statute of limitations is gone in the rearview. Plus the fact that they're both dead. Makes a conviction tough."

I tried the coffee. It was hot enough to kill any taste buds that dared to take a whack at it. "If you know Gut Burke's name, you must be up to speed on Sean. Your turn, Lieutenant."

"Not so fast," he said. "Let's go back to why you were around Burke's house."

"Learning what I could," I said.

"From the view standing on the sidewalk, I'm sure."

"Anything else would be trespassing."

Guerin shot me a flat look. "I don't like cute."

"Then don't ask when you already know how I'll answer. If you're just going to stonewall me, I'll get my breakfast to go and save us both some fucking time."

My attitude didn't piss Guerin off. Like any cop who worked for a living, he took abuse almost every day. The smart ones learned how to let it wash off their backs while they continued to look for an angle.

And Guerin must have had some idea of the emotions fueling my outburst.

"You're going to keep looking into Burke," he said.

I was waiting with the fork in my hand when the server put the plates down. Ravenous. I took a bite of the scramble and washed it down.

"All right," Guerin said. "I can tell you a limited amount. Maybe you already know what I know, thanks to those two hauling you in yesterday. But it's all you'll get."

I nodded.

"Burke has eyes on him," Guerin said. "High enough that there's a special joint task force. It's small and very contained. Podraski is state. There's federal involvement, too."

"ATF," I said.

He fixed me with a look. "However the hell you found that out, I can neither confirm nor deny it. SPD is out of the loop. But that doesn't mean I'm free to conjecture. Right?"

"Go on."

"Do you know who Gut Burke worked for, a few years after he made the move west?"

"Some mob. That's all people remember from thirty years ago."

"If you dug deeper into Seattle history and arrest records and bought some old print journalists a few beers, somebody might connect Burke to the name Liashko. Ever heard it?"

"Nuh-uh," I said around a mouthful. My hand and mouth managing the food while my mind was completely focused on Guerin.

"Anatoly Liashko," he said. "Ukrainian, originally, but raised mostly in western Russia. The eldest son of a homegrown mobster who started making inroads here in the Northwest just before the Wall came down, when things were going to shit for the Soviets."

"Running what?"

"Human trafficking to start, then drugs on a limited scale, whatever the slime could dredge up. After the collapse, young Anatoly expanded. Eventually into weapons during the Chechen wars. His eventual arms concession—legitimized thanks to the Russian oligarchs—made him a hundred times richer, with political influence to match. A lot of that money and clout evaporated when Putin started consolidating power. Maybe Liashko didn't bribe the right people at the right time."

"Did he still have connections over here? If he couldn't sell his goods at home . . ."

Guerin touched his nose. I'd hit the mark. The server came over and asked Guerin if there was anything wrong with his plate, which he hadn't touched. He shook his head and picked up his fork.

"Liashko doesn't come to the States often," he said. "He'll visit Vancouver, where most of his—'dealings,' you called them—seem to be centralized. But he's wary. You sure you don't know what business your grandfather was into with Gut Burke?"

"Dono didn't work for crime families."

"So you say. At any rate, Liashko still has American citizens on his payroll, too."

"Doing what? Arms smuggling?"

He ignored the question. "Podraski and his partner hauled you in yesterday to try and figure out who you work for. Liashko, or one of his enemies. They thought they could squeeze you."

From Guerin, that was almost a compliment.

"When it became clear that you wouldn't bend, they had a choice," he said. "They could book you for suspected B&E at Burke's house. You'd hide behind a lawyer and sooner or later they would have to explain to a judge why they are watching Burke. That could risk their whole operation, and one burglar just isn't worth it. So you walked. But if you cross their paths again, they will go back to Door Number One and stick you in a box for as long as they can twist the system to keep you there. They are motivated."

Guerin finally took a bite of his egg whites. "We've reached the end of story time. The point, in case you missed it, is that you would be all kinds of smart to stay the hell away from Sean Burke. For reasons both legal and familial." He raised his eyebrows. "If you really are related, the less you let this scum into your life, the better."

I still had a third of my meal left. I didn't want it.

"One last question," I said. "The doors in the patrol station aren't as thick as they could be. I caught the name Santora when Podraski and the ATF guy were arguing. Something about winding up like Santora."

The lieutenant stopped chewing. "I told you the department was out of the loop."

"Doesn't mean you don't recognize the name."

"Which you might also find background on, if you dug hard enough. Which you would. Damn it." He scowled. "Marcus Santora. An ATF agent. He's been missing and presumed dead for the past two years. No funeral yet, because the family is still holding out hope. His bureau isn't. When an agent disappears while on undercover assignment, there aren't a lot of alternative theories to the obvious one. We can only hope to find his body someday and give the family some peace. That's another reason why I don't want you kicking up dust."

"Santora was undercover on Liashko?" I stopped

myself. "Forget it; I know. Neither confirm nor deny. I can piece it together."

"Not quite." He tapped a fingertip on the counter. "Liashko was the target. But it was Sean Burke who's the prime suspect in killing Agent Santora. Burke also looks good for the murders of at least two more people we know of, on Liashko's orders. The Feds may not have evidence to prove it—not yet—but they'll get there soon enough."

Guerin pushed his plate away. Maybe his appetite had vanished as quickly as mine had.

"Burke is an assassin, Shaw. He's Liashko's gun in the United States and maybe elsewhere, and he will absolutely end anyone who gets too close. Anyone at all. You'd best keep that reality front and center in your head."

I couldn't think of one damn thing to say to that.

JUNIOR YEAR, PART FOUR

Broadway was home ground for street kids. The permanent homeless had Pioneer Square and the tent cities along I-5, but teenagers had gravitated to the Hill since before I was born, Dono once told me. They still did. Something about the compactness of the neighborhood, lots of people, lots of little shops, combined with the length of the street itself. Nearly a mile on the main drag left a lot of space if somebody ordered them to move along.

Prime panhandling was wherever foot traffic was thickest, off the bus stops and by the main intersections. The parking lot of the B of A was popular. Good foot traffic, easy to see cops coming. A couple of kids about my age had parked themselves there, mumbling the litany of "spare change" to every passerby. They weren't so high that I couldn't get a response out of them. I asked if they'd seen Candace tonight. The space cases didn't recognize her name right off, but after a quick description they knew what girl I meant.

Candace was what my granddad would call a do-gooder. He didn't mean it as a compliment, though I was never sure why not. If Candace wanted to spend her spare time talking with street kids, who gave a fuck? At least they could trust her not to rip them off.

After half an hour, I'd walked the length of Broadway until it started to curve at the north end. Nobody lucid had run into Candace tonight. I crossed the street and started back on the other side.

By the strip of shops called the Alley, I hit pay dirt. Candace herself, squatting outside a sushi place with another girl and her Chihuahua dog. The girl said "change" by reflex as I hunkered down next to them. Both her hair and her crusted eyes needed a rinse.

"Hey, Van," Candace said. "Good to see you." She sounded as though she meant it, like always. That was Candace. Ultra-skinny and scattered and she dressed like she'd picked the clothes randomly out of someone else's laundry, but you'd have to work damned hard to dislike her.

"You, too," I said. "I gotta talk to you. About Colten."

Alarm widened her hazel eyes, and I held up my hand. "I'm not with Singer Boeman. Swear."

"Okay." Her fear hadn't completely left. The fried girl caught the tense vibe and curled up around her dog.

"Singer's looking for him. And his gang. You know that, right?"

Candace nodded.

"I'll help. But I have to talk to Colten. Tonight."

"I can't."

"Candy. This isn't going to go away. At least tell me why Singer's so pissed off."

She glanced at her friend, who might as well have been on Venus. "Colt . . . He had some stuff to sell around school. Nothing really bad. I've told him to stop but he has such a hard time saying no to them . . ."

"What stuff?"

"Poppers. A whole bag of them, like two hundred. But someone stole the bag, and now they're blaming Colten."

"Okay." Davey had mentioned seeing little nitrite vials at a party he'd crashed recently, students mixing them with coke for a bigger rush. We figured it was the latest trend, old shit becoming new again. "So what's Colten's plan now?"

"I don't know." Candace was near to crying. "He can't go to his parents. They're terrible."

"Let me talk to him. I won't let anyone else know where he is. Promise. Cross my heart and hope to die."

The childish vow hit home. Candace said a few words to the girl, and we left. Half a block on, Candy pointed another group of teens she seemed to know well in the girl's direction, asking them to look after her. Then she led me on a long walk down the slope of Olive. Even with the breeze, the exhaust fumes of the constant traffic lingered in between blocks. She slowed at the little King of the Hill market, eyes wandering over the selection inside.

"You hungry?" I said.

She nodded, and we went in long enough to buy microwave burritos. Candace heated two up on the spot and ate one as we carried on.

We finally stopped at an ivy-covered apartment complex called the Biltmore, shaped like a block-letter C. The deep inside of the C formed the brick-accented entryway, lined with shrubs and small trees. While the brick exterior looked grand, like something built a hundred years ago, music from three different stereos on upper floors competed for dominance, and I could hear voices arguing from the nearest windows.

"My aunt lives here," Candace explained. "We're going to crash after she leaves for work." She turned to call out toward the apartments. "Colt?"

Colten Gulas emerged from behind a stand of trees at the far side. He was dressed for the cold in a tatty ski parka, gloves, and thick hoodie, but he didn't look comfortable at all. The only color on his drawn face came from his pink nose and red eyes. Baked, and maybe crying, too.

"Wha's he doing here?" Colten said.

"He's come to help," Candace said, handing him the warmed burrito she'd carried in her pocket. He didn't acknowledge it.

"How you doing, Colt?" I said, thinking that was the sort of thing Candace might say, and maybe I'd get further with kindness.

"Shitty, man."

"Candy told me about the poppers," I said. "That sucks."

"Fuck, Candace, why you have to talk?" he whined.

"I need to know something," I pressed. "And if you tell me, I'll see if I can help you like Candace said."

"Wha'd you want?"

"The quilt that went missing from the library last year. Who took it?"

"Aw, shit, man. That's not—nobody knows, man."

"You do. Straight trade. Tell me, and you've got me on your side."

"Help me first, then maybe." His bloodshot eyes looking as close to sly as they could get, being so clouded. I held myself back from grabbing Colten and shaking him like a bull terrier on a rat.

"Colten," said Candace, placing her hand on his chest, which managed to be hollow even with the parka. "This is a good deal." The way she said it made me suspect she knew more about the theft of the quilt than I did, but Colten was our focus right now.

"Tell me what happened with the poppers," I said.

Colten shrugged. "I picked them up. I went to school. When I came out, they were gone from my trunk. That's it."

"Came out where? To your car?"

"Yeah." Like that was obvious.

"Who knew they were there? Who saw you?"

"Nobody *saw* me, man. Somebody busted in. They kinda pushed the window down and opened the trunk and took them."

"But they didn't take anything else," I said. Colten shrugged. I took that for a yes. "Who'd you pick them up from?"

He shuffled his feet, reluctant to squeal. "Burn. He gave all the poppers to me that morning."

"Just Burn? No one else was around?"

"No way. I'm not stupid."

You passed stupid on the way to dumbfuck, I thought.

"You think Burn took them?" Candace said to me. "But he had the poppers in the first place."

And Burn wanted them, so he made Colten the scapegoat, giving him the poppers just long enough to hang their disappearance on him. But Burn hadn't been bright enough to reason that if he was the only one who saw Colten put them in his trunk, he would be the prime suspect. Granddad always told me ninety percent of crooks were dead in the head. Singer and his boys looked like poster children.

Moreover, I had a pretty good guess why Burn might have wanted to steal his own gang's supply.

"I can get you off the hook with Singer," I said, "but no going back on our deal."

"Sure," Colten said, shifting his feet again.

"Colt." I waited until his bleary eyes got a focus on me. "I'm a lot worse than Singer or Burn. A lot smarter. You'll tell me who took the quilt or I will make what you're going through now seem like summer vacation. Yeah?"

"Yeah. Okay."

I nodded.

"You didn't have to bully him," Candace said as I walked away.

Maybe not. But call it a little extra insurance. I was about to take a big gamble for Colten, and even if he didn't appreciate it, he'd sure as shit pay for my grief.

CHAPTER TWENTY-SEVEN

AFTER LEAVING GUERIN, I made a phone call. It was answered by a service. The lady at the other end took my name and number and said, with superb diction, that she would pass my information along to the party requested. No promises made or implied of any further contact.

I'd held the cryo bottle with its own promise of Aura's future children for twelve full hours now. I was conscious of that clock ticking, perhaps almost as much as Aura must be herself. If we couldn't make a deal within the next few days, what would I do? Rent space in some cryogenic bank somewhere? Tough job filling out those forms and explaining how I'd come into possession of human eggs.

Nothing for it but to set my only plan in motion, and find out if my persuasion skills were on par with my survival instincts.

ADDY'S FRIEND DOROTHY LIVED near Lincoln Park in West Seattle, the kind of location that Realtors would tout as being mere steps away from majestic views.

When I pulled up to the odd house—like someone had placed a Craftsman bungalow as a cap on two additional stories to maximize vertical space—the only view I had was of similar homes squashed into their own cramped lots.

Cyndra was playing with Stanley in the side yard, taking advantage of the unusually bright and dry winter day. The yard wasn't nearly big enough for a game of fetch, so she tossed a tennis ball high into the air and Stanley would try to catch it as it came down. More often than not the ball bounced off his nose or noggin, which didn't discourage him. He'd snatch it off the ground and run in happy circles, tearing through the bark landscaping until Cyndra ordered him to drop the toy so she could throw it again. Slobber spun from the thrown ball like rain off a whirling pinwheel.

"Look," Cyn said, once Stanley was running loops again. "Dorothy had those in her basement. She heard I was lifting weights and she made us take them." Boxes on the porch held pairs of dumbbells, each pair coated in pink or purple nonslip neoprene, in various weights up to eight pounds.

"You're already stronger than these," I said.

"I know," she said. "Isn't that cool? I'm gonna give them to the team."

I grinned and left her to Stanley, who was rolling on the ball like he wanted to fuse it with his pelt.

My knock at the door was answered by Addy's shout to let myself in. Inside, past a knickknack-laden sitting room still strewn with confetti from the night before, I found her puttering around the kitchen putting things in order. Like me, Ms. Proctor was not one for sitting idle.

She'd find something that required adjustment, at least to her way of thinking, and set to work.

"Where's Dorothy?" I said.

"She'd already made plans with her children for the day, so we have the house to ourselves for a few hours. A relief after staying up so late. Is there any news?"

I understood what she meant. "Still working on clearing the coast. But you and Cyn should be able to go home within a day or two."

Addy nodded but didn't look away from her work rinsing dishes.

"I'm sorry," I said. "It's not fair to either of you."

"As hideouts go, this could be shabbier," she said. "I'm too tired to debate you right now. Have you learned any more about who your father might be?"

"Nothing good." I told her all I had uncovered about Sean Burke and the murders he'd committed for his gangster boss. I didn't have to sugarcoat it for Addy. Or for myself. She settled on a blue divan in the living room. After another minute of pacing I made myself sit on the couch.

"Worse than you feared," she said when I'd finished talking.

"Yeah."

There were levels of bad, like shades of night. Dono had not been a good man, even if he'd tried to be a decent parent to me most of the time. I was somewhere on the murkier end of that spectrum myself.

But Burke was something else. Somewhere past what I, even with my sorry background and questionable choices, could justify. *Unredeemable* was the closest I could come to putting a name to it.

"So what now?" Addy said. "Do you let it go?"

"Everything tells me I should," I said. "That it would be smart to be Zen about the whole damn thing and release it to the universe, or whatever the hell the phrase is."

"But."

"But I still don't know if Burke is my father. And I hate not knowing. I have always hated not knowing." I clenched a fist. "At least with a definite answer, I won't have the question burning a hole in me."

"Could you talk to him? Or"—she shrugged—"get his DNA somehow? You could send it to one of those labs that verifies family relations. Just because you learn the truth doesn't mean Sean Burke has to."

I'd had that idea, even before breaking into Burke's house in Bitter Lake. That place had been so clean I'd wondered whether he intentionally kept it scoured of all genetic evidence.

"To do that," I said, "we'd have to at least meet."

"Something tells me I'm a step behind," Addy said.

"Only just."

Burke had found me once. I'd have to make sure our second encounter was on my terms.

"Pain is here!" Cyndra, calling from the porch.

It took me a second to grasp what she'd said. I looked out the window. Cyn's derby trainer—Wren, aka Pain Austen—stood on the sidewalk, holding a hand out for Stanley to sniff and lick in greeting. Her right hand, on the arm with the winding spiral of birds. Wren's hair was free of its braid today, the black-coffee waves cascading down to end just above the small of her back.

"I forgot to tell you," Addy said. "Cyndra invited

Wren over to pick up the weights before tonight's beginner class."

"Uh huh," I said, knowing there was more to Cyn's motives than that. Maybe Addy's, too. I was suddenly aware that I hadn't shaved today, and I was still wearing Hollis's T-shirt touting tourism in Mexico.

We stepped out onto the porch. Cyn had ordered Stanley to sit and behave while Wren opened the gate and joined us.

"Happy New Year," Addy greeted her.

"Happy New Year, and hello," Wren said to me. "Cyn didn't tell me you'd be here."

"There's a lot she's neglecting to mention today," I said.

Cyndra covered her sudden blush by asking if we'd all care for something to drink, automatically using the same inflection Addy would have used. We sat in three Mission-style chairs on the porch while Cyn escaped to the kitchen. Wren asked Addy how she'd spent the holiday, and Addy wove adventures of her faction of very active retirees.

Addy talked. Wren listened. I tried to do the same. But I was struck with a feeling of separation, of watching myself from outside my body with disbelief. The night before I'd been scaling a building and scrambling to keep Saleem from blowing my head off. Today I was sipping iced tea on a porch.

Returning home after a deployment overseas created a similar shock to the system. Between rotations I would dampen that blow to my psyche by staying immersed in Ranger life and training around Benning. If

I never fully wound down, I never had the challenge of gearing back up. But there was no escaping the anchor-like drag of civilian life.

Maybe that was a learned skill. Living in peacetime. I'd never had a chance to practice it much, even in childhood. Now that an opportunity for the quiet life presented itself, I was finding that I was a lousy student.

"Van?" Addy said, bringing me back to the now. "Did we lose you?"

"Sorry," I said. "New Year's Eve was rough."

"I kept my partying to a minimum. This time." Wren grinned. "Last year I felt like you do for three whole days."

"Speaking of recovery," Addy said, "there's nothing in the pantry. Cyndra dear, grab my keys and we'll visit the grocery store while it's quiet. Come on."

She headed off Cyn's protests, handing me a house key and bustling the kid to the driveway and into Addy's Subaru. They were gone as efficiently as if a helicopter had snatched them into the sky on a SPIE rope.

"That was awkward," I said.

Wren laughed. "Mortal Cyn is playing Tinder."

"Yeah. Sorry again. She's good at ambushing."

"I don't mind. And I've been stuck inside all weekend. Are you regretting last night too much for a walk?"

"It's not a hangover. And yeah, let's go."

Stanley would have battered down the door if we'd left him behind. I buckled the giant hound into his harness and we set off toward Lincoln Park. Wren was dressed lightly for the cool day in green cotton pants with slim cargo pockets, and a white polo and fleece vest that contrasted nicely with her skin.

"Cyn said you grew up here in Seattle," Wren said.

"Capitol Hill, born and raised. You?"

"Might as well throw a dart at a map. I was born in Algiers. Then when I started school we moved to my father's home in Marseilles. We came to the United States when I was ten. Since then, seven different states, if you only count the places we stayed longer than a year."

"Whoa. So you're—French Moroccan?"

"I'm American, like you. But I have my French citizenship as well."

I was reminded of Sean Burke's Russian passport, acquired no doubt to facilitate his work for Anatoly Liashko. I mentally shoved the intrusion away.

"I'm Irish," I said, "but that's the American version of Irish, which can be More Irish Than."

Wren laughed. "Performative heritage?"

"Exactly. My grandfather was the real thing, from Belfast. He got out during the bad times in the 1970s and made his way here."

An ambulance flew past as we reached Fauntleroy Way. I tugged at Stanley's lead. He wanted to race after the howling beast.

We crossed the road to enter the park and chose a trail that led to railroad-tie steps, down through the sparse forest of ferns and ponderosa pine. Scores of kids running and shouting on the nearby playing field sounded like colliding streams, splashing and bubbling with chaos.

"Seven different states, huh? And counting?" I said.

She looked at me, one dark eyebrow cocked. "Do you always find the heart of things so quickly?"

"I withdraw the question."

"No, it's all right. It's only—I've been thinking hard about that same question. I'll have been in Seattle for three years this spring. The first place I've lived, the longest I've been anywhere, without any of my family nearby. Most of them are in New Mexico now. I miss them. It's a good life here, though."

"But you're not sure if it's a permanent fit."

"Nothing is permanent, except change. I'm just deciding whether to make change happen, or let it happen on its own." Wren grinned. "You know about that kind of choice. When did you leave the military?"

"Cyndra told you?"

"No. One of my brothers is stationed down at Pendleton. There's a way of moving. Like"—she motioned—"the backpack is still there, and you're too light without it. Did you know you walk on the balls of your feet?"

It was my turn to laugh. "That's kinda witchy."

"A real witch could tell which kind of fighter you were. The Marines?"

"Army Rangers. I rolled out about a year ago." The thought made me stop. "Almost exactly one year, in fact."

"Your anniversary. And your birthday soon, too. Cyn did tell me that."

"Next week. I haven't had much time to think on it."

We reached the shore. A graded path ran along the rocky beach. We strolled north, letting Stanley sniff at each bush and random stick. The wind was in our faces, carrying the smells of salt and seaweed abandoned by the low tide.

Wren described growing up with her extended family, the bunch of them going wherever her father's job

as a solar engineer took them, then continuing that no-
madic life into adulthood. I gave her a very abbreviated
and slightly sanitized history of my own upbringing
with Dono. I said he'd been to prison and I'd been a foster kid for a time before we came back together.

And, suddenly, I found myself telling Wren about
Moira.

"I'm curious about her in a way I never was growing
up," I said. "Instead of what she was like when she was
with me, I'm wondering what she had planned for herself."

"As a person, not just your mother."

"Right. She was twenty-two when she died. I was
about to start school. Was she finally going to college?
Starting a career?" I shook my head. "All those things
she never got to do."

"Of course. You're working on your own direction,
seeing a reflection in her."

"Did you pick up a psych degree in your travels?"

"I've spent enough on therapy," she said, nudging me
with her elbow. "I might as well get something from it."

We turned inland, finding another path that would
take us out of the park. This trail was narrower than the
first. Hiking up the easy slope, Wren's shoulder brushed
mine every few steps.

"Your birds." I touched a fingertip to her arm and its
tattoos in flight. Despite the breeze, her skin was hot.
"From your name?"

She nodded. "A new one every time I migrate. Sometimes two. It's not a strict rule. Wren is a nickname for
Raina." She pronounced it as if there were an accent
over the *n*: *Rain-ya*.

"'Van' is short for 'Donovan.' My grandfather's name."

"And yours. You own it. Donovan. It's strong." She tilted her head. "What do you want for your birthday, Donovan Shaw?"

"I don't know your last name," I said, a little embarrassed at the realization.

"Marchand. That was an easy gift."

"Friday night, then," I said, "if you're free."

Wren considered. "I could be. I have something early in the evening, but it won't take long. You could meet me there."

Back at the house, we traded numbers and she said she'd be in touch about the time and place. She declined my offer of help and hefted the box of free weights without much effort. As she reached the sidewalk, Wren paused and turned back, pivoting as gracefully on one foot as if she wore her skates.

"Friday. The whole night?" she said, with a touch of a smile.

"Or as long as you can stand my company."

"We'll have to find out." She walked away and climbed into a well-dented camel-colored Jeep to drive away.

Damn. Maybe Hollis knew something I didn't. He had managed to make inroads with Doc Claybeck. And I was wearing Hollis's shirt today. I'd never make fun of his fashion choices again.

CHAPTER TWENTY-EIGHT

JUST AFTER TWO O'CLOCK, four of us met at Willard's house near Green Lake: me, Hollis, Elana, and Willard himself. The big man had owned the place for decades. Or maybe it would be more accurate to say he'd owned the land, as the house had been rebuilt from the ground up within the past three years. What used to be little more than a cottage—cozy for most, positively cramped for Willard—was now a two-story gabled home with solar panels on its bronzed metal roof.

I arrived in time to see Hollis's sky-blue Cadillac sailing down the street in search of a parking spot. The convertible top was up today. He waved a hand as he coasted past. Elana sat on a dining chair outside the front door, long legs crossed and propped on a garden planter as she vaped lightly from an ivory pen.

"No smoking inside," she said, "in case you were inclined."

"Good thing that's my resolution this year," I said.

I let myself in. The first story had been made an open design to maximize square footage. From the entry I could see the living room with a fireplace, dining area, and part of the kitchen beyond. Most of the furnishings were steel and cedar, and all of them were large enough to accommodate Willard's frame. The walls were papered in a putty-colored bamboo pattern that shouldn't have worked but somehow did. A tang of dark tea filled the space.

Willard came down the stairs, buttoning the cuffs of his shirt.

"Place looks good," I said.

"I had help."

"Interior designer?"

He shook his head. "Sonny. A friend with an eye. You want coffee? Tea?"

"Either." Passing by the mantel, I stopped to look at framed pictures of Elana and her parents when she was younger. And one of a tall, lean black man with a ring of silver hair around his temples. I guessed him for Willard's friend Sonny. Willard had always been very circumspect about his private life. His confirmed bachelorhood an open secret, but never stated, as if it were fifty years ago. I assumed that discretion worked for him. For them both, maybe.

Hollis and Elana came in, Elana exhaling her last drag in the rough direction of outside before closing the door. I set my rucksack down and extracted the cryo bottle with Aura's eggs.

"That's it?" Elana took it from me, weighing it in her hands. "Huh. I figured it would be heavier."

"Mostly padding and vapor," I said.

"And three lives," Hollis said. "Imagine."

We joined Willard at the dining table. He'd set a pot of coffee on a trivet and passed out mugs.

"I can't think about it that way," I said. "Like the eggs have any value beyond what Aura and Bilal give them."

Willard gave me a flat look. "So if you can't agree on a deal with them, you'll toss her eggs in the trash?"

"They'll deal. They'll never be more willing."

"You don't have to hand all three eggs over," Elana said. "Give them one. Keep the other two as insurance."

Willard looked at his niece like she'd sprouted horns. "That might be even colder."

She shrugged. "They started this."

"They did," I agreed, "and I thought about splitting up the eggs, too. But all three might be destroyed in the attempt. Even if we did it right, if Bilal and Aura are successful in having a kid with their first try, I've lost my leverage. If they can't, we're right back where we started. I don't want to do this again in a few months."

"Haven't these dickweeds heard of adoption?" Elana muttered.

Hollis hummed as he swallowed a mouthful of coffee. "I have to admire his commitment to her."

"You would," said Willard.

"It's true," Hollis protested. "Aura might only have one option, to get her eggs back. But Bilal doesn't. He could go off and have a kid with any willing woman before he kicks off if that's so damned important to him. Hell, he could sire a whole brood."

I stopped in midpour. "You're right."

"Of course I'm right. I know how children get made."

"About Aura being in a corner. She's the one who's truly desperate." I was looking out the window but not really seeing anything beyond the idea that was taking shape. "She's the one who'll be left alone when Bilal dies."

"Alone raising a brat," Elana said.

Hollis grimaced. "What is it you're thinking, Van?"

"Bilal has the money and the soldiers. But it's Aura I'll need to reach an agreement with," I said.

My first thought had been to talk face-to-face with Bilal and Aura, once I'd figured out exactly how to ensure my continued safety. Now I was peering down a path I hadn't spied before.

"We'll have to arrange a meeting," I said, as the idea occurred, "and let Bilal come heavy."

Willard rumbled. "Well, that sounds like ten kinds of crazy. You know if he sees a chance, he'll grab you and torture you until you surrender the eggs. After that . . ."

"That's what I'm counting on. Him seeing a chance. I'll need you and Hollis to be my eyes."

"You're not cutting me out again," said Elana.

"Nope. You'll be critical"—I stopped Willard before he started—"and out of the line of fire. You'll all be away from the heat."

"Speaking for myself, lad," Hollis said, "you walking in alone to meet those two and all the muscle they can hire is just mad-dog cowboy shit."

"Rabid, reckless, and all the rest," I agreed. "Let's pray Bilal Nath thinks so, too."

CHAPTER TWENTY-NINE

AFTER LEAVING WILLARD'S, I drove around the lake and wound my way toward downtown, the side roads giving me time to puzzle over a different problem, and a different threat. All my careful maneuvers with Aura and Bilal might come to an abrupt end if Sean Burke appeared and caught me by surprise once more.

My subconscious had been picking at the tangled knot of just how Burke had tracked me to the parking garage on the night of the museum gala. I had an inkling—my only idea this side of crazy notions like Burke following my car with a team of flying drones—but its implications were unnerving.

I'd used my personal credit card to purchase an evening pass when entering the garage that night. Burke knew my name and my car. If he'd somehow put a trace on my accounts, he might have known where I was within minutes. Perhaps even before I'd chosen a parking space.

Was that even possible? Burke's Russian boss, Liashko, had money, and pull. Did his reach extend to flunkies inside major American banks? Guerin had said the arms dealer wielded enough power to control his interests without setting foot on our shores. Wielded through men like Burke.

I was as realistic—Addy would say cynical—as anyone about the corruption of those in power. Hell, I'd bribed an FBI employee less than a week ago. But Liashko having that level of influence at his command gave me one very long pause.

And a theory I could put to the test.

Some car juggling was required. I drove my truck downtown. On the holiday, the streets were halfway to deserted and I had my choice of metered parking spots. I left the truck at the curb, not far from the museum. Caught a rideshare back to Addy's to retrieve the Barracuda. And drove the muscle car right back to the garage where Burke had aimed his gun at me. With intent, as the law would say.

I used the same credit card to buy a two-hour ticket. Wondering if, somewhere, the charge on the card was even now sending a flag to alert whoever might be watching.

Five minutes later the Barracuda sat nestled in a spot on the second level, copper paint gleaming in the low January sun, and I was back at street level, sitting in the truck. Watching the garage entrance.

I'd set the shiny lure. Now came the waiting.

If I was right, Burke had waited for me to return to the Barracuda after my visit to the museum. The more I thought about that, the less I figured he had stood outside on the roof of the garage, exposed to the cold and to witnesses. He'd have kept watch from a car of his own. Not his personal vehicle. Something untraceable to him, in the chance that he would have to leave me dead, with my rapidly cooling blood flowing down the slope of the garage ramp.

My phone rang, with the number of the answering service I had called early in the morning.

"It's Jessica," said a contralto voice. "You remember?" Ondine's bodyguard from the museum.

"Sensible shoes and a lethal purse," I said. "Can you speak for your boss, or are you just relaying messages?"

"This line's secure."

I took that to mean Jessica had some authority beyond being Ondine's flyswatter.

"Good. Let's cut to it. I need to set up a meeting with Bilal Nath. He knows it's coming. I figure he'll circle back to you to recruit more soldiers. Maybe he already has."

"Go on."

"Your boss told Nath I was unmanageable. Play that up. Make me out like some rabid dog. Encourage him to bring along a full team, racked and ready."

"Why?"

"That's my business."

"I'll state the obvious," Jessica said. "We don't take orders from you."

"No. But you are taking commands from Nath right now. Right? What's it worth to get Bilal off your back for good?"

I waited through the silence that followed. Jessica might be conferring with Ondine.

I'd sounded much more confident than I really was. In truth, I was playing a hunch, based on my hard-won experience with Ondine Long.

She had shared Bilal Nath's biography with me far

too easily. My confronting her at the museum had been like an opening bid, and she hadn't responded with a counteroffer. Instead she'd folded, telling me what she knew, and quickly, before the guards showed up to end our conversation.

So why would the most mercenary woman in Seattle be willing to give me intel on Bilal for free? Her client, who'd paid her for Claybeck's services?

Unless he wasn't a client. Bilal was very adept, Ondine had said. A bitter aftertaste in her statement. Maybe Nath had a leash around Ondine's neck, just as he had on mine. Had she been gambling a little herself, on the off chance my thrashing against Bilal might solve a problem for her?

Jessica came back on the line.

"Bilal has to stay alive," she said. "If he dies . . ."

"Agreed. This isn't that kind of op."

"But you want him protected?"

"I want him ready for a war. And if he demands a kidnap team to make me disappear, give him that, too."

Another moment passed.

"We can make that happen," Jessica said, "though we can't control what the teams do once they're in motion."

Meaning I was digging my own grave, from their perspective.

"It's on you if this goes wrong," Jessica continued. "In any way at all. Understand?"

"I'll tell Bilal where and when. Sometime tomorrow."

She hummed reflectively. "Whatever you have planned, I hope it's not as stupid as it looks from here."

I grinned. This was Jessica talking for herself, not as Ondine's mouthpiece.

"Nice to know you care," I said, and hung up.

During our call, a few cars had driven into the garage. A minivan with kids in the backseat watching movies on the fold-down screen. Teenagers in a Honda Civic adorned with the cheapest racing mods available from their local O'Reilly Auto, heavy beat pulsing the windows. Nothing that fit the right profile.

Until a black Ford F-250 with a bright silver toolbox across the full width of its bed, like a stripe over a thick beetle's wings, turned off Seneca and cruised slowly to the garage. Smoked windows obscured the interior.

The Ford stopped for a moment at the entrance, as if smelling the air, before pulling through the gate.

Five minutes passed, then another ten. No one walked out from the garage.

Okay. I hadn't seen Burke in the flesh. But I was sure he was there. Like the scent of another predator at the watering hole.

I was prepared. I had sandwiches from Addy's and water, and an open-necked bottle if I had to relieve myself. Mostly I had a lot of practice in waiting and watching. Casing jobs with Dono, back when I was a fidgety teen. Recon of targets in the Rangers, when moving at the wrong moment might bring a hell-storm of opposing fire.

My parking ticket had only been for two hours. I wondered if Burke knew that. He'd paused at the gate, maybe reading the hourly prices and comparing them to the small charge on my credit card. He might be expecting me to return to the Barracuda at any minute.

I hoped so. The more frustrated he became, the better. While my eyes did the work, my thoughts strayed to

Wren. I didn't know much about the woman yet. But what I did made me want to learn a lot more. She was intuitive as hell. And forthright. There hadn't been any question she'd been flirting with me, and I could admit I wasn't always the best at reading women's signals.

And sexy. Damn, Wren Marchand was an absolute smoke show. I wasn't positive which of us had asked the other out in the end, but I was glad either way.

I ate a sandwich made from Addy's leftover roast and some provolone. Sipped at the water. It had stayed plenty cold just from the ambient temperature. This time of year, the shade between downtown buildings was nearly round the clock. Even sheltered from the wind in the Dodge, I kept my watch cap on my head.

The Barracuda's parking pass had long since expired. Maybe an attendant had already placed a ticket under the wiper, informing me I'd have to pay for the full day. Maybe Burke had seen that and realized that I might not be returning as promptly as he'd imagined.

Another hour ticked by. The edges of the buildings around me began to soften, melding with the twilight sky. Their interior lights defined stripes and squares that grew ever brighter in contrast. Fewer lights than on a normal workday, so that each side of the avenue looked patchwork, incomplete.

The headlights coming down the garage ramp revealed the Ford's presence seconds before the truck itself hove into view. It stopped at the gate, which rose obediently to allow passage. As the Ford pulled out onto the avenue, beams from a passing delivery truck shone directly through the windshield, overcoming the tinted glass and giving me an instant's glimpse of the driver.

Sean Burke. Gotcha, asshole.

He turned left onto Spring Street. I U-turned to follow, staying at least one block behind and giving Burke plenty of room as he turned again onto 6th Ave and we made our way uptown.

Not far, as I soon learned. Burke pulled into a lot near the Westin. I drifted past, coming to a stop in a loading zone, watching in the rearview. A sign at the front of the lot had touted monthly parking rates. If the Ford was Burke's clean machine for work purposes, maybe this was where he kept it.

In another minute, a Lexus GS sedan in granite gray appeared from the lot. It continued on the same route, passing me and shimmering its way up 6th. Burke's broad frame was visible through the rear window.

I didn't follow right away. Burke might have marked the Dodge from his own truck. Pulling out behind him now could be a dead giveaway, accent on the *dead*.

He went left on Bell. In another second, I hurried after him. I passed through the intersection in time to see the Lexus cross under the monorail track at 5th and turn into an alleyway on the next block.

I stopped before the alley. Too easy to spot me in those close quarters. I left the truck at the curb and ran ahead to look down its length. The back of the Lexus was just vanishing from sight into a wide brightly lit rectangle. As I watched, the rectangle compressed until it was gone entirely. An automatic door had shut behind Burke's car.

After a slow count of twenty, I risked walking down the alley. The wide door was painted with the name EMPYREA.

I retraced my steps to the front of the block, on 4th Ave. The alley ran behind the Cinerama theater and a luminous high-rise, maybe forty stories or more.

The Empyrea. A newer addition to Seattle's skyline. Its lower six floors had been clad in backlit glass that shone a verdigris green. The same pale green highlighted each floor of the looming tower above. Discreet signs in the windows advertised units still available. On the other side of the doors, posters of happy families and conspicuously affluent professionals, enjoying the amenities within. The lower floors of the tower operated as a hotel under the same name.

I sent a text to a friend. More of a work acquaintance, really. I included the license plate number of Burke's Lexus GS. I'd had to lean on my newer colleague Panni to trace Special Agent Rick Martens's license. But for DMV checks on regular citizens, I had my own sources.

Ten minutes later the name Garrett Costello and an address matching the Empyrea Tower added to our text thread. Unit 3105. High living. I spent two more minutes wiring my acquaintance his fee for the service. Pays to know people.

Garrett Costello. A buddy of Burke's, lending him his car? Or the name Burke lived his daily life under, to keep people like me off his track?

I wasn't inclined to wait to find out. The security of the average hotel was no challenge. I made my way in through a utility door off the alley and then cut across at the quiet mezzanine level to find the elevator.

The elevator required a keycard to access the residential floors. I ignored the swipe pad. In my lockpick kit I carried a firefighter's service key, which allowed me to open the Phase 2 panel inside the elevator and override the keycard controls. The button for the thirty-first floor lit up on the first try.

Apartment 3105 was halfway down the hall, likely boasting unobstructed views of the southern skyline and the water beyond.

I listened at the door. I could hear faint voices from a television, a news channel. I debated whether to pick the deadbolt or to coax Burke into coming out somehow, maybe by leaving a package at the front desk. The television went quiet.

Then I heard muffled footsteps, close and coming closer, and had just enough time to get my hand on my Beretta before the door opened.

Burke. Dressed for going out, and with a look of stunned surprise. A gift horse with a gaping mouth. I shoved him back into the dark interior of the apartment and drew the gun.

"Hands," I said, kicking the door closed behind me. "Up."

He froze. I pointed the gun at his knee, just as he had to me, to underline the point. He laced his fingertips on top of his head.

I spun him around and quick-marched him up against the wall of the living room. His leg banged the glass table beside a black leather couch, knocking a full tumbler of water to the carpet.

My left hand patted him down while the right aimed the Beretta at his spine. I stayed off to one side with a few inches of extra space. No point signaling to him exactly where the gun was, inviting an attempt to disarm me. And I wasn't positive we were alone in the apartment. If anyone else suddenly appeared, I wanted Burke as a shield.

He had a small squarish automatic, maybe a Walther by the feel of it, in a soft concealed carry holster over his right kidney. A gravity knife with a four-inch blade in the pocket of his overcoat. And a backup piece, a subcompact Glock on his right ankle. Armed for a damned standoff. I tossed all the weapons toward the door. Fury radiated from Burke like heat off a reactor core.

"Get it over with," he said.

"You said it yourself: I'm not a shooter. But I will put a round through you if you step out of line."

"Then what the fuck is this?"

"My turn for picture time."

I tapped his shoulder with a half sheet of cardstock and the penlight from my pocket. Slowly, he reached a hand from his head to take them. I drifted back to give myself some space. This high in the sky, the city lights made more of a soft undertone to the darkness in the room than any illumination we could see by. The shadows worked to my advantage.

When he turned on the penlight, the beam bounced off the glossy print and into his face like a suntan reflector catching rays. Slashes of shadow trapped in the crags of his square face just served to emphasize his look of shock.

I said what we both already knew.

"Moira."

He didn't take his eyes from her yearbook picture. As his gaze moved slowly over the contours of Moira's image, motes of flashlight beam glimmered in his eyes.

"How do you have this?" he said. Something like wonder in his voice.

"She's my mother."

Burke turned the flashlight my way. I had anticipated the glare. With twelve feet between us, his blinding me and jumping to attack wasn't a practical option. Not that he seemed inclined. Flat-footed in both stance and attitude.

"You and Moira were friends," I said. "When you were both teenagers."

"And?"

I took a breath. "And I want to know if you're my father."

He stared at me for a long moment, before his lip curled in a snarling grin. If the laugh that followed had any humor in it, it was the kind that revealed itself when watching a video of someone you didn't like taking a nasty fall.

"You asking if I laid her? That it?"

"That's a first step."

"To what? Child support? Shit, you're bigger than I am."

"Did you?"

"Man, you really believe this. Dumb fuck." Burke shifted, his heel squashing on the wet carpet. "I never got in the bitch's pants. And without that, there's nothing. I haven't given two shits about her since. Happy?"

"Not yet. I want proof."

"Proof?"

"A hair sample. Including the roots."

The grin evaporated. "I should have known this was a cop trick." He dropped Moira's picture to the floor.

"I'm no cop."

"Oh, I heard that. You're just some snitch they told to break into my house to nab some DNA. What do they got over you? Another burglary rap?"

"You're wrong."

"Go fuck yourself. The only sample you're taking from me is blood." He nodded at the gun. "You got the stones?"

I did. On any other day. Popping one through the outer meat of Burke's thigh—a volcano of pain but nothing fatal, so long as he got help soon—and yanking out a fistful of his hair while he writhed on the floor might have been easy work. I didn't even have to go that far. Burke was strong, but I could whip him across the head with the Beretta and continue from there.

Except.

Except I'd seen the way Burke had looked at Moira's photo. Like you'd look at a childhood treasure you'd long believed lost.

Except he hadn't asked about Moira, or told me to take my fool questions to her. He already knew she was dead. Which meant he was lying about never giving her another thought.

There was something stopping me from hurting Burke. It didn't take a flash of genius to figure out what that was.

"Here." I took a burner phone from my pocket and tossed it to him. He caught it one-handed.

"In case you want to talk to Daddy?" he said, the predatory smile back in place.

"In case you decide to stop bullshitting me. Until then I've got other things to do."

"Other contenders, huh? Mom spread it around a little?"

I wasn't going to give Burke the pleasure of seeing my anger.

"Stay away from me, Shaw," he said, "or I'll finish this."

I backed toward the front door. Burke didn't bother shining the penlight in my direction. He stood with the beam illuminating the cuffs of his trousers and his shoes, and the white edge of Moira's photo on the frost-blue living room carpet. His shadowy outline only shifted once I began to close the door.

I left the Empyrea via the lobby. As I joined a stream of people letting out from a show at the movie theater, I had to step around a long-limbed dude inclined with almost sagging relaxation against a post, a cigarette like a piece of smudged chalk stuck in the black sand of his heavy beard stubble.

A few feet farther on, I caught the smoke. A pungent, deep-tar punch.

No way that was an American brand, not even hand-rolled.

I kept walking to the corner before looking back. The lean dude with the black overcoat and blacker stubble was still hanging there, eyeing the hotel lobby. He glanced vaguely in my direction. Then assiduously avoided doing so again.

Maybe Burke had been leaving to meet him. Or maybe the dude was watching the lobby, intent on following Burke when he left.

Podraski and Martens, the task force cops, had implied someone might have hired me to break into

Burke's house. Burke himself had demanded to know who I worked for. And if the smoking dude wasn't from Eastern Europe, I was a Martian. Was Burke somehow on the wrong side of his boss, Liashko?

I took my time returning to my truck, to make sure the smoking dude wasn't on *my* tail, and to take a moment to think about my last sight of Sean Burke.

As I had closed the door to 3105, he had moved. It had been hard to know for certain in the gloom, but I thought I'd seen Burke reaching down, rescuing the picture of my mother from the sodden floor.

JUNIOR YEAR, PART FIVE

I didn't skip classes often, not nearly as much as Davey. Part of my arrangement with Dono was that I could work with him so long as my grades maintained at least a three-point average and I stayed out of detention and other trouble. But today was a special case.

Not having a car of my own, I had to hide in the trees that bordered the school parking lots while I waited for first bell. Lurking like some perv. At least the woods smelled good, more like cedar than the spruce trees I guessed them to be from their mossy, scale-like bark. I wanted coffee and breakfast but I'd had to make do with a Coke grabbed from the fridge early this morning and some wintergreen gum.

When the lots were empty of students, I went looking. Burn Burkley's white GTO was in the farther lot, between a pickup truck and a Ford SUV. Perfect. No one could see me from the school as I used one of Dono's tools to pop the trunk.

No alarm sounded. Maybe Burn didn't have one,

or he had installed some aftermarket brand on his shitmobile that only went off if someone unlocked the doors. It wouldn't have mattered. What I was searching for took me ten seconds to find.

Under the spare tire, a plastic Safeway bag filled with pinkie-sized bottles wrapped in gold foil. A quick glance at one told me the little flasks had been mass-produced in England, where I guessed poppers must be legal. Maybe Singer or Burn had a relative willing to mail them over.

Twenty-two minutes until the end of first period. Time enough. I made one stop in the 400 block of classrooms, and another to wash my hands carefully in the bathroom. By the time the bell rang I was at my locker, picking up books as if it would be a nice, normal day ahead.

Word was all over school by lunchtime. Vice Principal Rikkard had opened up Burn Burkley's locker, and whatever he'd found there—rumors ranged from a sack full of airplane liquor bottles to a kilo of heroin—it had prompted a visit from not one but two police cars and the cops pulling Burn out of third period. No one had seen him since, but Lane March said he saw Burn in the back of one of the cop cars as they left, all snot-nosed and sweaty.

Yvette Friel didn't look much better. Like she was about to hurl, or had just hurled, or both. As I passed her in the hall at lunch I couldn't resist twisting the knife a little.

"Sorry about your party favors," I said.

She gaped at me like I'd grown fangs. Which it kinda felt like I had.

I'd puzzled over why Burn would steal the poppers back from Colten Gulas, when his whole sales market was in the high school. He couldn't have sold them at Watson without someone in Singer Boeman's circle noticing and making the connection.

But he could give them away. Maybe pour the liquid into dollar-store bottles for shampoo first so it wasn't so apparent they were the same supply. And Burn's sometime girlfriend Yvette was about to throw a huge bash tomorrow night. That was, if she didn't end up in a police station answering questions all weekend. I didn't put it past Burn to claim it was all Yvette's idea.

Colten and Candace met me after school, by the weird metal sculpture that the school had installed sometime during the 1970s. It was iron-gray and looked like sine waves had collided and broken into pieces. Like the artist had had a bad time in math class and wanted everyone to know it.

"What," Candace said before even saying hello, "*happened*? I mean, God. Everyone says there was an anonymous call to the fire department about a bomb or something. Or that the custodian found a puddle under Burn's locker."

"Spillage," I said. "Stuff leaked all over the floor in 400."

"You did it. How?"

"Doesn't matter. What matters is that by now even Singer has heard that Burn was busted with the goods. Colten is home free."

"I thought you were going to give them back to me," he said, hunching his shoulders so that his backpack rode up around his head. "That would have been better."

I waited. Stared.

"Colt, I think Van's done his part," Candace said.

Colten sighed.

"Who took the quilt?" I said.

Another sigh. "I did. Rebecca Hoff said she really liked it, and I thought she really liked me, and . . ."

"And you took it to give to her."

"She was graduating. If she had the quilt, she'd remember me. No one *cares* about the stupid thing, anyway."

I was back to staring. Keeping myself calm. Candace spoke even faster than before.

"Van clearly does, honey. Go on."

Colten took off the backpack and unzipped it. "Here."

He handed a thick folded mass to me. It was stained and tattered in multiple places, and nearly pulled apart in others, but unmistakably a hand-made quilt.

"We had it as a dog blanket," he said. "Fenster chewed a little."

Even if Colten hadn't said anything, I would have known that. The quilt reeked of canine.

"Go away," I said.

"I'm sorry," Candace said.

None of this was her fault, but I guess the look on my face must have spooked her a little, because she got Colten up and moving like he was on fire.

When they were out of sight, I unfolded the quilt. A couple of the fabric squares had representations of people, but most stuck to patterns of diamonds and triangles and smaller interlocked squares. I remembered the quilt better now that I saw it. Reminiscent of Easter, pastel colors like pinks and sky blues and soft yellows.

But I'd never seen the back before. Each student had stitched their name.

There it was: MOIRA SHAW, in green thread. One of the interior squares that weren't as frayed as the edges. I turned the quilt over to examine her square. It, too, was made in shades of green, with a central square and triangles angling off it like a sunburst. I liked it. I ran my fingers over it lightly, feeling the ripples in the fabric and the stitching. She'd had me in her belly when she made this.

I liked it a lot.

Ms. Nasgate and Mr. Lindhoff were together in her classroom. A nicer meeting place than his cramped office, I guessed.

"I found this," I said, placing the folded quilt on

one of the sewing tables. Ms. Nasgate was on her feet in an instant.

"Oh my," she said. "Look."

Lindhoff frowned. "Where'd you get that, Mr. Shaw?"

I pointed to the quilt's edge. "A dog's chewed on it."

"I asked you a question."

"That's no real concern, Milt," Ms. Nasgate said to him. She was already unfolding the quilt, spreading it to drape smoothly over the table. "It's very dirty, but the fabric we used is forgiving. A lot of these stains will come out." She spoke breathlessly to herself. "I think we can rescue most of them with a little patching. Which one was your mother's?"

"This one," I said. The speed of my answer wasn't lost on Lindhoff.

Ms. Nasgate smoothed the quilt's cloth with her hand, like she was soothing a nervous animal.

"Now, I wouldn't normally break up a project, Van, but this is a special circumstance," she said. "Would you like to keep your mother's square? We'll be reassembling much of this, anyway."

I shook my head. I'd taken some pictures of it. They would be enough.

"She made it to be part of something," I said.

"Well, thank you very, very much. You know this is the only senior project since I've been here that was lost? We'll take good care of it. And put it back in a place of honor."

"Mr. Shaw?" said Lindhoff. I inhaled, waiting for the shoe to drop. "I trust . . . no one was harmed in the recovery of this?"

Ms. Nasgate looked very puzzled by the question. I shrugged.

"No," I said, "but they deserved to be."

He chewed on that. "Then I suppose everything ended well."

Well as can be.

I left them there to talk over whatever they needed to talk over. I'd done all I could. Somewhere, Mom would know that.

CHAPTER THIRTY

WILLARD AND I STOOD in an unleased floor of an office building, across the street from a similarly empty and even more rundown warehouse on Seattle's north end. Rundown, but hardly quiet.

"You see them?" Willard said. "In the repair van."

I did. I had an even better view than Willard, once I'd adjusted the focus on my binoculars. Two men sitting in the front seat, and at least one more in the enclosed rear of the high-ceilinged van. The vehicle tilted slightly as the unseen third moved around.

Ondine had provided Bilal Nath with plenty of re-sources. All men in casual clothes, all moving with pur-pose, and every one of them armed. I'd counted four so far, carrying duffels long enough to allow for carbines or shotguns. They hadn't arrived all at once. The team had been taking positions around the warehouse since eight this morning, less than one hour after I'd texted him the address along with the time to meet: High noon.

They had set pairs of operatives at the corners of each intersection and already entered the warehouse. More than likely they were also on the roof of the building Willard and I were watching from.

I'd chosen our meeting place after searching through commercial listings. I didn't care much about the neglected warehouse itself. But I loved that the office building across the busy street had space available, giving us an excellent vantage point. And that its occupied floors were dedicated mostly to single-business suites, psychologists and massage therapists and chiropractic clinics, which buzzed with appointments after the holiday break. Lots of comings and goings. Lots of people for Bilal's team to try and keep track of.

It was a reasonable assumption that the repair van was planned for me. The kidnap team. Once they had me trapped, the team would bring the van around and they would efficiently force me out the side door of the warehouse and into the vehicle. What would happen after that wasn't worth thinking about.

Willard scanned the streets. "I'm up to eighteen so far. Think Ondine gave Bilal a bulk rate?"

I took my eyes away from the lenses. "A joke. From you. Amazing."

"Laughing in the face of death."

"Look at it this way: the more of them that are here, the better."

Eleven o'clock now. One hour to go. I called Elana.

"They haven't left the hotel," she said immediately. "But their Mercedes is in the roundabout, with two tight-asses in suits and crappy haircuts hanging at the entrance. How's the meeting spot?"

"Might as well have a giant bull's-eye painted on it."

We held the line open until something changed. It took less than ten minutes.

"He's here," Elana said, her voice an octave higher than usual. "Bilal. He and the two rejects and that bodyguard with the angry face are getting into their car."

"That's Saleem. No Aura?"

"No Aura."

"We're on our way."

Willard and I took the elevator to the ground-floor parking level. Hollis was in the passenger seat of Willard's Continental, from which he had been watching the eastern side of the warehouse.

"Are you sure it's too late to call in your Army compatriots?" he said as he climbed out and stretched. "I'm sure one of those lads carried a no-bullshit machine gun through that door."

"Keep your distance," I said, taking his seat. "And text me—"

"Once your man arrives. I'm on it. Good luck, boyo. I hope you know what you're doing."

Willard and I pulled out on the rear side of the office building and gave the warehouse a wide berth on our way to the interstate. I kept watch on the oncoming lanes as Willard sped south, on the off chance we'd spot Bilal's Mercedes as it passed. We didn't, but it didn't shake my confidence that Nath was headed where I wanted him.

Elana met us at the gate of the Neapolitan.

"I forgot to tell you: I haven't seen that walking cement truck who works for Bilal."

"Juwad. He's probably guarding Aura." I turned to Willard. "Think you can keep him from twisting my head off?"

Willard smiled. Humor didn't look at all natural for his Cro-Magnon features. As if a rock suddenly rippled like water.

"You're up," I said to Elana.

She smoothed her white blouse. Combined with the conservative skirt and efficient black pumps, and her hair drawn into a neat bun, she looked the very model of a hospitality professional. From the waistband of the skirt she removed a Neapolitan Hotel name pin that read NANCIE.

"Where'd you get that?" Willard asked.

"From Nancie, of course." She tapped the pin with her nails. "I'll put it on in the elevator."

"See you inside," I said.

Elana pivoted and walked away, a distinct spring in her step. Willard and I gave her a minute's head start before walking into the lobby and directly across to the hotel bar. It was lunchtime, and the handful of business travelers and affluent vacationers were doing their best to start the weekend a little early.

The Neapolitan's bar had a back room available for rental to parties of up to twenty people. It was closed for a private function. Ours. Hollis had reserved the space yesterday.

I left the door to the room ajar and chose a booth out of the direct line of sight. Willard stood outside at the bar as if waiting to order.

Elana would be knocking on the door of Bilal's suite by now. Helpful Nancie, conveying the message to Aura or, more likely, Juwad that Mr. Nath had mentioned on the way out that he would prefer they wait at the back of the hotel bar, and would Mrs. Nath please bring her computer and tablet in case they were required, and was there anything else she could do to make their stay more pleasant?

Aura might call her husband to check. Or maybe she would assume radio silence while Bilal was supposedly dealing with me. We had to roll the dice on that. She would have Juwad and the midday crowd in the nearby lobby for reassurance. Safe as houses, as Hollis would have said.

I set the cryo bottle at the edge of the booth's table, where it could be seen from the doorway, and watched the bar in the stripe of mirror that ran along the top of the artfully tiled wall.

We didn't have to wait long. Aura appeared in the entrance to the back room, her aqua-tipped blond hair framed by the broad expanse of Juwad's chest behind her. Both scanned the room. Her eyes lit on the cryo bottle. She rushed forward as if to stop the container from falling.

I placed my hand on it before Aura could reach the table.

"Let's talk," I said.

Juwad came up fast behind her, barreling toward me. Before he reached the table, Willard was there, draping a gigantic arm over the powerlifter's wide shoulders and taking hold of Juwad's bicep with the other hand. Juwad's neck muscles grew taut as he strained to pull away. Willard's fingers tightened. They stood, neither of them moving, two titans locked in an uncertain contest. Juwad's face contorted. Willard smiled grimly.

"You're safe," I said to Aura, "and if everybody stays calm, you and I can make a deal for these." I drummed my fingers on the bottle, looking pointedly at her guardian.

"Juwad," she said. "Please."

Willard stepped back. Juwad almost slumped into the booth, but he righted himself. His brow was shiny with sweat.

"Bilal is waiting for you by now," Aura said, her eyes on the cryo tube.

"Let him wait. These are yours, not his."

"What is it you want?"

"The same thing you do. A future for me and my family. Can we agree on that?"

She sat down opposite me in the booth, almost tossing her tablet and laptop aside, eyes flickering between me and the container. "You want our word you won't be touched."

"I want mutually assured destruction." I hefted the bottle. It was amazing, in a minor key, that only an inch of material separated my fingers from cold that would shatter them like peanut brittle. "I want enough hard evidence to send you and Bilal to jail forever, enough to make sure your future children are taken from you if it comes to light. If I have that, then I'll sleep soundly."

She blanched. "That's impossible."

"That's my price."

Aura touched her teeth together. The bottle pulled her gaze back as if her eyes were physically stitched to the slender tube. "Bilal has—clients. I could give you their names, and the materials he has on them."

"Not even close." I set my phone on the table, leaning against the cryo tube, angled so its lens would capture

Aura's every expression and gesture. "Three eggs, three stories. You, Bilal, and Ondine, too."

"Ondine? Why?"

"That's my business."

"Bilal—"

"He'll understand. But even if he doesn't, you'll have your children."

That was enough for Aura to look at me. "If you're lying to me, or if my eggs are already gone, I won't be able to stop him. I won't want to."

"I accept that, Aura. So let's figure out how to get past this."

After a moment, she leaned back. "I can—I can tell you about me."

I nodded. Baby steps.

"Timothy, my ex-husband. We were together when I was first diagnosed with cancer. He suggested harvesting my eggs. Our marriage was already—" She frowned. "It doesn't matter. The whys."

"Go ahead."

"Timothy oversaw my procedure. The head of the clinic, Jackson, was a friend of his. A friend of *ours*, I thought. We didn't have any money of our own— Timothy owed nearly a million dollars just for his school loans, all those crazy degrees, and everything was tied up in trying to get Ceres launched—so it was all done as a favor. I was so desperate, I was dumb. I never signed papers or even told my insurance company, just to keep it all under the table."

Aura closed her eyes, maybe berating herself out of habit.

"It wasn't long after that when I told Timothy I wanted out of the marriage. We fought, and when I saw that he was determined to draw our separation out for as long as possible, I demanded my eggs."

"He refused?"

"They told me that there had been an accident, that my eggs had been destroyed. I was sure at first that Timothy had arranged with Jackson to make the whole matter go away. They could have both lost their licenses if I went public."

"Why didn't you?"

"I had no proof. I have a criminal record, and time spent in psychiatric facilities when I was a teenager. Who would believe me compared to them? I'd already decided to fight back another way." Aura touched the sleeve that held her laptop. "It wasn't hard to hack into Jackson's home and work computers. I made some false trails, just to make it look right."

Her breath caught. I kept my mouth shut, allowing her space to say the next part.

"Pornography," she said. "Of children. There are horrible, horrible things available, just—out there. For the sick freaks who want it."

"You framed Jackson."

"I left one trail where it would be found. It was enough. The court sentenced him to six years." Aura's eyes flicked to the camera lens, to the cryo tube holding her eggs, to me. "Jackson didn't know about my skills, and I don't think he ever suspected me. But Timothy did, of course. He knew that I'd gone after Jackson first just to make him sweat it out. That he would be next."

I raised my eyebrows. Aura was, in her way, as merciless as her extortionist husband. "And that's when he told you he still had your eggs."

"I should have realized it sooner. If you're not with Timothy, you're against him. He would never destroy something that gave him so much control over me, even if it might save his career. And now he could use my eggs to keep me from ripping his life apart."

"You were trapped," I said. "Both of you."

"Until I met Bilal. I took some work with him, hacking into companies here in the States. When he came to Miami for treatment, we met in person. Our relationship was already serious. With his illness he didn't have time to spare, and I wanted him to be able to stay in the country. So we got married. I confessed to Bilal what I'd done. Ceres had completed construction of their new building by then. It made sense to us that he would hide my eggs there. Bilal's team and I searched through the company, looking for any coded items in their records without a paper trail back to R&D or vendors. Timothy wasn't as clever as he imagined."

I wondered again if that had been part of Aura's attraction to Bilal. Power, wealth. A chance for revenge against her abusive ex. And to be completely cold about it, only a temporary commitment, with Nath already showing signs of ALS.

"So now you know," Aura said. "If the police found out, I would take Jackson's place in prison."

"I have to have actual evidence." I pointed at my phone and its camera. "Something to back up your story."

I had expected Aura to kick at the final step, but she removed her laptop from its sleeve.

"There are the original logs and the ones I doctored to put on Jackson's computer," she said, "plus the hacked account from where I stole the—the pictures. Tell me where to send them, and they're yours."

Give her this: the woman was decisive as hell. We spoke for another thirty minutes while Willard kept watch on the entrance and Juwad grew increasingly agitated. The battery on my phone ran dangerously low as it videoed Aura's entire confession.

I learned about Bilal Nath fixing a provincial election in Pakistan, and two other instances where he'd bribed territorial leaders to get charges dropped against his informants. Aura also told me that Ondine Long had jumped a little too quickly to act on whispers of a company going public, with email messages that would be highly embarrassing at best and lead to charges of insider trading if the DA chose to make an example of her.

Aura was one of Bilal's best operatives, as well as his wife. She sent the evidence of their transgressions to the shared drop site I gave her. I'd already arranged that anything placed on that location would be automatically copied to a second private site in the cloud. Trust, but only so far.

"Ondine," I said to Aura. "I own the goods on her now. Forget you know her name."

"That's everything," she said. "Everything I have."

"Not quite," I said. I touched the white tablet that she'd used to hack my phone at Dr. Claybeck's. "I want this handy gadget."

Aura looked perplexed. "It's not perfect. And it requires recoding every time a phone model pushes an upgrade to its OS. Without updates, it will be obsolete within a month or two."

"I'll take it, anyway."

I turned off my camera and handed her the cryo tube. "It's safe to open it."

She did, as if the tube held the antidote to a poison already consuming her. I gave her a glove, and she used it like a rag to extract the slim steel rod with the vial of her eggs attached to its end. Wisps of escaping vapor curled almost protectively around the tiny crystal straw.

"Store them somewhere more permanent within two days," I said.

Aura nodded, but I was uncertain if she was paying full attention. I signaled Willard, who moved to the doorway separating the bar from the back room. Juwad remained on his stool as I stood up.

"Goodbye," I said to Aura.

"If Bilal sees you again," she said, delicately turning the seal to close the tube, "I don't know how he'll react."

"Then convince him to leave town," I said. "For your kids' sake, if not yours."

She nodded, as if she'd already thought of that. "Yes. I want to be gone. Tonight."

Willard and I walked through the bar to a utility hall that led to the alley behind the hotel. His Continental waited there, its engine idling, with Elana at the wheel.

"All good?" she said as we climbed in.

"Not all bad," I said. Elana hit the gas, and we were out of the alley before I took another breath.

CHAPTER THIRTY-ONE

I DIDN'T TAKE AURA'S WORD, of course. Willard and I took opposite corners of the block to watch the hotel entrance, Willard from the comfortable driver's seat of his car, and me from an apartment-block entryway that did little to block an adamant wind that smelled of impending ice sheer and car exhaust fumes.

Within half an hour, Bilal Nath's lunar blue Mercedes returned to the hotel roundabout. The vehicle bounced an extra inch as it nudged the curb, its suspension tested by all that hired muscle inside. Bilal's men quickly disembarked before Nath himself appeared from the rear seat. With his thin frame and cowl of dark hair, he looked like a chess-set bishop surrounded by bricks.

My phone buzzed. I didn't have to look to know who was calling.

"Ondine," I said.

"I imagine you already know that Nath has left the meeting place," she said. Her voice so calm, like the drop in air pressure just before a tornado hits.

"Yeah," I said. The rear guard of Bilal's host vanished into the lobby, leaving the SUV to the scurrying valet.

"Explain yourself."

"I'll cut to the finish. Aura Nath and I have reached an agreement. She and Bilal will be leaving town."

"With what guarantee of your safety?"

"That's my business. I've got everything I require. So will you, if we can cooperate."

"Meaning?"

"Insider trading must seem like small potatoes to a guy like Bilal. I wouldn't have thought you needed the dough."

Ondine's silence stretched long enough to read a page of hexes.

"What is your intention?" she said.

"I don't really give a crap about your stock market dabbling. Leave Dr. Claybeck out of any future business, and we can forget the whole thing."

Listening over the wind, I could almost hear the gears gnashing as Ondine pieced together how I could have met Paula Claybeck.

"You go too far," she said.

"Come on. Of all the things I might demand, this is easy."

"I'll be forced to take your word on it, I suppose?"

"So long as I stay hale and hearty, no one will ever know. And think how great it will be to never hear from Bilal Nath again."

"If I were truly fortunate, that would extend to you as well."

"We can dream," I said, and hung up.

I'd let Hollis tell Dr. Claybeck the good news. A token of his affection.

Shit, it was Friday. I was supposed to meet Wren tonight. She'd sent a text earlier this morning. I'd seen it but had been focused on Bilal and the warehouse.

8 o'clock @ Clifford's in SODO okay?

I replied with an apology that it had taken me so long and, yes, I'd meet her there.

Two hours later, as the wind worked on freezing my nose shut, the valet brought Bilal's SUV back. Only two of the blocky goons flanked Bilal and Aura this time, with Juwad taking the driver's seat.

The goons carried suitcases. Aura carried a black leather Gladstone bag, cradled under one arm. I could guess what was inside.

Saleem brought up the rear. He walked past the Mercedes and stopped to scan the street beyond the Neapolitan's gate. I knew I was invisible in the sheltered entryway, but it still felt as though his furious gaze paused on me for a moment. Did he suspect I'd be watching? A deep violet bruise marred the side of Saleem's face where I'd struck him. After another moment, he turned on his heel and stalked back to the car.

Within a minute they pulled away from the hotel. I called Willard.

"I'm on them," he said.

"Boeing Field," I said. "I'll bet a buck on it."

If I'd successfully convinced Aura to leave us alone. And if she had convinced Bilal. That was the trickier part. I wished we'd had time to bug their room. Having a fly on that particular wall might have helped me relax.

No point in continuing to freeze my ass off. I walked up Madison and found a pizza place that served lunch to the neighboring office workers locking its doors for the evening. A twenty convinced them to give me an unclaimed white pie and a bottle of Peroni lager to go. Not wanting to wait, I ate the warmish slices across the street in the partial shelter of a bus stop.

A scarlet sign on the building wall above the pizza place directed emergency vehicles to go around the block to access the E.R. at Virginia Mason.

That's where she died, a voice told me.

Moira. I hadn't even known that memory was in my skull. But there it was, as unyielding as any foundation block. After she'd been run over by the car downtown, the ambulance had taken her to the Mason E.R. Where the daycare worker had taken me. Where I got my earliest firm recollection of Dono, as he told me as plainly as he could manage that my mother, his daughter, was gone.

Willard called back. I tossed the remaining pizza and the unopened beer in the trash.

"I owe you a buck," Willard said. "Bilal just took the exit to BFI. The guy must have some pull to charter a flight this fast."

"He was prepared to leave tonight, no matter how it went down."

"I'll hang around until I'm sure he's gone."

"Thanks. Hey. You never knew Moira, right? My mother?"

There was a silence, which didn't prevent Willard's puzzlement from coming through loud and clear. "Naw. I started working with Dono not long after you were born, but I never met your mom. Hollis said something the other day about you tracing your roots."

"Did Dono ever mention what Moira did after she left high school? Besides raising me?"

"Dono never mentioned shit. He wasn't the kind for small talk, unless he was soused, and I hardly ever had tickets for that show. I remember we had some extra cash after one of our first scores together. He asked me to drop an envelope with some paperwork and a few bills off at a school on my way home. I think that was for Moira."

"What school?"

"Hell, Central? I don't know. One of the college buildings by Broadway. There was a woman's name on the envelope, but don't even try asking me what it was. Maybe just one of Dono's girlfriends."

Maybe.

"Thanks," I said. "I'll talk to you tomorrow."

"Keep your head on straight. Sure as shit this ain't over."

My apartment was a twenty-minute walk from the Neapolitan. I used every step of it to shake off the unpleasant energy that was powering me now. A combination of leftover adrenaline, too much stress during the past days, and the frustration of crossing paths twice with Sean Burke, both times with guns involved. I needed a shower and a catnap and food with some actual nutrition.

A mile later I caught myself grinning. I'd realized my jittery feelings weren't stemming completely from bad soil.

I was excited to go meet a girl. For the first time since Luce. Was it really that simple?

CHAPTER THIRTY-TWO

I FOUND MY WAY TO Clifford's Brewing Company without needing to check the address. South of the stadiums, near Holgate Street and the loose row of cannabis shops on the avenue competing for who could offer the widest variety of edibles. I'd driven past the brewery's neon orange sign with its yellow flames dancing where the apostrophe would be at least a dozen times but had never been inside.

Most of the weed purveyors were open late, their green crosses ablaze as if warding off Clifford's devilish fire. I left the Barracuda in an empty lot of a wholesale food distributor a block away and jogged toward the flames.

Friday night had the bar packed shoulder-to-shoulder, including the people smoking on the sidewalk. I bobbed and weaved through the door and went looking for Wren Marchand. It took a while, shuffling through the throng without knocking anyone's drink out of their hands or getting overly familiar. One girl in a sundress—maybe she'd planned for the crushing humidity in the crowd— laughed and raised her longneck bottle over her head to let me by. We about brushed noses as I edged past, and she winked.

Life was famine or feast. I seemed to be on the verge of the better half.

I'd just about completed my circuit when a combined shout of voices rolled out from somewhere beyond what I had thought was the back of the bar. Loud enough to carry over the freight-engine rumble of a hundred conversations. I changed direction, knowing somehow that Wren would be where the action was.

Halfway down a short hallway—also packed, here with people waiting for a restroom—I heard the THUMP of something very solid striking wood. The crowd in the room ahead groaned, but all I could make out were more people. I pressed closer. The throng shifted, and I saw what I was missing.

At the right side of the room, tall sheets of plywood lined the wall, each sheet painted with a classic target in blue, red, and yellow concentric circles. An instant later a short axe sailed through the air, landing with a THOCK this time as the blade hit properly and stuck. The audience whooped encouragement.

In another moment the mass of spectators undulated like an amoeba, and my guess was confirmed. Wren, grinning and holding a silver-bladed hatchet aloft like the cover of a fantasy novel, if warrior women wore black jeans and T-shirts advertising Cubana Perfecto cigars.

Her opponent looked much more the stereotype to wield an axe, in short-sleeved plaid flannel tight over his biceps and a full beard cut square at the bottom. A paisley handkerchief had been tied around his head as a blindfold.

Wren grasped his shoulders to turn him toward the target and handed him the hatchet. I couldn't say the crowd exactly hushed, but the din at least hit a lower register. The lumberjack drew back his arm and threw in a practiced, almost casual motion. His blade spun twice and hit home between the yellow center and the red stripe. The resultant roar caused beverages to slop from every glass.

The end of the match, it seemed. A Clifford's employee in his safety-orange polo began to collect the axes into a large bucket. Spectators drifted back toward the main room, and I found myself swimming upstream just to stay in place. In another minute I could make headway toward Wren and a circle of friends, still at the throwing line.

"You made it," Wren said.

"I'd have been here sooner but I didn't bring a bulldozer," I said, matching her volume to hear myself.

"This is Ulf." She squeezed the arm of the bearded axeman, who took the bucket of hatchets. "And Sara, Estrid, and Bo."

Bo arrived carrying two pints of ale, with another Clifford's staff member behind him toting four more. They began passing them out. I wound up with one somehow.

Ulf was selecting specific axes from the bucket, examining their edges for nicks before slipping the weapons into a leather carrying case. "Beer," he said. "Finally."

"'Drink and throw, lose a toe,'" Estrid said at my questioning look. "They don't serve until we're done."

"And done I am, beautiful people," said Wren, draping a leather jacket over her shoulders. "Thanks for the game." She toasted the group with her pint with one hand and took me lightly by the wrist with the other.

We snaked our way to a heavy wooden door, beyond which was a large enclosed patio handling overflow from the bar. Less crowded than the inside, thanks to the nighttime temperature, which threatened a frost before midnight. Wren set her pint on a flat plank railing to don her jacket. The heat lamps Clifford's had set on the patio kept the immediate surroundings thawed but a long way from warm.

"Hell of a show," I said.

"You caught me on a good night. I'm still getting the hang of it."

"Is it a league, like with roller derby?"

"Just with friends. I stumbled into it one night. Since my date was already throwing, I wanted to try it for myself."

"You and Ulf?"

"Me and Estrid. For a while." She gave me an assessing look. "I see who I want to see, and I don't apologize. Anyone I like. You cool with that?"

"Works for me."

"Okay. I'm glad."

"And I'm glad it's not Ulf. Never cross a guy who brings his own axe."

She laughed. We touched glasses.

"I don't know what you do," I said, "besides crush every sport you try."

"I'm an herbalist."

"That's . . . plants as medicine?"

"Botany, right. Everything from digestion to chronic pain relief. I have some private clients and classes now, but my friend Lettie and I are working on opening an online shop. It's the clinical part I really enjoy. Like with pharmaceuticals, you have to understand someone's history to consider what treatment might work for them, and know what drugs they might already be taking. You have to work with modern medicine, not against it."

"You like your job."

She shot me that self-aware grin. "I'm talking a lot, huh? It stokes me. We share a plot of land up in Skykomish where I grow what I can in this climate. I'll make the cures and consult with the patients, and Lettie will handle the inventory."

"I've used some of those remedies before. Addy has them. Calming essence drops, under the tongue when I don't want to knock myself out with trazodone or something like that."

"Do you have trouble sleeping?"

Not at all. But I couldn't explain to Wren why.

"Not as often anymore," I said.

"Can I ask something personal?"

"About my face?"

She dipped her chin, not quite daring a nod.

"It happened during my first deployment with the Rangers. Rock shrapnel off an RPG—a grenade—blowing up near us."

"Your first deployment? You had more after?"

"Lots. I was in the Army for ten years. Our rotations were usually around four months long each time. It adds up."

"How old were you?" Wren said, not to be deflected.

"Twenty."

"God. That's so young. I knew the wound must have happened when you were an adult, but I just assumed it was the reason you left the Army. Childhood scars look different. See?"

She turned around and pulled up her jacket and shirt to show me the small of her back. A slim pinkish line traced the soft humps of her lower vertebrae, vertically from her pelvis halfway to her shoulder blades. The scar was slightly wider at the middle, with tiny white notches every inch or so along the edges. On my pale Irish skin the line would have barely made an impression, but Wren's richer complexion gave it contrast.

"Spinal surgery, when I was eleven," she explained, "to correct a defect in my discs."

"That must have been terrifying as a kid."

"Yes. But it was very painful before, living with the condition. I was old enough to understand why I needed the operation. And that it wouldn't be a magic cure. Even if the surgery helped, it might not help forever. They fused three of the bones together back there. The recovery period was awful. Then it got better."

"Does it hurt now?"

"No, not at all. And every day I get up and I use my body. While it lasts." Wren smiled. It wasn't a rueful smile at all. She'd found honest joy in the reprieve.

Wren touched the lowest scar, the thin line along my jawbone. "Do you feel yours?"

"The opposite. My face is slightly numb on those

spots." I tapped my bisected eyebrow and the Y-shaped furrows at my cheekbone. "They filled in some of the bone and my back teeth with Bioglass. I can't grow a decent beard anymore."

"You're joking. How long were you in the hospital?"

"A week or two in country. Then they sent me to Italy for more cosmetic surgery. I rotated back to my platoon after a couple of months."

"So fast. And you were barely out of your teens. It's horrible."

"I wanted to get back to work. Waiting around was driving me batshit."

"No, I understand that part. Having to take control. To do something for yourself. I meant it was horrible being so young and having such—" She stopped herself. "How did you feel then?"

I took a moment to find the words. It had been almost the full ten years since I'd spoken out loud about that time after my injury, and I'd only said anything then because the Army made wounded soldiers jump through psych hoops before they would cut you loose. We all knew what to tell them. Feeling good, feeling strong, ready to go, Doc.

Which wasn't at all what I had really felt. Not since that first look in the mirror, once the doctor was done slathering me with caveats like *This will look much better once the swelling's down*, and *There's more we can do once your natural bone bonds to the new materials.* He'd finally removed the bandages and allowed me to see for myself.

A horrid puffed mass of purple and pink and black covered the left side of my face. So swollen that I could make out those livid colors at the corner of my eye without needing the mirror. Dozens of individual stitches protruded like tiny spines from a deep-sea creature. And an awful hollowness beneath it all, my face unable to feel, or refusing to accept, the alien material under the shredded flesh.

"I felt like a door had been slammed," I said to Wren. "Like normal life wasn't ever going to happen for me. So I might as well throw myself into my job."

"You couldn't be a regular person again. Because of your face."

I nodded. "I avoided mirrors. For a year or two, what I was seeing wasn't what I was seeing. Even after I'd healed, if that makes any sense."

"Body dysmorphia. Like what anorexics have, seeing themselves as fat no matter how thin they've become."

"Yeah. How was it for you? You were just a kid."

She shifted closer, tucking her head against the chill breeze. "I wouldn't show my back to anyone, all during school. I'd change shirts in the bathroom stalls if I had to, and I was late for P.E. all the time. It wasn't until I was in college that I dared to wear a bikini to go swimming. No one said a thing. And after a while I stopped being so self-conscious. But you"—Wren frowned—"you couldn't hide at all."

"Overseas, it didn't matter. There were plenty of other casualties around, some a lot worse than mine. Guys missing limbs and still doing their part. My Ranger buddies would maybe crack a joke. Happy it didn't happen to them, yeah, but so long as I could do the job, no one gave a shit."

"Acceptance." She tilted her head, considering. "You

couldn't stay overseas forever. What happened when they sent you home on vacation?"

"Leave," I corrected automatically. "Our battalion would deploy, rotate home for weeks of rest and training, and then do it again. So I didn't have to spend long stretches of time stateside. I usually hung around the barracks. Bachelor enlisted guys live on base."

"My brother lived at the bars near Pendleton." Wren laughed. "You can't tell me you never went out. Never wanted a girl."

I smiled. "I gave it a shot. I'd go drinking with my team, looking to hook up like anybody else. But . . . I could feel eyes on me. Whether people were really staring or not. After two beers, I'd make some excuse and head home."

"I'm sorry."

"That was a long time ago."

"You got over it eventually." She looked at me through her dark lashes. "I trust."

"Yes."

"How? A girlfriend?"

"Now, that's really getting personal."

Wren laughed. "I'll trade you secrets, then. Ask me anything you want. And just to be up front, I'm not going to bed with you tonight."

"No?"

"No. So whatever you tell me, you don't have to worry about it ruining your chances. Or that I won't see you again."

"You first?" She smirked agreement. I thought about it for a minute, my fingers prickling around the cold pint. "Okay. What are you most afraid of?"

Wren leaned back against the rail. "Here I was sure you were going to ask me a sex question."

"That would be too easy for you."

"You're right." She folded her arms. "I'm scared of playing things too safe. Of never knowing what's around the corner, because I didn't dare see it for myself. You know the Kipling book, with the mongoose and the cobras? There's a line from that: *The motto of all the mongoose family is, 'Run and find out.'* I loved that story."

"So you move around a lot."

"So I move around a lot." Wren nodded. "Your turn, Donovan Shaw. How'd you rejoin impolite society?"

"By seeking professional help."

"That's a cheat. I wasn't talking about your therapy."

"Me, either."

It took her a second. "You . . ."

"Hired a girl. Yeah. It was down to two days before my next deployment and I couldn't face going out to a bar again. I went online. Found a woman in the classifieds and wrote her about me, so she'd know what she was dealing with, wouldn't run away screaming. We met at a hotel a hundred miles from Benning, just to make sure no one I knew would see us."

"And how was it?" Wren looked more entertained than astounded.

"Businesslike. But she was kind. That's what I needed more than anything. It got me—"

"Over the hump."

"I was not going to say that."

"Sure you weren't."

"By the time our battalion rotated back again, I was

more myself. Or at least I cared less what people saw when they looked at me."

Wren raised her glass. "Here's to remedies."

"And understanding. Thanks."

"My pleasure. You want another round?"

I surely did.

CHAPTER THIRTY-THREE

I SPENT PART OF SATURDAY morning on the phone. It took a few calls to track down the person I was looking for, but fewer than I'd imagined. Even with a hundred other options there are still phone books, real and virtual, and plenty of people, especially of an older generation, still have their landlines listed.

My last call was to a retirement home in Mill Creek called Highland Hearth. The receptionist assured me that visitors were more than welcome between the hours of eight and four. I told him I'd be there within the hour. It took me less than half that before I was knocking on the open door of a room on the ground floor.

"Mr. Lindhoff?" I said.

The orderly behind me tapped my elbow. "You have to speak up. Mebbe go there in front of him, so he can see."

I took his advice, pulling the wicker guest chair from beside the narrow bedstead with its safety rails to a place in front of Milt Lindhoff's recliner. His eyes worked from behind his glasses to gain a focus on me. In the thirteen years since I'd seen him the lenses had widened and thickened, as if to balance the thinner, heavily creased face behind it. This close to him, a nostril-stinging smell of analgesic was strong and mixed with a sweeter note, like overripe fruit.

"You're not Louis," he said. His voice was husky, perhaps age or just from dryness. I didn't remember what it had used to sound like.

"I'm not," I said, louder than before. "My name is Van Shaw. I was a student at Watson High."

Lindhoff cleared his throat. Looked out the window of the little room at the path and kidney-shaped patch of lawn with its single crab apple tree, leafless now in winter. Single tree to match the room's single bed, single dresser, single recliner with attached folding tray where Lindhoff could take his meals when he wasn't up to joining the other residents in the dining room. On the walls and tucked up against the mirror on the dresser were paintings of people, all from the shoulders up, all on ten-by-ten prestretched canvases without frames. The paintings weren't sophisticated but were still intriguing. All of the people looked back at you with something like misgiving in their gaze.

"I got a lost quilt back for you once," I said. "You and Ms. Nasgate."

"Della."

"Right. Della." This had been a mistake. Lindhoff was not what he once was. "Sorry to have disturbed you."

"The tough boy," Lindhoff said. "The quiet one."

I eased back onto the thin pillow of the chair. "Do you remember me?"

"Sure. The only kid Harshbarger wouldn't yell at. Little creep was scared'a you."

Harshbarger had been the composition teacher. Short and short-tempered.

"My memory's slow. Not gone," Lindhoff said. "But I can't hear for a damn, son, so don't be afraid to rattle the windows. How'd you find me?"

"Ms. Nasgate's sister. You and Ms. N. got married, I found out."

"Second time for both of us. Ten good years 'fore she passed on."

"I'm sorry."

He waved the sentiment away. "Whatcha here for?"

"My mother, Moira, went to Watson before I did. That would be thirty years ago. Around the time you started."

"Jesus. If you say so. Thirty years ago I could still run marathons."

"Do you remember her at all? Dark hair like mine, very pretty. She was good at English and wanted to go to college before I came along. When I was a student you told me you'd talked to her about community college, and—a friend of mine remembers dropping off what might have been tuition later at Seattle Central." I held out my phone with the image of Moira from the yearbook.

Lindhoff peered at the phone. I wasn't sure if his cataracts allowed him much of a view. His hand, gnarled but clear of liver spots or lesions, worried at where the crease of his pants might have been.

"No," he said finally. "I know the girl you mean. Got pregnant." He waved it off again. "With you, I know. That kind of thing didn't happen so often I wouldn't remember. But I don't know her face. Central, you said?"

"Yeah."

"Then it's Shelly Rudkin you want. Shelly was the rep for the Seattle community colleges, came around to Watson twice every year. Usually stopped for dinner with me and Della. Call Della's sister June back. She'll have Shelly's number in the book."

He motioned for me to comply. I did. June Nasgate, perplexed but willing, looked up the contact information. I copied it down.

"Shelly's a good saleswoman," Lindhoff said once I'd hung up. "I expect if your mom went to Central, they would have had a talk at some point before that."

"Thanks," I said.

"I may not remember her, but I remember you some," he said. "The talk that went around the teachers' lounge about you. Odds on whether you'd wind up in jail before long. Didja?"

"Army," I said. "Right after graduation."

He grunted. "Good. You might be suited to that. Your mother finished her senior year at Watson, is that right? Pregnant and all?"

"Yes."

"Thought so. That kind of thing didn't happen often, girls expecting and staying in school. I already said that." The hand fluttered again and pointed at me. "Hell. That must have been a lot for her to handle. She wouldn't have sacrificed so much if she hadn't thought it worth the fight."

"Guess not."

"That quilt," he said, as if remembering for the first time. "One of Della's projects."

"Yes. My mom had worked on it."

"Della loved those sorts of undertakings. Said people working together to create something good was our highest calling. Art especially. You do any art?"

"Nope. You?" I already had the answer, of course.

"Painting, when the brush'll stay in my hand. I like portraits, but mine never look like the subjects much. Doesn't matter. I just say I'm capturing their inner self, like the brush is possessed or something. Nine times out of ten they buy it." He shook his head. "You believe that? Angels and all that horseshit?"

"Not anymore," I said.

Lindhoff coughed, and it took me a second to realize he was laughing.

"Not anymore. Isn't that the living truth?" he cackled. "Isn't that just true of everything?"

SHELLY RUDKIN STILL WORKED for Seattle Colleges, and she was dedicating her Saturday afternoon preparing for the new quarter starting the next week. She told me over the phone that if I could make it to her office off Harvard Avenue within the next hour, she would speak with me today. The address was barely two blocks from Bully Betty's. I knew exactly which lights to run to make it there with time to spare.

"Your question put me right into the Wayback Machine," she said once she'd let me into the building and we'd shaken hands. "The high school circuit was my very first job with the district. By the time Moira contacted me a few years later, I had transferred to Admissions. Good timing for her, I must say."

I had to stretch my stride to keep up with Rudkin;

she walked like she was trying to keep pace with her words. She had pale hair and paler skin, but her eyes were nearly as dark as mine, in a face shaped like a generous heart.

"Do you remember Moira?" I said.

"I do. We only spoke a few times, but I processed her application. The school hasn't transferred all our backlog from twenty-five years ago to the new system, but transcripts and student registrations? Those we have. Schools prioritize money and credits. Here we are."

She sidestepped through a shared office crowded by at least one more desk than the room had been intended to hold. Rudkin had stacked copier-paper boxes on her desk to elevate the monitor and keyboard, creating a standing workspace. The absence of a chair gave her another foot of elbow room. I hovered to one side as she typed ferociously with two fingers, then swiveled the monitor to show me. It was Moira's transcript, with columns for dates and course codes and grades and credits earned.

"She completed two quarters and had registered for a third," Rudkin said.

I looked at the span of dates. Moira had died before the spring quarter began. To have something else to think about, I pointed to the list of codes. "What are these classes?"

"The course IDs are out of date, but that one was Intro to Public Policy. And that one in the second quarter is Group Counseling."

"Like what, psychology?"

"Social work. Moira was on a track to eventually earn an MSW. I know because of this."

She scrolled down to show a scanned document. A letter of recommendation, addressed to SCC Admissions, from the director of something called New Road Outreach. It was a lengthy letter. Moira had been volunteering her time, and the NRO director had written two paragraphs about her empathy and aptitude and resilience in dealing with some of the tougher cases in their program.

A program for the children of prison inmates.

Rudkin hummed thoughtfully. "That's unusual. My guess was that Moira was applying for grants for her education, and the letter was to help make her case."

Grants. Maybe Moira hadn't been comfortable having Dono pay her freight. "Do you know these people? New Road?"

"I used to. It's defunct, has been for at least twenty years. A victim of budget cuts and competition for charity and who knows. Their director left for Austin or someplace not long after. New Road served at-risk kids, most of them in foster care or stuck somewhere else in the system. Some in juvenile detention. Or kids just needing counseling with one or more parents incarcerated."

Kids from criminal families.

Just like Moira. Just like me.

"Would you make a copy of these?" I asked. My voice more hushed than I'd expected.

Rudkin spun the monitor back and got to typing. "Normally there would be a formal request and a fee for a transcript, but honestly, who has more right to it than you?"

A printer in the hallway between offices hissed and

buzzed. I followed Rudkin out to take the papers off the tray as they appeared. Each sheet warm from the rollers.

"Hope this was what you were looking for," she said.

I looked at the copy of the letter, sent by a long-shuttered charity on behalf of a woman who had been killed only a few weeks after. Both more and less than what I'd imagined I might find here. An idea of what Moira had wanted to do with her life, and the dead end I'd known would come eventually.

CHAPTER THIRTY-FOUR

IT HAD BEEN A full week since I'd been to work at
Bully Betty's. The crowd placid enough now that the
holidays were over that no one on either side of the bar
was moving at more than half speed. A-Plus granted
me a half-lidded gaze of curiosity at my unexpected appearance, showing off her brilliant blue eye shadow, as
I walked behind the counter to take over the taps and
the menial work.

As my hands got to cleaning, I thought back to what
Milt Lindhoff had told me. That Moira wouldn't have
sacrificed so much if she hadn't thought it worth the
struggle. The *it* being me, her baby boy.

His implication was clear enough: Did you grow into
a person worth everything she gave up?

Those concerns passed the time, going around and
around in my head, until late in the evening, when my
phone rang with a blocked number.

"Shaw?" a man's voice said. I waited. "This is the
guy who met you at the airport lot. Yeah?"

Yeah. I grasped the voice now. Rick Martens, the
ATF Fed. Working very late, apparently.

"I remember," I said.

"Let's meet. It's good news."

Sure it was. "I'm busy."

"No bullshit. This is something you want to hear. I'm on Queen Anne at a place called Uncle C's. You know it?"

A cop bar. "Pass."

He chuckled. "Guess you do know it. Okay, then where?"

Martens's insistence annoyed me. And I had to admit, I couldn't guess what he thought was so urgent that he needed to find me after midnight.

"You know where I work," I said. He probably had my file open in front of him, including Betty's W-2 filing for employee taxes.

"Uh, yeah. Cap Hill, right?" Martens must have transferred to Seattle from another division. I'd never heard anyone call it that.

"I'll be here for another hour."

Out in the main room, a dozen night owls roosted in the booths. Two other birds of undefined gender made out at one of the center tables while their friend went on with their story, seemingly oblivious. The Fed would stand out like a terrier here, and perhaps be just as skittish.

I stuck my head out the door to wake up Mo.

"You'll see a white guy here before long, looking like he just strolled off the driving range."

"Should I hiss at his spikes?"

I grinned. "Just let him in. Even if we're past last call."

Martens made it before that. I'd taken over dishware duties for closing, letting A-Plus finish stocking the stirrers and toothpicks and parasols with hasty dexterity, before gliding away with the entourage that always materialized to greet her when she went off duty. She blew me a kiss, as Martens turned sideways to gawk at the passing bevy of magazine-gloss perfections.

"Holy shit. Who was that?" he said, taking a stool at the counter.

"The most beautiful bartender in Seattle, according to the *Weekly*. And the *Stranger*." Though the *Stranger* had tactfully called A-Plus their "Favorite," probably to avoid accusations of objectification.

"And she's—uh—here?" Martens glanced around at the bar's late-night menagerie and the ceiling beam with its line of human hair braids and ponytails, souvenirs of the old location. I set the tumblers out of the dishwasher in rows to dry overnight. The middle-aged Fed was attracting a few baffled looks himself. Maybe it was the Brooks Brothers tie. So uptight it was almost ironic.

"When I learned you worked at a bar, I was picturing something different," he said. "MGD on tap and MMA on the screen."

"We got a regular here who's seven-and-one in her pro fights, if that's your type." I took a last pull off the bottle of Reuben's Porter I'd been nursing and tossed it into the recycling bucket with a clank.

"Sorry I said it. Can I get a cola? So damn cold outside I need some caffeine to get my blood going." As I drew one from the soda gun, Martens took off his blue jacket and folded it neatly to place it on the counter. "And get yourself whatever you want. On me."

When cops are this polite, start sniffing for the trap.

Mo flicked the lights to signal last call. Quiana at the other end of the bar made a couple of dirty martinis for the lovebirds while a few customers made half-hearted moves toward the exit. Martens fetched a paper napkin from the rack A-Plus had just filled. There was no one within hearing range of us.

I finished with the dishware and poured myself a healthy shot of Redbreast. "Once this is empty, I'm gone."

"Fine, fine. Here's what it's about: Podraski and I pulled you in the other day because you were spotted in Bitter Lake." He held up a hand. "I won't rehash our debate from the other day, I promise. But can we at least agree that Podraski and I were *told* that you were seen? Whether or not it was really you?"

I waited.

"So let's build on that," Martens continued. "Let's say that if someone was in Bitter Lake that night, breaking into a particular house, then perhaps that wasn't a random burglary. Perhaps this very skilled dude was hired to do that job."

He took a sip of his Coke while looking pointedly at my shot of whiskey. "I don't have to tell you how these things work. We aren't interested in the hired hand in this scenario. We want his boss, the guy at the top. Especially if that boss has a lot of other activities rolling that pique our interest."

"You want a snitch."

The agent's mouth twisted in a rueful frown. "A snitch squeals on everything and everyone, hoping to shake himself loose from jail time. We're looking for a man on the inside. If his information is gold, he might write his own ticket. Immunity from prosecution. Perhaps a few dollars in his pocket, too. You aren't drinking."

I sipped at the shot, taking a few ticks to think about Martens's setup. He followed the progress of my glass all the way back to the counter. My radar pinged Recovering Alcoholic. No one else was so focused on another man's booze.

"What happens when there's enough information to lower the hammer?" I said.

"Then we bring that sucker down. But for our man, he's free and clear. Protection and a new life if he thinks he needs it."

"A hell of a deal," I said.

"All of this hinges on whether our man has the kind of information we need. That's where I'd need some proof."

"What sort?"

"Start with a name. If it's the right name, we're off and running."

I finished my whiskey. How far to pull this thread? I wasn't the hired gun Martens imagined me to be.

But there might be an advantage to his task force thinking I was. At least long enough to confirm once and for all whether Sean Burke was as poisonous as his rep suggested.

"Liashko." I mouthed the word, on the off chance that there was a cell phone recording our talk from Martens's jacket, placed so conveniently between us.

"There we go," Martens said.

"And as far as we go. Until I see the details in writing."

"We will make that happen." Martens pointed. He

scooped his suit coat. "I gotta visit the can, meet you at the door."

I killed the chili-pepper lights and walked around to check that no one had left their belongings in the booths. Quiana let the last straggle of customers out. I bolted the emergency exit at the side for the night. Martens rejoined me at the door.

"I'll call you tomorrow. We're moving fast on this," he said, plunging out into the cold.

I watched him cross the street and hurry to his Acura, hunched against the wind.

Something was seriously warped here. I didn't fully buy Special Agent Martens's offer to make me a confidential informant, out of the blue. Even odder, I was halfway to certain that he didn't believe me when I'd told him I'd take the deal. So why in hell had he come all this way in the dead of night?

I decided to take the truck from its space near Bully Betty's and crash tonight at the marina, in my speedboat. Maybe talking to Hollis in the morning could help me make sense of this. I fetched my coat and said good night.

My long-term parking spot for the Dodge was on Union, serving denizens of new residential buildings that had been built or converted to condominiums on the west side of the hill during the past couple of years. As my truck rattled down the ramp and onto the street, I passed a metallic-green Buick sedan, which had stopped to let a long-limbed dude hop into its backseat.

I'd seen the guy before. This time he was wearing a hat pulled low and had the jacket collar popped to ward off the cold, but it wasn't enough to fully hide his thick shadow of beard stubble. He'd been outside Sean Burke's apartment building two nights before, smoking foreign cigarettes and watching the lobby.

The smoker wasn't alone this time. The Buick pulled out again, a hundred yards behind me. And closing.

CHAPTER THIRTY-FIVE

WHO WERE THESE BASTARDS? Burke's crew? Or working for Liashko himself?

Whoever they were, I wasn't going to let them follow me home. Shaking the Buick would be tough on the nearly empty roads at two in the morning. The grid of one-way streets in downtown might be my best chance. I turned left and at the next intersection jogged one block west to Boren. Not pushing my speed. Not yet. The Buick stayed with me, green paint glittering under the streetlamps. Like a blowfly keen to find a carcass. The Beretta in my pocket made a comforting weight.

They followed me over the freeway and into downtown, drifting southward. I knew of an alley off Columbia that ran for two long blocks. If I could put some extra yards between me and the Buick, I'd veer into the alley without them spotting me and have my choice of half a dozen escape routes at the other end.

I turned down the slope of Columbia. Two intersections away, the stoplight flashed red at 2nd Ave. The Buick drifted confidently behind me, one block back. I looked for a gap in the traffic, ready to run the light and leave them hanging.

A black Taurus launched itself from the curb and past me in an instant, turning sharply to block my path. I jogged right by reflex. The truck's grill slid off the Taurus's fender with an agonized scrape.

My engine sputtered and nearly stalled. The gas pedal felt as soft as butter. I downshifted and managed to keep the old Dodge moving, down the hill, more coasting than driving. Men were out of the Taurus now. Running to catch up. The truck's engine finally gulped fuel and the Dodge lunged forward.

The green Buick roared past me, trying to cut off my escape. I turned hard left and nearly brained myself on the ceiling as the truck bounded onto the sidewalk, then swung right again before I crashed into the building. The truck flew off the curb, screaming across 2nd, the Buick roaring after me through a blare of frightened car horns.

The black Taurus caught up to me on my left side, the Buick now on the right. I couldn't outrun them in the old Dodge.

And ahead, a nightmare: Columbia Street closed to all traffic by a chain-link fence, readying for the viaduct demolition. If I stopped I was dead.

I swung the wheel right. The side of the truck banged off the green Buick, once, twice, but the heavy car barely moved.

I was out of road. All the way out.

A chained gate blocked the on-ramp to the viaduct. The Dodge crashed through, sending the gate half off its hinges and links of chain flying like fastballs. I shifted again and the truck howled in protest as it tore up the ramp. Behind me, a screech and a low crunch of impact as the Taurus slammed into a solid plastic barrier at the side of the gate.

The truck climbed, so slowly that I yelled at it out loud. Headlights in the rearview. They were coming.

The on-ramp curved left to become the lower level of the abandoned highway, the southbound lanes. Demolition had already begun. I swung the wheel to avoid a pile of concrete rubble torn from the lanes above and left in pieces on this level for salvage teams to cart away.

Another heap of debris ahead, a larger one. The truck bounced as I hit a loose chunk of old asphalt. Moonlight streamed through missing portions of the upper level, where tearing down the guardrails had also demolished huge shark bites of the pavement underneath.

At the other end of the viaduct, a mile south, there must be another gate. A way out. The headlights of the Buick were closer now, the faster car eating up the distance despite the ragged road.

I'd picked the wrong instant to check the rearview. The truck struck another chunk of highway and the wheel spun. Only stomping on the brake kept me from hitting the guardrail. I sped forward again, but the Buick was right on top of me.

Ahead, just coming into full view in my headlights, a short wall of smashed concrete and twisted rebar blocked the entire road.

No way around. No way over. The truck could never climb that crumbling, spiky mass, not even with all four wheels churning.

I could make it on foot. I swung right to put the truck between me and the Buick. As I slammed the brake, the

Beretta skidded from the seat where it had jostled from my pocket during the havoc and onto the floor of the truck. I unclipped my seatbelt to reach for it.

A bullet shattered the passenger window, making me flinch from the flying shards. A second round punctured the door. I ducked and rolled away from the barrage, falling out of the truck to land next to the wall of destroyed highway.

Shouts in what might be Russian or Ukrainian followed me as I half ran, half crawled up and over the bank of rubble, loose hunks tumbling and crumbling under my feet. One chunk tipped over, threatening to crush my ankle beneath it. I sprung away and fell to my hands and knees on the other side of the wreckage.

Demolition of the highway was further along in this section. The road in front of me had become more a collection of huge mounds of cracked pavement than any kind of passable route. The night sky showed in patches ahead. I was up and running, even as I heard another pistol shot and more shouts from behind.

The mounds of concrete would offer some cover. How many men would be chasing me? Four, maybe five. Too many to fight even if I still had the Beretta. I'd have to run for it, all the way to the far end. Pray none of these thugs were competitive marathoners when they weren't busy killing people for Burke and Liashko.

No, I realized as I sprinted. Running was no good. There was no way to get off the viaduct until it ended all the way down near the stadium. Too far away, too many minutes to get there. They would send half their team with the car to head me off at the other gate. Maybe they already had.

I was boxed in, just as surely as a bull in a slaughter-house chute.

Continuing to run would just exhaust my energy. Already my breath was tight in my chest, lactic acid building in my legs, the adrenal rush from the ambush having peaked. I needed a place to hide. Get a second wind. Attack with surprise and take a weapon from one of their crew.

There. A taller pile of rubble than most, broken sections of roadside barrier heaped on their sides against one another, forming a crude low pyramid. I looked behind me to make sure none of my pursuers were in sight before I ducked behind the pile.

I concentrated on slowing my breath. To ready myself for a fight, and so that I might hear something more than the pounding of my own heart. I peered between the leaning chunks of crumbled pavement to watch the road. Dust of decades-old cement filled my nose, as powdery as clouds from a chalkboard.

They came at a fast walk. Two of them, one on either side of the four-lane highway. Both with hand-guns. Scuttling like spiders from mound to mound and avoiding the brighter spots of moonlit road. Searching. Maybe they'd found the Beretta and were more confident that I was unarmed. They circled each mound separately to flank anyone on the other side. Like me.

I felt strangely calm. The part of my mind that emotionlessly calculated tactical options narrowed that list to one and ordered the rest of me to get on with it.

I reached down to pick up a heart-sized chunk of rubble. With melting slowness, I made myself as flat as I could at the base of the outer side of the pyramid, near the guardrail, one leg coiled underneath.

The two men were moving too fast to be silent. Each footfall made a distinct scrape on the pebble-strewn pavement. Twenty yards away now, checking the nearest mound of debris. Coming toward mine.

They would move together around the pyramid where I lay. I listened as each rustling step closed the distance.

A shoe landed three feet from my head. I sprung up, half blindly swinging the chunk of rubble in my fist with all my force to where his head should be. It nearly missed, striking the man high on his skull, tearing the fabric of his hood. He went sideways with a cry of pain and terror, almost leaping away in his panic. Away from me, and over the rail. He vanished.

A second cry then, shorter and ending cruelly. There was surely a sound when he hit the street thirty feet below, but it did not carry.

The other man shouted, "Stop!" behind me. Any instant now his bullets would rip through me, turning my heart and lungs into so much paste.

They didn't come. I turned. The lean dude with the midnight stubble stood twelve feet away, his face a sweated mask of hate.

"You. Down," he said, in heavily accented English.

I stayed where I was. Might as well die on my feet.

"Down."

I waited. He didn't move, either. Maybe too smart to get close.

Our little contest of wills didn't last. A single headlight appeared to the south, weaving between the piles of debris. Their team had come through the gate at the far end. The Taurus stopped, its lone beam illuminating my angry foe and me, the other headlight and a good portion of the front grill crumpled by whatever the car had struck earlier.

Three men scrambled from the car. All of them drawing guns, training them on me.

A fourth emerged from the passenger's seat. I didn't need the moonlight to recognize his dark visage immediately.

Sean Burke.

He looked at me. The killer with the permanent five o'clock shadow said something to him in Russian. Burke walked to the rail and looked down at the body of his soldier on the street below.

"Take him," Burke said. His man stepped forward to whip a leather sap I hadn't seen across my forehead.

He got his wish. I went down, all the way. The last that any of my senses registered was a scouring rasp of grit against my cheek, and the strange sweet taste of powder from ammunition.

CHAPTER THIRTY-SIX

I WOKE TO A SHRIEK of metal against metal. Far enough into consciousness that I felt the brush of fabric shrouding my head. Hands grabbed me, lifted me out of a car—the clunk of the door closing, a thousand miles off—and the toe of my boot scraping dirt as they dragged me along.

But I wasn't truly alert until they threw me onto a table. Its surface frigid and so hard that the tap of my wristbone against it sent a crackle of pain up to my elbow. My bound elbow. My arms and hands were stuck tight to my sides. The stutter of duct tape coming off a roll snapped me to full attention.

And brought the first wave of panic. I bit down on the rag that filled my mouth, stifling an instinctive cry of alarm. Where had they taken me? A more frightening question followed close on that thought: Why wasn't I dead yet?

The cloth bag over my head was infused with the sickly powder I'd tasted before blacking out. Powder from pistols, recently fired. The scent had filled my nose past the point of smelling it directly, to where I felt it like a physical mass in my forehead, pressing back against the ache of where I'd been sapped.

A metal toolbox clanged down on the table by my ear. I tried moving my feet, without success. More tape at my ankles. Another pressure now, over my thighs, tightened until my quadricep muscles were crushed against bone. They were strapping me down. I sat up, lunging against the bindings. Futile. A hand gripped my throat and shoved me down so abruptly that my head bounced off the steel surface of the table. Before the impact stopped shooting sparks into my brain, they had me immobilized.

Then came a ratcheting click. My feet rose, my head lowered. I yelled into the gag, a rasping caw barely audible above the machine sound. The table stopped halfway to vertical. Halfway to upside-down, my blood pounding my head from the inside.

Someone pulled the bag off. I turned to see the tip-tilted world.

Two men in twill workpants and zip-front athletic jackets pushed at a heavy rolling door, closing it. The squeal of tortured metal returned as the door's wheels ground against their track. A visible square of night narrowed quickly to a sliver and was gone with a bang.

Someone behind me swore in English. The lean killer with the heavy stubble came around where I could see him. He glared and yanked the rag from my mouth before walking away.

The room was large, maybe twenty feet by more, depending on how far it went back behind me. Even craning my head, I couldn't make out the far end of the room in my peripheral. Wooden rafters, high overhead, and a sloped roof like a barn. A floor of poured concrete.

And a huge vat behind and to my left, pipes running from the vat into the wall. An acrid reek wafted from its direction, sharp enough to carve away the last of the powder smell.

Think, Shaw. Two exits, one beside the rolling door and one to my left. No windows. I might have seen a flash of the green Buick before they'd closed the rolling door. If I could get free . . . They had removed my jacket and pullover, leaving only my T-shirt. Was my multitool with its blade still in the pocket of my jeans? I squirmed, trying to press my hip against my arm to feel it.

The door to the outside opened and Burke walked in, another man with him. That made five. Burke was more sharply dressed than his thugs, in an ash-gray suit and black shirt.

"Stepan. Have you called it in?" he said to the man with the stubble.

"No."

"I'll do it. Don't start on him until I return. Anatoly may want to hear what this punk has to say, straight from the rat's mouth."

Stepan nodded assent. Burke motioned to two of the other men and the three of them left through the side door, to what I perceived was deeper into the interior.

When Burke was gone, Stepan exhaled minutely. Burke's reputation must have extended across both sides of the Pacific.

"Scared?" I said.

Stepan said something I assumed was another curse. "No one here is frightened of you."

"But you're not all here, are you? At least one missing."

He glared balefully at me. Maybe deciding whether to cut my throat and be done with it. Instead he walked away to a table against the wall. I had to work to focus, the upside-down angle messing with my eyes.

Stepan's partner, a gangly man with a hoop earring in his right lobe, watched him and grinned. When Stepan returned he carried what looked like a gallon paint can. He set the can down close to my head. A puff of the bitter fumes I'd smelled before seared my nostrils.

"Gennady was a good boy," Stepan said. "Very excited about visiting America. His first time."

"A hunting trip."

"You joke. This is not funny."

"So do something about it. Cut me loose, and you and your buddy can beat the shit out of me like real men. If you've got any guts, even two against one."

"Not funny yet," he clarified, waving a finger and then drawing a circle in the air to indicate the room. "Burke tells us about this place. Where he makes people go away. Even policemen."

Guerin had told me about the ATF agent who'd disappeared while working undercover on Liashko. Marcus Santora. This had been his last stop.

"Look." Stepan drew something from his chest pocket to show me. An eyedropper. His hand dipped to the can and returned, the dropper held delicately between thumb and forefinger.

The open tip of the eyedropper showed a trace of milk-white fluid. A fresh reek rose from the disturbed can.

Some kind of lye compound, I guessed. Sodium hydroxide or a similar mix. Readily available and incredibly corrosive, especially when heated.

"Very bad," Stepan said, turning the dropper to make sure I would see the caustic liquid. "And much more, there." He pointed at the huge steel pressure vat.

That would be for later. To dispose of my body, after they'd wrung me dry.

"Starting before your boss gets here. Not smart," I said, the words threatening to catch in my throat.

"For Gennady," he said. He gripped my hair and jerked my head backward. My neck strained to pull away, to thrash, but I had no leverage.

I had a perfect view of the eyedropper, three inches from my eye. The rounded edge of the first pearlescent drop expanded, grew fat.

It fell onto my cheek. For a moment nothing changed. I had an instant's relief that they had gotten the mixture wrong, or that this had been some psych game to see if I broke down immediately.

Then the heat rose, shockingly fast. Like the red tip of a cigarette touched to my skin, but far from being smothered, the fire only increased with each second. My breath hissed through my teeth. The room went watery, tears rising as my body sought any way to expel the torment.

Another drop fell, adding to the first, the trickle now running up toward my clenched eye. My neck muscles strained to move, only succeeding in shivering and making the trickle run faster.

Stepan released my head. I shook violently, trying to throw any remaining lye away before it reached my eyelid. Beads of sweat popped from my scalp.

"Hold it." Burke's voice.

I blinked the water from my eyes as Burke and Stepan had a short, angry conversation in Russian. It ended with Stepan marching away to join his friend at the worktable, heels of his boots communicating fury with every step.

"I told you to stay the fuck away," Burke said to me. From upside down, his form looked monolithic against the barn ceiling.

"Message received," I said. "Let me walk and I'm gone."

He didn't bother to answer. Instead he leaned in to study the chemical burn on my cheek.

"Stepan doesn't think ahead," Burke said. "Normally, the face is where to start if we just want one piece of information. Melt a guy's nose off, fry one of his eyes, and the fear does half the work for you. But—" He shrugged. "Terror scrambles people's brains. They can't piece thoughts together and tell you anything complicated. And your face is pretty fucked up already. I'm surprised you can even feel much through that scar tissue."

If what I'd felt had been blunted, I couldn't imagine what the full treatment would be like.

"Just put a bullet in my head," I said. "There's nothing I know that you want your buddies to hear."

Burke moved to the center of the table to begin turning a crank. The table tilted back to horizontal and continued, my head rising.

"If Stepan had any sense he'd know it's better to start slow," Burke said. "With the feet."

He said something in Russian to Stepan and the other man. Stepan walked over to the wall of the room and began to uncoil a thick green hose from a reel on the wall. The man with the earring brought a deep steel tray and set it down on the floor under my boots before jogging to help Stepan.

Burke continued his lecture. "Not just leaving the victim's feet in the mix. That's for shit. Once a few drops of this gets into your blood, that's it—dead within minutes. No, you have to hose the feet down between dunks. The water helps activate the solution. Makes it even more corrosive. Painful, yeah, but it's seeing it work that makes magic happen. Nobody alive can stay quiet while they're watching their own feet drip off the bone."

I spoke under my breath: "If I talk, they'll know why I found you."

Burke gestured: *So what?*

"Even if you really were my kid," he said, "nothing I can do about it now."

Stepan and his buddy dragged the water hose close while his partner took out a paper painter's mask and pair of latex gloves. Burke didn't move to put them on.

"His shoes," Burke said, pointing. Stepan sneered, maybe at me, maybe at Burke, and knelt to start unlacing my boots. Burke said something in Russian, and the second man dropped the hose and picked up the roll of duct tape from the floor. He stepped behind me and began to unstrip the tape, winding a length around my shins to completely bind them to the table. There would be no thrashing and tipping over the tray during what was to follow.

Stepan pulled off one boot and looked up at me.

"After the feet we do your hands," he said. "Glug glug." His friend with the earring laughed as he came around in front to wind another loop over me.

Burke shot him in the back of the head. He fell forward, onto my legs.

Stepan turned at the sharp pop of the suppressed explosion. I saw his left eye widen in shock even as Burke's second round shattered his skull. A spray of blood and pieces more solid than blood blinded me. Hot in my mouth. I spat, reflexively.

"Hold still," Burke said, stopping me from trying to wipe my face with my shoulder.

I heard the whispery clink of a gravity blade and felt tension on the tape at my wrists as Burke sliced through it. I raised my hands to scrape the gore from my brow. I could see again. Stepan's blood was already growing sticky. I felt it thick on my lids with every blink.

Burke bent over the two bodies, checking. Stepan's leg twitched, but neither man would move again on their own.

"Why?" I croaked, my throat impossibly dry.

"I only had two bullets left," Burke said.

Not the question I was asking. He didn't elaborate, just resumed cutting me loose. The instant my ankles were free I stood up, tearing at the remaining tape, not waiting for him to finish. I wanted off that fucking table.

Burke crossed the room to a panel of gauges on the wall. I knelt to grab the hose. A spray nozzle at its end controlled the flow. I pulled the trigger and stuck my head under the gushing water. Through the splashing I made out the rhythmic clangs of Burke climbing a set of metal steps to the top of the vat.

By the time I was satisfied that the last of Stepan had been sluiced off me, he'd returned and was going through the pockets of the dead men, collecting their belongings in the same bag that had hooded me.

"Another ten minutes and the mix will be hot enough," he said.

"What are we doing?" I retrieved my boot that Stepan had removed.

"What does it look like? Getting rid of these assholes." He jabbed a thumb at the vat. "It's already heated up. For you. Twenty, thirty hours in there and these boys will be goop."

I started to protest, and then my brain caught up to reality. We sure as hell weren't going to call the cops and try to explain what had happened. Stepan and his buddy were dead, thanks to Burke.

Killed with what he'd said were his last two rounds. Where had the others gone?

I went to open the interior door. A smaller room lay behind it, an office space with smeared whiteboards and one aged desk in cracked blue plastic and peeling metal. No chairs.

Another door waited, opposite the one I'd just come through. I opened it, knowing what I would find.

The third and fourth men from Stepan's team lay on the smooth concrete floor of an empty two-car garage. Wide blooms of blood stained their running jackets; the chest of one, the spine of the other. The man who was faceup had had time to draw his gun. It lay a few feet from his outstretched hand.

Burke had killed these when he'd stepped out, supposedly to call Anatoly Liashko. He'd arranged for Stepan and the last man to have their backs to him, their hands busy, before he closed the deal on them, too.

He could have taken one of the pistols from the dead men. But maybe he only trusted his own weapon when it really counted. I followed that same rule.

CHAPTER THIRTY-SEVEN

I RETURNED TO THE VAT room. Burke was using his knife to strip Stepan of his clothing.

"What is this place?" I said.

"Private property. The tank here came from a paint factory."

"And you . . . repurposed it."

"Gus did. He wanted a place out of the city nobody knew about, for this kinda work. It took him a couple of years to build. I've kept it up."

Jesus. The question of just how many bodies had found their way into the vat, melting into a caustic slurry, came into my head before I shoved it away. No point to dwelling on it. Not when we were about to add four more to the total.

"Your jacket and blade and shit are over there." Burke nodded to the table. "Cut the clothes off Iosef. The metal zipper and rivets won't break down in the vat. We'll bag 'em."

"What did you tell Liashko? Or did you call him at all?"

He looked up, his expression almost amused.

"You know about Anatoly, huh? Thought so. Maybe

there's more to you dogging me than your little story about lookin' for Daddy." Burke brought his knife up the back of Stepan's shirt, parting the fabric like water.

"Stepan said they flew in this week. To kill me?"

"Don't flatter yourself. If this was just about killin' you, Liashko would have left it to me. Come on."

I helped Burke carry the bodies of the other two men from the empty garage into the main room. We stripped them and stuffed their shredded clothes into a heavy-duty plastic trash sack. All of the Russians' personal effects—passports, phones, wallets, knives, guns—Burke tossed into the bag. He removed the American cash from the wallets first.

Four naked bloody corpses lay in as neat a row as could be expected at the base of the vat. Christ. I inhaled, not caring about the smell of fresh death that was making its first appearance.

"I actually do gotta call Anatoly," Burke said. "He's waiting. Fuck knows what I'm going to tell him."

"Say that I killed them. And you killed me."

"Some shithead burglar killed all four of his boys? All Anatoly knows about you is that you busted into my place. Stepan's no lightweight. Liashko won't buy that story. Not without a news story showing the cops fishing your body out of the harbor."

I looked at the row of dead men. The idea that bloomed in my head was less a flower than a black, poisonous mold.

"What if he saw me for himself?" I said.

"Saw how?"

"If you have to call him." I stripped off my T-shirt. "You can send pictures, too."

"The fuck are you doing?"

He watched as I tossed my boots and socks aside, my jeans and underwear following just as quickly. Getting it over with. I walked barefoot over to Stepan. Burke's bullet had come out through the killer's left-rear skull, taking enough bone and brain along with it to fill a generous ice cream cone. I'd just washed some of it off my face. Now I dipped my fingers back into the gore.

Stepan's blood was cooling but still viscous. I scooped small globs of it onto my chest. Not wiping like paint, just daubing, trying to keep the horrible red as thick as possible. I could feel gritty flecks of bone matter on my fingertips. When I'd taken what I could from Stepan, I moved to Iosef, and then the others, stealing some from each.

Burke stared. I'd learned what it took to sicken a stone killer.

The lumpy red patina extended from the hollow of my throat to my armpit. It dried rapidly against the heat of my body. I shaped the larger blobs as best I could into a rough simulation of an exit wound, as if I'd been shot in the back and the round had exploded out through my breastbone. Trickles of watery pink dripped down my ribs to my groin and thigh. I ignored them, along with the voice in my head shouting to stop. I was busy.

When I'd done what I could, I lay down next to Stepan's body. The floor was cold enough to have made my skin prickle if my hair weren't already standing on end. Stepan's arm and leg felt like a partially deflated inner tube against my own limbs. Rubbery and cool. They warmed horribly against my flesh. I turned my head to one side and forced myself to relax.

"Do I pass for a cadaver?" I said, as much to distract myself as to ask.

"More than you wanna know." Burke stepped forward with his phone held high, to capture the moment. "Hold your breath. And move your arm, it looks too— living."

I half lidded my eyes and let them go out of focus. Burke shot pictures of the full row of bodies, then two of me, closer in. The flash blazed in my peripheral vision.

"Fuck me, that's creepy," Burke said, holding out the phone. I sat up to look.

My body was a shade darker than that of the dead Russians. The difference could be chalked up to genetics. The impressionistic artwork of viscera on my chest looked as violent as any of their fatal wounds. But my face in profile really hit home, the slackness and the rusty flecks around my mouth and neck that I'd missed with the hose. It looked as though my destroyed lungs had coughed out one final bloody breath. A final touch that sold the deception.

That, and my nakedness. The horrible indignity of being stripped and lined up like so many pigs for butchering. Even though that effect had been what I'd been aiming for, that my corpse must be real because no one would subject themselves to that primal disgrace, it still made me feel something close to shame.

I stood up and went to turn on the hose and spray myself clean for a second time.

"I'm calling him," Burke said after I'd rinsed the last of the red from my body. One of the Russians' shirts was clean of blood. I used it to towel off.

"Anatoly," Burke said into the phone. "We have to talk."

During the pause that followed, I gathered my clothes and mimed for Burke to turn up the volume.

"—where we may discuss," Liashko's voice came from the phone as I leaned closer. It was a resonant voice, even made tinny by the digital transformation. Careful enunciation cut through the thicker swaths of his accent. "Where is Stepan?"

"That's why I'm calling," Burke said. "Stepan is dead. So are Gennady and the others. They walked into a trap and that housebreaker you sent them after killed them."

"No." A flat refusal rather than an exclamation of shock. "I spoke to Stepan tonight. He said preparations were ready."

"And where was he going after that?" Burke asked dryly.

Liashko didn't answer.

Burke grunted to emphasize the point. "Gennady called me when they spotted Shaw. All hyper to run him down. When I got there the shooting was already over. Shaw was wounded. I finished him off."

"The police?"

"I got them out before any cops showed," Burke said. "Or most of them: Gennady took a fall and I couldn't reach him. I'm at the barn now. You remember?"

"Yes. Your father's place."

"Here." Burke pressed buttons on his phone. Sending

his boss our impromptu photo shoot. "I have to put them in the vat, Anatoly. I'm sorry."

There was another pause, longer. I imagined Liashko studying the row of naked, grisly bodies, with mine making a kind of exclamation point at the end.

"I must tell Iosef's family," he said finally.

Burke grunted assent. "At least Shaw's dead."

"And who hired this man? This thief?"

"Near as I can tell, Shaw works for himself. The cops held him awhile back on suspicion in a diamond robbery. His grandfather used to pull the same kinda jobs. High-end burglary. And Anatoly," Burke chided, "you've put my name on a lot of those wire transfers under the import business, and had me withdrawing it in cash to grease a lot of palms. Somebody at the bank could be throwing up signals. Maybe alerting a partner like Shaw to check houses where there might be cash around. I've told you that's a risky way to move your money."

Liashko made a rumbling sound. Maybe disagreeing, maybe just chewing on the thought. "The police will investigate Gennady."

"I'll get rid of the traces tonight," Burke said. He glanced at me and walked away. "It's lousy, but we have bigger concerns," I heard before he stepped out of earshot.

I went to the table to gather my things. My wallet and multitool and everything from my pockets, including the Beretta I'd lost at the truck. One of the men must have fumbled the pistol into the rubble on the viaduct; it needed a serious cleaning to remove the grit in its barrel and works.

Burke had left the bag holding the belongings of the four killers on the floor nearby. On impulse, I slipped my hand inside to find the phone with a black enameled case we had taken off Stepan.

He'd said Liashko's team had flown here for more than just killing me. The arms dealer had something brewing in the States. Even with my clothes back on, I was still cold.

After hanging up, Burke stood at the corner of the barn for a moment. Staring at nothing. I pretended to be engrossed in checking the pockets of my jacket.

Was his hand shaking? Fear, or rage?

As if he sensed my attention, Burke stuffed his phone in his pocket and marched to a standing supply cabinet. He returned with two respirators, green masks with twin charcoal filters like stubby white tusks.

"Put this on," he said.

I didn't have to ask why. If I tried, I could still smell the lye residue on my cheek.

Burke had kept the dead men's belts separate when we'd stripped the bodies. He knotted two of them together, then did the same for the second pair. One makeshift leather rope he looped around Iosef's ankles. The other went around his chest. I had to lift the body by the head to allow Burke to fix the belts in place. When he was done, we had two crude handles for the corpse.

Without a word we lifted Iosef and carried his limp form up the stairs one careful step at a time. A thick hinged lid on the roof of the huge vat was held shut by twist handles and sealed with a rubberized gasket. It looked like a windowless porthole. Burke adjusted his mask before turning the handles to open the lid. He stepped back as he did so, letting the first billow of fumes have its space.

I looked at Iosef. "Small opening."

"Gus told me once he had to cut bigger guys up 'fore he put them in the mix."

I was sorry I'd said anything.

Iosef went in feet first, Burke removing the belt strap from around his ankles. I lifted the torso. Burke arranged his hands at his sides, almost delicately, like we were about to lay Iosef to rest in a coffin. But it was simply to allow his upper body to slide smoothly along the rubber gasket.

The surface of the caustic pool was five feet below, the vat only half full of the mixture. Iosef hit with a splash that echoed briefly off the stainless-steel walls.

Disposing of the other three men went faster. We were practiced now. The only hitch was Stepan, the last, whose shoulders caught briefly on the sides of the porthole. Burke held on to the railing and raised his foot to push hard on one shoulder, then the other, and finally on the top of the stubbled, bloody head until the body broke loose.

Stepan didn't make as large a splash as he struck the liquid. *Landed on his friends*, a voice whispered. Burke closed the lid and tightened the handles.

We walked down the stairs. I pulled my respirator off. Burke followed suit. The mask had left his face creased and drenched in sweat. He wiped his forehead on his sleeve.

"Once they're all the way gone, I drain the liquid into drums and bury those a long ways from here," he said. "The vat gets scoured. Floors, too. Nothing any lab could detect."

I hadn't asked. Burke was talking just to release tension, distract himself, whatever. It was my first hint of anything like human emotion from him, apart from anger or mockery.

He grabbed the trash sack of torn clothes and the bag of the Russians' possessions. I retrieved my jacket from the table. My T-shirt, stained with blood and worse, I rolled into a tight ball to carry away and dispose of later. I wouldn't put it with the other men's clothes.

"Why am I still alive?" I said.

"Because I didn't want you dead."

"That's no answer." I looked at the vat. "You've killed plenty, just on Liashko's orders. You've killed cops. I heard about Santora, the ATF agent. Why not me?"

Burke grimaced. "You think it's 'cause I'm your daddy? I already told you that's crap."

"So what's the reason?"

"Fuck off. That's the reason." Spit flew from Burke's mouth. "You owe me, Shaw. I just put my neck out for you. You owe it to me to be dead."

He pointed. "Your truck's outside. Take it and drive until you run out of land. Nobody sees you, hears you, smells you until I say so. I'll let you know when you can play fucking Lazarus. Take it before I change my goddamn mind and burn you down to nothing with the rest of them."

His right hand had drifted behind him. Nearer the holster on his belt. It might just be a reflex.

I left before I found out.

CHAPTER THIRTY-EIGHT

MY SHAMBLING STEPS BROUGHT me to the truck before my higher brain functions reminded me that I had no idea where I was. Or exactly when. It was still nighttime. Gut Burke's barn, his personal abattoir, was the only structure in sight, surrounded by acres of what looked like fallow farmland. To both my left and right, horizons of low black hills marked the borders of a valley.

My fingers fumbled with the phone. Just past five in the morning, and the map placed me in the southern part of Snohomish County. Stepan and his men had driven over an hour from where the luckless Gennady had fallen from the viaduct.

At least they'd brought the Dodge with them. Burke probably had a convenient way of disposing of cars, too.

My truck was missing most of a window and all of the air vent on the passenger's side. A crack the width of my thumb ran through the dashboard like a sideways lightning bolt. Fragments of glass and blue plastic littered the seat and floor.

But the engine started. And the truck moved when I

touched the gas. And my hands and feet kept moving, too, just as mechanically.

Wind blasted through the destroyed window on the highway. I was desperately thirsty, but if I stopped now there was no guarantee I could start again. Momentum was everything.

Both the Dodge and I made it to the marina, though if someone were to ask me what route I'd chosen, they might as well have been asking me the way to the moon that had sluggishly sunk below the horizon during the drive.

Hollis nearly ran to meet me as I tottered toward the dock gate. Had I called him and forgotten?

"Did you know your headlight—" He stopped. "What happened to your face?"

I stared, not understanding. My scars?

"No, there." He tapped his own cheek. I felt my face and wished I hadn't. The burn line made by the trickling lye flamed anew.

"Long night," I said. I reached into my pocket for my keys and found Stepan's phone instead. The sight of it lent me a sudden surge of energy.

Stepan and his men had come to America. To handle important business for Anatoly Liashko. Lieutenant Guerin had told me Liashko was an arms trafficker. What had that business been? Or—I corrected myself— what was it still? Burke would surely pick up where Stepan had left off. Did the task force tracking Burke know about this yet?

"You look . . . like a coffee would help," Hollis said.

"Water. Thanks. Meet you there."

But he stayed put, watching me as I returned to the truck.

Good. Stepan's crew hadn't searched the Dodge. Aura Nath's tablet, her hacker's special, was still hidden under the backseat. I kept a USB and other charging cables in the center console. I grabbed them all and walked back, cords dangling from my fist like slain snakes.

Inside the *Francesca*, Hollis cleared a pile of clothes and random junk off the settee—a beach towel covered the cushion dappled with the Finnish sailor Jaak's blood—to allow me to sit down. I was already preoccupied with plugging Stepan's phone into the tablet.

The application within responded immediately, filling and refilling the tablet's screen with rows of information—contacts, search history, times of use. I had to hand it to Aura. Her tool even translated the Cyrillic letters on the phone's screen into English for my convenience.

Within two minutes, the tablet pinged to mark completion of its task. I looked first for emails or texts. The earliest dated from only a week ago. Stepan had kept his use of the phone to a minimum. Maybe a byproduct of his boss, Liashko's, penchant for security.

"Paula was very pleased to know that Ondine won't require her services any longer," Hollis said, handing me a glass of water and putting a pitcher on the table.

I mumbled some vague agreement in response, all my concentration on the phone's single text message from an international number, consisting of fifteen characters: BTZU 742669 0 22G1.

The pattern of characters was familiar, though I

couldn't place it right away. An account number? The text had been sent to Stepan yesterday morning, only hours before he and his crew had come after me. I wrote down the letters and numbers on a notepad.

Stepan hadn't used the phone's map feature to find his way around Seattle. I scrolled farther down the pages of data. The SIM card had dutifully recorded each cellular tower that the phone had pinged while active, and every corresponding update of the location services. It made for reams of information, much of which was numeric coordinates and cell tower authentication keys.

Most of the coordinates were the same. Stepan had remained stationary for at least half the day, and then he was on the move just after 3:00 P.M. local time. He'd stopped again one hour later, where he'd stayed until well after dark. I plugged those coordinates into my own phone. They matched the far south of the city, close by the Duwamish Waterway.

"What's the shipment?" Hollis said.

Off my puzzled glance he pointed to the fifteen characters I'd written on the notepad. "That's an ID for a freight container. A twenty-footer, general use model. See, you can tell from these numbers here."

I looked at him. "You're a genius. Can you tell where it is?"

"At least who owns it. BTZ, that'll be the company. The U just means standard freight. Hold on." He found his own phone. I finished the water in two gulps and refilled the glass while Hollis typed.

"Blacksea Tradepartners, a German firm," he said. "But I suspect what you really want to know is who's leased it. That's nearly impossible without having the company's own records."

"Maybe we can narrow it down." I sat down to show Hollis the coordinates by the waterway. "A ship near here."

He screwed up his face in mock pain. "It'll have to be a smaller freighter, if it's on the river. Or we could be looking for a train. Thousands of containers go through there every day."

Damn it. Of course that was true, in the heart of the city's international shipping. One twenty-foot steel box in a virtual sea of them.

"Can you tell me anything more?" Hollis pressed. "What's the cargo, or where it's from?"

"The owner is Ukrainian. The cargo is almost certainly weapons. I assume something packing more punch than small arms, if he bothered to send them all the way to the decadent West to sell them."

Hollis sat down. "You come across the most interesting people."

And sometimes I murdered them. A wave of fatigue threatened to knock me sideways.

"Are you all right, Van? Your hand?"

I looked. The glass Hollis had given me rested on my knee. Despite that, the surface of the water within bobbed and rippled as my forearm trembled in near synchronization.

"Grab a bunk down below," he said. "I'll see what my friends down the docks can tell me."

"I'll crash in the speedboat."

"You sure?"

I was. For one reason, the sun would be up soon. The

enclosed interior of the small craft effectively blocked nearly all light from outside, making it ideal for rest at any hour.

For another, the sight of my shaking hand had brought back the memory of Stepan's arm, in the vat, being inexorably swallowed by the corrosive solution as the bodies beneath his own shifted and settled deeper.

It was entirely possible that I might start screaming, any second now.

"Call me if you learn anything," I said, carefully.

Hollis frowned. "Not too soon. You need downtime."

All the way off the *Francesca* and down the dock, I kept my jaw shut tight, in case any sound tried to escape.

CHAPTER THIRTY-NINE

My PHONE WAS RINGING, and I fumbled to grab it from the radio shelf.

"Hollis?" I said automatically.

"No, it's Wren. Were you asleep?"

I blinked at my watch. In the pitch black of the speedboat cabin, its hands refused to resolve into anything more than a slim luminous triangle. "What time is it?"

"About six-thirty. I texted earlier."

I pulled my phone away from my ear to look. Two unread messages. I'd slept for nearly twelve hours.

"Shit," I said.

Wren laughed. "Well, I get now why you didn't message me back. You sound really out of it."

"Feels that way." I rubbed my face, trying to massage some sharpness back into my senses, and hissed at the sudden pain. The burn on my cheek had scabbed over during my hours of oblivion. The first rub cracked the scab wide open.

Then my brain finally kicked in to remind me why Wren was calling. "It's Sunday. We were supposed to get together."

"But that's not happening. Hey, another time."

"Wait," I said.

"You're not going to try to talk me into still hanging tonight."

"No. Just . . ." What was I doing? "Just hold on with me for a minute. At least until I can apologize like somebody normal."

She didn't say anything. During the pause I opened the cabin doors and slid back the hatch. Any warmth that had accumulated in the cabin from my body heat fled in a rush, replaced instantly by frigid evening air accentuated by the lightest possible drizzle, barely more than a fog. Welcome goose bumps popped to life on every inch of me.

"Okay," she said at last. "I'll ride along. Are you all right?"

"Getting there. I wasn't thinking I would sleep so long, and—" I paused for a second, even though I'd already made the decision to come clean. "And I spaced our date. Last night wasn't good."

"You want to tell me about it?"

I had my face raised to the sky. Could practically feel my parched skin soaking in the water.

"We don't know each other, not yet," I said. "I'd like to get there. Loading you down with a lot of my baggage might not be the way to start."

There was another pause. "I can stop just by hanging up. Hard to get safer than that."

"You know about me tracing my mother, Moira. I found a guy, here in Seattle, who might be my father."

"Oh. That's loaded."

"Yeah. He denies it, barely admits he ever knew

Moira, but . . . it feels right. Which is the shitty part of the whole situation."

"How?"

"He's not one of the good guys. I don't know what to call him; he might be a full-on psychopath. Last night was violent. He wasn't coming after me but I saw up close what he was capable of. Sorry. I don't know why I'm telling you this."

"Because you need to tell somebody, and I'm almost a stranger. It's easier," she said, like the answer was obvious. "So now you know. What he is. And you never have to get near him again."

I didn't say anything.

"What?" Wren asked.

"I know him, yeah. I know part of him real well. The killing. Hard to keep him completely out of my life when that instinct is also a part of me."

"Do you mean what you did in the Army?"

I was sharing a lot with Wren. More than I'd thought I could. But there had to be a line.

"Right," I said, and I hated myself a little for it.

"Is . . . Is there somebody you talk to about that? Your time overseas? I know just enough to know when I'm over my head."

"There's a shrink I saw for a while. And I've talked with brothers from the regiment. But this—" I wasn't finding the right words. Maybe there weren't any, if I couldn't go all the way. "This is just new to me."

"You noticed what you and this man had in common. You must have differences, too."

"Yes. Hey, I learned something about Moira. She was

taking college classes. In social work, maybe toward a job with kids in juvie or foster care."

"That's great." She sounded enthused. Or relieved that our conversation was on a more positive beat. "Did you know she had an interest in that?"

"I didn't know anything about her as an adult." And this might be all I'd ever learn. "It seems to fit. She was stubborn enough for the job."

"A trait she clearly passed on." I could hear Wren's smile.

"Thanks for not hanging up. If I can push my luck, can we try again?"

"I'm free Tuesday."

"I'll set an alarm this time."

"Damn right."

I kept the speedboat stocked with spare clothes and other essentials. Including ammunition of various calibers and a Colt Commander automatic I'd taken off a guy less trained and less restrained in proper handgun usage than me.

Liashko thought I was dead. That didn't mean I was safe. I clipped the holster to the back of my waistband and wore a heavy flannel shirt like a coat to conceal the weapon.

I was starved. The diner on Seaview might still be open, or I could hit Oaxaca in Ballard. My appetite could conquer an entire platter of pork with mole sauce, and beer.

But the cabin lights of the *Francesca* beckoned first. I wolfed a protein bar to keep my stomach from eating my liver and jogged over.

"Any word on the ship?" I said to Hollis from the dock.

"Ukrainian, you told me. I've checked with two different fellows who might know. They say the same: there are no Ukrainian vessels currently at port anywhere in Seattle."

"Dammit."

"Hold on, now. I'm warming up. There's a Moldovan freighter traveling under a Belize flag of convenience moored on the same stretch of shore you indicated. The *Oxana M.*"

"Moldova is next to the Ukraine."

"That much I knew. The name of the home port is beyond my ken. Gweer-goo-lesti?"

"Giurgiule ti."

"Impressive. I expect the Army briefed you lads on all manner of fun places you might see. The ship sailed from Jeer-whatever the long way, out through the Black Sea and the Mediterranean, across the Atlantic, through the Canal, and back up again. Taking short-hop jobs as they went, as most of these small cargo freighters do."

"Any chance you can get your hands on the *Oxana M*'s cargo manifest?"

"A good chance, but that will be a long list. She's not a big ship, as they go. A hundred meters or so in length, no more than thirty thousand deadweight tonnes in her belly."

"All right, I get your point." It would take me half a week to search the *Oxana M*'s holds, even if I could do it in broad daylight. "Let's look at the manifest. Maybe lightning will strike."

As if in answer, my phone buzzed on Hollis's table. An incoming video call from a blocked number. An instant later, Aura Nath's face appeared on the screen.

We both stared at it. How the hell—?

I stopped my own thought; the answer was obvious: Aura and Bilal had an unsettling amount of tech wizardry. Of course they might be able to jack my phone's controls.

"Are you there?" she said, looking into the lens. From our side, all she might see was the ceiling of the *Francesca*'s cabin.

"What is it?" I said, picking up the phone.

"Thank God." Aura spoke softly. "I don't have much time. Saleem is missing. I think he might be coming after you."

Hollis and I exchanged a look.

"Why would your man do that," I said, "unless Bilal ordered him to?"

"No. Just the opposite." Aura's words came rushing one upon another. "Bilal and Saleem argued on our flight back to Miami. We told Saleem that we had what we needed now. Our time in Seattle is done. But Saleem insisted that you were an unacceptable risk, that you knew too much about us. He wanted to return. Bilal refused. Saleem became furious. I've never seen him like this. He's never challenged Bilal this way."

I remembered Saleem's maddened eyes when I dropped his hog-tied body onto the deck outside Ceres.

"And he left?" Hollis asked.

"Sometime during the night. He took Juwad's gun and some clothes."

Neither Hollis nor I said anything. I was wondering

whether this could be some ploy. But even if Bilal and Aura had decided to renege on our deal, and risk their secrets coming to light, why warn me that their vicious servant was on his way to kill me?

Aura spoke again, maybe thinking we were still unconvinced. "Saleem left his phone behind. He probably expects we might track him that way."

"If he took the gun," I said, half to myself, "he must not be planning to fly. Does Saleem have a car?"

"Not one of his own. I suppose he could steal one."

A foreign visitor driving a stolen car across the continental U.S. I suspected Saleem was smarter than to try that.

"Does he know anyone in the States? Someone who could provide him with transport?"

Aura considered it. "He has relatives in New Jersey. Middlesex, I think."

Too far to drive down and pick up Saleem in Florida. But it was a place to start.

"Check them," I said. "Their accounts, their phones, whatever you can hack into. Do it fast. And anyone else Saleem might rely on."

She hesitated. "Bilal doesn't know I'm telling you this. He would—are you still there?"

My image had disappeared because I'd switched to a different app, to send something to Aura. I heard her phone beep as it arrived.

"What's this?" she asked.

"Who," I corrected. "Cyndra. She's one of the people Bilal threatened the first night I met you."

Aura was quiet. I switched back to the phone app and saw her staring, absorbed in the short clip Cyn had taken of herself, lifting weights and waving at the camera with that half-abashed, half-cocky grin on her face.

I leaned closer to the camera. "Saleem knows where this girl lives. She's what's at stake."

"I understand," Aura said.

"Find a way to find Saleem or everyone loses."

"Yes," she said again. "I'll make it happen."

She ended the call.

"We're a long way from Miami," Hollis said. "You sure Saleem is coming?"

I nodded. His eyes had told me. Too many humiliations for the volatile gunman. First his boss marrying Aura and having to take orders from her. Then Bilal choosing me to break into the biotech firm instead of trusting the job to his right-hand man. And the cherry on top: my knocking him cold and tying him like a rodeo calf in the cryobank. I could imagine all of those events fueling Saleem's resentful fire.

What did he know about me, besides where Addy's house was? He'd seen the *Francesca*, though without access to Aura's magic tablet he likely didn't know where it was moored. He may have seen the address of Bully Betty's where I worked. But Addy was the likeliest tack. Even if Saleem didn't find me there, he could still make good use of a hostage or two.

"That was a nice trick," Hollis said, tapping my phone and the video playing on repeat. The clip of Cyn deadlifting the barbell, setting it down, saluting ironically, over and over. "Showing her the girl. The soft touch, instead of pressuring her."

"It wasn't a trick," I said.

Aura understood my desperation to protect Cyn.

She'd lived with that feeling for weeks while her un-born children had been used as collateral. First by her ex-husband and then by me. Now that our fortunes had reversed, an appeal to her empathy was my best shot at stopping Saleem.

And in case that went sideways, I had to get Addy and Cyn out of the line of fire. For the second time in a week.

Shit, Addy was going to eviscerate me.

CHAPTER FORTY

THE MORE I THOUGHT about the *Oxana M* on the drive to Addy's, the more I liked it. If Liashko had smuggled arms out of the conflict in the Ukraine, and if he was truly desperate to make this deal happen, he'd have played it very safe. Air travel was a nonstarter. Anything flying out of that war zone might have been searched down to the fuselage. He wouldn't have sent the arms by land across all of Asia to the Pacific. Too many hostile checkpoints, too many rolls of the dice.

Moldova was a friendly neighbor, and just a rock-skip away from the peninsula. Find a suitable freighter with a bribable captain—I couldn't imagine that had been tough—conceal the arms in a deep hold stacked under tons of identical shipping containers, and have patience while the *Oxana M* made its long journey halfway around the world to the western U.S.

Burke had ordered me to keep my head down. Implying whatever deal he had planned with Liashko was happening soon. And I already knew that Special Agent Martens's task force was aiming to catch Liashko on American ground.

If I could find the container that held the arms, I

could pass that information along to Martens. The ATF could follow the weapons off the freighter and have a SWAT team ready to spring when Liashko arrived.

Closing the net on him, and on Sean Burke, too. I might have met my father just in time to see him imprisoned forever.

It was true that Burke had saved my life. But my life had limited value, even to me. I couldn't stick my head in the sand if a little recon work might mean ensuring Liashko's weapons never left the *Oxana M*.

ADDY SAT AT HER dining-room table, writing a note by hand. Probably a thank-you to Dorothy. From Cyndra's room I heard the competing discord of music and Cyndra talking to a friend who might have different music playing on her side.

The roller bag from their stay was still out, waiting on its wheels by the hall closet. I took it into the living room and unzipped it to lay it open.

"Are you packing?" Addy said.

"For you and Cyn. We have to relocate you for a while."

She slowly capped the pen and placed it in perfect alignment with the stationery. Her deliberate movement as palpable as a shout. "Absurd."

"I know it's bad news—"

"I mean you. What on earth is the matter with you?" She kept her voice low, so as not to alert Cyndra. Regardless, Stanley caught the shift in her tone and grumbled confusedly as he paced between the back door and the living room. "It wasn't a day ago that you told us it was safe to come back here. Now you're coming in like a rhinoceros, trying to charge right through any objections."

"We can argue later. Let's get you to a hotel. I'll explain on the way."

"No. If the situation is that dire, then we'll go to the police. I refuse to live on the run. Or to subject Cyndra to that. She starts school in the morning, for Lord's sake."

"Addy."

"I'm not having it, Van. I don't know what's happened lately, but you look twisted into knots. Certainly you're not in your right mind."

"I'm scared," I said.

"Well if you're frightened, how do you think I feel? Tell me what's going on."

I sat down on the floor next to Stanley. Laying my hand on the dog's panting ribs may not have given him much comfort, but it did some for me. As briefly as I could, I told Addy about Bilal Nath, and Aura and her eggs, and about the danger of Saleem returning.

"I don't know if Saleem will use you to get to me," I said, "but we have to plan for anything he might do."

"Anything and everything," Addy mused. "Small wonder you're twitchy. You can't protect everyone all the time."

"I don't care about everyone," I said.

"Yes, you do. Despite your many faults, you do give a damn, Van." She sighed. "Cyndra and I are going to go about our lives. I can tell the police we've had menacing telephone calls or somesuch, so they'll keep an eye on the house. We'll be careful."

A cop car cruising past every couple of hours wasn't going to make me breathe easier. "What if Hollis or Willard and I stay close the next couple of days? I can take Cyn to school and pick her up."

"Willard? He's your very large friend? I imagine any trouble would give him a wide berth."

"They're both smart. They'll know what to watch for."

"All right. I won't let my own obstinacy make things worse. But only for a day or two."

"I hope that's all I'll need."

"Where have I heard that before? And once Cyndra's home from school tomorrow, we'll both sit down with her and explain the situation. She's old enough, and it's unfair to keep her in the dark about her own life."

Old enough, and tough enough. Cyndra had come through harder times.

"Deal," I said. "I'll take the night watch and see if Hollis can relieve me tomorrow."

"Now I think we'll be sufficiently safe for twenty minutes while you make yourself useful and run Stanley around the block. Tire him out some so we can all sleep. Three days at Dorothy's and the poor boy is ready to dig a hole through the floor."

I sympathized. Every minute I would be guarding the house was a minute I wasn't solving the root cause of the problem. But it was what had to be done. What was I fighting so hard for, if not this cobbled-together duct-tape-and-baling-wire family we'd made?

CHAPTER FORTY-ONE

Harbor Island formed the heart of the city's commercial shipping, and the Duwamish River was its primary artery, winding from the terminals off West Seattle to taper and scrawl crazily into smaller waterways south of the city. Industries reliant on merchant vessels crowded its shores: landscaping materials, food products, biodiesel plants. And dozens more boatyards and maintenance docks to service the tugs, barges, and tankers that sailed at every hour of every day.

Hollis's notes on the *Oxana M* told me the freighter was moored south of the Georgetown reach, across the river in the industrial part of South Park. I drove half a mile farther to a stunted avenue ending in a high razor-wired fence. The closest any car could come to the water on a public street.

No company sign hung from the spiked gate. If you didn't know what the place was, you weren't supposed to be there. Past a collection of corrugated buildings, rust eating each of them from the ground up, I could see lifting cranes on cargo ships and multicolored stacks of twenty- and forty-foot steel containers, like a giant toddler's toy blocks left to fade in the sun.

Hollis had tracked down the *Oxana M*'s manifest, duly filed with U.S. Customs and Border Protection and a copy to the Port of Seattle. The freighter had arrived three days ago, offloading more than two hundred containers of industrial machinery and steel from Eastern Europe, textiles from North Africa, wooden furniture from Central America, and a thousand other goods. All from small companies, bartering on the cheap for a sliver of space in the *Oxana M*'s holds and accepting that it would arrive when it arrived, with no expectation of speed.

A check of the local map showed a small park just south of the shipping yard. I left the Barracuda and backtracked to find it. The half acre of community land had more dead grass than living, but it let me walk right up to the water. Looking north, I had a sidelong view of the shipyard.

Three freighters had been moored in a tight row along the yard's long concrete dock. The biggest was the *Oxana M*. Over three hundred feet long, the white block letters of her name at the bow stark against the black paint of her hull. Two loading cranes extending from her deck nearly touched at their highest points, like a praying mantis's forelegs. A white three-story-high superstructure enclosed the bridge and crew's quarters at her stern.

She floated high on the water, showing nearly as much red underbelly as black hull. Not completely empty of her burden. The container I wanted might still be aboard. If it was, it might be easier to find with the freighter's legit cargo already offloaded and out of the way.

Might, might, might. One assumption piled on all the others. I had nothing but a shipping container ID from a dead thug's texts. No proof that the *Oxana M* was the ship that had carried it, or that the container was still aboard, or even that Liashko was smuggling arms at all. I was chasing phantoms.

If I handed what little I knew over to Special Agent Martens, would it be enough to make the Feds hold to their deal and let Burke into WITSEC? Could I adequately explain where I'd gotten the shipping container code? Or would that be tainted evidence?

I hadn't signed any papers officially making me a C.I. for the task force. And no way could I tell Martens about the four men his good buddy Burke had murdered in saving my life, much less my own slaying of Gennady.

And if they believed me about the ship? And all of my guesswork turned out to be right? It was too easy to imagine U.S. Attorney Stratton weighing his options, opting for the safer bet, securing the smuggled weapons, and declaring victory. With a little spin the bust would undoubtedly lend him a rocket in the polls— "CANDIDATE FOILS TERROR PLOT" would be a dream headline for any politician—even without arresting Liashko.

An inner voice told me that would be best. Securing smuggled arms was a no-bullshit matter of national security. The life of one hitman couldn't compare. No matter what he might be to me.

I stayed in the small park and watched the freighter for the rest of the afternoon. Nothing was lifted on or off. Beyond the occasional ant-like speck of a sailor walking her deck, she might have been a ghost ship.

When the evening grew too dim to see more than the wan yellow deck lamps and the white arms of the cranes, I gave up. The only way to determine if the *Oxana M* carried anything of interest would be to take a much closer look. Which would require some thinking. I couldn't bluff my way aboard.

At a pub on Cloverdale I ordered a Cubano sandwich and a pint of brown ale while mulling over the problem. Before the food arrived, my phone chimed with a video chat request: Aura Nath. At least this time she waited before popping onto the screen, unasked. I mimed to the guy working the counter that I'd be right back and stepped outside to answer the call.

"I've got something," Aura said. Less hushed than her previous call; her husband must not be near. "Saleem's brother in New Jersey FedExed an overnight envelope not long after we arrived in Florida. His emails had the tracking number, so I was able to place it. The envelope went to a shipping outlet in a strip mall less than a mile from our hotel here."

"That must be it," I said. "Money, maybe, or identification."

"I'm ahead of you," Aura said. "The brother's credit card bought an Amtrak ticket here in Miami early yesterday morning. One adult in a Viewliner bedroom, going all the way to King Street Station in Seattle. Saleem must have boarded almost immediately."

Meaning Saleem had timed his departure to make a fast exit. Maybe he and his brother resembled each other enough that he could pass using the same ID and charge cards. Traveling by train fit my theory that Saleem wanted to hang on to the gun he'd lifted from his buddy Juwad. "Where's the train now?"

Aura paused while she looked over her notes. "Outside Washington, D.C. It'll go through Chicago and Salt Lake on its way to Seattle. Arriving Wednesday morning at 10:25."

Good. Two nights and a day for me to devise a suitable welcome. For once Bilal's people had me on a timeline that worked to my advantage.

And Saleem would know that.

"He must suspect Bilal might warn me he's coming," I said, "if they argued, and Saleem cut ties."

"That wouldn't be like Bilal to hand him over," Aura said, with a glance over her shoulder. "He prizes loyalty. He's mad at Saleem for going against his orders, yeah, but he gets Saleem's pride. They have that in common."

I thought about that. "Does your team have a secure way of communicating? If you're staying off phones?"

"Of course," Aura said, like the question was Hacker 101. "We use portable networks sometimes to share information and stay off the Internet. Or remotely, we can use private drop sites."

Like dead drops in espionage. One party leaves information for another to retrieve without direct contact. "Would Saleem be checking those?"

Her face hardened. "You're asking me to pretend to be Bilal."

"I'm asking you to help me. To prevent Saleem from doing something we'll all regret."

"But you already know where he'll be: King Street Station, Wednesday morning."

"And I could miss catching him there. If that happens, I want a contingency plan." I sent Aura coordinates of a location in Snohomish County. "Put this out on your drops for Saleem to find. Make him think it's from Bilal."

"He's my husband. It's like betraying him myself."

"We've both got a gut check here, Aura. Because I don't know how far I'll have to go to keep all of us safe. Your family and mine. If you want me to believe Saleem's acting alone, then help me stop him." That was as close as I would get to premeditation on an open line.

She was quiet for a long count. "I won't know if Saleem sees it."

"It's enough."

After another moment, she nodded. "All right. I'll do it. And I'll keep checking his brother's credit card and other accounts."

"Thank you. We'll get through this."

She nodded once more and hung up.

A few days before, Aura and Bilal Nath had been my worst enemies. Now events compelled us to cooperate. Those circumstances might include my holding their future over a barrel, and them trying to keep their unhinged bodyguard from blowing me away. Still, a reluctant ally was better than none.

I'd implied to Aura that I was wrestling with whether to kill Saleem outright. That had been a half truth. I'd already decided on a plan of action.

Tomorrow I would tip Lieutenant Guerin to the arrival of an armed individual traveling with false identification on the incoming Amtrak Wednesday morning. That should be enough to get Saleem arrested and likely deported after a long tour of various holding cells. Not a permanent solution, but enough to get the gunman out of the way while my attention was on Sean Burke and Liashko.

And if Saleem somehow slipped past Guerin at the station? The location I'd given Aura was Burke's barn in rural Snohomish. Isolated. And designed to make people vanish for good.

The idea of returning to that slaughterhouse, opening that vat once more to see what might remain within, made sweat rise on my scalp despite the outdoor chill.

But I could do it. For Cyndra and Addy, no question.

DRIVING UPTOWN, I WAS about to enter the underground tunnel when my phone rang again. Not Aura this time; the calling number had a 721 prefix. The burner that I'd tossed to Sean Burke.

Speak of the devil, and he shall telephone.

"You around?" he said.

"Depends what you mean."

"Get here. My apartment. You remember where."

And he hung up. Less than ten words, most of them sounding pulled from his throat. Was he drunk? Being forced to talk? Or was there something else going on?

I wouldn't waste any minutes getting there to find out. I did allow one extra second, however, to make sure the Colt had a round chambered.

CHAPTER FORTY-TWO

I RAN THE LIGHTS DOWN Dexter Avenue and into Belltown until I reached the burnished spike of Sean Burke's building. I pressed 3-1-0-5 on the intercom and he—or someone—buzzed me in without a word.

I took the elevator off the residential lobby to the twenty-ninth floor, got off, and checked the stairwell. It was clear. Two flights up, the hallway outside Burke's door was equally quiet.

Without leaving the stairwell, I tapped the button to reply to my last call. Burke answered on the third ring.

"I'm outside," I said.

Ten full seconds later, the apartment door opened. Burke walked out into the hallway. He held a rocks glass full of ice and a dark brown liquid. It took him a second to find me and another tick to focus his eyes.

"Huh," he said. "Cautious cat, ain't you?"

He returned to his apartment. I followed. The double-paned French doors to the balcony were wide open and the wind at thirty stories brushed my hair back before I took my first step over the threshold.

It was my first look at the place with the lights on. Five grand a month in rent, easy, half of that paying for the view. The furnishings were slightly lower market, and so much of a piece I suspected Burke had bought them based on a catalog display. Sturdy and masculine and showing minimal signs of wear. I guessed Burke wasn't home a lot.

He plopped down in a leather club chair arranged where he could look out through the railing at the city beyond. Divots of perfect circles in the Persian rug marked where the chair normally stood. I shut the door and bolted it.

"You want coffee?" he said, brandishing his glass. "Something with teeth? Bar's over there."

It *was* coffee swirling around the ice cubes. A sharp aroma of burned beans persisted even through the breeze ruffling the curtains.

"You called me," I said, wondering if he might have forgotten.

"I did. Siddown."

There were no chairs near his. I crossed the expanse of living room to the dining area, taking an extra few steps to glance into the bedroom. No one there, unless they were hiding in the walk-in. I dragged a straight-backed chair from its place at the table and placed it where I could see the hall and the front door. The view could take care of itself. Cautious cat.

Burke sipped his coffee, licking stray drops from his lips. "You asked me why I didn't let Stepan kill you."

I nodded.

"If you found me, an' you know about Anatoly Liashko, that means you got some buddy-bud in the cops letting you peek at their files. Right?"

I didn't say anything.

"So I guess you must know all about Gus, too. My dad. Right?" The second *right* was spat out, like I'd insulted the man's memory.

"Gut Burke. Used to be a Westie in New York."

"That's Pops. Gus wanted me to have an education, which for him meant he spent stupid money for me to go to private school. Me with a buncha rich brats never walked more than a quarter mile at one time. I hated it. But I finished, 'cause that's what Gus wanted."

Some kind of painkiller in Burke's veins. Or maybe a muscle relaxant. No indicators of long-term addiction, no weight loss or tipsy balance. The action at the barn had proven Burke's reflexes were just fine.

Whatever he was popping tonight, it had relaxed his tongue well enough.

"After school I went back to what I'd been doing with Gus. Stealing, mostly. He'd started taking jobs for Russian multimillionaire fucks, looking to get their hands on American products that hadn't been cleared for export. After a few years he got in with Anatoly, and that was real money."

"Doing what?"

"Whatever needed doing. Gus kept me out of the hard stuff back then." Burke pointed in the general direction. "I think he still had ideas of me going legit someday. But I knew what he did. And he knew I didn't mind."

"Back then."

"Things change. Gus got older. Slower. Whether he changed his mind about bringing me in or jus' realized he needed my help, I don't know. Pretty soon I learned about everything, even the barn."

We both listened as a high, sustained whisper came

into the room. The sound of a siren, some four hundred feet below us on the street, its wail stretched to the breaking point by the night wind.

"And you were still okay with all of it," I said. Making a connection between us I would have ignored if I could. "Sleeping soundly."

"Is that a crack?"

"No. It's a resemblance."

Burke shrugged. He didn't catch my meaning, but he didn't give a shit, either. "Anatoly had swerved from smuggling into selling weapons by then. Our job on this side of the water was about making deals run smooth. Cash drop-offs. Leaning on bent lawyers and money men who wouldn't take a hint. Sometimes there was work in Russia besides."

"So you got a passport."

"You know that, too, huh? Anatoly found Natalia for me, bribed somebody in the right directorate over there to approve my residency and attest to my living in Russia for years." Burke snapped his fingers, like describing a magician's illusion. "I bought a house with backdated estate papers. Only met the girl once, at the wedding. Never even fucked her. Done and done. But I'm getting ahead. All that came after."

He blinked, slowly. "Gus fouled up a job. A big one. Anatoly let it go. We thought."

Burke downed the last of the coffee and reached into his rocks glass to pluck an ice cube from the stack. He didn't put it in his mouth, just held it between thumb and forefinger, letting the melted drops fall to the rug. I waited.

"A year later Gus gets hit by a car in a casino parking

lot. Crushed the whole side of him. Cops never found the guy. Never found the car. Don't know how hard they looked. Stupid Sean, I go on a tear trying to find Gus's killer by checking local body shops for repairs, before I wised up."

I was tracking Burke's tone, the pattern of his strange mood, as much as his words. "You stayed dumb. To stay close."

He grunted and tossed the ice cube out the window to a long, long fall.

"Sticking a blade right through Anatoly's neck was my first idea. *Whap.* Just enough time before he kicked so he'd realize why I'd done it. But getting next to him would be impossible in Russia. And Liashko comes to America about as often as I visit fuckin' Africa. He's a paranoid. Going to jail over there doesn't scare him. If they send his ass to a corrective camp, he's wired enough to buy himself a comfortable reeducation. But here? All the race shit and the other gangs? He'd be meat. He knows it. Our prisons freak Anatoly out."

"You've been waiting for a chance at him this long?" I said. According to the FBI file, Gut Burke had died almost a dozen years ago.

"I found other work." Burke couldn't help but glance at his fine apartment.

"Must pay well."

"Somebody owed. They signed their paid lease over to me instead."

Instead of the alternative. *Whap.*

"But I kept on bugging Anatoly," he said. "Telling him there was plenty of money to be made in the U.S. of A., the way the country's going to shit. And his cash flow's been squeezed ever since Putin started jailing his old sponsors on corruption charges. Now he's fucking frantic. It's beautiful."

"Stepan's crew was here to set up a deal," I said. "Is Liashko coming stateside?"

Burke sneered his affirmation, mouth a little slack from the pills. "I know that son of a whore. His mistrust cuts both ways. Any big transaction, Anatoly has to know every fucking thing."

He stopped, maybe noting how intently I was following his story.

"You an' me, we got—what do you call it? Commonalities. We can both keep it together when shit goes down."

"Yeah," I said.

"Plus I think I've got you scoped, Shaw. I tell you to take a long vacation away from Seattle, there's no better way to make sure you'll stay around. Keep stirring up trouble. And I'll keep trippin' over you." Burke laughed harshly. "So fuck it. You've already got me by the balls 'cause I let you live. If telling you to screw off doesn't work, maybe the truth will."

"Maybe."

"After too many years I finally figured out I'd never get my shot, a chance to take out Anatoly the way Gus might have. Dropping him into the vat still alive with his hands and feet tied. No gag, though. I'd wanna hear him."

He said it with the same flat tone he might have used when ordering the furniture from the catalog. Talk to Burke long enough, and you started to notice the shallow pools in his emotions.

He settled back into his leather chair. "I'd have to get Liashko another way. I needed help. So I called a friend of mine. A guy I've known since we were just kids. His life turned out different than mine. Better. I figured if there was anybody in this world I could trust, it would be him."

Holy shit. I gave the moment the space it needed, the space I needed to wrap my head around it.

"Burke," I said. It was the first time I'd called him by name. "Are you telling me you're working with the cops?"

He crushed the last ice cube between his teeth.

"Funny, isn't it? Gut Burke's kid, a fuckin' rat. Nobody knows about it except me and a coupla Feds. For my own safety. And now you."

"That's how you found me at the garage by the museum," I said. My face was probably stupid with astonishment, but right then I didn't give a damn. "The Feds have traces on my accounts. And your buddy is keeping you in the loop on my movements. In case— what, I might be hunting you?"

"You coulda been from one of Anatoly's competitors. Or who knew, maybe from the man himself. I wouldn't put it past that fucker to hire somebody to snoop into my business."

"I thought the task force was trying to nail you. For the dead ATF agent."

"Santora? Hell." Burke chuckled. "Marcus Santora's alive and kicking, somewhere. My guy put him undercover for months as a dealer. Had a whole trailer full of rocket grenades as bait. He got damn close, I'll give him that. But like I told you, Liashko's a bugout. He smelled something wrong. The next thing I know, he's fled back to Russia." Burke flipped the imaginary Liashko the finger. "I had to do something to save face. So we made the best of it. Santora vanished, and I told Anatoly I was the reason why."

"And he believed you."

"I had some cred. A few years ago, two Bratva shit-heads ripped off Anatoly's summer house for spending money before they fled to the States. Busted up his housekeeper while they were at it. Anatoly sent me to find them. Wasn't hard. The idiots had holed up in a Long Beach fleapit owned by the brotherhood. But when I got there, they were already dead and stinking, overdosed on some laced heroin. Lucky opportunity. I made it look like I'd tied up the two punks and spiked them myself."

Burke had a different definition of luck than I did. If the two gangsters hadn't already been cold, would he have taken care of that minor detail, too?

Or maybe he had killed them after all. And lying to me about it was just second nature. Maybe he was lying about everything, including his status with the federal task force.

"So what now?" I said.

"Now you stay as low as the deepest roots under the tall trees, until Anatoly comes to America and we nail his ass. Don't say shit to anybody, just vanish. I can contact you when it's safe."

"No. Liashko's boys tried to burn my face off. Tell your guy on the task force that I want in."

"Get bent. He'll never go for it, and sure as hell I

don't want you neither. You're gonna get me killed or something worse, stumbling around."

"So aim me where I can do some good. Even if it's watching your back in case your paranoid freak boss decides to have you whacked on general principle."

He slapped his glass down on the side table, hard enough to make the ice cubes jitter and bounce. "Fuck whether or not he takes me out. There's pressure here. My guy put his ass on the line, you understand? He's the only guy in the world would do that. I ain't taking him down with me."

Despite his loose tongue, Burke had kept his handler's name out of our conversation. But I could put the pieces together into a rough picture. The supposedly dead Santora had been ATF. And ATF Special Agent Rick Martens had offered me a similar deal as Burke's, to turn informant. Martens was in his late forties, about the right age to be a childhood friend of Sean Burke.

One plus one plus one. Burke had sent Agent Martens to Bully Betty's to offer me a deal, right after I'd told Burke about Moira.

Which might mean he wasn't as positive as he claimed about whether he might be my father.

"If you have enough faith to tell me all this," I said, "you can tell me about Moira."

Burke sighed. "I figured you'd circle back to her. You're like a pit bull on a fuckin' pork chop."

I waited. Without taking his eyes off me, Burke reached into the pocket of his trousers and removed a rectangular piece of clear plastic. A sealed bag. He unfolded it to show me. Inside the bag was a Q-tip. One tip of the swab was wet.

He held out the bag. I took it.

"You knew her," I said.

"Of course I knew her. I never forgot her. And before I spend the rest of my life in WITSEC, I guess you and I better sort this out, huh?"

CHAPTER FORTY-THREE

I CALLED PAULA CLAYBECK THE instant I was back at the car. She picked up, thank God.

"Dr. Claybeck," I said. "Van Shaw. Hollis's friend."

"Oh, I'm aware. You said you would lose my number."

"I need a small favor."

"Color me surprised." Claybeck didn't seem too grateful that I'd helped extricate her from Ondine's clutches. But then, maybe the good doctor felt she'd traded the frying pan for the fire.

"I need to compare two DNA samples for paternity," I said.

"Honestly, dragging me into your baby mama troubles?"

In a few sentences I laid out what I needed. A long pause followed.

"That's not something I can do here at any rate," Claybeck said. "DNA comparison requires specialized equipment to separate the fragments and review the profiles."

"I guessed."

"I'll call a friend and see if he would be willing to fit the analysis into his day. Take down this address." She read it off. A street in the southern part of the Central District. "Unless I call and tell you differently, meet me there at seven o'clock in the morning. The process will require at least a few hours. Hours unencumbered by you hanging over his shoulder."

"Understood." I almost had to stop myself from adding "ma'am." Claybeck had that superior officer vibe down cold.

"Don't be late."

Un-damn-likely. I would be counting the minutes. Sleep might be impossible. It was like a twisted version of Christmas Eve as a child, agonizing through the hours until morning and time to see what presents had appeared under the tree.

Not that the yuletide had ever been so showy with Dono. My grandfather had kept our festivities to an extra slab of meat and some dessert on the dinner table, with a gift or two wrapped crudely in newspaper and garden twine as the centerpiece. Usually winter clothes or something I needed for school. But there was always cash on Christmas morning, too, and Dono never gave a crap what I spent it on. Spider-Man comics and a candy feast for me and Davey Tolan from the 7-Eleven later that same afternoon was the standard spree.

Now I held what might be the conclusive link to my father in my hand, and there was nothing to do but wait.

STANLEY SNUFFED FROM HIS tractor-tire-sized bed in the corner, battling some dreamland adversary. Normally he'd be in Cyndra's room, occupying ninety percent of the mattress, but when I'd spread blankets on the couch around midnight he had padded out to join me, a yawn stretching his huge maw. The dog had apparently determined that he and I were guarding the castle gates together.

It was near five o'clock in the morning. For the past hour, my mind had been turning over what Burke had said about his buddy in law enforcement, how the Fed had put everything on the line to help Burke. That if the bust of Liashko went south, they would all be finished.

Burke saw his C.I. status as transactional. I had the same opinion. If Liashko wasn't caught, Martens's career might be flushed and Burke's chances of survival would follow it down the same drain. No criminal trial equaled no escape into WITSEC. The man in charge, U.S. Attorney Palmer Stratton, would wipe his hands clean of the whole debacle.

It was the smart move, politically. Burke would be abandoned, forced to run. Anatoly Liashko didn't seem to lack for trigger men to chase after him.

I finally tossed the sheets aside. Better to get something done than to fruitlessly pursue rest that I knew wasn't coming.

Addy kept her home computer perched incongruously on a delicate secretary desk that she'd owned for fifty years. Her original computer had been a creaker, close to joining the desk in antiquity, until Cyndra had insisted on a model that could handle a teenage-sized gaming habit.

I switched on the PC and pulled up a browser, searching for news on the recall election for governor.

The race had narrowed to three contenders. Stratton,

the Democratic candidate, still showed a narrow lead in the polls. His Republican challenger, Fulcher, had made headway by trumpeting his ties to business growth as a congressman in Spokane. The independent third party, Barrish, had no chance judging from the poll numbers. She had barely pulled enough donors to be included in the debates two nights before.

I clicked on a KIRO-TV news video to skim through the latest debate. It was about as enlightening as I'd expected, meaning not at all. Every question the moderator threw to the candidates was quickly spun into whatever sound bites the politician wanted to repeat.

From what I saw, there wasn't a whole lot of difference between the two front-runners. Both white guys around fifty, with the sleek look of weekly grooming and well-rehearsed hand gestures. Stratton's money came from his family, Fulcher's from his corporate career before he climbed the rungs of the state and national legislature.

I focused more on the verbal combat. Fulcher was on the attack, implying Stratton was an entitled kid from a long line of career politicians. Stratton parried by emphasizing his job putting crooks behind bars and counterpunched with Fulcher's voting record, as evidence that Fulcher was far more right-wing than he claimed. Barrish ignored them both and appealed to the voters for action on corporate tax reform and housing inequality. Of the three, she seemed to be the one stressing her actual platform. Fulcher and Stratton were too busy fighting tooth and nail for every undecided voter.

Addy came into the room, swathed in her white Turkish robe with navy piping. Her silver hair stuck out in conical clumps instead of its usual slim spikes. Stanley's tail thumped the armrest.

"I didn't think you cared about politics," Addy said, closing one eye against the blue-white glare of the screen.

"I don't." I muted the video. The debate raged on in silence.

"Could have fooled me. It's usually Cyndra I'm telling to not sit so close."

It was true that I hadn't taken my eyes off the arguing candidates. Addy sat down on the couch, shooing Stanley to curl himself onto the remaining cushions.

"Have you learned any more about—your father?" she said.

My jacket was hanging on the dowel pegs by the door. I retrieved it and took the sealed plastic bag with the swab from Burke from the pocket to show Addy.

"He gave me this. To have it tested."

"Oh, my. That's huge. So he and your mother were a couple."

"I doubt Burke would put it like that. And," I admitted, "maybe Moira had other boys, too. But something makes me doubt it. If she and Burke hooked up as kids, my guess is that he's the only one."

"And your father. How do you feel about that?"

Like I'd opened a treasure chest to find that the gold doubloons inside carried a curse. Like I was sorry I'd ever asked.

"Burke's right in the middle of bad times, with bad people. I talked to Wren about him some last night. She implied knowledge is power. That by understanding the kind of person Burke is, I can make sure I'm different."

Addy didn't say anything. She knew me well enough to imagine that drawing that line could be so easy.

"Wren, eh?" she said with an upbeat tone. "She's quite something."

"Yeah. I like her. She's . . . direct."

"It's nice you're looking to the future. Not that I assume you two will become soulmates. But all of this"— Addy handed back the sealed bag—"is really just talking about what's already passed. It's not the same as leading your own life."

"Whatever happened, I'll find out the truth today." I pocketed the swab.

Addy idly scratched Stanley's ear. "You don't have to. I'm not sure I would, in your place."

The computer was still running the video of the debate. Candidates shook hands and waved to the crowd, each of them beaming a huge smile to communicate victory. I switched it off.

"I've come too far to let this go now," I said.

CHAPTER FORTY-FOUR

CLAYBECK WAS WAITING AT the address she'd given me, a drably functional tinted-glass and chrome-steel building at the outskirts of a college campus. Its four stories had probably been the height of workspace design in the 1990s. Raised letters above the door read: SEATTLE STATE UNIVERSITY WEGNER HALL.

"Med school?" I guessed, touching a finger to the pitted metal frame around the keycard entry plate.

"Forensic sciences," Claybeck said, waving to a lanky man who was already hurrying from the back end of the lobby to meet us. "Don't let the facilities mislead you. The school produces some of the top analysts in the country."

The door's automatic lock clunked as the man drew within range of its motion sensor, allowing him to push the plexiglass door open.

"Paula," he said to Claybeck, shaking hands, "great to see you. And weird." He blinked happily at her, like the strangeness of our morning meeting was the most entertainment he'd had in ages. He was a touch over six feet, with long limbs and a neck framing a pronounced

Adam's apple. In his plaid shirt and slim-cut jeans, a mannequin for the Northwest Professional Type.

"I appreciate the help," Claybeck said. "This is Mr. Shaw. He's the one in a hurry."

"Jay Corrigan," he greeted me. "I'm a professor of forensic biology here. Most of the time. I also do some consulting for state and King County police labs."

I caught the implication. Don't ask Corrigan to do anything that he would have to report.

"It's a paternity check," I said, handing him two baggies, one containing a swab from my own cheek, the other Burke's similar swab. Samples A and B. I explained what I wanted. His eyes took on that tickled expression again.

"How long will it take?" I said.

"Premium rush, right? I can start later this morning, and we can handle the short-tandem repeat here," he said, holding the samples against the light for a better look. "We apply reagents and heat to release the DNA. If there's enough to work with, I'll make a few million copies and separate those out. We've got a genetic analyzer on the third floor. To make a profile—"

"O'clock," I said.

"Ten o'clock," he said, with a staccato chuckle at my urgency. "About twelve hours after I start, we should be looking at the profiles and seeing if all twenty-one locations—that's half—match. That's proof of paternity. And that's as fast as the analysis can be done. Can't force it."

"I'll call you at ten." He told me his phone number. "What do I owe you?"

"It's a barter job," he said, jabbing a thumb at Claybeck. "Paula's gonna be a guest speaker."

Claybeck's mouth pursed. I was getting better at reading her moods. Less disapproval than concern. "I hope the results are worth the trouble."

The doctor had only a hint as to how much trouble obtaining that tiny swab had been. Or how much more grief it might lead to, if the results confirmed a killer like Sean Burke was my father.

I FOLLOWED CLAYBECK AROUND the university building to the staff parking lot in the rear. The holiday break meant only half a dozen spots were occupied. Off to one side of the paved area, a large plot surrounded by ivy-covered wooden fences had been dedicated to a communal garden for the student body. Raised beds for vegetables and herbs were mostly just soil now, stiff and brittle with the night's frost. Waiting for the season of growth. I wondered if Wren knew of plants that would flourish in the cold months. Past the garden, a long row of groundskeeping sheds covered the space between the parking lot and the street beyond.

"I'll be staying in town tonight," Claybeck said as she removed her keys from her purse. "Once you hear the results from Jay, you're not obligated to let me know, of course. But I'd be lying if I said I wasn't curious."

Maybe it was the unexpected movement twenty feet ahead of Claybeck that sparked me. Or maybe I'd caught a ripple of something wrong on the light breeze. Either way, I was dodging left, behind the cover of the garden fence, before a cogent thought had formed.

Saleem stepped partway out from between the sheds to aim a large automatic at Claybeck's head.

"Be silent," he said. She stood frozen.

The Colt was in my hand and I was concealed, but the fence's wooden slats wouldn't be much proof against high-caliber rounds. Saleem and I were at a standoff. Doc Claybeck in the middle.

I didn't have a clear shot. Saleem took advantage and moved first, shifting his aim to me and closing the half-dozen steps to the doctor in a heartbeat.

"Move back," he said to me, wheeling Claybeck around and grabbing her by the coat collar. She was a tall woman. I had even less of a target than before. "Back. I will kill her if I must."

I retreated into the lawned garden. It was a stupid move, tactically. My cover went from inadequate to almost nonexistent in the open space. The walled plot of land offered more privacy for Saleem to finish us off.

But I believed him. He would risk a shootout in the open with Claybeck as his shield if I didn't comply.

My only chance would be to dive for the ground behind one of the raised planting beds. If Claybeck struggled, there might be a sliver of a second for a kill shot. I moved backward, stretching the yards between us as Saleem pushed Claybeck forward and into the garden. Stepping every time she stepped, as if they were dancing. She still clutched her purse and keys. In another few seconds, I would be out of room.

The doctor's fingers pressed urgently at her keyfob.

Her eyes sought out mine, pleading, even as I leveled the Colt at a spot over her shoulder and prepared to jump.

I realized what she was doing. And kept walking, until my back was pressed against the ivy. Inviting Saleem to follow.

"Throw away your gun," he called to me as they took another step. He started to say more, but his time was up.

I already knew Claybeck's dogs didn't bark. And on the lawn, their sprinting feet were as silent and swift as the wind.

Saleem managed one stunted scream of terror and agony as they brought him down. He thrashed and kicked madly, not slowing the beasts for an instant. Claybeck recovered from her shock, tried calling them off. But nature would not be denied. Her dogs had smelled fear on their mistress, and that was enough. One lunged to clamp its jaws around Saleem's head. He kicked more, each time weaker than the last, and fell still.

Then all that remained were feral growls and the sounds of rending, like pork from bone and gristle. By the time the dogs finally responded to her commands, releasing their grips and running circles as they whined in horrible excitement, what was left on the dappled grass looked like a rag effigy dipped in carmine ink.

I didn't approach. In fact I had done my best impression of a stone, moving only to slowly hide my gun, in case the sight of it might be an attack trigger.

In another moment, Claybeck had them sitting, one

hand on each of their heads. She was sobbing. Praising them. They panted and smiled behind their blood-drenched muzzles. They knew they were good dogs.

WHEN I WAS SURE Claybeck had them calmed, I walked around the edge of the fence to close the gate. Then I picked the clearest path I could through the reddened grass to Saleem's body. In one of his pockets I found the keys to an Impala, identifiable by a key tag that had the dealership's name along with the license number and model.

A locked shed at one side of the garden contained hoses and irrigation-system controls. I opened the valves and let the spray wash over the lawn, and Saleem's corpse. Claybeck took charge of the dogs, hosing each of them down. I went in search of the car. We hadn't said a word to one another.

The Impala turned out to be one of the handful of cars in the staff lot, and the oldest by at least half a dozen years. In its glove compartment I discovered Saleem's brother's passport and credit cards, along with a bill of sale showing the junker had been acquired for twelve hundred dollars in cash from the dealer in Salt Lake yesterday.

Saleem must have jumped the train and driven half the night to Claybeck's home before tailing her here. Maybe aiming to take her prisoner—once she was separated from her dogs—and ensnare me or Hollis by using her. Perhaps Saleem had planned to leave the train before it reached Seattle all along, or maybe my attempt at luring him to Sean Burke's barn had only served to arouse his suspicions. I guessed that he'd paid cash to keep the car off his brother's charges.

He'd probably paid cash for the plastic sheeting that lined the Impala's roomy trunk, too. Ready for our dead bodies. Now it would serve for his. I backed the Impala right up to the garden gate, grateful for the deserted campus.

Inside, Claybeck had finished cleaning her dogs and was doing her best to rinse blood from her sleeves and pants where they had brushed against her. The hounds lay on the dry grass to one side, watching curiously. Their black-brown fur stood out in lustrous wet spikes. I turned off the sprinklers and removed my jacket and shirt. Putting Saleem in the trunk would be messy work.

"Are you all right?" I said.

"No." Claybeck tugged forcefully at her pants cuff, wringing it out. "But as the gravedigger said, I'd rather be on this end of the shovel."

Her dark joke surprised me so much I nearly laughed. "Christ. You would have made a good soldier."

"Right now I wish I had been." She shuddered, not just from the cold water, and tossed the hose aside. The dogs rose to investigate and lap at the running stream.

"They were in your car," I said.

Claybeck nodded, a touch frantically. "I was planning to stay in the city overnight. I can't leave them at home. Of all the uses for a minivan with automatic doors . . ."

"I'm very glad. Thanks."

"What about—" Claybeck gestured but did not turn toward Saleem's body. She hadn't looked directly at it since she'd called the dogs off, I guessed.

"We can't tell the cops. For one thing, the courts would probably insist on putting your dogs down."

"I wasn't intending to involve them."

"I'll handle it."

"Yes. I suppose you would know how." Her expression was hard to read.

"You should stay with friends tonight," I said. "Don't be alone."

Claybeck nodded.

"Maybe not tomorrow, either. You're going to need some time, and somebody you can confide in."

"I'll be all right."

"Yeah. You will."

Her eyes were wet again. "Hollis asked if I would accompany him on a trip down the coast this week. I think I might just."

THERE WAS A QUIET marsh off the Black River near Renton where I could dump Saleem. Wildlife and water would go to work on his remains. The blood-smeared plastic sheeting would be stuffed into a dumpster behind any grocery store with a butcher. The creaky Impala, clean and empty, I'd leave on a city street with the keys in it.

The corpse would be found eventually. But without papers—without much of a face either—it might never be identified or linked with the car. Once the job was done, I'd call Aura Nath and tell her the gunman was no longer a danger. Leaving Claybeck out of the story.

Driving south in the Impala with the shrouded body in the trunk, I thought about the doctor and her dogs, and what they had done to Saleem. I pondered whether Stanley might have done the same, if it were Addy or Cyndra who had been in danger.

He would, I decided. The huge mixed breed was not a trained weapon like Claybeck's hounds. Stanley was friendly by nature. Despite that, the predatory instinct to bite and rip and kill lay just beneath, peeking out whenever Stanley tore after a squirrel or into a chew rope.

But killing a man would have changed Stanley. After such an experience, I doubted he could ever be the joyous overgrown pup that he was now, not completely. Dogs could suffer trauma, too.

Burke was akin to Claybeck's dogs. Merciless, and happy to be so. I wasn't quite as savage, but I knew full well I could get into that headspace when I chose. That I could live with the consequences and sleep well, just like Burke did. Maybe it was in our blood.

CHAPTER FORTY-FIVE

THE CLOCK ON THE wall of the Sol Liquor Lounge read a quarter to ten, to the best of my knowledge. Hard to know for sure, because the interior light was soft and the wall entirely covered with a world map that perhaps explained why the lounge's décor was stuck somewhere between China and Polynesia. Also because the clock might not actually exist. My vision was a little impaired.

I tried focusing on the aged J. Baum of Cincinnati combination safe that rested in a place of honor atop the vintage glass-fronted cooler behind the bar. The safe was the main reason I liked the lounge. The bartender on my first visit had told me the staff had never succeeded in opening it. I was sure I could. Maybe I should do it right now.

To keep myself from trying, I called Professor Corrigan.

"You're a little early," he said. "But I got it done. You want the results now? Forget it, of course you do, I'm just wiped out." His stuttering chuckle did sound ragged. "It's definite. Matches across the board on the profile. Sample B is the father of Sample A. I'm guessing you're B? Is this congratulations or commiserations?"

"I'm A," I said, my voice sounding a long way away.

His amusement vanished. "Your dad, huh? Whoa. Okay. I suppose the same question applies."

It did. I just didn't have an answer.

"I've got the full profile; I can send that to you," Corrigan said. "It's not anything that can be used in court, just so you know. For that a lab tech would have to witness the samples directly—"

"Not necessary," I said.

"Cool. I gotta get out of here, get some sleep. It's been a minute since I've pulled an all-nighter."

I hung up.

Sean Burke, seventeen. Boyfriend of Moira Shaw, sixteen. A relationship doomed to fail, but it had lasted long enough to permanently change at least one of their lives, not to mention starting mine.

God.

Burke had wanted to know. I wasn't up for sharing the news. Not yet.

A notion of ordering another Boxer's Fracture tequila drink or six occurred. I let it slide past. Getting bombed—more thoroughly bombed—wasn't going to help my mood. I was still figuring out what the hell my mood was.

Of all the fathers I might have imagined, Burke wasn't even on the list. If the man had any redeeming qualities other than his faith in his friend Martens, I hadn't seen them.

I owed Burke my life. I wasn't sure I owed him the truth.

AN HOUR LATER I surrendered my stool at the counter and wandered outside into an unexpected sleet. The slush fell at an angle that spoke of intentional spite, working its shivering way under collars and into gloves. While the cold didn't instantly sober me, it ensured my body would be burning every bit of fuel to stay warm, sugary alcohol included.

I needed clean clothes if I was going to stay at Addy's for any longer. I'd stop at my apartment, pack a bag.

But once I got there, I found myself sitting in my leather wingback chair, an extravagant piece that I'd bought because it reminded me of one Dono had once owned. I began looking up gubernatorial candidate Palmer Stratton on my laptop. He was the man in charge. The one who would decide whether Sean Burke—*my father*, my brain insisted on adding—would live or die, indirectly.

I didn't like Stratton's face. Or his Holy Order, Ivy League, yacht-and-country-club background. Even his mom, Margaret, pissed me off, with her endless causes, every one of them hyping the Stratton name.

I knew it was classist. I knew my opinion of Stratton was powered by booze. But fuck the guy. Whatever good he'd done as a prosecutor was just to balance the scales, make him more palatable to voters before he leapt into the political arena. He practically had CRUSADER stamped on his Botoxed forehead. With all the morally superior fervor that word implied.

Stratton was the man I needed to convince. Or barter with. I had knowledge that might be crucial to bringing down Liashko. Stratton was the only guy who could assure me that whatever happened, even if that didn't include the arms trafficker in handcuffs, the Feds would get Burke to safety.

His campaign webpage listed a private fund-raiser at the Alexis Hotel tomorrow night. For key donors and potentials, no doubt. Security would be tight. I'd have to think how to clear those hurdles, once my thoughts were back in full working order.

A text lit up my phone on the armrest of the chair.

ANYTHING?

It was from Burke. Maybe he was as curious, in his own sociopathic way, to know the results as I had been.

I could keep delaying the inevitable, or get it over with. I chose the latter.

Anderson Park reservoir. Half an hour.

The park would be closed at one o'clock in the morning, but I doubted Sean Burke would be put off by city ordinances any more than I was. Plus the reservoir was practically on my doorstep. Home field advantage.

HE CAME FROM THE north side, past the volcano-shaped fountain that had been turned off for the winter. Enough glistening frost from the earlier rush of sleet remained that his shoes made crunching sounds on the pathway.

"So?" he said, while still ten yards off.

I nodded confirmation.

He stopped short. "Damn."

"Can't put it better than that."

A curved concrete border around the dormant fountain served double duty as a bench. We sat. Burke seemed no worse for wear from his binge on downers the night before. His grizzly-brown hair shone wetly. Too long since the sleet had fallen; maybe he'd showered before going out. In his black windbreaker and khakis, he might have been about to tee off a very late round of night golf at the Jefferson course.

"I dunno what to do about it, now that we know," he said.

"Now you tell me about you and Moira. No bullshit this time."

Burke took a long breath. "It's been thirty years. More."

I waited.

"Gus brought me along one day when he came to see your old guy, Dono. Pops was buying something from him. Some sort of whatsit that would help Gus get past a burglar alarm. That sound right?"

It did. Dono could make such a tool in his sleep. Though Gut Burke must have been willing to pay a small fortune for my grandfather to bend his rules and deal directly with a mob enforcer.

"Moira was at the house that day," Burke said. "Damn. Gut had to slap my skull, I was staring so hard at her. I know she's your ma and all, and I don't mean no disrespect, but shit, I was a teenage boy. I managed to talk to her some. She wouldn't give me her phone number at the house. But she said she'd call me."

And she had. Moira Shaw, straight-A student, apparently had a thing for bad boys. I couldn't muster any surprise, given our family. My mouth was dry.

"We had to sneak around," Burke continued, "and we hardly ever went anywhere when it was just the two of us. We'd go to the movies or hang with friends of mine from school."

"She ever talk about herself? Her plans?"

"College for sure, I know that much. But Moira was . . . her mom had died like a couple of years before. She was kinda distant."

"Not too distant."

"Well, yeah. When she, ah—when she said she wanted to get with me, it was a surprise, you know? I figured she still had her cherry. Sorry."

I shook my head. We were past protecting anyone's memory.

"Then she called me a week after and broke it off. That was it."

"What about later? The letters she wrote you?"

Burke's head snapped around. "Jesus. You've seen those? What, did she keep copies?"

"Her best friend caught her. That's how I learned your name."

He relaxed. "Well, shit. Yeah, she wrote me. I was wanting to get back together. She sent a letter: Thanks but No Thanks. Embarrassing as fuck. I'm glad you didn't see it."

"And that was all?"

"Almost." He took out his keys and began to remove something from the ring, slipping it off an inch-long ball chain of metal, like a tiny dogtag necklace. He handed the object to me.

It was a round brass disc about the size and shape of a fifty-cent piece. Tarnished half green from inattention. My religious education was nonexistent, but I recognized it as a Catholic medallion for a saint. The image etched in relief showed a bearded man standing ramrod straight, with a lighthouse in the background on his left side and a twin-masted sailing ship on the right.

"Saint Brendan," Burke said. "Built a boat and sailed around spreading the gospel. Moira sent that to me a few weeks after her kiss-off letter. She didn't explain why. I figured it was 'cause Gus and I got around a lot, we needed protecting."

She might have sent the medal to Burke after she realized she was pregnant with me. The timing was right. Stopping short of telling him about the baby—maybe she'd already judged Burke as a rock-bottom choice to raise a kid—but wanting her child's father to be safe nonetheless.

Moira had been sixteen. Hard to fathom exactly what she might have been thinking, or the stress she was under.

I could sympathize with her desire to keep Burke safe, though. Lousy daddy material or not.

He looked at the frost on the ground, sparkling in the lamplight. "I wish she'd said something."

The brass medallion fit in the key pocket of my coat like it had been crafted for it.

"What's Liashko bringing into the country?" I said.

Burke frowned. "I told you to keep out of that."

"Stepan and his team are dead, you're taking over. That makes you more valuable to the Feds now. Do you have any written guarantee they won't cut you loose?"

"Leave it."

"Not now I won't. Not after this."

"I'm askin' you. For Moira."

Angry as I was at Burke, laughter nearly won the moment. His cheap fucking ploy.

I tapped the medal in my pocket. "All this means is that a teenage girl gave a damn. Don't start pretending Moira was more to you than she was."

Burke looked at me like I'd sprouted antennae.

"I'm on Liashko's hit list, too," I said. "You want payback for Gus? Let's get it. Liashko will rot in a super-max cell twenty-three hours a day for the rest of his life. He'll know every minute that you're the reason. Give me something."

"You're crazy," he said. "I mean you're really fuckin' bughouse."

"But not stupid. I found you. I can do a lot more. What don't you know about Liashko's deal? Where can't the Feds go?"

Burke just kept staring. "I know what he's selling, but not where he's got them stashed. Yet. The paranoid fuck isn't trusting me." His hands tightened around his knees. "You really think you can find his stuff?"

"I got a knack for it. What am I looking for?"

He looked at the dry fountain, like it might help him decide. Grunted a laugh.

"Shit, I've gambled this far," he said. "Might as well go all in. You know what a Verba is?"

It was my turn to be stunned. "Russian surface-to-air missile launchers. Portable, for ground troops."

"That's right. When things really started to slide for Anatoly, he found a way to lift a bunch of those babies from some separatist group backed by his old Russian masters and blame their disappearance on the Ukrainian armed forces. Forty missiles with reusable trigger mechanisms and sights. I saw 'em myself, in Moldova, more than a year ago. Liashko's looking to close up shop. Everything he stole out of the war in the Donbass region, in one go."

Jesus. Like most modern missile launchers, the Verba had seeking and guidance tech built right in. Designed for infantry grunts who might have to fire the weapon after only a few spare minutes of training in the field. The missiles came with ultraviolet and infrared sensors both, to engage targets with even minimal radar signatures.

Just one of those could bring down a jetliner, or a military chopper, or a cruise missile. Damn near anything in the sky. Forty, deployed strategically, could temporarily cripple a nation.

Burke must have read my shock. "Ease up before you have a stroke. We're all over this."

"We?"

"Anatoly's buyer, the guy I've set him up with, is ATF." Burke spat on the ground in satisfaction. "An agent pretending to be a cartel go-between. We'll have a hundred Feds in combat gear swarming that piece of shit like ants on a dead rat the second he shows his face."

Because they didn't know where the Verbas were.

For once, I was ahead of Burke and the task force both.

"This could still go sideways," I said, "if Liashko never lets on where he's got the missiles."

"Like I said, I'll take that chance. Anatoly has fifteen million comin' to him, he thinks. That's a fucking big incentive. If you can really point me to those missiles, that's all we need. Once we nail this asswipe, you're home free."

"And you'll have a new name."

Burke grunted. "Yeah. It may not be much of a life in whatever podunk shithole they stick me in. But I'll be livin'."

He stood up.

"For whatever it's worth, I liked her," he said, and he pointed to my pocket with the medal of Saint Brendan. "Hang on to that. She woulda wanted you to have it."

"If I don't see you . . ."

"You won't." He smiled grimly. "One more week, and I'm as gone as gone can be."

BETTY CLOSED HER BAR early on Mondays. I let myself in the back and went directly to the alcove where she kept the DVR that captured the feed off the security cameras.

The cameras had been a debate between us in the old location. Betty didn't want her customers to feel watched. I wanted a positive ID on anyone who made trouble. Taking that side had felt odd at the time: Van Shaw, Crimestopper. But I'd persevered. That same week a brawl had broken out in one of the U District watering holes, resulting in everyone threatening to sue everyone else. That had probably helped my argument.

The DVR stored a week's worth of high-def from eight different cameras I'd installed at key angles. Right now, I was concerned about the one to the right of the main bar. I clicked on last Saturday and sped through the captured feed until just before closing time.

There I was, with Special Agent Martens across the bar from me. His blue rep tie in full color. I let the silent video play at normal speed, as Martens gathered his coat and left the screen toward the back of the bar, as I went in the opposite direction to close up.

Martens returned almost immediately to the screen. Crouching very low, hiding from the rest of the bar behind the high counter. I watched as his image pulled out the recycling bin from underneath, removed something, and crept back the way he'd come.

A beer bottle. My beer bottle, the Reuben's Porter I had tossed during our little talk about me becoming an informant for the ATF task force.

Martens already had easy access to my fingerprints. I'd been booked before, plus my prints had been taken during military service. The only other use for that bottle was a sample of my DNA. But that could also be obtained by an official request to the Army. They had snagged a blood specimen from me when I was first inducted, same as any recruit. So what the hell was Martens after?

Burke might have confessed to his old friend why I'd sought Burke out, and that young Sean might have fathered me three decades ago. Martens and the task force could be checking that evidence for themselves. But if the task force wanted my DNA to find out the truth about Burke and me, why would Burke have given me his swab? Were the two sides operating independently, not sharing information?

There was another possible reason, besides my parentage. The task force was looking to match my DNA to evidence found at a crime scene. Maybe they didn't want to wait while the Army processed the request through its endless channels.

The break-in at Burke's house? Or somewhere else? I thought back, wondering if I had slipped up somewhere. I couldn't think of any crime I'd committed that might intersect with the task force's aims. But then, I'd broken into plenty of places since my return to Seattle. And my crimes hadn't stopped at B&E, either. Maybe Martens and his team had their sights on nailing me on another charge. Force my cooperation.

If a federal task force had added me to their list of suspects, I could wind up working for the law whether I liked it or not. That was the best-case scenario. The other would be a long stay in maximum security, maybe right alongside Anatoly Liashko.

CHAPTER FORTY-SIX

ONLINE REGISTRATION FOR THE night's fundraiser for Palmer Stratton, candidate for governor of the great state of Washington, had closed the day before. But a morning call to Stratton's campaign HQ produced a volunteer who had clearly downed plenty of coffee despite the early hour. He passed me on to a senior coordinator, to whom I breathlessly explained that I'd seen the candidate's performance in the debates and heartily *agreed* with his positions and would be *delighted* to purchase a pair of seats at one of the premier tables at tonight's little gathering, if any of those might still be available. She didn't squander a second in taking down my debit card number and held the line until the charge for ten thousand dollars cleared.

It did, barely. As fast as I'd made my substantial nest egg from selling my family land and from less legitimate means, it had evaporated.

Worth it, if my most recent spending spree got me close enough to Stratton to say a few words.

My next call was to Wren.

"How do you feel about incredibly overpriced chicken with a side of political speeches?" I said.

"I get enough punishment on the derby track. Is this our date tonight?"

"Sort of. A fund-raiser for the governor's race."

She made a humming sound of consideration. "You don't seem the type of guy to go to partisan rallies."

"No."

"Am I . . . camouflage?"

"Yes. But not for anything illegal. I need to speak to the candidate, and this is the fastest way."

"You take your activism seriously. This has something to do with your dad, yeah?"

"It does. Are you up for it?"

I heard her moving, then the sound of Janelle Monáe singing in the background dimmed.

"Two conditions," Wren said. "Tell me why this is so important."

"That's a long story, and I'm late to meet someone up in Everett. I'll call you after and tell you what's going on. If you don't like anything about it, you can bail. No hard feelings."

"You have a really weird way of flirting. How dressy is this fund-raiser?"

I hadn't even thought about clothes. The blue checked suit I'd acquired from the grumpy Giuseppe hung in my closet, back in its bag. "I'm guessing jackets and ties?"

Wren laughed. "Why is it guys never know? Doesn't matter. I have a dress that's conformist enough for any political stripe."

"Was that your second condition?"

"No. We'll get into that later. What time does the dinner start?"

"Six o'clock."

"Pick me up at five-thirty." She gave me her address, a house in Fauntleroy. "And don't forget to call me. This is a story I have to hear."

I'd already told Wren about my relationship to Burke and hinted at the kind of work he did. I could give her the rundown on Liashko and the task force without naming names or putting the investigation at risk.

Wren had seemed fascinated by my criminal past. I wanted to be up front with her about my life now, as harrowing as it was.

Would the truth push her away? Or was that part of my attraction for her?

THE REST OF THE daylight hours were spent shopping, and cooking, after a fashion.

My early appointment in Everett was with a salvage yard owner, who'd been willing to open on his day off to let me purchase a small and barely seaworthy rowboat for a hundred bucks cash. I'd brought my own rope to tie the boat to the top of my truck's canopy. Secure while I made multiple stops in the northern tip of King County.

At each hardware store I bought a quart or two of kerosene. From pharmacies and outdoor shops and a janitorial supply company I acquired chemicals and other materials, including a box of shotgun shells and what eventually amounted to two full cases of antacid tablets. All purchased with cash. It took me two trips from the truck to carry everything up to my apartment.

Back in my kitchen, I filled the bottom of a large

baking tray with clay cat litter and soaked it with a pint of gasoline mixed with cleaning solution, setting the granules to dry under the stove fan while I carried on in the living area.

The kerosene I poured one can at a time into five-gallon buckets, steadily adding the antacid tablets with their active calcium carbonate and a mix of other chemicals. What I was left with, after an hour of very careful stirring, was a thick pungent slurry roughly the color of a rotting peach, a byproduct of the rainbow assortment of tablets.

I had all the windows open and fans blowing to ward off the fumes. It helped, marginally. When my phone rang, I went out into the hall before I dared to take off my painter's mask and safety goggles to answer.

"Hollis," I said. "Are you where you can talk?"

"No one for a quarter mile but us, if you don't count the fish." Hollis was practically shouting. "I'm on the satellite phone, halfway up Juan de Fuca with the good Doctor Paula."

"How's she doing?" I'd filled Hollis in on the last moments of Saleem.

"A strong woman. She's quiet a lot, but that might just be her nature. Having the dogs at her side seems to help. The mutts and I are actually getting along, if you can believe that."

Believe it I did. Hollis Brant could make friends with a tiger shark.

"Hollis, I need to talk to your buddy Jaak today, along with someone who can translate the tougher parts. If you think we can trust him a short distance."

"You saved his life and his job, Van. I expect Jaak would take holy orders and become your father confessor if you asked. But, ah, you know he's still recovering—"

"There shouldn't be any danger. In fact, he might find it fun."

I explained what I had in mind. By the time I finished Hollis was laughing.

"Hell, I'd be up for that myself, if I were there. Sorry to miss it. I'll have Jaak's man call you."

I thanked him and returned to the miasma within my apartment. I sealed the buckets of flammable slurry, having already punched holes in the plastic lids with an awl to make sure the fumes didn't build up pressure. One more task, and then I would be ready.

The powder from the shotgun shells became the key ingredient in an oversized firecracker, packed into a cardboard tube with the dried and highly toxic cat litter. A long bit of waterproof fuse from the model rocket section of a hobby store capped the tube.

Not exactly a shaped charge with C-4, but I didn't have the Army providing toys for me anymore. It would serve just fine. Like Hollis, I was a little sorry I wouldn't be there to see it go off.

CHAPTER FORTY-SEVEN

THE LOBBY OF THE Alexis Hotel had been partitioned by velvet ropes and concrete security guards. A pair of crisp concierges in eggshell blouses and skirts ushered guests of the hotel toward the marble-topped reception desk. The rest of us, the politically minded affluent, were allowed past the ropes and welcomed into a barroom decked out like a bookseller's, with leatherbound editions lining the shelves in place of bottles. A cocktail reception was in full swing. A campaign staffer checked our names off a clipboard and handed us a card, which noted we would be at table 7.

Wren placed the card in her clutch purse. "A souvenir," she said.

She wore a beautifully simple midnight-blue sheath dress. With its sleeves covering her tattoos, and her dark hair gathered into a twist that managed to be both elegant and casual enough to allow stray curls to frame her face, Wren might have been a candidate herself. Only the bemused smirk at the corner of her mouth spoiled the effect.

"This is nuts," she said as she took my arm.

"Really? I feel right at home." We moved into the

reception crowd, as two of the security guards changed position to get a better angle on us.

It had been a smart choice to bring Wren. Her earlier assessment was spot-on; I couldn't pass for a political patron. Nor even much like the clean-cut security detail in their blazers and gray slacks currently giving me the eyeball. Concealed weapons would be their main concern. Hidden cameras a close second. Indiscreet footage could be more damaging than a bullet, at least to a candidate's poll numbers.

Had I been alone, I would have been discreetly pulled aside, queried, probably searched, and almost certainly denied access once they performed a cursory check and noted that I had bought my seats the same day and had no connection to either the party nor anyone at the event. Better to refund a few thousand bucks than to invite very public outbursts from some disgruntled vet.

But Wren attracted the eye, to put it mildly. Once the guards had decided my presence was an acceptable risk, no one paid me any heed.

"Drink?" I asked. Wren agreed and we drifted toward a gold-draped table covered with trays of canapes and tiny quiches. Two servers stood at parade rest, offering prepoured champagne as guests drew near.

I didn't see Palmer Stratton among the fluted glasses and speckled neckties. Only five weeks until the election. I knew just enough about campaigns to assume Stratton would have an event scheduled every available minute of his day. He would probably appear through some private entrance after the dinner, make his stump speech and shake a few hands, half of his mind already on whatever function was scheduled right after this.

If all went well, I'd have ten seconds to grab his attention. Ideally without getting the rental cops involved.

"Ladies and gentlemen, if you'll take your seats," a staffer near us proclaimed, his arm outstretched toward the banquet room. Wren and I joined the migration and wound through a small jungle of circular tables to the front row. Table 7 was set near stage left, with an unobstructed view of the podium.

Hotel waiters circled, doling out bread baskets and pitchers of iced tea. The other guests at the table began to exchange names. They were all middle-aged couples, save for one lean older woman to Wren's left, in a dress-and-jacket combo whose shimmering gray color emphasized her nimbus of white hair.

"Margaret Stratton," she said to us as the introductions came around.

I'd already placed her, from the news videos. Palmer Stratton's mother. As the wife of the late congressman and mother of the Democratic hopeful, she'd been in front of the cameras nearly as much as her son recently. Breeding and probably something like equestrian sports had kept her posture youthful.

"I'm Van, this is Wren," I said.

"A Sounders game," Wren said with a note of surprise. "Sorry, but I just realized that's where I've seen you before, Mrs. Stratton. Last June. You were introducing a youth group at halftime."

"The Junior Strikers," said Mrs. Stratton. "You certainly have a good memory. My husband, James, started that team for underprivileged children, after he left Congress. Part of our Stratton Foundation."

"Soccer and sailboats," I said. "The Stratton Regatta

was a few weeks ago. I saw the coverage." The cynical part of me wanted to ask if the deprived kids served as deckhands, but I figured that would be unproductive.

"Anything we can do for our city." Margaret Stratton nodded magnanimously. The royal "we," perhaps. "Are you involved with the campaign?"

"I aim to be," I said. "Your son is something else."

She smiled. "I happen to agree."

A three-person camera crew had set up at stage right, running prechecks at the podium. Ready to get a clip from Stratton's speech for the late news. The ambient jazz music dimmed and a woman with a blond pageboy and scarlet dress spoke into the podium's microphone.

"Good evening, and welcome," she said, beaming at the assembled donors. "I'm very pleased to announce a change for tonight. We've moved up our guest of honor's schedule so that he can take the time to meet you personally." A few people in the crowd murmured appreciatively. "Please welcome the next governor of the great state of Washington, United States Attorney Palmer Stratton!"

Stratton strode out of the wings and gave a big wave and even bigger smile to the room, as the guests obediently burst into applause.

In person, he looked tanned and nearly overflowing with good health. His indigo suit had been expertly tailored to encompass his college-wrestler shoulders and to conceal the stubborn few pounds around his middle that had accumulated in the quarter century since. Combined with a jewel-toned red tie and the gray at his temples that might have been tamed by a careful dye job, Stratton's whole image walked a line between old-money confidence and new-economy flash.

After a moment of Stratton soaking in the welcome, a brunette woman who was his equal for glossy attractiveness joined him onstage. I wondered if her dress had been chosen to match his tie, or if the tie had been made to match the dress. The blonde with the pageboy handed Stratton a microphone.

"Thank you for coming, everyone," he said. "Carolyn and I are delighted to be here, and even happier that we'll have a chance to thank you for your support in person. But I won't make you wait for your meals all the way through a stump speech. Not even mine." A ripple of laughter from the audience. "We'll say a quick hello while you enjoy the hors d'oeuvres and then get back to what's important." Stratton waved once more and took his wife's hand. On cue, the boisterous jazz music swelled again.

They came down the steps from the stage and immediately began shaking hands at the first VIP table. Everyone around us rose to their feet. Wren looked at me in amusement—*I guess this is how this works*—as we stood, too.

The campaign staffers quickly combined forces to herd the premier guests at the front into something resembling a queue. Rather than us filing past Stratton, he moved along the loose row, both preceded and followed at a discreet few feet by two of the blue blazers, who kept their eyes on the crowd. I pasted a smile on my face.

Stratton and his wife took no more than thirty seconds to greet each guest, and the donor had the full focus of his attention during that time. It seemed to be enough. Each guest went away looking a little dazed. I'd heard once that Bill Clinton had a similar effect on people, making them feel, however temporarily, like the most important individual in the room.

Busy with each VIP in turn, Stratton never looked to the next person. Never saw my face until he was already shaking my hand. Give him due credit. He had only seen me once before, in the state patrol station, but there was no question that he recognized me in that first instant.

"Mr. Stratton, Donovan Shaw," I said immediately, hoping security wouldn't notice the astonished expression that had swept the candidate's persistent smile away. "I've followed your time as our federal attorney, and it's made a huge impression."

"Well," Stratton said. His shake of my hand was much slower than the quick three-beat clasp he'd delivered to others. "That's very good to hear, Mr. . . . Shaw."

"Building a platform on your prosecution record, that's a solid foundation. I know a lot of people who put crime safety as their number one priority."

The candidate's eyes narrowed in calculation. This close, I could tell the suntan was mostly makeup, expertly applied for the cameras. Was I here to disrupt the event? Embarrass him somehow? "What sort of work do you do?"

"Freelance journalism. A new line for me, covering trade with Eastern Europe."

Stratton nodded, ignoring the staffer who was subtly trying to herd him onward. His public mask was back, but even as his body turned to greet Wren, his gaze stayed on me. "That sounds very interesting. Hello."

"Hello," Wren said, as poised as if there was no tension in the air at all. "Raina Marchand."

"Very pleased. How did you come to be involved, Ms. Marchand?" Stratton's laser attention had redirected to Wren, but I expected the question applied to us both.

"I'm active in environmental causes," she said. "My friends and I have a kind of task force."

I nearly snorted. Wren was a natural at sticking the jab.

"I see," said Stratton. His teeth behind the smile might have been gritted. "Very nice to meet you both."

After an extremely brief acknowledgment from Stratton's wife, Carolyn, who looked slightly confused by our exchange, the couple moved on to the next table. Wren and I sat. Margaret Stratton had disappeared during the receiving line—I imagine she'd had her fill of those recently—and we could speak without being overheard.

"That was strangely fun, poking the bear," she murmured to me. "Now what?"

I was watching Stratton. He glanced once in our direction, then leaned to speak a few quiet words in the ear of a campaign sheepdog. The staffer nodded briskly before hustling up the steps and backstage.

"Now we think about what restaurant we'll go to," I said. "I don't expect we'll be staying for dinner."

It took ten minutes for Stratton to finish greeting the donors at the premier tables. The blond assistant murmured in Stratton's ear, and he gave a quick wave to the camera crew before exiting into the wings.

A security man tapped my shoulder.

"Would you accompany me, sir?" he said.

I nodded as if I'd been expecting the summons since I first arrived. Our friends at the table looked uncertain, not sure if I was receiving preferential treatment or the bum's rush. Neither was I, but I smiled like I held the winning hand.

Wren cocked an eyebrow. "I'll make sure the champagne doesn't get lonely."

The security man led me around the far side of the stage to a door used by hotel staff. Beyond it was a short hallway with the sounds of a kitchen in full swing coming from the end, a melody of clattering pans and shouted orders. I was hit with the scents of vinaigrette and searing beef. The guard led me halfway down the hall and stepped aside to allow me to enter a side room, then closed its door behind me.

The room might have normally served as a meeting space for hotel staff, with framed Alexis promotional materials from years past on the taupe fabric walls. Now the furniture had been cleared to allow room for a studio-quality interview. Lamps and broad white fabric reflectors formed a loose circle around two high chairs at one end.

A makeup station, its mirror emblazoned with glowing bulbs, waited to one side. I walked over to it, noting the stained applicators and sweat pads and hairbrush neatly arrayed in case the candidate required a touch-up during the filming.

Stratton entered as I was adjusting my new tie in the mirror. He motioned to another guard in the hall before shutting the door.

"We can speak privately. And I'll spare two minutes, so let's dispense with the bullshit." His natural speaking voice was flatter and less resonant than the baritone he used for the public. "Why are you here, Shaw?"

"To reach an agreement. About Anatoly Liashko, and your task force."

"Stop there. I'm not discussing any part of any investigation with you."

"So I'll do the talking. Your ATF agent, Martens. He has an informant." I glanced at the door, conscious of the guard somewhere outside. "I won't say his name out in the open, but you know who he is. You'd have to know, as head prosecutor."

He stared. Hard to interpret the look on his face, but it might have been dread peeking through.

"No matter what happens with your case," I said, "I want that inside man protected."

Stratton reassembled his hard expression. "What's your interest?"

I shook my head. Burke and I could keep our questions of family to ourselves.

"Martens already made you an offer," Stratton said. "You didn't follow through. You've done jack to demand any concessions."

"What if I could find where Liashko is holding weapons? On U.S. soil?"

His face tightened. "If you have information pertinent to this case, you'll give it to us. Immediately. Or I promise I will bust you as an accessory and find a way to make it stick."

"In which case you get nothing. My way, at least you

secure the arms. Maybe even get the drop on Liashko when he shows."

"This is national security, Shaw. You could wind up in ADX Florence for the next twenty years, playing checkers using scraps of felt alongside domestic terrorists. You lump yourself in with those traitors?"

My expression was another answer.

"So prove it to me," Stratton pressed.

"Your inside man," I said. "Arrest, no arrest, complete clusterfuck, I don't care—no backing out on your deal with him."

"Just assuming there was a source, that person would be protected. My word on it."

"Not enough. I want that protection guaranteed. Otherwise he's dead. You know that's the only outcome if Liashko goes free. And then you'll have a new problem."

"A threat," Stratton scoffed.

"I'd never threaten a federal prosecutor. But it's just as dumb to expect I'll keep quiet if this goes off the rails. *'U.S. Attorney Abandons Federal Informant to Mobster from Russia.'* It'll look like you manipulated the task force to try and score a political win in time for the election."

"That's completely false." The candidate's brow furrowed. His makeup would definitely need a retouch.

"I don't care. I have enough provable facts to point CNN and Fox and everyone else in the right direction. Like you said, I'll find a way to make it stick."

He crossed his arms. "There's a natural reaction to that action. State investigators will rake over everything you've done and everywhere you've been since the

Army kicked your ass home. Including whatever went down in Oregon last year. Griffon County still has a few unanswered questions." He nodded. "There's no need for us to be on opposite sides. Give me what you have, and I'll do everything I can."

"Including the WITSEC deal in writing. If I locate Liashko's stash, I'll give you all you need to nail him. If I can't find it, you've lost nothing."

"Don't play brinksmanship with me, Shaw. You'll lose."

"We'll both go down." I knocked on the door, and the guard dutifully opened it. "You just have farther to fall."

CHAPTER FORTY-EIGHT

THE GUARD ESCORTED ME around the back hall-ways of the Alexis, emerging at the lobby. Wren met me by the revolving doors.

"Well, you're not in handcuffs," she said, "and I didn't see a SWAT team run past while they were passing out the salads. Was it a win?"

"It was a draw," I said.

"Always take the draw. Tell people the refs made bad calls."

"Sorry if they hustled you out."

"They were very polite. The blond woman with the diamond studs and the DNC pin told me you'd be in the lobby in five minutes. I saw the entrees on a tray as I left. I'm sorry to miss out on the salmon."

"I'm hungry, too."

"Which raises the topic of my second condition for attending this crazy night with you."

"You want to pick where we have dinner?"

"I want room service."

"From the Alexis? I'm not sure we're *persona grata* here anymore."

"From another place. The Hotel Max is nice."

"So to get room service, we'd have to have . . ."

"A room. Yes. You said your place is kind of trashed, and I share my house with three other people. You're grinning. Is that good?"

"I told Addy you were direct. *That's* good."

"Then let's go. The sooner we're checked in, the sooner we order. I'm famished."

DINNER WAS DELAYED. BY the time Wren and I walked to the Max and got a room and exchanged jokes about the dramatic black-and-white photographs that swathed every door on the hallway of the fifth floor, we'd distracted one another from the idea of food. Those intentions were sidetracked even further once she passed close to me entering the room, and I kissed her. Then all other plans went completely off the rails, as her dress slid off in one soft rustle to form a midnight-blue pool around her heels.

LATER, LYING ATOP THE bedspread we'd never gotten around to pulling down, I discovered that Wren's spiral of eponymous tattoos ended at her shoulder blade. I touched the last bird in the line—intentionally blurred ink mimicking watercolor paint—and traced the natural evolution of where future birds might join the procession. The line made a path down and across her spine, nearly touching the top of her childhood scar.

"If you left Seattle, where would you go next?" I said.

"Getting rid of me already? I see how this is," Wren murmured into the sheet.

"Do you keep heading west? Hawaii? The Philippines?"

She laughed. "I've never been to Alaska. Not sure what medicines I could grow there." She rolled onto her side and moved back to lean against me. "You came back to Seattle after the Army."

"Yeah. That was almost happenstance. I came home on leave, took up with somebody when I was here. So when my time was up, I came back to Seattle to keep seeing her."

"Are you still?"

"No."

"But you call it home."

"I guess I do. I never thought about where I'd settle once I was a civilian again, because I never thought I'd *be* a civilian again. Now that I'm here . . ." I shrugged. "It feels right. I like the city. I like how I can find almost anything but still run across people I recognize every day, like it's a small town. I like how insane the landscape is."

"Lettie says it's changed so much just in the past few years. All the industry coming in, people who started here can't afford to live here anymore."

"True. I sold a plot of land in the city last year for what would buy a new house most places."

Wren turned her head. The sharp outline of her profile looked like a cameo against the snow-white pillow we'd tossed aside earlier. Her hair smelled of limes and something like honey.

"You don't have to worry I'll vanish," she said. "If that's what you were asking."

"Good to know. Who would pay the hotel bill?"

"Not tonight." She laughed. "I mean Seattle. I don't do that, leave all at once. There's a whole decision tree and a lot of conversation with my tribe."

"Tribe?"

"My friends. You call your Rangers brothers, my friends are my tribe. Occasionally people decide to move together. A built-in support network when you get to wherever you're going."

"I hear Montreal is nice."

"It is. *Parles-tu français*?"

"Not a word," I said. "The Army had no plans to send me and my brothers into Quebec. At least not that they shared. How many languages do you know?"

"Five if I stretch the truth. My Spanish didn't get far after we left Morocco. Speaking of stretching . . ."

My hand had been cupping Wren's breast, and she unfolded her arms to reach splendidly toward the headboard. I trailed my fingertips lower.

"That's nice," she whispered after a few moments. "A little harder."

"Like that?" I said into the nape of her neck.

Wren hummed assent. "I'm getting the strong impression"—her breath hitched and gasped before continuing—"that we're postponing dinner for dessert again."

"I can wait."

She rolled over so that we faced one another. Her pupils so wide and dark, the irises showing around them were mere halos of chestnut brown, sparkling with amber.

"Prove it," she said.

CHAPTER FORTY-NINE

At THREE MINUTES TO midnight, the only sounds in the boatyard of the *Oxana M* were the deep rumble from a recycling plant farther up the stunted street and the almost musical clink created by the chain-link fence each time I cut one of its wires. Past the fence, towers of shipping containers in the gloom made a kind of huge metal maze, with each stack standing in for a hedge. Or a tombstone.

The tiny snap as the last wire parted was lost in the echoing boom of an explosion from the far side of the freighter. A rage of light threw the massive span of the *Oxana M* into dark relief and deepened the shadows for a quarter mile, including those around me.

Perfect. In black clothes and a balaclava over my head to hide my face, the dark was on my side tonight.

It wasn't much of a blast in terms of concussive force. But it was loud and blindingly bright, thanks to the flammable slurry I'd cooked up filling half of my new rowboat. New, and now destroyed. The fireworks had provided the boom and enough flame to ignite the rest of the boat into a miniature but very garish Viking funeral, lacking only the corpse.

Crude, but I'd needed something quick and easy for Jaak and his buddies. When we'd met that afternoon to discuss my idea over a lunch of meat pies and beer, Jaak's shipmate Harri had done the translating. The sailors couldn't keep the grins off their faces, and they toasted the audacity of the notion, or maybe just the chance to raise some hell.

His crew had used my speedboat to tow the rowboat up the Duwamish. When they were a few dozen yards off the *Oxana M*, they'd lit the long fuse on the giant firecracker, cut the rowboat loose, and hauled ass out of there. Right on time.

I twisted the fence aside and wormed my way under, ducking low to keep my small rucksack from catching on the cut wires. Then I ran like hell through the towers of cargo containers toward the looming hull of the ship.

The first burst of light from the explosion had dimmed into a flickering glow that danced off the *Oxana M*'s twin cranes. By now the freighter's crew would be gathered at starboard, staring at the impromptu show. I hoped. The fire wouldn't burn forever. Speed was as important as silence in getting aboard unseen. I took the steep gangway stairs to the deck three at a time.

At the top, the passage was clear. I could see the heads of crew members twenty yards across the deck at the far rail. Words in a Slavic language drifted my way in between laughter and shouts of encouragement to the blaze.

Between us, the broad gap of the aft hold yawned. A sharply sloped lip as tall as my shoulder ringed its edge, prevention against any sailor stumbling and falling a hundred feet from the deck to the very bottom of the open hold, well below the ship's waterline.

That was where I needed to be. I slipped away toward the bow, in search of the nearest stairwell.

Most of the ship's living and working spaces were housed in the three-story superstructure at the stern. Any crew not watching the burning boat from the deck should be there. Nevertheless, I cat-footed my way down an access corridor and four spiraling flights of stairs, then softly twisted both handles to unlock a watertight door to the aft hold.

It was like opening the door to a cathedral. A vast vertical emptiness seemed to extend high enough to touch the overcast sky. The lowest levels of the hold were stepped, three gigantic stairs on each side climbing the curve of the hull, adding to the sudden feeling of insignificance. I held on to the door for an extra moment to steady myself. Voices from the men high overhead might as well have been jeering at me.

This hold was empty, save for stifling vapors of fuel and oil that had sunk to the lowest part of the vessel. The *Oxana M* had two more holds the same size, each large enough to carry nearly a hundred forty-foot shipping containers in tight stacks.

I didn't need a hundred, just one, half that size. So long as it was the right one.

At the forward end of the immense interior was another watertight door, to allow crew to move between holds without retreating to the upper decks. I ran to it, conscious of the fact that any sailor who grew bored of watching the blaze outside might cast his eye downward into the hold and spot me scurrying around its sides like a mouse in an empty trash dumpster.

The door opened into a passageway cutting across

the ship. I shut it behind me and tried the one opposite, to enter the midship hold.

There. One twenty-foot steel box, painted dark green, alone in the cavernous space. Liashko's smuggled container. I was sure I'd found it, even before my eyes had pieced together the identification code stenciled on its door. The white paint of each letter and number virtually glowed through the murk.

A C-shaped padlock sealed the container. I felt in my sleeve for the leather wrist brace I'd fashioned recently. The brace held my basic set of lockpicks on the inside of my forearm, for quicker access than fumbling in my pocket. I selected the right pick and opened the lock purely by feel.

Before touching the twin handles on the container door, I paused to listen. The voices above had quieted. The fire would have burned out, maybe even sunk the sorry rowboat entirely. I cautiously pulled at the handles to turn the door's lock rods, grateful to whatever dockworker had greased the rods half a world away.

The door came loose with a hollow reverberation, signaling that the steel box wasn't completely full. I entered and pulled the door closed behind me.

My arm brushed something flat and solid as I removed my flashlight from my belt. The beam bounced off long black crates stacked high on both sides. Plastic straps secured each individual crate to the container's sides, proof against foul weather. A gap down the center between the two stacks let me estimate their dimensions. Each crate was about seven feet long and eighteen inches square at the ends.

Just about the right size to hold what I'd expected.

I pushed the crate at the top, testing its weight. It shifted, barely. Two quick slices and its plastic restraints fell aside, allowing me to ease the crate—well over a hundred pounds, the cords in my neck standing out with the strain—silently off the stack to set it on the floor.

Twists of wire sealed the crate's latches. My blade cut those nearly as fast as it had the straps. I opened the lid.

The six-foot tube of the Verba missile launcher cushioned in molded foam padding looked deceptively innocent. Not much different than a length of metal pipe painted olive green. A trigger mechanism like an oversized pistol grip was detached and waiting in its own foam slot.

I lifted the tube out to look into its muzzle.

There was no mistaking the intent of the slim gray dart housed within. The surface-to-air missile was nearly as long as the launching tube itself, a malevolent needle packing enough speed and power to bring down damn near anything flying below fifteen thousand feet.

Under the tube, the crate held two more missiles just like it. Three to a box. Forty crates. One hundred and twenty in all.

That was three times as many as Burke had said the task force was buying. Which meant Liashko must have other customers. Jesus. Did Burke know?

There was something else here, too, at the very back of the container between the stacks. A silver metal case, smaller than the crates holding the missiles. Not much larger than my rucksack. I left the Verba to cut the case's straps and latches, then opened the lid for a look.

And nearly choked. I removed my hands from the

case and stepped back immediately. A reaction as instinctive as if I'd opened the lid to find a cobra.

Nestled within the foam pads were twelve slim canisters of light, clear plastic. Every one of them bearing a large red-and-white label with the unmistakable tripod symbol for chemical weapons.

Nerve gas.

I told myself that it was safe to breathe. That the canisters couldn't be armed. My body didn't seem convinced, and my next few inhalations came shallow and quick.

Each canister was bisected by a slim metallic layer, with a pull-tab extending from it like a stubby tail. Their tops contained a blue-tinged liquid. At the bottom, a gray granular substance.

I remembered a few basics of bioweapon chemistry from the Army's defensive training. Nerve agents had a limited shelf life. Their components would have to be combined shortly before use. Pull the tab, allow the two halves to mix, and the canister was armed and ready to be deployed.

Deployed by missile, maybe. I comprehended an even more horrific use for the Verbas resting in their dark beds.

Anatoly's looking to close up shop, Burke had said. *Everything he stole, in one go.*

The task force had assumed they were buying Liashko's entire job lot. They weren't even close. The arms dealer apparently had other deals to make, other customers here in the land of opportunity. He'd kept Burke in the dark because that was the paranoid's MO.

What was the chemical? Sarin? VX? My stomach

twisted, imagining how many dozens or hundreds of people would die in agony if even one of these canisters was detonated and dispersed over a crowded area.

Screw the arms deal. Time for the cavalry—ATF, National Guard, whoever could secure the nerve gas and transport it to where it could be safely destroyed.

I checked my phone. No signal. The steel container and the ship's hull beyond were impenetrable.

The whirring of an engine from above brought me out of my shocked reflection. I closed the case just as a second noise followed, a heavy reverberating clank of metal on metal. Close. Closer than something moving up on deck. I killed the flashlight.

Pushing the container door open an inch, I looked up toward the open hatch. The heads of crewmen at the lip of the hold showed as silhouettes against the deck lights and the night sky. I ducked back and silently shut the door again.

Shit. I would have to wait until they'd finished whatever work had them so busy at midnight. Maybe setting the rowboat on fire had prompted some kind of safety drill—

BANG

I flinched and nearly stumbled. The impact had been right over my head, on the roof of the container.

Oh, hell no. I realized what the sound meant, even as the sides of the container creaked with sudden pressure. I reached for the loose door and grabbed the retaining straps of the stacked crates with my other hand. Only an instant before the container with me inside it soared skyward, borne by the crane that clutched the big steel box like a scorpion claw on a doomed cricket.

CHAPTER FIFTY

THE ABRUPT ACCELERATION THREATENED to swing the container's heavy door open. I threw all my weight into holding it shut. The missile crates shifted against the straps, mashing my hand. I gritted my teeth until the pain in them matched that in my finger bones.

In another five seconds the vertical motion abruptly stopped, only to be replaced by a seesawing tilt and a feeling of acceleration that dropped my stomach down to my knees. The Stygian dark inside the container added to the sudden vertigo. But the slant of the huge steel box kept the loose door closed. For the moment. Any tip in the other direction, and the door would fly wide open, with me sailing out after it.

The container dropped in a barely controlled descent. I had an instant to brace myself before it hit the deck of the *Oxana M* with a scraping thud that must have removed metal along with paint. With another creak and the whir of moving cable, the crane released its hold on the roof.

I yanked my hand out from under the crushing straps, flexing my fingers and willing some feeling back into them. A slender glowing line appeared at the top of the container door, drawn by powerful deck lamps high on the comm tower at the ship's bow.

Almost taunting, that sliver of light, with the rest of the interior so dark I couldn't see the wall inches from my face.

Someone might approach at any second. They couldn't miss noticing that the container wasn't locked tight. Then they would check the cargo.

Or, worse, just lock me in.

I would have to break for it the instant they came near the door. Count on surprise to buy me a second, maybe two. Run toward the gangway or jump for the water? Whichever direction looked less likely to get my head smashed in with a wrench.

A moment passed. I heard voices only yards away. I crouched, ready to spring.

Then the floor of the container buzzed, vibrated, rumbled. The feeling of the ship's propellers, surging into action.

The *Oxana M* was moving.

Christ. I was out of options. It would have to be the water. Jump off the port side and swim to shore. The river wasn't so wide that I couldn't make it, even through the bone-chilling cold.

I was about to launch myself out of the blackness when I remembered the nerve gas.

I couldn't leave the canisters behind. My escape and the havoc it would raise would undoubtedly force Liashko to change all of his plans. Including the deal Burke had arranged with Agent Martens and the Feds. Liashko would escape on the next flight across the Pacific, and who knew where his lethal stock would wind up?

Even if it meant never catching the evil bastard, I couldn't let this chance slip away. The nerve agent was too dangerous. Too easy to hide. Secure the chemical weapons now and let fate sort out Liashko. And Burke, too, if it came to that.

I moved to the rear of the container and knelt to open the crate again by touch. The steel floor quivered with the ship as the engines increased speed, pushing the freighter faster toward the Sound.

With my jacket wrapped around the flashlight to narrow its beam, I set each cylinder of nerve gas—very carefully—to one side. The foam pads I tore into chunks to line my rucksack. Working as fast as I dared, it took fifteen minutes to pack the canisters firmly into place.

I shone the beam around the container to make sure I'd found them all. My ruck stuffed full of padding and poison looked like a nest. I'd stolen real eggs, Aura's eggs, only a week before. Those had held the infinite promise of new life. These would birth only horror, and anguish, and death. I strapped the ruck to my back and peered out through the cracked door to the deck.

Empty. Maybe fifteen long paces to the starboard side. Beyond the rail, the lights of the city had receded into glittering specks, as if borne away in the freighter's wake.

Too far for me to swim to shore now. I would never survive, especially not loaded down with the rucksack. Its twenty kilos might not bear me under the waves immediately, but after a quarter mile or more, with the cold sapping my strength . . .

A boat. I would slip away to another part of the deck,

steal a lifeboat with an engine or even just an emergency zodiac inflatable and some oars. Anything would do now.

I slipped out of the container, closed the door to refasten its padlock, and walked directly to the rail. Voices and the faintest hint of cigarette smoke drifted back to me. The wind so frigid that the skin around my eyes creased defensively.

A steel ladder led to the deck immediately below. I stole down the rungs and into a passage that led along the port side of the ship.

We were changing course. The curved phosphorescent wake off the stern showed our path turning northwest. Moving fast, fifteen knots at least, out of Elliott Bay and into the open Sound.

The *Oxana M* was in a rush. To where? To meet Liashko? Or had Liashko decided to abandon Seattle and the arms deals altogether?

It wouldn't change my plan. Find a boat and escape and call the cavalry. I crept along the passageway.

Footsteps. Clanging on stairs forty feet ahead, descending from the deck above. More than one person. I tried the nearest door. Unlocked. I ducked into the darkened room and shut the door again, just as the steps reached the passageway.

The steps were heavy but not fast. Two men, ambling along the deck, talking in what I took to be Russian. They halted just outside.

"I see you," the voice said in English.

I froze. My hand was on the Colt in its holster. I wasn't about to shoot any of the crew—hell, the sailors aboard may not even know who they were working for—but the sight of the gun might at least keep anyone from getting aggressive.

"Follow us out," the voice continued. A thick Slavic accent. "No, farther than so little. Another ten minutes. Anatoly is here."

Anatoly. The room had a porthole. I risked a look.

The one speaking held a phone to his ear with one hand and a powerful set of binoculars to his eyes with the other, looking somewhere northwest of the ship. I guessed him for an officer, probably the captain. He wore a brimmed cap and a thick blue coat and pants as wards against the cold, along with a bristly beard that started at his cheekbones and extended to his chest.

The second man stepped into view to snatch the phone. Big all over, with rolls of fat on the back of his bull neck and a belly that pushed out his fine black overcoat like it had been draped over a globe.

"Do you have it?" he said into the phone. I knew that resonant voice. The last time I'd heard it, I'd been covered in the gore of the killers he'd sent after me. Liashko.

An errant gust pushed his sparse black hair vertical, and he turned to impatiently smooth it back down. His head was round and his cheeks pink and hairless, like an infant's. But the glaring piggish eyes conveyed as much malice as the poison I carried in my ruck.

"And the landing?" Liashko said to the caller. "We will not be seen when the barge goes to shore?"

A barge. They must be rendezvousing offshore with another vessel, making an exchange there.

It made sense. The *Oxana M* had its own cranes to offload the shipping container, if that was their aim. In the dead of night, miles off land, the chances of being seen were minuscule.

I heard the captain speaking quietly into a radio. Almost simultaneously, the lights in the passage outside went out. Dimming the ship to running lights only for their clandestine meeting. The two men walked away. I exited the room a moment later.

The captain had said he could see the other ship, the barge. On the western side of the Sound. I couldn't spot it myself. Off the port rail, ebony water tipped with silver from reflected moonlight stretched for miles. A low strip of peninsula in the distance almost part of the horizon.

I tried my phone again. Nothing. Too far from shore. Liashko and the captain had been using a satellite phone. If I could find another like it on board, or get to a radio—

The steady hum of the engines lowered in pitch. We were slowing. Preparing to heave to and meet the barge.

Footsteps again, on the deck above. If I was too late to stop what was happening, I could at least get a look at who was taking ownership of the missiles. Enough to give the Feds a proper description as soon as I found a way off this heap.

The shipping container with the arms was near the bow. It followed that most of the crew would be either working there or staying warm inside the superstructure at the stern, walking a direct path back and forth on the main deck. This lower level should be clear.

But the long passageway on the port side offered no hiding places. I hunched low and headed forward on the ship, looking for a vantage point.

Farther along, the passageway opened out to span the full width of the ship. Two winches like huge toadstools, each as tall as my chest, flanked an open hatch on the deck floor. With the deck lights turned off, it took my eyes a moment to adjust and see what lay within the hatch. Heavy mooring rope, as thick as my arm. Another coiled pile of rope made a mound near the port siderail. The rail at this part of the deck had a two-foot-high gap underneath, to allow the mooring lines to run from the winches off the ship to a dock.

It would have to suffice for cover. Already the thrum of the propellers had changed again, becoming hollow. The engine in reverse, to stop the ship's leviathan momentum. I squatted beside the mound of coiled rope and looked out through the mooring gap in the rail.

A boat was drawing along the port side of the *Oxana M*. Liashko had called it a barge, and I had pictured something like a trash scow in my mind.

But this was something different. A vehicle ferry, made to transport a dozen or more cars and trucks. With the pilot's cabin at the rear and a ramp at the bow, almost the entire deck was usable smooth space for passengers.

The barge carried only two vehicles. A heavy-duty flatbed truck and a car.

A *cop* car. What the hell?

The cruiser was a chalk-white Chevy Caprice PPV, its push bumper and LED light bar on the roof readily visible from my bird's-eye view. I squinted to make out the dark blue insignia on its door: Washington State Patrol.

Was the sting already running? Had I stumbled into the middle of it?

Footsteps and voices overlapped on the deck above as the crew ran to throw lines to the waiting barge. A guy in coveralls emerged from the pilothouse of the barge to catch and secure one line to the barge's bow. A second man, a state trooper in a black winter coat and gray Smokey Bear hat, stepped out from between the vehicles to grab the line dangling at the stern.

No. Not a trooper. Just a man wearing the uniform.

Sean Burke.

CHAPTER FIFTY-ONE

BURKE WAS HERE. WORKING for Liashko, helping to smuggle the container of weapons ashore. He must have known the missiles were on board to prepare this rendezvous on the water. There would be no tactical team coming. If Burke had signaled Martens, they would have descended on the *Oxana M* before it cast off the first mooring line. He'd sold us out.

Above me, I heard the whir of cables and clank of the crane's jaws as it grabbed hold of the cargo again.

It wasn't tough to predict their next moves. They would place the container on the flatbed truck. Take the barge to shore. The boat had a shallow draft and the extendable loading ramp at its bow. They could set ashore at any boat launch, or even on a beach. And simply drive away, with Burke in his WSP disguise and stolen patrol car running interference, making sure that the truck reached whatever destination they intended. A hiding place? A buyer?

It didn't matter now. All that mattered was making sure I got the cops here before that truck reached shore. After that, the missiles might vanish.

A radio. There would be one on the bridge, and

backup handheld sets around with the crew. I'd take the whole place hostage if I had to, set off every flare gun on board, just to hail the Coast Guard.

But I was already too late.

I never knew whether I had been spotted, or whether the four men had simply been taking an alternate path down the starboard passageway to cut across the deck. But they had been quiet. Even as I whipped around, they were already raising their guns, overcoming the shock of spotting me and yelling in multiple languages for me to halt.

Sailors, two of them, from their oil-stained weather gear. The other two wore street clothes, puffed vests and turtlenecks and woolen pants. Handguns for the sailors, AK-12 assault rifles in pixelated khaki camo for the city boys. Liashko's men, I was sure.

They grabbed me and threw me to the deck. Hands relieved me of my gun, emptied my pockets, and tore the balaclava off my head and the rucksack from my back. I yelled for them to be careful with it, and one of them kicked me in the side. After that I was no trouble at all. The crewmen hauled me to my feet and manhandled me up to the main deck.

Dazed, for an instant I thought I was lying on the ground again. But it was the container that was high, swooping overhead on its journey to the barge.

The wind at the bow whipped at our hair and clothes and even blew the last of my dizziness away. Liashko stood at the ship's rail, looking down at the barge as his steel box filled with one hundred and twenty Verba missiles was lowered to the waiting truck.

One of his men stepped forward to speak to him in

Russian, before handing over the rucksack. Liashko's face, already glowering, began to seethe. He tore at the top flap, yanking the ruck open to look inside. His eyes went wide with terror. But he managed to keep a grip on the ruck and the canisters of death staring him in the face.

He turned to look at the green shipping container on the barge, then back at me.

"How do you have this?" he said, holding out the rucksack as if for me to look inside.

I didn't answer. Liashko said a word and one of his bodyguards punched me in the gut. I'd already tightened in expectation, but the blow still hurt like hell coming right after the kick to my ribs. I might have fallen if the sailors weren't still holding my arms. When I looked up again Liashko was pointing, ordering the crew to do something. The captain, standing behind me, spoke as well. From the side deck, a gangway began to lower to the barge.

Liashko and the captain got into a shouting match. The arms trafficker was furious about the stowaway and the near loss of his property. Around me, I could feel the bodyguards edging back, uncertain about the sudden tension from the crew all around them. Then the captain was marching down the gangplank to the barge, followed by Liashko and his two men, who herded me in front of them like a reluctant sheep.

Should I dive for it? The water here had to be something like forty-five degrees. A bullet would be much faster, and no less certain to end it all.

We reached the barge. A chop had risen with the wind, and the barge bobbed on the waves. Each man wavered unsteadily for a moment as they acclimated to the motion.

"Who the fuck is he?" Burke said, stepping forward. His eyes met mine. Rage? Or fear that I would give him away?

"It's him. Shaw, the thief," Liashko said.

"Can't be," Burke said. "Shaw's dead."

Liashko stared at me. Was I the same man? My scars hadn't been showing in the pictures he'd seen of my dead body. My standing here, very much alive, gave him cause to doubt his memory.

"Hiding aboard and looking to steal money," the captain said.

"No." Liashko brandished the rucksack. "He took these."

From his pocket he removed a set of keys and handed them to Burke. "Open it."

The barge pilot had been busy securing the container to the flatbed with chains and restraining straps. Burke stepped around him to climb onto the truck and remove the padlock. Liashko shouted at the pilot, who hurried to turn on the headlights of the state patrol car and illuminate the container just as Burke swung its door wide. Liashko stepped closer to see. I was shunted along by the muzzles of the armed bodyguards.

If the two thugs split up and I could take one by surprise, I'd have a chance. A lousy one, on this small boat with nearly no cover, but something.

Liashko swore at the sight of the open missile crate. He turned to grab me with both hands by the throat.

"Who are you?" he hollered, flecks of spit flying. He was strong. Even with my neck muscles tensed, his

thumbs crushed my windpipe. Shining spots materialized in my vision, a mottled constellation on Liashko's
enraged pink face.

Fuck it. Go down swinging. I went limp, sagging
against the arms of the crewmen holding me, and just
as abruptly sprang back up to headbutt Liashko in the
teeth. He fell back and his hands dropped from my neck.

I didn't get to enjoy the moment. Something hard
smacked me on the skull, and this time I folded for real.
Another kick sent me over sideways.

"Don't!" Burke's voice. "Don't shoot him yet. He
might have stolen more. Or booby-trapped it."

Liashko cursed again and spat on the deck. His
men yanked my arms behind me once more and I felt
handcuffs—probably taken from Burke's WSP service
belt—click tight around my wrists. The sailors yanked
me upright and frog-marched me to the patrol cruiser.
One of the bodyguards opened the back door and I
ducked just in time to save my head another bad knock
as they tossed me headlong inside.

I wrestled myself upright. My side ached from the
kicks. Looking through the clear plastic barrier between
the backseat and the front compartment and the car's
windshield I had a view of the back of the flatbed, and
the collection of angry men standing between the truck
and the freighter's massive hull. Burke and the captain
were arguing now. Liashko held a handkerchief to his
face. Red dappled the ivory cloth. Good. *A gift from me,
you son of a bitch.*

Bravado. I'd failed, and now both the missiles and the
nerve gas were back in Liashko's hands. And Burke's.
My wave of hatred for both men almost overwhelmed

the dread of the bad ending I knew must be in store for me. Soon.

Liashko shouted both men down, and now the captain seemed to be on the receiving end of his rage again. The barge pilot in the coveralls was inside the container, maybe checking the arms. He leaned out to show the Verba launching tube from the crate I'd opened, which seemed to infuriate Liashko further. His bodyguards had fanned out.

I saw what was about to happen before the crewmen did. Even before Burke did, and he began to move in the next instant. The bodyguards raised their rifles and fired. The two sailors didn't even have time for a look of surprise before they died. That left the captain, who lifted his hands as if to wave away the oncoming rounds half a second before they tore open his chest. He fell between the barge and his ship, into the water.

More gunfire now. Coming from above, from the deck of the freighter. I hit the floor of the cruiser. One bullet spider-webbed the car's windshield and another punched a tiny hole through the roof of the cruiser, two feet from my head.

I looked sideways out the window. The bodyguards had Liashko shielded from fire around the other side of the truck. They leaned out to exchange chattering bursts from their AKs with the continued assault coming from the ship.

Shifting in my seat, I tried to reach into my sleeve, to the leather brace with my picks. The cuffs hindered my hands. I could touch my wrist but no farther. I kept struggling, straining for a different angle.

In the corner of my eye, I saw the mooring lines fall limp from the freighter. They'd cut the barge loose. A few seconds later both sides stopped shooting. Engines surged and water frothed as the *Oxana M* began to pull away.

Liashko was screaming at his men. The barge pilot had wisely taken cover from the barrage inside the steel container. He obeyed his boss, jumping out and running to the pilothouse of the barge. The bodyguards checked the freighter's progress—too far away now to shoot at us again—before they risked moving to the open side of the truck.

They shouldered their rifles and bent down to lift something. Burke. Facedown and unmoving. Was he dead?

The two men dragged his limp body to the cruiser. They opened the back door and threw Burke inside with me, more onto the floor than the seat. The back of Burke's trooper jacket was torn in two places over his shoulder blades. The black fabric gleamed wetly. Blood. He'd been hit, probably in the first wild volley from the deck.

But he was breathing. Raspy, but there. I twisted to get my cuffed hands lower, to feel at his jacket. Yes. A lightweight ballistic vest, maybe stolen along with the uniform. He'd come prepared.

Body armor or no, Burke was wounded. Though he may not have enough time remaining for the bullets to prove fatal.

Liashko came to the open door.

"Your man is shot," I said.

He didn't bother to look. "Sean would die tonight, anyway. I know his plans. I know he is the reason you are stealing from me."

I didn't say anything.

"He is too excited to have me come here," Liashko said. "I know him, like his father. They smell blood. They turn on their masters." He spat on Burke's prone body, his lips stained red from my headbutt.

Liashko motioned to a bodyguard, who handed him an automatic pistol. He aimed it at my head.

"You will tell me who you are, if you and Sean have other partners. Then it will be quick. Instead."

He spoke to the bodyguards. One of them came around to the driver's side. I watched him through the clear barrier. He opened the door, leaned in to release the emergency brake, and shifted the car into neutral. The car eased fractionally on its shocks. Wheels ready to roll.

Liashko waited, his deep-set eyes expectant.

I didn't say anything. Just attempted a defiant grin, which was probably closer to a baring of teeth.

Liashko nodded like that was an answer he'd already known. He closed the car door and motioned. The bodyguards smiled and bent into the glare of the headlights to push at the front of the car, getting it rolling backward toward the open bow. A bump, as the tires hit the slight rise of the retracted loading ramp. It didn't slow our progress.

The back wheels rolled off the deck. The cruiser's chassis dropped to hit the bow edge with a grinding crash. I tumbled backward, Burke rolling from the floor onto the hard black plastic seat.

For an instant, it seemed like the car would be stuck there. Then the combined force of its momentum and the grinning bodyguards' shoves slid it one inch, three more—

We were falling.

CHAPTER FIFTY-TWO

THE BLACK WATER SPLASHED and gurgled as if hungrily devouring the car's front compartment. It found tiny crevices, entry points between the seats and the caged rear. Icy gouts sprayed over me and the unconscious Burke. My feet were under now. So cold it felt like stepping on an electrified wire.

Ignore it. Set everything else from my mind and keep searching for the fallen lockpick. I'd had a hold on it, was already picking the handcuffs, when the car's rear tires banged off the barge and threw everything inside ass-backward. The pick was still here. It had to be. My fingertips brushed across the seamless hard plastic of the seat, even as the car tilted farther forward and the water rose to meet my touch.

Burke might have the keys to the handcuffs on his belt. Or in his pocket. Or not at all. No time and no way to search him now. Find the pick.

There. A tap of metal, brushing against my knuckles as a first wave lapped across the seat. I stretched, touched it, got the pick between two fingers that were already growing numb. I twisted around. The end of the metal pick scraped the cuffs, missing the lock. Water at my chest now, squeezing my ribs. Burke was half floating, his face bobbing just above the roiling surface. My head touched the roof, and the surface of the water rose fast to catch up.

Breathe, Shaw. You have all the time you need. Just like catching a line drive, or taking your shot at five hundred yards with iron sights alone. Nothing else exists. I closed my eyes.

The pick found the handcuff lock. Eased in. Turned, gently. All like my fingers had nothing to do with it.

My wrists were free. And my mouth underwater. I pushed with my legs, toward the last vanishing inches of air at the rear window. The car was near to vertical. Sinking fast. By turning my neck I found air, gasped twice, held it. Outside the window, I could see plumes of bubbles escaping from the car's trunk.

Burke was under now. His autonomic response keeping him from inhaling water into his lungs. I crawled hand-over-hand down his body to his ankle. Working by feel. The world was growing dark, and squeezing tighter.

He'd worn it. His backup Glock. *Bless your homicidal habits, you maniac.*

I yanked the gun from his holster and spun to shove it against the side window and began pulling the trigger, the explosions in the enclosed underwater space hammering on my ears. Two rounds, three, four. I reached out blindly to shove with both hands and the splintered window fell outward, more like fabric than glass.

Burke's legs were closest. I grabbed his foot and clambered out of the window. The cruiser's headlights still shone, silt and foam swirling frantically past the beams as we dropped. How deep were we now? I got myself free, and the sinking car immediately pulled at Burke, threatening to tear him from my grasp. It turned me upside-down, borne deeper by the car and my grip on Burke's pants cuff.

I reached in, finding his other leg, twisting to push against the car with my feet and force Burke's reluctant body from the car. Was he alive? The water pressure pounded at my skull. His legs were out, then his torso, and then suddenly we were floating loose.

Below us, the police cruiser flew toward the void, its headlights seeking, white paint as luminescent as some deep-sea creature returning home.

I kicked. Burke's body rose, too slowly. His body armor. I kicked harder, dragging at him. If there was an end to the water above, I couldn't see it. If the crushing pressure was lessening, I couldn't tell.

My heart stuttered in my chest, desperately pushing blood in search of oxygen that wasn't there. Somehow my head was expanding from the inside out. Every-thing was pain. Any second now I would lose the fight and my body would inhale, reflexively, and then there would be a moment of horrible agony before it was over.

Kick, damn you.

Was that a light? The moon? Or the light of the end? *Kick.*

We broke the surface.

I coughed, retched, my lungs so desperate they had

forgotten their job. Burke bobbed up next to me. His face to the sky. I grabbed at him, thumped on his chest.

He let out a strangled gasp. Clutched at me. Clawed my face. Pulled me underwater in his atavistic terror of waking to dark and pain and bone-deep cold.

I fought free from his thrashing limbs to surface again. He reached for me again, eyes wide and unseeing. I thrust him back with one arm, reached up with the other, and clubbed him as hard as I could.

Just enough. Burke went limp once more, floating on his back. I got behind him in a lifeguard carry, where I could keep him from drowning me if he revived.

If. I looked into the distance for the first time. I could see the sliver of black that signified land and sparse fairy dots from the brightest lights onshore. A long, long distance. Four miles or more to the closest point in the west.

Already my teeth had stopped chattering. I couldn't feel my hands or feet.

We were going to die.

And with that decision made for us, I swam.

It was a very slow process. My limbs like planks of wood. One arm, two legs, moving as well as I could convince them to move, a conscious debate each time. Towing Burke with me like driftwood.

A waspish buzzing sound filled my ears. An engine. Somewhere east of us, getting closer. Still out of my sight. I tried to raise my unfeeling arm to wave. It barely lifted above the surface. Tried again, and the arm pointed skyward.

The sound was coming fast from behind. I flailed

to turn myself, just in time to see the spearhead of the gray hull bearing down on us. I blinked stupidly. I knew that boat.

A round bristled head appeared over the side.

Jaak.

"Shaw, man," he said, grinning. "You have crazy days, I tell you."

CHAPTER FIFTY-THREE

JAAK'S TWO CREWMATES FISHED us out, working in tandem to haul our soaked and uncooperative bodies aboard my boat. Jaak apologized for not helping. Given he'd been stabbed barely a week before, I could forgive him slacking off. I pointed more than I spoke to show them where clothes and towels were stored. My lips and tongue felt like so much dead fish.

West. The barge had gone west. Damn it, why hadn't I told them that first? I pushed my way past them to take the wheel, pushing the throttle forward with my elbow. The speedboat leapt forward and the sailors stumbled back, protesting.

"Shaw," Jaak said. "You're too cold."

"Nerve gas," I said. "They have nerve gas. Poison. You understand?"

Jaak's mate Harri translated into Finnish. Jaak blanched.

The gunfight between the ships might have been seen. Liashko must know he could put the barge ashore anywhere with a boat ramp or even a shallow beach. They'd headed west, toward the closest land. Probably aiming to get off the water before police boats or the Coast Guard came hunting.

That land was the Kitsap Peninsula. Did Liashko know the area? The peninsula would be quiet, with plenty of beaches. But it was also remote. A long drive south and around the Sound until he'd be back on the mainland.

The cops could corner him. If we called it in now.

I told Jaak to take the helm while I stripped and fumbled myself into a dry turtleneck and paint-spattered jeans, my urgency and rage combining to warm my bones. My mouth still carried the taste of brine. I spat over the transom into the speedboat's thrashing wake. Jaak pressed coffee on me, and I gratefully downed half a pint straight from the thermos.

The Finns already had the groggy Burke half out of his sopping trooper uniform. The wounds on his back had bled but not profusely. Cuts and punctures. I guessed that the vest had mushroomed the rounds and Burke had caught a few splinters along with the impact that had knocked him cold. Lucky. Lucky that the gunfire had come from a distance, and that the rounds weren't jacketed with something harder.

"He's dangerous," I said, pointing. "Once he's in dry clothes, tie his hands and feet. And watch him close."

The VHF radio was on the shelf just inside the cabin door. I reached in to switch it to Channel 16 and handed the receiver to Harri, the one with the stronger English.

"Call for the Coast Guard. Say you saw a lot of gunfire between two ships on Puget Sound. A cargo ship and a smaller craft. The cargo ship headed out of the Sound and—" I checked our heading. The beam of a small lighthouse shone like a low star, maybe two miles off now.

"—and the smaller ship is going toward Point No Point," I finished. "Say that back to me."

He did, perfectly. The Finnish crew was adept at handling emergencies.

"Good," I said. "If they ask, tell them who you are and that you borrowed this boat from your friend Hollis Brant. There won't be trouble."

As Harri hailed the emergency line, I dove into the cabin, tossing the sleeping cushions aside to reach the compartment underneath. Inside was my worn set of hiking boots. And, wrapped in a waxed cotton sheet, a Mossberg pump shotgun and two boxes of shells. The shotgun was kept loaded. I filled my pockets with shells and grabbed a burner phone and a flashlight from the chart locker.

When I emerged, Burke was alert.

"Let me go," he said.

"I should've let you drown. You sold us out."

"The hell I did." He looked around at the sailors.

"You can talk," I said. "They're with me."

"Anatoly changed the plan tonight. The deal was supposed to go down three days from now."

"Then you should have told Martens. Called the task force in."

He sneered. "If I did that, I'd miss my shot at Anatoly."

The truth was so obvious I felt like my pounding head was some sort of divine penance for not realizing it earlier. "You were never going into WITSEC."

"Shit no. I'd kill Anatoly and his two pussies and

call the Feds to come pick up the arms. My boy gets the bust, and I'm gone. Disappearing ain't hard when you've been preparing as long as I have." He showed me his bound wrists. "Cut me loose."

"Not a prayer."

Burke swore. At length, as I finished tying the laces on my boots. I imagined even Harri learned a few new words. "You owe me."

I glanced at the vast stretch of Sound to our stern. "Remember where you were ten minutes ago and say that again."

"You're going to take him out, right? I can help you. You can't do it without me."

Ahead of us, the torch of the lighthouse burned. It might have been my imagination, but I thought I glimpsed a reflection off green metal, at the beach mere yards from the short tower. I hefted the shotgun.

"Fuck I can't," I said.

CHAPTER FIFTY-FOUR

I HAD THE FINNS PUT me ashore on the beach, half a mile south of the point. Or what passed for one. Point No Point had earned its name because, from a distance, it tricked the eye into thinking a mere bump in the land was something more substantial.

But it was enough of a bend that the short lighthouse was out of my view as I waded through the low surf. And I would be just as hidden, running along the beach.

Liashko and his men would watch the single road that led visitors to the lighthouse. With an eye on the water, too. Those were the places where cops might approach. They would pay less attention to the shoreline.

They couldn't have arrived too many minutes ahead of us. The speedboat was a hell of a lot faster than any barge, and I had pushed her throttle all the way open. How long would it take them to offload the truck? The pilot could run the barge hard into the shore—I guessed they planned to abandon the vessel—and then lower its ramp. Picking the right spot would be critical. If the truck with its heavy load floundered in loose sand, they were finished.

A path off the beach led to a hiking trail. Tall thickets

and bramble bushes shielded me on both sides. Ahead, a flash of yellow light from behind the building. Too low for even the undersized lighthouse. Headlights. I slowed my run, hunching over and keeping the shotgun butt tucked tight to my shoulder.

As I neared the end of the trail, the rev of a diesel engine temporarily covered the soft crunch of my footfalls on the gravel. I looked through a gap in the reeds. The truck, on the other side of the lighthouse. Already moving.

I kicked into high gear, tearing off the path, full tilt toward the stubby black-capped tower. Angling left to follow the moving target of the engine.

I stopped at the corner of the white building that abutted the lighthouse itself. The beams of headlights came into view. The truck was still on the beach, making its steady way forward on the harder-packed sand, parallel to the water. Steering to avoid chunks of flotsam and larger logs that had washed onto land over the years. Along with a line of small boulders, the timber formed a natural barrier that prevented them from simply driving straight off the shore.

Another hundred yards down the beach, lampposts illuminated a red-roofed house and nearby parking lot. The log barrier ended there. Liashko and his men would turn onto the paved lot and then to the road, and then they would be gone. The truck passed my corner at a runner's pace. They were careful. Not losing their nerve. Not getting stuck.

I sprinted out from the shelter of the building, racing toward the driver's side of the truck as it trundled away. Veering into an angle of approach I hoped matched the blind spot in its side mirror. Only thirty yards away from their taillights and closing fast. Jumping the boulders and the line of bleached logs like huge bones, my boots digging into the sand as I ran faster.

At fifteen feet they slammed on the brakes. They'd seen me. Too late for them.

The first blast from my shotgun exploded the left front tire of the truck. The second tore the side mirror from its brackets. I faded back, racking another shell and blowing out the two rear tires on the left side with one shot.

They floored the gas. Trying to escape the sudden onslaught. The big flatbed with its cargo sagged heavily to one side on flattened tires and dug in. Sand sprayed from under the shredded rubber for an instant before the front wheel became mired too deep to do even that. The truck's right tires pushed forward, the left side stayed stuck. The truck began to grind a slow painful circle in the dirt and sand.

I dove behind the nearest driftwood log. Knelt into shooting position. Over the howl of the straining engine I caught a loud creak from the passenger door on the far side. In another second, the silhouette of legs came into view under the flatbed. One of the bodyguards moving to the rear of the truck.

I shot the legs under the truck bed, racked, and fired again at the same spot over a scream of pain or fear I barely heard over the ringing in my ears. Half deaf and half blind on the dark beach with muzzle flashes still hot in my vision. I put one more blast through the driver's window. Not hearing the shatter.

Keep them guessing. Don't give the guards a chance

to sight in with their assault weapons. I retreated, running to crouch behind one of the jagged boulders. The driver's door opened and the barge pilot fell out to scramble to his feet. He ran clumsily up the beach, into the beams of the headlights and away. I let him go, watching the truck as I loaded shells into the underside of the Mossberg by feel.

Liashko, and the second bodyguard. They were my concern. Both still in the cab?

I looked at the door of the steel shipping container. One thin black vertical stripe appeared on the wall of green.

The truck's engine stalled. My ears cleared enough to hear waves lapping on the shore. A gull screeched overhead, furious at the intrusion into its peaceful territory.

The stripe widened fractionally. A long tube extended out like a questing finger.

I hit the dirt, covering my head with my arms. But unable to resist the temptation to watch.

The Verba missile launcher was not designed for short-range work, by any stretch of the imagination. Aiming it by sight alone, at a ground-level target barely twenty yards away, was like tossing a grenade blindly in the same room in which you were standing. Maybe the bodyguard had fired a rocket launcher in the field and thought he had the procedure down. Or maybe he'd just reached for the biggest, baddest gun in his panic.

A searing orange flash of light erupted out of the open container door. The backblast from the launcher. It must have singed everything in the steel box, including the man. The missile itself ejected ten feet from the tube before its propellant engaged. That brighter glare of light had only an instant's life—which I barely glimpsed as I stuck my face into the crook of my elbow, my retinas already stinging—before the slender dart struck the logs from which I'd fired the shotgun a minute before, and the world erupted into flame and heat. Chunks of wood struck the boulder beside me. More pieces landed on the sand, blasted and smoldering.

I looked up. The logjam was mostly gone, replaced by a blackened and still burning shallow crater. A fire blazed in the grass farther up the shore, and leaves in a stand of trees just beyond glowed orange as they curled and died.

I waited.

Another minute passed. The door to the container widened. A figure slipped out, black against the red of the truck's taillights and the yellow bonfires the missile had ignited. He bent low, using the container as cover from where he thought I was. Wondering if he'd succeeded in blowing me to pieces.

Liashko's voice called from the front of the truck. The bodyguard didn't answer. Not giving away his location. As I watched, he moved around the truck on the water side, maybe to check his fallen comrade, maybe to whisper to his boss.

The truck's lights went dark. An instant later, the interior light of the cab followed.

I couldn't see them from here. I low-crawled toward the surf, the ground scraping my stomach. Sand fleas jumped and popped out of my path. The reek of rotten kelp grew stronger as I wormed my silent way forward, to a better position behind a low dune, fifteen yards from the rear bumper.

With the truck's lights off, the only illumination came from the small dying fires. And the moon. Near to full tonight, low in the sky on the western horizon. Its pale glow made the two men look like puppets in a shadow play. One huge and round, one lean and stooped and edging ahead of the other. Perhaps to check for the remnants of my corpse in the burning driftwood. The bodyguard's cautious steps as soft as rustling leaves.

I fired straight into the center of his shadow, racked to fire again. The shadow crumpled.

Liashko fled. A terrified and surprisingly fast run, over the smoking logs and toward the lighthouse. Instinctively seeking the nearest place to hide. I didn't shoot. In the firelight I saw the arms dealer clutching my rucksack to his chest with both arms, like an infant he was protecting from harm.

I caught him at the base of the lighthouse tower. He heard me coming, turned just as my shotgun butt was swinging for his bull neck. It clocked him on the cheek instead. He fell, even as I wrenched the ruck with its deadly nerve agent from his grasp.

I checked it. Nothing leaking. Nothing broken. I was breathing hard, but I still managed to exhale a little more in relief.

Liashko stared up at me from the ground. His face white around the punctuations of blood.

Of course. He'd last seen me half an hour ago, as the black waves consumed the sinking patrol car. Seconds from death. The second time I'd come back from the grave, a scarred and bloody specter haunting him.

Surprise, you evil fuck. I smiled at Liashko, and this

time my grin wasn't forced at all. He shrank away from my reach.

I hauled the quivering man to his feet and marched him back to the truck to sit on his ass in the dazzling headlights, once I'd turned them on.

His bodyguards were alive. They might even stay that way, if the cops got here fast enough. Like Burke, they wore their own tactical vests under the seasonal outerwear, and the armor had saved them from the worst of the buckshot. One of them hung on to my arm and said something in Russian, maybe asking for help, maybe still trying to fight. The other might never walk right again. I handed him his own belt and motioned for him to make a tourniquet above his shredded quad muscles, not sticking around to see if he understood. I flung their rifles far out into the lapping surf.

While rifling through the truck cab, I found a long security cable with a padlock in the glove compartment. I used it to bind Liashko's wrists and ankles together behind his back and looped the cable around the truck's bumper before locking it. He wound up lying on his side, the damp sand and bits of seaweed painting one side of his big head. The padlock key followed the guns into the Sound.

I took out my burner phone and dialed a number I'd memorized.

Special Agent Rick Martens answered, his voice thick with sleep. "Wha—Whoizit?"

I held the phone out to Liashko and pointed the muzzle of the Mossberg at his groin.

"Say your name," I said.

It took him a few seconds to find his voice. "Anatoly Fedorovych Liashko."

I took the phone back. "Point No Point lighthouse. Get here fast."

The phone stayed on the truck's hood, the line still open in case Martens needed to trace the signal. My rucksack with the canisters of nerve gas next to it.

I ran back down the beach the way I had come, feeling exhausted, feeling unsteady, feeling like I could race the brilliant beam the lighthouse cast over the waves, and beat it.

CHAPTER FIFTY-FIVE

AFTER SOME DISCUSSION WITH the anxious Finns, we agreed to chart a course south along the coast before turning across the Sound to Seattle. Giving the second wave of chaos at Point No Point a wide berth.

I watched the invasion through my set of field glasses. An SPD helicopter arrived first, then a sudden blossoming of lights onshore, red and blue and white, a second chopper, and what might have been a Coast Guard cutter. It was hard to tell; by that time we were miles away.

Burke had gone silent and pale. Aware that his opportunity for revenge was gone forever. And maybe his injuries and the near drowning had stripped everything from him but his defiance. Harri had patched his lacerations with gauze and tape from my well-stocked first aid kit in the cabin.

Now Burke sagged against the cabin wall, looking ten years older than he had an hour ago.

"What was your plan?" I said over the drone of the big outboard. "To get away after Liashko?"

Burke grimaced. "Anatoly was going to put the truck ashore at Edmonds. I'd ace him and his two lunks the second we touched land. Drive off in the cop car and call Martens to come get the weapons."

I hefted his torn WSP coat, my next question obvious.

"I already had the uniform," Burke said. "Looking like the law can be useful sometimes. The car I boosted earlier tonight from a substation in Auburn. Hardly anyone around during the regular week, they might not miss the car till Friday. After I was done with Anatoly I'd swap it for a clean vehicle I stashed in Shoreline with everything I need. Out of the state before dawn, out of the country by noon tomorrow. Spain to start. Maybe Mauritius once I got bored."

"Why was Liashko headed for Edmonds?"

"Anatoly had a plane at Paine Field, ready to fly with the sarin."

Sarin. So that was the chemical weapon that we'd been playing Capture the Flag with all night.

"You knew he had that lethal shit all along?" I said.

Burke nodded. "A bargaining chip for me, in case I needed some extra clout with the cops."

"You're insane."

He shrugged indifference. Jaak and his friends had found other places to be. Tough to do on a slim twenty-foot boat.

Burke looked toward the jagged line of lights that defined the city ahead. "You turning me in?"

"Why? You're a damned hero."

He looked at me, puzzled. I jabbed a thumb back toward the blaze of activity on the point.

"Liashko and the missiles in federal hands, and captured bioweapons as the cherry. You've disappeared.

The prevailing theory will be that you took out Liashko and his men and drove away, almost like you planned."

Burke blinked. Started to say something, then thought about it for another few seconds. "He'll finger you."

"Maybe. But he's not a fool. If Liashko admits he knows me, he's also opening up the part where he tried to murder us. For all he knows, you're dead and deep underwater. The cops will find the sunken car only if they know to look for it. If he's shrewd, he'll claim he never got a look at the guy who shot up his truck and hog-tied him."

"The sailors on the cargo ship saw you, too."

"For a hot second. And the ones who got the closest look at me are dead now, thanks to Liashko's firefight. Maybe I was Sean Burke, and the guy in the trooper uniform was just another grunt. I think their stories will be confused as hell. The simplest answer is that you learned Liashko was moving the arms early, and you decided to handle it yourself and disappear. That seems about your level of crazy."

"The Feds will never buy it."

"I think they'll find a way to believe. Martens and the rest have what they want, and more. Why spread shit in front of the ticker-tape parade?"

"Now who's nuts?" Burke shook his head.

I took a diving knife from the cockpit locker to cut the bonds at his ankles and wrists.

"We'll let you off downtown," I said. "Get to Shoreline, get in your car, don't look back."

We watched the city manifest as the speedboat sliced through the soft chop. The Needle in the north, the stadiums south. A rough bell curve of skyscrapers between. The moon had dipped out of sight, and there was nothing to dilute the shimmering reflection of the city lights on the water.

"There's something I gotta tell you," Burke said, his voice barely carrying above the thrum of the outboard. "About Moira."

I looked at him.

"I already know," I said.

CHAPTER FIFTY-SIX

PALMER STRATTON'S CAMPAIGN HEADQUARTERS occupied the first two stories of a narrow office tower near Denny Park, squashed between apartments on one side and a medical center on the other. I counted four different coffeehouses within sight of the entrance. Caffeine to keep the volunteers going, and paramedics nearby when they finally collapsed.

I let myself in through the small loading dock in the rear of the building, took a freight elevator up four stories, found a stairwell, and walked down to the second floor of the campaign offices. It wasn't difficult. Stratton had a private security team, but they were downstairs now with the man himself, along with all of the workers to hear Stratton's latest pep talk. No cops. The U.S. attorney wasn't governor yet.

His personal office was in the rear. I knew that thanks to the half-dozen videos of tours granted to news services and community organizations, all readily available on YouTube. I think the campaign's intent was to demonstrate that despite his blue-blooded upbringing, Stratton's HQ looked like almost any busy office in America, with cubicles and cluttered desks and stacks of boxes and inspirational posters. All the volunteers smiling as they worked the phones and checked the latest social media impressions. One wall had been covered in pictures from rallies and other appearances. Another displayed a variety of graphic designs for Stratton's official photos and his slogan: COURAGE—CHARACTER—COMMUNITY.

The office was locked. I opened the door, locked it again behind me, and drew the blinds. Stratton had allowed himself a large window and enough space for a small conference table and a couch. Clutter from the outside cubicle farm had not stormed the ramparts of the candidate's sanctum. The only pictures of himself here were framed family snaps of his wife, Carolyn, and their college-age twins, all smiling at the camera with an abundance of health and teeth.

His rolling chair behind the L-shaped faux-walnut desk was comfortable. I enjoyed it while I waited, looking out the window at the bright clear January day.

My birthday, as it happened.

Ten minutes later, a swell of noise on the second floor rolled steadily toward the back of the building. I heard Palmer Stratton's voice, talking jovially with his staff. The door opened and Stratton came in, with the blond campaign lead I'd seen at his fund-raiser and another two workers close on his heels.

He stopped midsentence. "How did you get in here?" he said. I smiled, all modesty.

The workers were staring, just as dumbfounded. The blonde turned to her boss. "Should I—?" She gestured back toward the office, and the guards who were no doubt minding the perimeter downstairs.

I held up the brass medallion of Saint Brendan that Burke had given me. Suspended between thumb and forefinger, like I was about to perform a magic trick for Stratton. Watch carefully. Something might just vanish.

Stratton stared, with the same look of foreboding he'd had when I'd told him to protect his inside man, Burke. Then he composed himself and turned to the staff.

"It's fine, Grace. I'd just forgotten our appointment. Would you tell Lyle and the others that I'll be a few minutes?"

Grace nodded, perhaps unconvinced, but she left nonetheless.

Stratton shut the door and waited until he was sure no one was hovering outside.

"We've been looking for you," he said. "You're more than halfway to an arrest warrant."

"Sounds like you're still undecided."

He frowned sternly. "This isn't a joke, Shaw. You'll answer our questions. Has Sean Burke been in touch with you?"

"I was wondering the same thing about you. Did Burke tell you he was going to disappear? That's the kind of thing you'd want a friend to know. So they didn't worry."

Stratton didn't say anything.

"My mother, Moira, gave this to my father, a long time ago," I said, setting the medallion on his desk. "And Burke gave the medal to me," I said, staying on course. "Saint Brendan. A patron of travelers, like Saint Christopher. But mostly of sailors."

"I read in your file that she died when you were a child."

"She'd been exploring her faith at the time, I've learned. I guess she wanted some reassurance. Tough on a girl, being knocked up in high school."

Stratton slid a chair from the conference table out, sat down across from me. Changing tack. "Liashko made noise about an American coming aboard the *Oxana M* and planting all of the arms, trying to frame him, before his lawyer buttoned his mouth. He may not persist with that alibi, but it's sure that his team will try to muddy the waters."

"Keep me out of it," I said.

"Sorry." He shook his head in mock regret. "You may not do time, but you have to be brought in. Tonight. It's up to you whether you leave here in handcuffs. And you'll testify if necessary. I want answers."

"Like father, like son."

His hand gripped the chair's armrest. "Excuse me?"

"I take after Moira's side. Black hair, black eyes. Burke is dark complexioned, too; it threw me for a while. But you and I are about the same size, and back in your wrestler days we were probably the same build. Plus there's this." I tapped the etched image of Saint Brendan. "Sailors. You and your family. Regatta races, service in the Navy. And you're Catholic. Why would she send a saint to protect an agnostic thug like Sean Burke?"

"That—that's a fantasy."

A rap at the door made him jump. The person on the other side opened it without waiting for a response. Margaret Stratton stepped partway into the room.

"Palmer?" she said, then realized it wasn't her son behind the desk. "Oh."

"Afternoon, Mrs. Stratton," I said.

"Mother, would you excuse us?" Stratton said. "We're just finishing up some business."

Instead of leaving, Margaret entered and shut the door.

"What was it you were discussing?" she said. To me, not to her son.

"Family legacies," I said.

Her minuscule smile evaporated entirely. "I don't understand."

"Palmer does. Tell her."

"Mr. Shaw," Stratton began, before clearing his throat. "Shaw seems to labor under the impression that I'm his father."

"Ridiculous," Margaret said.

"That's what I was about to tell him. Sean Burke has already admitted to being Shaw's father. He informed Agent Martens of that, when he explained why Shaw had sought him out. And Burke also informed us about the DNA test that confirmed his parentage." He nodded emphatically, back on message.

"The tests confirmed parentage," I agreed, "but it wasn't Burke's DNA on the swab he gave me. It was yours. He was covering for you."

"What are you saying?" Margaret's pallor came close to matching her silver-white hair.

"Burke told me that when he decided to turn informant, he reached out to the one guy in law enforcement he thought he could trust. Agent Martens was Burke's handler on the case. I'd just assumed Martens was also his childhood buddy. Martens couldn't have kept their prior history a secret from you, the man in charge of the task force. That would jeopardize any investigation."

Stratton and his mother exchanged a look.

"But I had it backward," I said. "You and Burke were the ones who knew each other in private school. Martens was his primary contact, as a go-between. Keeping things kosher for the eventual trial."

"I'm calling security," Margaret said, turning away.

"Don't," said Stratton. His mother stopped, one hand on the doorknob.

"When I started getting close, Palmer and Burke went over their options," I said to her. "It was clear to them that I wouldn't stop until I had answers. Burke knew that before long I'd steal a bit of food or a water bottle he'd tossed in the trash and have tests run. If that test came up negative for my father, I'd keep digging. Maybe I'd even find out the names of other friends of Moira's from back in the day. Like Palmer."

"That's wrong. Palmer never knew—your mother," Margaret said, as if that settled things.

"So they got out ahead of the problem," I continued. "Palmer gave Burke a swab from his cheek. Burke gave it to me. It would come up positive and I'd think Burke was my father. And it worked, for a day or two."

They were silent now. Waiting to see what cards I turned over, so they would know if they had any of their own left to play.

"I was already half convinced that Moira went for the bad-boy type. Then I remembered Burke had mentioned something else, about the two of them hanging with his friends from school. So I made some calls. Sean went to Whitaker Academy, I learned. Moira met someone else in that group, someone she liked more." I pointed at Stratton. "You. One of the academy's most distinguished graduates, and that's saying something."

"Whitaker has a lot of alumni," he said. "Your mother may have taken up with someone, but it wasn't me."

"There were other things that bothered me, too. Agent Martens had come to the bar where I work just a couple of nights prior to Burke giving me the swab. He lifted a bottle of beer I'd been drinking from out of the recycling bin. I have him on camera, skulking around. That got me puzzling. Why would Burke give me his swab if his C.I. handler had already stolen a sample from me? Unless someone on the task force was running a test for themselves. Maybe in private. Did you tell Martens you wanted my DNA for the case?"

"Conjecture," Stratton said, "and wishful thinking. I'm sorry Sean Burke doesn't meet with your image of what your father should be—"

"But he did," I interrupted. "Burke and I have more in common than I'd like. We're both raised by criminals. Both with a history of violence. And we're loyal to a damned fault. Burke was about to disappear into WITSEC. You two would work together to take down Liashko, who had killed his father, Gus."

I shrugged. "Tricking me, pretending to be my dad for a month or two, was a small price for Burke to pay. Especially since a shitstorm in the news about U.S. Attorney Stratton's out-of-wedlock kid could sink the task force, and ruin Burke's chance to nail Liashko right along with it."

"You've no proof—" Stratton began, and then stopped. Maybe guessing what was coming.

"Your makeup table at the fund-raiser," I said, pointing a finger-gun at him in confirmation. "I lifted a few hairs out of the brush. Too bad your dye job doesn't mask genetic testing. I've got a whole profile rundown. One of the state's leading authorities explained it to me earlier this morning, but I have to confess I only understood about half of what he said. The conclusion spoke for itself, though."

"If you say anything," Margaret said, "we will sue you into oblivion."

"That's the spirit, Grandma."

Her lips curled back. "Don't you dare call me that."

"What do you want?" said Stratton.

"Palmer—" said Margaret.

"It's over, Mother," he said, "except for the negotiating." He turned back to me. "How much?"

"You think this is a transaction? I'd say it's more of a plea bargain."

Margaret would not be denied. "I was sure this would come to pass. From the first moment I heard about that horrid girl. You're all malignant."

I stopped, and Stratton's mouth dropped open. Both of us caught off-guard this time.

"You knew about Moira," I said.

"Of course we knew. Do you imagine Palmer could be involved with people like you and we wouldn't know?"

Stratton stiffened. "Mom. What did you do?"

"What you should have. I told that girl to stay away from you. That if she didn't, James and I would make sure that monstrous father of hers went to prison where he belonged for the rest of his days. The child had just enough sense to know I meant what I said."

I looked at Stratton. He still stared at Margaret, aghast.

"Moira wasn't protecting you from Dono by breaking up," I said to him. "She was protecting Dono from you. Your family."

"James and I had people keeping watch after Palmer left for college," Margaret said, "in case she had lied. We found out she was *expecting.*" The word was cyanide. "I couldn't believe it might be Palmer's. But I warned her again, in case the little witch thought she could lay any claim on you. I told her we would arrange for a medical procedure to clean things up. That if she even hinted that Palmer was involved she would regret it forever. She said—it doesn't bear repeating what she said."

Good for you, Mom.

"You knew," Stratton said to Margaret, as if his thoughts had become trapped at that point. "All these years. Moira was pregnant and had our child and you *knew*?"

"It doesn't matter," she replied, going to him. "It didn't matter then. Or now."

Stratton stood and brushed her questing hand away. "Don't. Don't pretend this is nothing. That what you tried to do . . ." Words apparently failed him.

She talked past him to me, an edge of desperation in her voice. "We will pay you a reasonable amount. But then it's done. Do you understand?"

I understood, all right. The teenage Moira was leaps and bounds tougher than any of them. I bet that had scared the hell out of Margaret Stratton and the honorable congressman.

"Get out," Stratton said to his mother.

"Palmer, this is unaccep—"

"Get out of my sight right now."

Margaret's face paled. She looked at her son, then back to me.

It was cruel, but I didn't even try to resist smiling at her.

"Dads and I have some catching up to do," I said.

Margaret went, immediately and directly, as if fury had given her wings.

Stratton closed the door behind her. When he came back to the chair I realized he was nearly as pale as Margaret had been.

"God," he said. With a tone of honesty directing his words upstairs. "How can this be?"

"The how explains itself," I said. "It's the why I'm wondering about."

Stratton was staring at the medal of Saint Brendan, still resting on the desk.

"Confession's good for the soul," I said.

He closed his eyes before he began speaking.

"Moira. She and I—we met when she came out with Sean. It was immediate between us. Even Sean saw it. He punched me in the gut, but he couldn't get too mad. It was just one of those things. And Sean had had a lot of girls. Moira was the first one I cared about."

He might be weaving me a story. Politicians were good at that, creating empathy out of nothing. But I didn't think so.

"We both accepted I'd be going east for college at the end of the summer," Stratton said, easing back into his chair. "We'd even talked about her coming to visit, once she got up the nerve to tell her dad she was seeing me. Then she stopped calling. I got a letter. Moira had sent it through Sean, and now I understand why. My parents might have intercepted it otherwise. Moira said she had to end things between us, that she hoped I understood. I didn't. At all. I suspected it was because of Dono, but I didn't care if he came after me."

Foolhardy. But Stratton had been young and in love.

"I went to her house one day, when I knew Dono was away, but Moira refused to let me in. I finally got the picture. She wasn't coming back. Then a couple of months later, at Cornell, I received another letter forwarded through Sean. With that inside."

He nodded to Saint Brendan. "I'd seen it before, the one time she allowed me into the house. Moira had told me then that the medal was a sort of heirloom she'd inherited, from back when the family were regular Catholics. Before Dono moved to America. I'd—encouraged her to start up again while we had been dating. But then . . ." Stratton folded his hands. "She wished me well in the letter and said she was okay. And that she hoped I'd keep it."

She had learned she was pregnant. And said nothing, to Dono or to Palmer, to keep the Strattons from using all of their influence to bury my grandfather.

"I nearly threw the damn thing into Beebe Lake the day I got it," Stratton said. "But no. The medallion was the only thing I had from her. Eventually I met Carolyn, and everything worked out." Stratton's interlaced fingers fiddled with his wedding ring, twisting it by habit around his finger.

"Until Burke."

"When Sean told me about you last week, I couldn't believe it. I thought it was a trick. Liashko trying to pull something over on Sean, getting him to trust you. I'd found out Moira had died years after it happened. I was still in the Navy, and overseas. It never occurred to me that she might have—that you might exist."

"Must have been a hell of a shock."

"The more I thought about it, the more I wanted to know the truth. Even if I couldn't do or say anything about it. Sean and I cooked up the idea of having you run the test on my DNA, believing it was his. I sent Martens to get a sample from you if he could, to find out privately for myself, and, well . . ."

"To keep me from upsetting the apple cart."

He had the decency to look abashed. "Yes. Moira was gone. Past helping. If I had known about you when you were young, perhaps—" He exhaled. "I gave Sean the medal to give to you. To sell the lie. And because of all people you should have it."

I picked up the brass disc. It felt heavier than I knew it was.

Stratton shifted uncertainly. "If you want money—"

"Not yours."

He flushed.

"You'll leave my name out of the investigation," I said. "No interrogation, no deposition, nothing. Sean Burke took down Liashko and his men and chose to disappear rather than suffer through life in WITSEC. You make sure Liashko gets the worst hellhole the Feds can arrange for him."

Stratton hesitated. But his mind was back in gear. Making deals was his wheelhouse. "You'll have to sign nondisclosure agreements."

I laughed. "For what? I don't exist."

"That's all? Nothing more than to stay out of it?" said Stratton.

"What price freedom?" I said. "I don't like attention. Notoriety is even worse."

Updates on the Liashko case would be scrolling on cable news chyrons for weeks. A Ukrainian arms trafficker arrested with stolen Russian bioweapons on American soil. There would be think pieces and committees at every level of government. Seattle would become the temporary base of every national news service and true-crime podcast, and everyone remotely involved would have their moment in the spotlight. Like it or not.

"You should—you should have *something*," Stratton tried again.

He wanted to make amends, maybe feel absolved through his generosity if not his suffering. But Stratton wasn't the one who'd sinned, any more than Moira had.

I stood and put the medal of Saint Brendan in my pocket. "Good luck in February. Not that you'll need it."

Stratton nodded. When I closed the door, he was staring at nothing, still turning his ring around his finger like it might rewind time.

THAT NIGHT, I SLEPT. That night, I finally dreamed. Or remembered.

"MOM?" I SAID. "MOMMA? What's this?"

If the box had been on Mom's shelf before, I hadn't seen it. But she had a lot of little things, and I wasn't allowed to touch them unless she said.

"What's what, honey?" She was in the kitchen and couldn't see.

"This. Um." Like quarters but bigger, and yellow. "Coins. In the box?"

"Oh. Those are saints, baby. Do you know what saints are?"

"Nuh-uh."

"Well, they protect people, kind of. Each medallion there is a different saint."

I looked closer. There were—I counted—five of them. Four men and one woman. And one missing. Leaving a circle in the wooden box, like a puzzle that wasn't finished.

"Can I play with them?"

"Yes. But on the table and wash your hands after. You'll remember?"

"Uh huh." I lifted the box carefully over some little glass horses and brought it to the table, setting it down before I pulled out the chair and climbed up to see.

The coins fell out all at once when I tipped the box over, clinking and clattering real loud onto the table. Mom didn't say anything, so I guessed that was okay. I picked them up. They were much heavier than the loose change in my elephant bank. Like pirate money.

I lined them up to look at the pictures. One man held a book, and the woman carried something hard to tell, maybe flowers, but two of the men had long sticks like wizards. They all wore long clothes, and one man had a big tall hat, which was funny.

"Are you excited about first grade, Van?" The kitchen timer beeped like it was answering for me.

"Yeah." The coins spun best if I used two hands and pushed on them first with my fingers. Soon I could make them go for a long time, spinning upright until they started to tilt, making circles on the table and getting louder and faster. I counted to twenty-seven before the last one finally shuddered to a stop.

"The school's closed for the summer, so I'm going downtown to the district office tomorrow to get your forms," Mom said. "We'll find out who your teacher will be. And then I think you and I should get a lunch-box for you. Your kindergarten one is Worn. Out. Too many cookies broke the handle!"

I giggled. Maybe the lunchbox would have Hulk on it. Superstrong to hold more cookies. That made me laugh more. I spun the coins some more and stacked them and made them bounce off each other until Mom said over the sound of the oven closing that it was time for dinner. Something smelled good, maybe pork chops. When I put the coins back in the box with all their faces showing, I remembered the missing one.

"Um, Mom? There are only five. One was gone before," I said.

"I know."

"Did you lose it?"

Mom didn't answer. Maybe she hadn't heard. "Momma?"

"I didn't lose it, baby. I gave it to someone who . . . who could use a little help. That's what they're for."

"Help how?"

"Maybe . . . maybe knowing the right thing to do when they're not sure. We can all use that sometimes."

I looked at the coins again. Did they have powers? "Did it? Help them?"

"I'm gonna say yes, it did."

"Okay." Cool. I put the box back careful behind the horses.

"What were you going to do next?" She brought in plates and forks and set them on the table.

I was still looking at the coins in the box. One was tilted, and I fixed it. "Wash my hands."

"Right." She kissed me on the top of the head. "I love you, baby."

"I love you, too, Momma."

I went to wash up. The coins would be there tomorrow, after we came back from getting my new lunchbox. I bet I could get one to spin till I counted to a hundred.

EPILOGUE

BULLY BETTY HAD ALLOWED me to take over the back room for a private party. It was a small enough group that on a Tuesday night in early February we all could have easily gathered in the main bar, but putting it in a separate space allowed Cyndra to be present with some deniability. The kid, me, Addy Proctor, Oscar and Cannonball and Twelvetrees from the gym. My usual suspects Hollis, Willard, and Elana. Betty and A-Plus and Mo and a few others wandered through to say hello. Hollis and Willard sat across from one another, regaling my fellow gym rats with stories of youthful indiscretions. Which for them usually involved a large quantity of alcohol with a dash of felony.

And Wren. I looked across the room. She and Elana had hit it off, and Cyndra watched every move and joke the two women made with rapt fascination.

The party was supposedly for me, in honor of my thirtieth spin around the sun. I'd put Addy and Cyndra off planning anything until I was certain Palmer Stratton would keep his word and I wouldn't find myself in a holding cell, biding time between interrogations by everyone from Homeland Security to Parks and Rec.

Now Palmer Stratton's image appeared on the muted screen in the corner. Waving to the crowd in whatever hotel ballroom his campaign had rented for election night. A much larger room than for the fund-raiser at the Alexis. The Stratton bandwagon had swelled exponentially during the month since Liashko's arrest.

It was only eight in the evening. Votes would be counted for hours yet, if not days. But every poll during the past week had shown U.S. Attorney Stratton leading the race, most by double-digit percentages. The candidate was just marking time until his acceptance speech.

On the screen, Palmer Stratton held his wife, Carolyn's, hand. He waved, she waved, their twins behind them beamed, both boy and girl looking a little dazzled by the lights and the adulation.

Margaret Stratton shared the stage with her family. She stood to one side, graciously leaning down to accept the proffered handshakes of people in the crowd. Was it me, or had she aged since I'd seen her at campaign headquarters? She moved hesitantly, responded to the well-wishers slowly. Maybe it was just the stress of the race.

I waved to Addy Proctor, who'd stepped out to use the restroom and had returned with a pint of stout for me and a shot of vodka for herself. Addy was the only person with whom I'd shared the truth about Palmer Stratton, and Moira.

She joined me at the wall counter, and both of us watched events unfold on the television.

"Your father is our new governor," Addy said softly after a few moments, shaking her head. "Isn't life amazing?"

"I always felt like a black sheep. Nice to know it's from a good flock."

She snorted. "Sheep's clothing, maybe. Scratch that. You don't look like anything other than what you are."

"Thanks."

"I meant it as a compliment."

"It is," I said. "I'm my mother's son."

Addy looked at me quizzically. "Perhaps that's why you broke away from your grandfather's way of life. Moira's influence, for however long she had you."

"I'd had that same thought. It occurred to me that all my stress about what I might have inherited from Sean Burke was a clue in itself. Burke's a damn sociopath, or spitting distance from it. Not capable of that kind of introspection. For all the similarities in our lives, at the core I've got something he's missing. Chalk that up to Mom."

The stout tasted like coffee and smoke. Perfect.

Addy nodded to the three young women laughing, slapping their hands on the table made from a repurposed door. "I like Wren. She's got focus."

"Yeah."

Me, too, it seemed. I knew what I wanted now.

Wren may have sensed our attention. She looked up and smiled at us. I toasted her with the pint.

"Addy," I said. "Your cabal of friends. You mentioned one of them used to run the United Way around here."

"That would be Connie," said Addy, "and she used to run the United Way. Of America."

"Ah." Addy's network never ceased to surprise. "So she would know something about setting up a charity."

"You could safely say that, yes. Why? Are you thinking of starting a benevolent fund for burglars?"

"Their children, actually."

She set down the vodka she'd barely been tasting. "You're serious."

"I am. Moira was a volunteer with something similar. Foster kids and others whose parents are doing time. Like Cyndra was. I was thinking about how to create an organization like that."

"Define 'create.'"

"Hire somebody who knows what to do. Give them funding."

"Funding from . . . ? You can't start a charity with stolen money."

"Depends on who it's stolen from. But let's work on the assumption that any proceeds can be legitimately explained."

"That sounds like a very gray area."

"I'm very comfortable with very gray. Can you help me?"

She took an actual drink of her vodka this time. "I'm willing to consult. That's as far as I'll go for now."

"Thank you." We clinked glasses, and I started a circuit of the room to say hello to everyone. Wren met me halfway, at the stained-glass window that gave the regulars a nicer thing to look at than the alley beyond.

"Hey," she said. "You throw a good party."

"I dunno. I might not stay too late."

"No? There's somewhere else to be?"

"A christening." I took a set of keys from my pocket, showed them to her. "I got a late birthday present. A lawyer contacted me yesterday. He asked me to come to his office to go over a mess of papers and other things, but the upshot is that for the next twenty months I hold the prepaid lease to a high-rise apartment in Belltown. And a new truck. An inheritance, kind of."

She took the keys to give them a closer look. "This is . . . from the guy you thought was your dad? Burke?"

"Yeah. He's skipped town. For good. But after he left he arranged this little surprise. I'm still wrapping my head around it."

"So you have a new place to live."

"I do."

Wren stood close. She seemed to radiate something more than warmth. I could feel it down to my marrow. "And when you say you want to christen it, you mean . . ."

"I do."

"Hah. I'd better let Elana know we need to ease back on the tequila shots, then. Too many more and I'll be no good to you."

I grinned at her. Enjoying the challenge in her eyes.

"I have faith," I said.

ACKNOWLEDGMENTS

With gratitude to the people who unleashed *A Dangerous Breed*:

Lisa Erbach Vance of the Aaron Priest Literary Agency, a wonderful agent and first through the door in representing this and all my other works. Taking point takes courage and competence, and Lisa has both in spades.

Lyssa Keusch at William Morrow, a brilliant editor who hones and polishes every novel for the better, while making it seem like any improvements were my idea. And to the team at Morrow who steer and power the creative machine: our renowned publisher Liate Stehlik, Danielle Bartlett, Pamela Jaffee, Kaitlin Harri, Bob Castillo, Kyle O'Brien, and Mireya Chiriboga.

Caspian Dennis of the Abner Stein Agency, Van Shaw's top operative in the UK.

And to those who lent their knowledge and technical expertise. They offered their time and energy to make the story richer, sometimes only to find their hours of conversation distilled into a single line in the final draft. Any mistakes are my own darn fault.

Patricia Powell, MD, and Dave "Doc" Powell, USN, for specifics on field medicine, pharmaceuticals, oncology, and all things related to the healing sciences.

Christian Hockman, Bco 1/75 Ranger Regiment, for his military and tactical support.

John N. Nassikas III, Partner at Arnold & Porter and former federal prosecutor, for the structure and operations of joint task forces and their work with confidential informants.

Jeannette Wentworth and Betsy Glick of the FBI, for lessons on the science of DNA collection, profiling, and analysis.

Sheryl Moss of the Office of the Secretary of State, for insights into Washington State's political processes.

Los Anarchists Junior Roller Derby in Los Angeles, where our own young jammer skated hard.

And finally, for support both emotional and spiritual:

Jerrilyn Farmer, and the Saturday Gang— Beverly Graf, Alexandra Jamison, and John McMahon. Fighting the good fight, word by word.

Rick Martens, charity auction "character name" winner. Rick, for the benefit of anyone reading this first, I won't spoil whether your fictional counterpart makes it out alive.

My sincere thanks to every reader who gave this book a try; I hope you enjoyed the tale. And to the booksellers, reviewers, and fans who might have helped that reader find the novel in the first place. Your dedication transforms a solitary pursuit into a warm and welcoming community of friends.

Amy, Mia, and Madeline, I love you so much. Thank you for your unwavering faith and for making our home a peaceful harbor from any storm, including the occasional tempest inside my head.

AUTHOR'S NOTE

This novel is fiction, which means I get to make up anything and everything, including but not limited to businesses real or imagined, jurisdictions, history, or anything else that might keep the story moving, keep the lawyers bored, and keep potentially dangerous information where and with whom it belongs.

That said, it's worth recognizing a few of the more egregious liberties taken:

Sharp-eyed Seattle residents may have noticed that I've compressed and slightly accelerated the timeline of the long-awaited opening of the Alaskan Way underground tunnel, and the subsequent demolition of the old elevated viaduct. Neither had happened during January of the same year.

Washington State gubernatorial recalls, regardless of the circumstances, do not result in a runoff election between parties. The order of succession is a sedate process, where the duties would automatically fall upon the lieutenant governor. My way is more fun.

The beautiful Japanese Garden in Seattle's Washington Park Arboretum is closed to visitors during the winter months. Nor does it admit dogs at any time. Not even Stanley. These limitations aside, a peaceful hour spent in the garden is like a day's vacation anywhere else. If circumstances permit, I encourage you to see it for yourself.

IF YOU ENJOYED VAN SHAW'S LATEST ADVENTURE, WAIT UNTIL YOU SEE WHAT'S NEXT.

While his hometown is under lockdown, Van Shaw deals with the cabin fever of quarantine in his own fashion . . .

TURN THE PAGE FOR A BONUS SHORT STORY.

ESSENTIAL BUSINESS

VAN SHAW LOOKED DOWN at the streets of Seattle from thirty stories above and counted the seconds between pedestrians. Whenever a new person appeared from around a corner or emerged from a building, he restarted the count at one. His personal best after a full hour of watching was twenty-six.

Twenty-six ticks was a long time for any stretch of downtown blocks to be completely empty. Even at close to midnight. Nearly half a minute during which you could easily imagine yourself the last person on Earth.

Cabin fever. That must be it, Shaw decided. He had been inside for most of the past three weeks, complying with the governor's stay-at-home order during the pandemic. On the rare instances that he'd ventured out during daylight hours, it had usually been a rapid sortie to grab bread and meat and beer—whatever cuts and brands the corner market had managed to restock overnight—before returning directly to his apartment. He'd wipe the packages down with disinfectant and scrub the hell out of his hands, as per the guidelines on every reputable news media. His clothes went straight into the wash, every time, including the bandanna he used as a makeshift mask. His friend Addy Proctor had said the red kerchief made him look like an Old West pistolero.

The last time Shaw had taken an order so seriously, he'd still been in the Rangers. Then again, he considered, those orders had *also* been intended to keep himself and others alive, so maybe that was the key.

Nights were better. Shaw would take his car from the high-rise's underground garage and drive the highways, with no destination required and no chance he might meet anyone up close.

He had no fever, no cough. Probably wasn't infected at all. Two guys on the same volunteer crew had tested positive so far, so said the grapevine, but Shaw hadn't run into either of those men on the motel job weeks ago. By that time, they had all had been keeping the requisite six feet or more away from one another, as if someone might take a wild swing with a hatchet at any moment.

Still, it was possible he'd caught the virus. The crew had been moving damned fast. The county had bought the rundown Travelodge in Renton knowing it would need a ton of work, as quickly as it could be done, to retrofit the motel's eighty units for isolation and quarantine. All the carpet torn out and replaced with sterilizable tile. All beds removed and the showers modified for the mobility impaired. One of the veterans' groups around Fort Lewis had heard the county's plea, desperate for anyone with construction experience.

Shaw had been roped in by a former 1st Battalion lieutenant who owned the gym Shaw worked out at. He'd shown up for the volunteer team the very next day. Maybe during the rush to get materials off the truck somebody had breathed in his direction, or coughed into their hand and touched the same wooden palette moments before he had, and that was all it took, wasn't it?

It could be worse. Shaw hadn't visited Addy Proctor and her foster kid Cyndra in the days immediately after the motel job. That was good luck. Or maybe Addy's smarts were the real blessing. She'd put her house into quarantine well before most of the city. At eighty years old, the crafty woman wasn't taking chances. Cyn hadn't kicked at the sudden confinement as much as Shaw had thought she would. The teenager lived most of her life online anyway.

So Shaw lived alone. The bar he worked at was closed for the duration, and it wasn't like he'd been pulling a ton of hours lately anyway. He had enough money squirreled away to hold out for a few weeks. Maybe months, if he kept living like a monk.

That longer timeframe looked like the most probable outcome as the number of reported cases of the virus in the state climbed steadily toward quintuple digits. Shaw burned the days checking in with friends like Hollis Brant on the phone, or binging TV shows he'd missed during his years in the Army, or playing board games over Zoom with Cyndra and Addy. Cyndra liked King of Tokyo, and usually won. Addy preferred chess for the same reason. They'd all mutually agreed that the game of Pandemic could be set aside for a while.

On the fourth night of his isolation, Shaw had climbed the stairwell to the top level and deactivated the alarm on the door to the roof. The wide expanses of rubbery bitumen flooring between the shed-sized air conditioning units offered plenty of room for jumping rope or jogging around the perimeter. Every night since, he'd visited the roof again, even if just for a few minutes of fresh springtime air on his face. He reset the alarm when he left each time, in case some bored child wandering the building happened upon the same door.

The ping of an incoming video call summoned Shaw from the balcony. He set his bottle of Deschutes on the cracked pine veneer of the only table in the apartment. In the two months since he'd moved in, he hadn't gotten around to finding better furniture than had served for his old studio off Broadway. Hollis had said it was like putting a half-dozen rustbucket Chevettes in a Tesla showroom.

Shaw retrieved his laptop from the antique leather wingback chair and sat down to look. He stared at the caller's name for another three pings before he clicked Accept.

"Luce," he said when she appeared on the screen.

"Hi, Van."

She looked good. No makeup that he could detect, but Shaw had never thought Luce Boylan needed embellishment.

"How are you holding up?" he said it even as Luce began to speak the same words.

"That's everyone's question now, right?" she replied. "We're— I'm all right. Safe. Plenty of food and supplies, and no one at work has come down with it yet, thank God."

From the corkboard covered with photos over Luce's shoulder, Shaw could tell that she was in the bedroom of her small apartment. Probably sitting on the bed. He wondered briefly if it was the same queen-sized bed he'd known, and if it still squeaked, before he kicked that line of thought far away.

"Same here. Except for the work part." Shaw told her about the motel job. "So all of us on the LT's group text are just waiting, hoping nobody else wakes up with a temperature of a hundred and four."

"Addy's okay?"

"Yeah. Tougher than ever."

"Great," said Luce. "And Hollis?"

"Sailing offshore most of the time, like he's on vacation."

"Good."

Shaw waited. Stalling like this wasn't Luce's way.

"I want to ask a favor," she said.

He nodded.

"It's about Carter," she said.

And there it was. Carter was Luce's new husband. The guy she'd been with before Van, and after.

"He's working at Harborview. Part of the team they brought in to deal with the surge," Luce said.

Shaw recalled that Carter was an EMT and in medical school. Maybe doing his internship by now. A baptism of fire.

"How bad off are they?" he said.

"You should see the place. They've got tents outside to triage anyone with symptoms. With the ICU beds full up they're using any space that can be safely cordoned off from exposure. The doctors and nurses have outfits like hazmat suits with piped-in air, so awkward it takes two people to put them on."

Luce paused for a breath. Even with the limited resolution of her laptop camera, Shaw could see the fine lines of long-held strain around her oceanic eyes.

"Carter's in the middle of it?" he asked.

"Like a bullseye. At least that's what it feels like to me. He was already training for respiratory care when all this started, so they've got him shadowing specialists in the COVID-19 unit now."

"What's the favor?"

"You don't have to do it. There probably isn't anything you *can* do."

"Luce."

"Yes. Okay." She tucked a stray lock of blonde hair behind her ear. "The hospital was going to receive two high-pressure ventilators from a clinic near Spokane today, along with protective equipment. Masks and gloves, mostly. You know about the shortage of ventilators?"

Shaw nodded. Everybody had become familiar with the worldwide scarcity of machines to keep critical care patients breathing in the worst cases. The next-to-worst cases, he corrected himself. The worst cases were already past help.

"Then you know how much those machines mean right now, I guess. How much good they could do." Luce rubbed her brow, as if to wipe the worry from it. "The truck was hijacked outside of Ellensburg. Its driver had pulled off the freeway to get coffee at a drive-thru. When he stopped at a light, two cars boxed him in and men with guns forced him out of the truck. Left him standing there and drove the truck away."

"Uh huh."

"You say that like you already saw the story on the news."

"No. But I figured it had to be something like that."

"Or else I wouldn't be calling you. Of course. I'm just— it's been a hard time."

Luce was underselling it, Shaw thought. Married only a couple of months, and suddenly her new husband is working the plague ward and only coming home on those rare hours they could spare him. All while she never dared to see anyone else in person, because how could Luce take the chance that neither of them had caught the virus yet, with Carter on the front lines?

She closed her eyes. "I keep thinking if Harborview had those ventilators, that might tip the balance somehow. The hospital isn't turning people away, but they already have to make hard decisions about who's on the machines and who isn't. Most critical patients need assisted breathing for something like two or three weeks, Carter told me. Three whole weeks where that machine can't help anyone else. And if they had more protective stuff, then he might not have to keep wearing the same mask—"

"It's all right," Shaw said, and then amended his statement. "It will be."

"I wouldn't have called if I knew what else to do. Sorry. That sounded like talking to you was the last thing I'd ever want, and that's not true." She swept her hair back from her forehead. "You know it isn't."

But Shaw and Luce had agreed to be apart. All the way apart, because that was easier than trying to toe some line that seemed to be made of quicksilver. Social distancing, before that was a thing.

"What do the cops say?" he asked.

"From what Carter can glean through his friends in administration, the sheriff in Kittitas County will be investigating, but nobody's holding out much hope. For one thing, the jurisdiction is complicated by the ventilators being in transit across the state. And every police department has their hands full with the lockdown and all that comes with it. The county cops can't spare much manpower."

"Is the driver from Spokane?"

"No, Seattle. He was on a round trip to pick up the ventilators and return."

A full day, driving across the wide part of the state and back. At least he'd had the advantage of sparse traffic on the freeways.

"The first person the cops will look at is the driver," Shaw said, half to himself. "He knew the route and the cargo. And he'd have had plenty of lead time with the long drive, if he and some friends got ideas. That's assuming there was any hijacking at all. Maybe he stashed the ventilators before he left Spokane and lost the truck somewhere in Ellensburg before calling 911."

But Luce shook her head. "I know him. Aurelio. He's an ER nurse at Harborview, and he was using his off-duty day to make the run to Spokane so they'd get the masks and other things as soon as possible."

"Not exactly a low-life."

"There's no way I can picture Aurelio stealing. He's devastated. And it's not like the trip was a secret. Everyone in the ICU knew the ventilators and masks were on their way, just like I'm sure the Spokane people knew too."

"Get Aurelio to call me. Tell him—just tell him I'm a volunteer. That's accurate enough."

"Thank you. Really. I don't actually expect this to lead anywhere, but . . ." Luce shrugged.

"It's something we can do," Shaw finished the thought, "when we're out of other options."

"Yes. Exactly."

Aurelio called ten minutes later. The ER nurse had a resonant baritone voice that stretched into tenor as he recounted his very stressful afternoon.

"Three dudes, or maybe four. I don't know for sure. I pulled off I-90 and right then a car raced past me on the ramp, driving halfway onto the shoulder and kicking up all kinds of dirt. I figured it was some little punk gone crazy staying at home with his parents, blowing off steam. Then he slammed on the brakes and I stopped of course and the next thing there's a gun in my face."

"What did they say?"

"'Get out. Go that way. Don't look back.' Literally that much, eight words out of the guy pointing the gun at me. As chill as if he was ordering lunch. So I walked back down the ramp toward the freeway like he told me. I thought sure he was going to shoot me any second, even after I heard them drive away. It took a moment for me to dare turning around and going the other direction. There was a gas station a quarter-mile up the road and somebody there called 911 for me."

"You did the right thing, staying calm."

"I don't know how calm I was. I felt numb mostly, until I got the shakes. Shock, you know? Funny. When I saw them get out of the car in front of me with masks over their faces, I didn't think anything was weird at all. Everybody has masks on all day now, right? We're used to it."

"Tell me what you remember about them."

"I only really saw the guy at my window. And with the mask and sunglasses, his face was down to nothing. White dude with brown hair. And big, bigger than me anyway, and I'm six-two. His hoodie was gray without any writing on it. The sunglasses were Oakleys, not like that could be a clue. I told all this to the cops. You're working with them?"

"If I learn anything useful."

"About the only thing that really sticks was when the dude waved me out of the truck. The light shone kinda sideways through his glasses and I could see through them for a second, you know how that is?" Shaw said he did. "Well, one of the dude's eyes looked all milky. Like a cataract, but he wasn't an old guy so maybe not."

"But his eye was clouded?"

"I think so. If I had to swear on a Bible, I'd have to say I was only mostly sure. Maybe it'll give the cops a way to find him. I didn't have a chance to get the car's license number."

Shaw suspected that wouldn't have mattered. This crew sounded like they'd had some experience pointing guns and relieving people of their possessions. The cars were probably stolen and wiped clean, though if the gang had worn gloves it wouldn't strike anybody as strange nowadays. Maybe the whole bunch had followed Aurelio all the way from Seattle, a small convoy, or maybe they'd had one half of the team ID the truck in Seattle and call ahead to their partners in Spokane, who'd wait for Aurelio to show at the clinic. No need to tail him for hours when they could keep some distance and move in when they saw their chance.

And Aurelio was a dead end. Shaw would have to try to find a lead on the other side of the supply chain.

The ER nurse's voice, deep once again, cut into his line of thought. "What kind of assholes would do this right now?" he was saying. "I mean Jesus, don't they give a shit at all?"

Shaw didn't have an answer for that. Market forces, he figured. The demand reached a certain point and whatever reservations this crew might have had about stealing from deathly ill people, if they had ever had any qualms to begin with, were overruled. Everybody had a price.

Once he'd ended the call with Aurelio, Shaw prepared to go streetside for the first time in five days. He put on a shirt and hiking vest as proof against the cold. After a moment's thought he added a compact Colt in a clip-on holster as proof against other things. He wasn't expecting trouble, but it was a time when everyone was taking extra precautions.

He drove south, a winding course through the empty streets. Three miles on he passed CenturyLink Field. A line of refrigerated trucks stood in close formation just outside the north entrance, on the paved plaza normally reserved for fans walking from the nearest parking lot. The trucks' gleaming paint jobs glowed pale in the night.

No prizes for guessing why the cold storage trucks were there, Shaw thought. The Army was converting CenturyLink into a field hospital, to handle overflow when and if—looking more like when and less like if every day—medical centers like Harborview became overwhelmed. The trucks could be the final stop for many. Potentially a long stop, too, until funeral homes found a way to manage the crisis.

There had been no trucks for extended storage in Afghanistan. Body bags came in by air or road and the soldier in question would be swiftly prepared for transport. Any personal effects removed and bagged. The remains placed into an ice-packed aluminum case already draped with the flag, to be sent off with a ramp ceremony—seeing the body onto the aircraft home—as soon as schedules allowed. Shaw had stood in a few of those ceremonies, saluting as a brass quintet played and a short parade of Humvees drove slowly across the hot tarmac toward the ramp of a giant C-17, each vehicle carrying one transfer case, one soldier going home.

Dignified. Efficient. But the Army had the benefit of years of practice. Shaw prayed his hometown wouldn't have to learn the same lessons.

THE DUGOUT TAVERN WAS closed, of course. Which was not the same as saying it was unoccupied. When the city was told to stay at home, Shaw figured certain people would consider the Dugout their home far more than whatever house or apartment happened to contain their possessions.

The tavern wasn't near a ballpark, either, though someone had once told him that the Seattle Pilots had played at a nearby stadium, both team and venue vanishing long before Shaw was born. A Lowe's hardware store occupied the site now. The plywood sheet with painted letters pronouncing the Dugout CLOSED FOR THE DURATION had probably been purchased there.

Gold dots spelled out the tavern's name on the face of the building, like the bulbs in an old-time light-up scoreboard. The doors carried the letters G and O. He adjusted the red bandanna over his face and knocked hard in the center of the G. Half a minute later a male voice called from within.

"Who is it?"

"Van Shaw. Looking for Milford."

"Ain't here." The answer coming so fast it might have been reflex. Ask the voice if he was awake, he'd deny it instantly.

"His car's at the curb," Shaw said. "I'll wait."

Another minute passed while a debate presumably raged inside. The Dugout's door cracked open and a rotund man with a blue paisley scarf concealing his nose and the top half of a bushy beard looked out. "You can't come in."

"Don't need to."

Shaw waited. The man glared over the top of his scarf before retreating to shout into the depths of the tavern. "Mill."

The three-inch opening stayed black for a moment. Then Milford Kettering appeared. He was less round than the doorman, but only in the way an egg is less round than a cantaloupe. The old fence wore no mask, but Shaw imagined Kettering pulling up the fold of his yellow turtleneck if he felt the need, like a turtle retreating into its shell.

"Van," Milford said, sounding as surprised as if he hadn't been told Shaw was at the door. "How wonderful. Are you here to check on my welfare?"

"Business."

"Even better, even better. I didn't realize you were back in the game, though certainly when I heard you'd returned to Seattle after so long away . . ." Kettering fluttered his fingers. "One hopes. You and your grandfather were always a welcome sight, and profitable. What have you brought me?"

"I want information."

Kettering's face, pitted with scars from acne that had vanished fifty years before, looked crestfallen. "Van. Surely."

"Call it a public service. Medical equipment was stolen. Two COVID-suitable ventilators, and personal safety gear."

"And you're looking to . . . re-acquire these?"

"I am."

Something in Shaw's tone made the purveyor of illegal goods blanch a little.

"Quite like your grandfather, now that you're full-grown, I see," Kettering mumbled. He cleared his throat. "What can you tell me about the theft?"

Shaw described every detail Aurelio the nurse had told him, right down to the cloudy-eyed leader's plain grey sweatshirt. Kettering listened intently, his fingers playing idly with the buttons on his corduroy sport coat.

"I'd owe you a favor, if it works out," Shaw finished.

"Certainly, certainly," Kettering said, still half in thought. "Do you mind occupying yourself while I make some calls? I believe the people I'm trying to reach may still be up at this hour."

"And home."

"Yes. That's almost guaranteed, isn't it?"

Kettering vanished into the interior. Shaw spent twenty minutes waiting, during which only half a dozen cars drove past. One was a police SUV. The cop in the shotgun seat turned to give him a once-over. Shaw tensed reflexively, expecting the Interceptor to stop, but it cruised northward without pause.

On another night they'd have braced him, a lone man standing outside a closed business in a low-traffic area. Priorities.

It was good being out, Shaw mused, before clarifying the thought. It was good to be on the hunt.

Milford Kettering reappeared, bold enough now to step out onto the sidewalk.

"I may have something," he said. "A favor, you said?"

"Of comparable size. I won't knock over a jewelry exchange for you."

"I suppose you're a fellow of your word, though what could I do if you weren't? Regardless, your mention of the gentleman with the eye problem sparked a memory. McReynolds was his name. I bought a shipment of DVD players from him, back when people still wanted such things. McReynolds was a strong-arm thief, and perhaps worse, at least until recently."

"What changed?"

"The eye changed, certainly. Some disease of the optic nerve. I don't know if he's the same man who robbed your poor nurse, but I do know who he works for now. Harold Vulpe."

Shaw stared at Kettering. "You say that like I should know the name."

"Perhaps not. Though if you and your grandfather were still working together, the name might be as familiar as mine. Mr. Vulpe works a similar line as me, only he deals primarily in technology. Counterfeit software licenses or illegal duplications of intellectual properties. It's very lucrative. Were I young again and knowledgeable about such things I might be tempted. As it is," Kettering glanced at the Dugout's unimpressive exterior, "I'm content to ease into retirement."

"Medical supplies are a weird jump from bootleg movies," Shaw said. "Maybe McReynolds is in business for himself."

"If you're intending to confront either of them, I would advise extreme caution. Harold wouldn't employ a man like McReynolds if he were given to reasonable discourse."

"And if I felt reckless?"

Kettering smiled. "I took the liberty of acquiring his address. Harold Vulpe lives in Dash Point, near Tacoma. You know where that is?"

Shaw did. He checked his watch. Sunrise was three hours off yet.

Time enough.

HAROLD VULPE'S HOUSE WAS simple enough to find and proved even easier to approach. Trees bordered the grounds and a broad swath of lawn, allowing the occupants privacy from the neighbors but also giving Shaw an unobstructed view of the rear of the home from fifty yards away without fear of being spotted.

The home consisted of three separate structures connected by enclosed hallways of glass windows atop short stone walls. Those modernist halls didn't quite match the Tudor style of the grand house in the center, and Shaw supposed they'd been added years later when the outer buildings were constructed. The farthest building from him was a four-car garage. The closest, even larger than the garage, might be guest quarters or perhaps an oversized home office. Lights shone from the main house. The guest quarters were dark.

It was a long shot that the ventilators would be in Vulpe's house, Shaw knew. But better odds than it might have been weeks ago. Everyone was sticking close to home lately. Even if the stolen machines were elsewhere, and even if Vulpe had nothing to do with their theft, he might be able to steal a cell phone or laptop and get a lead on McReynolds.

Motion detectors had been planted every few yards around the perimeter of the lawn, like white toadstools. Set to trigger exterior lights, or maybe more. He took a wrench from a pocket kit he'd retrieved from a hidden compartment in his car, and disabled two of the detectors before beating a path across the grass to the rear of the guest house.

Looking through the window into the dark interior, Shaw could make out the shape of a simple contact pad alarm on the top edge of the door. He used a snap gun to unlock the deadbolt within seconds, and a magnet to disable the alarm sensor. A job he could have handled when he was twelve years old and just starting out. If the rest of the house was this soft, he estimated he'd be back on the road within half an hour.

The space inside was a laundry room, and beyond it an entertainment area, complete with pool table and a ceiling-mounted projector aimed at a movie screen. Billiard balls and cue sticks remained on the green felt as if a game had been interrupted. Shaw moved through the room to the opposite entryway, which led him to the guest house's foyer. Coats hung from pegs just inside the front door. Shoes and boots formed a neat line underneath. And standing like an attentive butler beside the bannister of the stairs leading to the second floor, the tall rolling cart of a ventilator.

Son of a bitch, Shaw thought. There it was.

In the reflection off the machine's display screen, he caught a shadowy image of his own startled expression. Along with something else behind him.

Shaw ducked right, just as the swinging pool cue whipped past where his head had been. He went for the Colt on his hip, but his attacker's backswing came too fast, hitting Shaw's elbow. His gun clattered to the tile floor. Shaw flung himself at his attacker, more out of desperation than coordination. Their bodies thudded together, stumbled. The two men fell back into the darkened game room, Shaw half on top. He punched with both hands, hitting the man in the chest and arms. The slim end of the cue stick smacked him hard across the temple.

Thrashing, the attacker tumbled free. Shaw lost him in his daze and the dim. He scrambled madly, expecting another swing to fracture his skull at any second. A vicious kick caught his left shoulder instead, numbing Shaw down to the fingertips. But the force of the blow got him rolling the right direction, under the shelter of the pool table. The descending cue cracked against the table's stout leg.

The man rushed away, rounding the broad table, eager to end the fight. Shaw got to his feet on the other side. He grabbed the 9-ball from the felt surface and threw it with all his strength, a frantic heater that struck the attacker's forehead with a note two octaves lower than the wooden cue had made hitting the table leg. The man's head snapped back and he fell, bouncing off the lip of the table and down to the floor. The cue stick rolled from his grip.

Shaw, gasping for breath, replaced his skewed bandanna and knelt to check if his enemy was still alive. Blood had already begun to trickle from the purpling spot where the ball had caromed off the attacker's skull. The trickle changed direction as Shaw turned the man's head to check his pupils. He lifted the eyelid and saw a cloudy gray-white orb.

McReynolds. He must have seen Shaw coming across the lawn towards the guest quarters and circled around to sneak in through the same door. Lucky that the thug hadn't brought a gun. But maybe his boss Harold Vulpe or another person in the main house was calling for backup right now. Best to grab the ventilator—both if he could find the second machine—and get the hell out.

He returned to the foyer. The Colt had tumbled under the caster wheels of the ventilator cart. As Shaw holstered the pistol, he looked out the windows at the Tudor house. No sign of movement, nobody staring back at him from the well-lit first story. McReynolds might have been alone. Or the only one awake in the wee hours.

Where was the second ventilator? Vulpe may have already passed it off to a buyer. The first machine had been set by the stairs. It would only take seconds to check the upper floor. Shaw took the stairs two at a time, only to halt abruptly at the reedy sound of a man's voice calling from the rooms ahead.

"Harold?" the voice said. "I heard a noise."

A cough followed. A dry rasp and the wheeze of labored inhalation.

"Harold?"

Shaw knew he should retreat, take the single ventilator and count himself lucky. But the unseen man's cough had nudged his curiosity.

He padded silently down the carpeted hallway to look through the first open doorway. A bedroom, antique in decor, with oaken wainscoting and floral wallpaper. But instead of a four-poster, he saw a modern hospital bed, set so that its occupant sat up at an angle. Oxygen tanks had been fixed to the safety railing of the bed, and trays holding prescriptions and other care rested on a vintage dresser. Against the far wall, the second stolen ventilator, ready like its brother on a rolling cart.

A small lamp on the elevated bedside table cast the only light in the room. The man on the bed peered at Shaw. He was tall and as thin as a heron, and even in the low illumination Shaw could tell that his color was bad. A pallor washed out even the liver spots on his neck and scalp while his cheeks remained flush with fever. If the patient seemed frightened by the sudden appearance of a large masked stranger in his doorway, he didn't show it.

"Who are you?" the man said. "One of Harold's men?"

His spindly fingers pressed a button on a cord. Calling for help, and stalling until it arrives, Shaw reasoned.

"I'm here for this, not you," Shaw said, crossing the room to the ventilator on its cart. The screen folded down flat for easy transport.

"My eyes are for crap. What is it?"

"A ventilator. Helps people breathe."

"I know that. What's the damn thing doing here?"

Shaw loosened the straps holding the ventilator to the cart and hefted it. Twenty pounds, at most. He could carry both machines in one trip, one under each arm. If he didn't have to worry about interference.

A door opened downstairs. The old man heard it too.

Shaw set the ventilator back on the cart. "You're Harold Vulpe's father? Uncle?"

"He's my boy."

"Your boy stole two of these from an ICU. From people who need them to survive."

The old man grunted and glanced at the oxygen tanks at the side of the bed.

"I'm taking them back," Shaw said. "Sorry."

"Screw your sorry," the man said, then called out again with surprising volume. "Harold?"

Shaw drew the Colt.

"Dad?" Vulpe shouted from the stairs. "You okay?"

"I'm peachy. This bandit here has a gun, so maybe you don't come charging in like a fool, hah?"

"Cops are already here and I've got a gun too," Vulpe shouted to Shaw. "There's nowhere for you to go, asshole."

"Hell," the old man said. "Harold, put that thing away and get your ass up here." He coughed again and managed another curse between breaths.

A pause followed. Shaw moved to a more defensible position behind the wall of the attached bathroom. The old man watched him but said nothing.

Vulpe appeared at the doorway. He'd obeyed half of his father's instructions; he still clutched a nickel plated 9-millimeter automatic with pearl grips. Shaw thought the gun looked oddly formal for a man wearing sweatpants and a V-neck sweater, the uniform of the quarantined.

"You two idiots can shoot each other," the old man said, wheezing a little, "but first I wanna know where that came from." He waved a finger at the ventilator on its cart.

"You need it," Vulpe said. "You're getting worse."

"That's not what I asked. I know I'm getting worse, I'm the one who's in this damn body. And I know I've got the sick, too. Probably caught it from that attendant you hired who keeps taking my food away before I'm done. You take that gadget from a hospital?"

Vulpe looked stricken. "I had to. They'll turn us away if you go. Let somebody younger take your place. You know they will."

"I don't know that and neither do you. And it's beside the damn point," the old man said. "You wouldn't remember this, Harold, but when I was a kid, your grandmother went to work at the shipyards building destroyers for the Navy. Not for money. Because she thought it was her duty. Then when I was about your age and Boeing nearly went bust, I was on the committee that put bonds together to hire some of those laid-off workers to build parks." The old man coughed again, nearly doubling over.

"Dad," Vulpe said. His father waved a palm impatiently and Vulpe and Shaw both waited, guns drawn but at their sides, until he recovered.

"Shut up a minute, Harold. I know you're into some criminal garbage, now that I live here and I've seen the kind of people you've got coming around at all hours. It's stupid but I let it go 'cause it's your life. But this is my life. My integrity. You can't take from people in need to benefit me. I won't have it. This guy"—the man gestured toward Van—"is going to take those machines back."

"And the masks," Van said.

"And the masks or whatever," the old man agreed. "And if I die like I figure I will, so what? At least I won't be dragging any souls along behind me. That's one last thing I can do for this town. You follow, son?"

Vulpe stood stock still for a long moment. Then he set the automatic on the dresser beside the cornucopia of prescription bottles.

"Go on," Vulpe said to Shaw. "Take the shit and get the hell out before I change my mind."

His father nodded. "Come sit by me, kid," he said to Vulpe. His final reserves of energy spent, he sank as far into the pillow as his emaciated frame allowed. "Keep me company a while."

"What's your name?" Shaw asked.

"Francis," the old man said. "I'd ask yours, but maybe it's better you stay anonymous, hah?"

Shaw agreed. "Thanks, Francis."

"Nothing to it," said Francis Vulpe and took his son's hand.

THE YOUNGER VULPE POINTED Shaw to a cardboard box in the bedroom closet. Inside were individual boxes of wrapped sterile masks, fifty per box. Shaw wrapped each ventilator in a towel and placed them on a blanket, which he bundled up to make a crude sack. With the cardboard box under one arm and the ventilators slung over his back like Santa Claus, he stepped over the snoring bulk of McReynolds and out the back door.

Driving to Harborview, Shaw thought about what he'd said to Luce hours before. About how tracking down the stolen ventilators was something for him to do when there were no other options left. But that hadn't quite been true. He'd made a choice. An easy choice, true, between doing something that might save lives and sitting on his ass. But still a decision.

Francis Vulpe had made a choice as well. Maybe his final one. And maybe he'd turned over the goods just to keep his crooked son Harold from getting shot, though Shaw doubted that. The old man had seemed resolute, even when the life in question was his own.

Enough, Shaw thought. You chose a path, and you walked it. Right now, his path led to a fast and very discreet stop at the hospital and then home for sleep and more sleep. No need to call Luce. She would find out about the mysterious reappearance of the stolen gear soon enough through her husband, and she would understand why Shaw hadn't told her himself.

And tomorrow, he would spend another day inside. And the day after, and the day after, until this thing was dead and gone and the world started spinning again.

Shaw didn't mind. It was what he could do.

I frequently miss my hometown. No more so than during the pandemic. But I've also been tremendously heartened and proud of how Seattle has faced up to a challenge that makes the fire of 1889, a blaze that gutted the town's entire center, look like a minor inconvenience. Most residents made the smart choice to isolate themselves for their safety and for others' and to flatten the curve. When they ventured out, it was usually to handle critical work, keeping the rest of the community healthy and secure and fed.

While following the local news, I got to wondering how another hometown boy would be faring during the quarantine. Van Shaw might be more aggressive in his actions, but he cares just as much. He'd want to do something. I wanted to do something. So I wrote this story.

And if this story is anything, it's a love letter.

In the days following that 1889 conflagration, Seattle rebuilt. Bricks and stone instead of wood. An improved water supply. The city's first professional fire department. Stronger—and more importantly, safer—than ever.

I hope that we, too, will rebuild—locally, nationally, and globally. With improved crisis management protocols, more stockpiles and supply chains, expanded medical services and increased personnel, and economic guardrails. Our children will know how to handle a crisis from our examples and our mistakes. If you'd like to help, please reach out to your own city's non-profit organizations to support families in need, the homeless, and first responders.

Stronger and safer. I hope that's true for you and your families as well.

GEH, June 2020

When it comes to Van Shaw, there is no rest for the formerly wicked, even when he thinks he's finally on the straight and narrow.

When a new security gig turns into a setup, expert thief Van Shaw finds himself the prey in a cross-country pursuit that launches from the Island of Thieves . . .

Van Shaw is hired by eccentric business magnate Sebastian Rohner to evaluate the security of his art collection. When Van arrives at Rohner's expansive island estate, Rohner reveals to Van the real reason he's been recruited: to prevent another professional burglar from stealing the art. Rohner wants to set a thief to catch a thief.

Van, while questioning the bizarre nature of the job, takes it seriously and surveils the highly secure gallery wing, only to stumble across a murdered body on the rocky shore beyond. Van knows the homicide detectives on the case—and perhaps Rohner as well—mark him for the prime suspect and will turn his life upside down in their search for evidence.

Van begins to hunt for the killer himself, but scrutiny only digs his hole deeper. With no other options, he goes on the run, alone and unaided. He's hunted by the cops, the enraged Rohner, and by a pair of psychopathic hitmen who chase Van from one coast to the next. To clear his name, Van Shaw will have to uncover the truth, even with a band of killers on his tail, determined to add Van to their growing list of victims.

Don't Miss
ISLAND OF THIEVES
Coming Summer 2021